TRAPPED

A novel of Parapsychological Suspense

GEORGE A BERNSTEIN

{Amazon Top 100 Author}

TRAPPED
Copyright © 2013 by George A Bernstein
ISBN-13: 978-0-9894681-1-4

GnD Publishing

GnD Publishing LLC
72 Saint James Terrace
Palm Beach Gardens, Florida 33418

http://GnDpublishingllc.com
info@GnDpublishingllc.com

Cover Design & Interior Layout *Laura Shinn Designs*

2nd Edition

Other novels by
George A Bernstein

A 3rd Time to Die
(Available in ebook and print)

<u>Coming Soon!</u>

Death's Angel
(A Detective Al Warner Suspense)

Officially Inactive
(The 2nd Al Warner Suspense)

Dedication

I'd like to first dedicate this book to my wife, Dolores, whose fount of ideas spawned the original idea for this story. It was she who suggested, over 20 years ago, that I apply my story-telling talents into writing a novel.

"*Trapped*" is the first of four I've completed. Dolores even attended several writers' conferences with me, which had mixed results. On the plus side, she learned what makes good writing. She became my first editor and unrelenting critic. The negative side was that she learned what makes good writing (!!!)... and that ruined a lot of books and movies for her that she once would have enjoyed.

Good story-telling is an art not practiced often enough.

My thanks to Dolores for her continued patience and encouragement.

I also want to thank the editor(s) (Name unknown) from my previous publisher whose insightful suggestions helped make TRAPPED the best it could be.

PROLOGUE

Turn signal flashing, she eases into the right lane in front of a large, battered pick-up, with less than a half-mile to the Old Orchard Exit Ramp. Jackee Maren rarely drives so aggressively, but first delayed by her two sons' late departure from school, and then navigating around a minor fender bender on Dundee Road, she is already ten minutes behind, and she's *never* late. The Northern Illinois Chapter of the United Way won't start their planning session without their chairwoman, and Jackee hates the idea of keeping so many busy people waiting.

Peeling onto the ramp, her attention is drawn to her two boys, bickering and shoving in the back seat. Glancing back at the road, a ridge of goose bumps cascades down her spine. They're hurtled toward a string of glaring taillights... cars unexpectedly stopped by a red light at the first intersection off the expressway.

Jamming a foot on the brakes, she's stunned when the big Mercedes slews sharply right, smack into the path of the huge pickup truck, which had exited behind her. It slams into the rear fender of the sedan, sending it careening off the road, the seatbelts gouging her shoulder, crushing the breath from her lungs.

"Hang on boys," she gasps.

Oh God! My sons! They can't die here.

They spin down the embankment like an eccentric top, ricocheting off a bridge column. The wheel torn from her grip, the air filled with the screech of rending metal and the stench of burning rubber, the car rears like a great angry beast, its rear legs hamstrung. Slamming down, it hurtles backward into the culvert, bucking and skipping along the steep embankment.

Despite seatbelts, Jackee is flung around like a rag doll in the jaws of some huge terrier. The air bag erupts in the midst of their tumultuous downward plunge, rushing out at 200 MPH, just as frontal impact slings her forward.

Her face catches the brunt of the blow, skewering lips on her teeth, smashing her nose. A searing bolt of pain fires across her brain, igniting a burst of red heat behind her tearing eyes. A sharp pitch right crushes her left cheek against the window, knocking her momentarily senseless. The sedan teeters, enveloped in a cloud of dust, hunkering precariously on its haunches before crashing down on its wheels, coming to a thunderous, grinding stop.

She awakens to wailing and blubbering from the two small boys in the rear seat.

"Mommy!" The call gasped through ragged breathing.

"Mommy!" Now a frantic screech.

"I'm...I'm here."

We're alive! Thank God, we're all still alive.

She sags against the seatbelt, every joint singed with agony, unable to will herself into action.

Help should be coming. She moans. *Gotta hang on...* She slips out of consciousness.

The continued bawling and moaning of her sons stir her, drawing her out of the fog of semi-consciousness. One of her eyes is swollen shut, but the other flickers open, glazed with shock.

Where the Hell's Fire/Rescue.

She winces, her whole body racked by pain.

Seems like we've been trapped down here for...

The warble of a fast arriving rescue vehicle answers that question. She closes her eye, struggling to control the thunder in her head and the molten bands of fire across her chest.

"Lady? You with me?" A hatchet-faced EMT materializes at the shattered passenger-side window. She strives to focus on the man, who is futilely struggling with the door.

"Malcolm, Bryan," the words slurred through blood stained lips. "Sons...back seat..."

"Yeah, they're still strapped in. We're gonna take care of everybody, but it's you I'm focused on."

Jackee's head lolls forward, her emerald eye fluttering closed as she struggles to remain conscious. The swell and ebb of her breast confirms that, while battered, she still lives. Her sons in the back continue their chorus of terror, though it's winding down to a pattern of whimpers as their surge of adrenaline burns out.

"Can't budge this damned door," the EMT, grunts. He's joined by his thick-shouldered partner, hefting a crowbar.

"Move over and give me room to work." forcing one end of the steel into the jamb, struggling to lever it open, he glances at his partner. "Those kids look okay?"

"Probably. All that loud wailing is a good sign, but we'll check 'em out once we get everyone free. The woman's obviously suffered some airbag trauma and...Oh, oh, she's coming around."

Jackee's eye blinks, her head inches up, and she tastes the blood oozing from her nose and lips.

"Oohhh. What...what..." She makes a feeble effort to turn her head.

Oh! My sons. The brakes...bad crash...are they...?"

"Mommy." Malcolm's voice a hoarse squeak. "Are you hurt? We're okay, I think." His voice and Bryan's whimpering through ragged breathing is reassuring.

Thank God. So close. Don't know how I could..." She sags, her thoughts fading again.

"We're gettin' nowhere with this bar." He looks back.

"We need the hydraulics down here, and in a fuckin' hurry," he screams up at the road.

"On the way. How 'bout a power saw now?"

"No way. Too dangerous."

Ten minutes later, a hydraulic pry bar dispense with the door. Frantic minutes drag by as they disentangle Jackee from the air bags, and her two sobbing, shaken sons, from their seatbelts.

Jackee smells the fuel that continues to seep from the ruptured tank, pooling beneath the wreckage.

Fire...or worse...is an eminent threat.

She floats to full awareness. Her body is festooned with welts, and her face feels like she'd gone ten rounds with Joe Frazier. Strapped to a gurney, her head and neck immobilized, one medic checks her vitals, which, despite her tattered façade, are surprisingly robust.

"Looks like you're gonna be okay, lady. Got someone you want me to call?" he asks.

"Husband. Phil Maren." Mumbled with a thick lisp over a swollen tongue and lacerated lips.

"North Chicago Printing. In city. My sons?"

"They're shaken and bruised, but don't seem to have any major problems. We're checking 'em out now. They'll come to the hospital as a precaution, and your husband can pick 'em up there."

Moments later the ambulance races toward Skokie Valley Hospital.

A freak thing. Was it the brakes? Phil just serviced the car.

She sighs.

How did it...?" She slips off into a sedative induced slumber.

Jackee Maren had no idea that this terrifying accident was but a small taste of the true horror soon awaiting her.

CHAPTER ONE

Five Months Later

Where am I?

Intense, deep-cave blackness envelops her... smothering, almost thick enough to touch. She seems adrift, suspended a pool of dark, still water.

A bath? That doesn't make sense.

Despite a shroud of absolute darkness, she senses herself rising, finally breaching the inky surface, floating weightlessly.

And she is awake.

What was that? A dream? It seemed so real!

Jackee Maren lay very still, confused by the eerie perception of bobbing gently on tepid, calm waters. Despite a sense of warmth lapping at her, she shudders.

What's happened to...? Oh... how stupid of me.

My surgery! It's finally over. Five months since the accident, and breathing hadn't gotten any easier. But why is it so... so dark in... where? A recovery room?

Why have they left me alone?

A pungency unique to hospitals floods her with unpleasant memories: momma, daddy, and her own last visit. Not a happy moment in the bunch.

Icy tentacles caress her spine, kindling a mountain range of goose bumps.

What's going on? Why... oh...

Voices murmuring, bare whispers, apparently close by. What are they saying?

Spooky, laying here in this... this black place. Why haven't they taken me to my room? Phil'll be worried.

Won't he? He promised to take time from work to care for their sons... to be supportive for a change... while she recovers from this reconstructive facial surgery he seemed so eager for her to have. She shivers, momentarily reliving that scary car accident.

Spinning, lurching, crashing down that embankment. The shriek of rending steel.

God, it was terrifying.

The boys tussling in back, and I was distracted, worried at being late... and wondering about Phil's frequent late nights. He was seldom home evenings before then. But that changed after I spun the Mercedes into that ditch.

Whatever. That was then. Gotta figure out the now... why I'm still in Recovery. Get someone's attention. If she moves, will stitches tear? The undercurrent of voices pulls at her.

Why are they whispering?

She shivers again, her skin peppered by an icy sleet of uncertainty.

Has something happened... something bad? No one's here... no one to check on me. Did something go wrong?

Oh God, it must be terrible!

Her heart tumbles, skipping into high gear. This crushing darkness robs her of any sense of place.

Maybe I'm dead, locked away in the Morgue, lying on a slab, waiting to be cut up? It's so black, and they... Oh, shut up!

Jeez, it was only reconstructive surgery after the accident. Dead people don't lie around, thinking. Always ready to worry if there's a little hitch somewhere. Nothing bad happened. Still, I've gotta get someone's attention.

Hey! Why didn't I see that before?

How had she missed what was right in front of her... two shaded windows, a bare sliver of light glimmering at their lower edges. Dare she move, seeking aid? Still stymied by the strange aura of weightless floating on a glassy film of water, she tentatively stretches out a hand.

Am I actually moving? Eerie! I can't really tell in this utter darkness. Her unseen fingers trip lightly across the base of the shades.

Success! Both spool noiselessly upward.

Finally! She winces, blinking at the sudden light, before her vision clears.

There, three men, standing in a small white room, two wearing blue surgeon's scrubs, the other, the tallest, a dark suit. No second bed, no moveable tables, no guest chairs anywhere. No outside windows, either. Stark illumination from flickering fluorescent fixtures cast demonic shadows across their faces. She shivers, unassured by the sight of the trio of apparent doctors.

What is this place? A recovery room? Suddenly their voices are clear.

"I spoke to her husband," says the one in the dark suit, fingering the stethoscope looped around his neck. "He said she occasionally took both amphetamines and tranquilizers."

He said that? It was just this one time, and he said...

"Damn," from the taller of the two, "that wasn't on the admitting form. We could've rescheduled. Drugs and anesthetics always cause problems."

Problems? God, I knew it. Damned hospitals! Damn, damn, damn!

"We're checking," the third man says. "I'm not convinced tests will tell us anything that will do us much good in court, if it comes to that."

What are they talking about?

She is suddenly struggling to breathe, her heart pummeling her breast.

Oh Jesus, something did happen! Something bad!

Head spinning, her world lurches surreally askew. She shudders.

I'm so cold! Her little lagoon churns from comfortable warmth into a bed of ice.

Something's terribly wrong! Hospitals are supposed to fix things, but I had the same scary feeling while waiting for Daddy's test results... and I was right!

Gotta find out what's happened. Sucking in a ragged breath... worried about damaging her facial surgery...she grits her teeth before calling out.

"Hey!"

Don't panic. They'll see me in a minute.

But they *don't.* Are they deaf?

"Over here!" Louder now, willing them to look at her.

"You, out there! Please help me."

The taller surgeon cocks his head and turns.

Thank God! He'll see me now.

He pauses, still as stone. Then his eyes flare wide, his jaw dropping. Snatching at the other doctor's sleeve, he thrusts an almost accusing finger at her.

"Look," he shouts. "Look!"

"Her eyes! Her eyes! "They're open!"

Chapter Two

The three men rush to the two little windows, the sports jacket of the tallest flapping in his haste.

My eyes? What about my eyes? Why is he so damned excited?

The taller of the two surgeons pushes in front, very close to the glass, his head seeming to fill both openings. She winces, blinking, from a bright light shined into her eyes.

"Mrs. Maren, can you hear me? Are you all right?"

"Of course I hear you! You're standing right there, aren't you?" He squints, bushy dark brow creased, lips pursing, but doesn't respond.

Is he deaf?

"Mrs. Maren, if you hear me, please signal somehow." A furtive glance at the other men, then back to her, his brown eyes boring into her. "Can you move anything?"

OhmyGod! She shivers, the truth crashing over her, sending her heart on a rumba rampage inside her breast.

I wasn't talking! Were they... oh, God... they were only thoughts inside my head!

I didn't... Oh, Jesus. I can talk, can't I? Stomach roiling, she gags back rising gorge, acid burning her gullet. Another reality stabs her, freezing her mind. She gasps... or did she?

Did I actually swallow? Despite the bitter taste, she senses no connection to her throat, her tongue, her lips. She feels nothing! The sour taste of bile fills her head, not her mouth, as if everything is disjointed. She can sense, but can she *feel*?

No! There's only this ethereal aura of weightless floating.

What's happened to me? Why can't I talk? Why can't I feel anything?

"Mrs. Maren?" His voice breaks through the jumbled panic surging through her head. "I'm sure you hear me. I see your eyes moving. Can you do anything else? Please, try."

Struggling to clear her mind, she focuses on his face, so close to the two little windows.

Move? Yes, I must be able to wiggle something!

Oh, God! Oh, God! Why can't I... Something! I gotta do something! Twitch, finger. Nothing. *Move arm... move.* It refuses.

Wag a foot! Make a fist! Nothing cooperates. She grunts silently, straining at the effort.

Scrunch, toes. No luck there, either. No need to see them to know the results.

Nothing! She tries to shake her head. *Stupid! Can't do that either.*

Oh, God! Can't move! Can't talk! Can't do anything! Nothing at all! Her mind spins dizzily, whirling down... down... down, into a black, chaotic whirlpool of terror.

"No physical activity," the other man in blue scrubs says, glancing at an electronic monitor, "but her heart rate's way up. She's agitated."

"I'm not surprised." The taller man studies his patient. Shrugging, he reaches for her hand. It's beyond her vision, and she feels nothing.

"Can't you signal us somehow? Maybe blink your eyes?"

Jesus! What have they done to me? What have they done?

Only she hears the screams of terror echoing through her head.

Nothing works. Gotta do something. Gotta get control. Fix this, somehow.

Tenuously in charge of her fractured psyche, she concentrates on the simple task of shutting her eyes.

They close.

Thank God. At least that's something, and... What the Hell!

Those emerald orbs fly wide, the "window shades" closing and opening at the same time.

My God! They're not windows. They're my eyes!

"She did it! She did it! Mrs. Maren, please blink twice if you understand me."

OhmyGod! It was simple surgery. What's gone wrong? This can't be happening!

Can't panic. These are good doctors. Gotta calm down and cooperate.

Her heart still jackhammering at her ribs, she musters fractured courage, willing her eyes to blink twice. The "shades" closed both times!

"She did it," said the taller one. "She understands. Get an EEG on her. Let's find out what's going on." The other doctor hurries away.

Oh, Jesus! She pants, her throat closing, choking her breath, crushing her lungs.

I'm gonna be sick! Gasping for breath, she struggles against rising gorge swamps her.

What's gone wrong? Why can't I even wiggle a finger, or make any sound? Not even a grunt. It's like a bad dream.

That's it! I'm having a nightmare. Wake up, Jackee. Wake up!

"Heart rate and BP are really spiking. She's panicking."

"Can't blame her," the dark suit says. Leaning close, he speaks with a quiet firmness.

"Mrs. Maren, I know you're scared, but you've got to control your panic. I don't want to be forced to give you a sedative."

No, this isn't a bad dream, is it? The scary truth is I'm living the nightmare.

"Now we know you're alert, we can take care of you. Try to calm down. We need to ask you some questions and do further tests on your condition."

My condition? You call this a condition?

"Blink once for 'yes,' and twice for 'no.' Okay?"

Oh, God! What did you bastards do to me? A banshee's wail echoes inside the soundproof vault of her beautiful, blonde head. Purged, she struggles to stifle her panic.

Gotta calm down. Daddy taught me to be tougher than that. You can do this. Finally, precariously in charge, she blinks once.

"Good," says the doctor she labeled Number One.

"Now concentrate hard and try again to move something. Even a small twitch of a finger or a toe. Anything. Can you do that?"

*Okay. Gotta stop acting like a crazy dog, chasing its tail. Take a slow, deep breath, just like Daddy taught me when I was little and afraid from a bad drea*m. But this is no dream, and she seems unable to govern her breathing.

Another damned thing that doesn't work! Mentally gritting her teeth, she bears down on the minor task of jiggling a tiny digit. Her thumping heart slows as concentration supplants fear.

But controlling her emotions seems all she can do. No twitch anywhere... not even a millimeter. Closing her eyes, focusing her mind, she wills just one finger to curl. No success. She gives a mental sigh, as reality sweeps over her.

Gotta accept the facts, no matter how terrible.

Strangely calm now in the face of unassailable truth, Jackee's green eyes find the doctor's, blinking twice.

"No? You can't move anything except your eyes or eyelids? Okay, don't worry. I'm sure there's something....." The clippity-clop of fast approaching wheeled carts cuts him off. Several white-coated people, led by Number Two, burst into the room.

"I've got the EEG team and the head of neurology," he says. An efficient group of newcomers, a conglomerate of men and women in blue scrubs and white uniforms, bustle about, setting up their equipment. Number One nods, taking her hand.

"We're going to run some tests to see what's going on. Figure out how to get you well. You're our top priority."

Jackee supposes he's giving a reassuring squeeze or patting her hand. It's out of sight. No way to tilt her head to look.

God, how scary. I can't even feel that!

She "shivers," chilled, as if lying in a snow. How is *that*? Physically, nothing changed.

"I'm Dr. Hersch," he continues, "and this (gesturing toward Number Two) is Dr. Lambini, Chief of Surgery. Our boss, the man in the suit, is Dr. Markowitz. We're doing our best to figure this out. Get you better so you can go home."

What a jerk! If that were to be reassuring...well, not very convincing.

His hollow charade is ridiculous enough to fracture her dam of tension, spilling the frigid bath of panic and terror into the ether, leaving her slack and listless. She's again bobbing gently, sending ripples across the newfound watery cove of her mind, no longer cold.

His words sow no confidence. Nothing they can do will actually work.

She blinks once through welling tears.

At least I can still cry.

CHAPTER THREE

Jackee floats on the surface of her mind, mentally numb, which seems appropriate, considering her physical condition. Strange, having the "bees" (the myriad technicians, swarming around her) pushing, prodding, bending, and sticking her, with absolutely no tactile sensation. She hovers, totally disconnected, in a sensory void.

Eleven "bees" flit around her, tending their shiny chrome machines, which hum and scratch quietly, producing yard after yard of paper charts. The tests seemed to go on for hours, although she has no real sense of time. They have long since packed up and left.

She is alone, running on empty... cold terror supplanted by an even more frigid calm.

No doubt anymore. It's hopeless. Daddy taught me to be an optimist, but I've never faced anything like this.

Daddy protected his "Countess" throughout most of her worry-free life. Her greatest problems were whether to attend Vassar or Smith. She rarely wanted for anything. Then she married Phil, and life's specter changed.

Then Daddy died, and nothing was ever the same, especially after Arthur read his Will. Everything was in trusts for the boys and me. Phil raged at not getting a dime, sulking for months. Was money all he married me for? During that terrible time, she attributed much of the stress between them to her devastation at the loss of her beloved father.

Oh, Daddy! Why did you die? I need you desperately! Strange, it's her father she seeks when she needs solace, even after he died. Phil seems less capable of compassion.

Tears fill her eyes.

This is a disaster for everyone. How'll Phil care for our sons? His job never gave him much time for his family. He hasn't even come to visit me yet.

As if summoned by her anguished thoughts, her husband peeks in from the door, his sapphire eyes almost cold, and she is strangely chilled.

What's that look? Anger? Bitterness? Why not? Look what they've done to his wife. She represses a clawing uneasiness, peppered by a sudden aura of animus flooding her senses, as he saunters to her bedside. *Foolish imagination.*

What now? Will he stick by me? He's so young to be saddled by this. Why would anyone want to care for a living corpse? Tiny teardrops make emerald pools of her eyes.

"Thank God you're awake." The passion of his word made hollow by a voice flat and devoid of emotion.

"Jesus, what the Hell have these bastards done? They're feeding me this crap it's the anesthesia, combined with the tranquilizers you didn't list on the admittance form. They would have rescheduled if they knew."

Admittance forms? I don't even remember filling them out. I was so scared this morning (was it only this morning?), I took those two Valium Phil gave me before we left for the hospital. How should we know that's not safe? I hated being back here so soon after the accident. Shouldn't they warn you about things like that? Little rivulets slide over her bandaged cheek.

Is this the end? Am I going to die... so young? Who'll raise our sons?

She visualizes nine-year-old Malcolm, with his corn-silk hair and emerald eyes, a mischievous grin tickling his mouth as he pulls an innocent prank on his younger brother. And little, cheerful Bryan, the spitting image of his older brother, except for his ocean blue eyes. Rarely jealous, always happy at his brother's accomplishments.

I so wish they'd come to visit. How will they react at seeing me like this?

She blinks away moisture, as doctors Hersch and Lefkowitz ease into the room.

"I'm glad you're here, Mr. Maren." Lefkowitz shuffles his feet, avoiding Phil's eyes. "May we talk to you in the hallway for a moment?"

Phil glances at her, shrugs, and follows the doctors, the heavy doors swishing closed behind them. Propped up in bed, Jackee sees their heads through glass panels in each door.

"We've gone over our test results several times," Doctor Hersch says. "I've even e-mailed a set to a world-renowned neurologist at the Mayo Clinic."

They don't want me to... hey, wait! Jackee blinks. *There's no way I should hear them through those thick doors, but it's like they're standing right next to me. What's going on?* Confused, she tries to harness her suddenly galloping heart and concentrate on what they are saying.

"We're looking for answers, but what's happened to your wife, while not unprecedented, seems very unusual." Doctor Lefkowitz says.

"What? Putting her in a coma is unique?" The doctor tugs at his collar, shaking his head.

"That's just it," he says. "She's *not* in a coma. With complications like this, brain impairment is not uncommon. Drugs and anesthesia just don't mix."

Oh, Jesus! No!

"Damage is usually pretty complete. A few basic functions may survive, like breathing and heartbeat. Even then, mechanical life-support is often needed."

"Yeah, that's a ventilator she's sporting, isn't it?" Phil asks.

"Right. The patient is usually reduced to a vegetative state, only kept alive by life-support systems. There's never any cognitive function."

Listen to him! Saying such scary things in front of me.

She quivers... mentally at least... fear blending with anger.

But they're not in front of me! This is weird. There's really no way I should hear them.

Her eyes water.

This can't be happening. Why am I being punished like this?

The doctor gazes at her through the glass, clearing his throat.

"Mrs. Maren's condition is caused by the same situation," he continues. "But, her results are different. There *has* been brain death..."

Ohmygod!

"...but it has been... well, it's been selective."

No! No! Brain dead. Vegetative. Useless. Might as well be totally dead. Tear blur her view of Phil, who glances her way and shrugs. He seems calm, or maybe in shock.

"Partial brain death happens occasionally," Lefkowitz continues. "In your wife's case, the centers controlling voluntary motor functions have apparently died. The one exception seems to be

Ophthalmic Nerve V1, which controls the eyes and eyelids. There's little likelihood of cell regeneration. It's what you'd expect when sedatives are accidentally mixed with anesthesia."

Angry fascination transcends her fear.

They're discussing me as if I were some medical textbook, not a living (more or less), breathing being. The insensitive jerk!

But they probably don't realize I can hear them.

"What's different here is all of the cognitive portions of the brain, centered in the Neocortex, seem perfectly intact," Doctor Hirsh says.

"That happens occasionally, and the Neocortex is what most often survives. We call it 'Locked-in Syndrome.' Mrs. Maren appears able to think, see, hear, and possibly even smell. Our preliminary tests indicate her brain activity is quite high. While voluntary motor functions have ceased, her cognitive abilities actually may have been enhanced. The centers controlling involuntary responses like heart, breathing and possibly even digestion, also seem somewhat intact. Nature often has a way of making trade-offs."

Phil studies her through the glass, lips pursed, his gaze almost icy. He turns to Dr. Hersch, shaking his head.

"You're saying she's totally paralyzed, but she can still think, hear and see like anyone else? And that's it? She'll never improve?"

"Highly doubtful," Doctor Lefkowitz answers. "We'll run a complete PET scan to see what's really going on in there, but it seems likely most of the Neocortex lobes and neocortical columns are intact. As I said, those process thought, sound, sight, smell and hearing. I won't bury you with technical jargon. Simply, we'll inject a radioactive dye, highlighting which areas are responding, and how well they're doing that. We'll learn if she'll continue to need life support or if the centers handling that are operating well enough on their own.

"Functional Magnetic Resonance Imaging is the newest system for evaluating brain activity, but we don't have it at Highland Park Medical yet. If it seems warranted, we'll send Mrs. Maren to a lab in Skokie that has the equipment, but I think we'll get all we need from our PET scan."

Phil looks again at Jackee. "Christ, what a screwed-up mess. How the Hell do you feed her, if she can't even move her mouth too chew?"

"Through a tube through her nose and down her esophagus into her stomach," Doctor Hersch says. "We can go directly through the stomach wall, but I like this better for long term care. In her present condition, it won't be uncomfortable, and there's less room for infection.

"It's a liquid diet, but quite nourishing. She'll need care-givers for feeding, bathing and physical therapy, but with proper attention, she could easily live another twenty years."

"Twenty years? Twenty years like this?" Shaking his head, Phil hunches his shoulders, raking the doctor with hooded eyes.

"She'll never recover?"

"I've never seen it. As I said, brain death rarely reverses itself."

"What a mess. How'll I care for our sons? They need a mother. Jesus! You guys really screwed up my... uh... our lives."

Bitter words, but still with no heat in them... no real conviction. *It's like he's reading lines. And was he smiling? Should I be surprise he's more worried about himself then the boys and me? Well, why not? My life is over. They'll have to forge something for themselves without me. I'll be an expensive inconvenience.*

The doctors, glancing at each other pensively, follow Phil as he pushes through the doors, coming to Jackee's bed side.

"Luckily there are her father's trusts." Phil mutters, taking her hand, pressing it softly to his lips. She feels absolutely nothing, but the slight smell of Musk cologne wafts over her.

"There's plenty of money to see she's properly cared for," he continues.

Yes, Daddy's trusts. Phil's got them now, after all.

"I'll have to draft a governess for our team to care for our sons. We'll cope. For us, it's a major inconvenience. But for Jackee... Jesus. I can't imagine what Hell she's going through."

His eyes find hers.

"There's no way for us to even know your needs, Jacks." He turns to the doctor.

"Will she even *have* any needs, like... this?"

"Other than physical care? It's hard to say. I'd think you'll have to find *something* for mental stimulation... something to fill her mind in place of physical activity. It won't be easy."

A strange look flitters across his eyes. Fidgeting, he drops his gaze.

Poor Phil. He never bargained for an anchor around his neck.

In spite of her own disaster, compassion floods her. He'll stick it out for the love of his family... or for its money. She is uncertain which matters more... especially after that tirade after the reading of Daddy's will, but either is reason enough for him to stay.

His life's ruined, almost as much as mine. But knowing him, he'll keep going... more for himself, I think, then for our children. Still, he's too young to resign from living because this.

Better if I were dead, instead of trapped inside this motionless shell for the rest of my years... whatever they may be. Twenty years! God! How horrible!

CHAPTER FOUR

Apache high-steps nervously as she rides onto the field, scanning the course. She's never seen such towering fences. A quick glance at the bleachers, where Daddy and Mama are watching.

Snorting steam, the horse springs forward. She's frozen erect in the saddle, rigid and immobile, as they hurtle on, driving hard toward an enormous wall

Oh, God, I'll be killed. Her legs are stone, her knees locked, unable to squeeze, signaling him to leap. Now is the time, but she can't move or utter a sound.

Jump! Jump! Apache, as if hearing her mental urging, vaults high into the air.

Still stiffly upright, powerless to lean into the jump, she grits her teeth, expecting to be thrown from the saddle by the beast's powerful upward surge.

Miraculously, that never happened, as they clear that wall and race on toward the next. Again she commands, *Jump*, and they soar high above the shiny white rails.

Wow! I forgot how exhilarating this is. She chances a peek at the stands. Daddy is still there, smiling but alone now.

"Go on, Countess!" he calls. "Keep fighting! You can achieve whatever you put your mind to. Don't quit now!"

Another fence looms ahead, but she is gaining confidence she might clear any hurdle, if she wills it hard enough.

◆ ❖ ◆

Jackee opens her eyes, struggling to focus, dispelling the last vestiges of the dream.

What was that? Daddy talking to me from heaven? I don't think so.

Blinking away the lingering fog of sleep, the real world, filled with bitter truths, slides into focus.

Still in the hospital. Still can't move, like in the dream. A nurse lingers by her bed, studying her chart.

"Ah, you're awake." She smiles. "The doctor wants to talk to you."

Now what? I've been here twelve endless days. First that PET scan, which didn't turn up anything encouraging. Then so many doctors and nurses pushing, poking and sticking me, all day, every day. Weird to feel absolutely nothing... not even the injections. Always hated needles. Might as well be watching a movie.

They are pursuing everything to find some answer to her "condition," but she knows the truth.

There's no magic wand.

My body's basically dead, and that's that! The old heart's pumping, and my brain and eyes work fine. Got me hooked to some kind of machine to help me breathe, but they say it's only precautionary.

The scan showed what Dr. Hersch called "minor deterioration" to my involuntary systems, but they're working well enough to do the job, since there's no physical activity to support.

"Hello, Mrs. Maren. How are we doing today?" Doctor Hersch saunters in, dapper in a rust-brown silk suit, the collar of his beige dress shirt open with a loosened, red and brown striped tie.

We? Speaking for myself, things aren't exactly great. You know, paralyzed and all, thanks to you and all the other incompetent jerks that work here! What's this "we" you're always tossing at me?

She sighs in her head. She *never* threw abuse at anyone, but she's doing it a lot now. Who has more right? Besides, no one can hear her.

She blinks her eyes once, acknowledging him.

"Good. Your husband will be by later. We've finished our tests, and you're ready to go home. We're skipping the fMRI. We don't believe it will add anything we don't already know, and Mr. Maren feels it's an unnecessary expense. Your quarters at home will surely be more comfortable, and you'll be surrounded by family."

My boys! I can't wait to see them. Her eyes tear.

Phil's never brought them to visit. What will they think of their "zombie" mama?

"We'll continue doing research, but honestly, this is a pretty rare situation. Happens maybe once in many thousands of times. We're fortunate you can still think. You're lucky to have a loving family to care for you and keep you stimulated." His smile is anything but reassuring.

Lucky? You bastard! This is 'lucky?' You've ruined all our lives with your incompetent blundering, and you call me lucky? I hate you! Her eyes blaze emerald daggers. He flinches, edging backward, as if struck by their angry points. Perspiration beads on his forehead.

"Uh... yes." Sounding much less confident, he mops his brow.

"Anyhow, you'll be leaving soon. You're still our top priority, but I don't want to give any false hopes that anything will change for the better. Try to make the best of things.

"I understand the therapist you're husband hired has visited you. It'll be his job to keep your muscles in shape, and there'll be a nurse to feed you and tend to your needs."

Yes, they visited two days ago. Deciding whether to take my case, I guess. What an interesting pair, the therapist and the nurse – a giant Southerner...an ex-boxer, I think, based on that battle-scarred face... and a wiry little Filipina with such serious eyes.

Her eyes found the doctor's, blinking once.

"Right. You've met them. You're lucky..." *Damn you and your Goddamned 'lucky'* "...your husband can provide that care for you at home. It'll be much nicer than even the very best maximum care facility."

Sure, but it's really Daddy and his trust funds watching out for me, even from his grave. Her eyes glitter wetly at the memory of her father, and how he always cared for his Countess.

I love you, Daddy, wherever you are!

"I'll let you rest. Mr. Maren said he'd be by in an hour or so. I'll stop by again later tonight." He spins on his heel, hurrying away, leaving Jackee with her thoughts.

This is it! This how I'll spend the rest of my life... an empty shell with a brain. I'll have to do something...think of something...to keep from going crazy. Thank God Phil's sticking it out, but I'm not sure for how long. Things with us were less than perfect when this happened so I don't know how long he'll keep up appearances. Still, I... I sense something deeper there that's not right. Something I can't quite put my finger on.

What am I going to do? I can't even talk to my boys. Tell them how much they mean to me. It isn't fair.

Tired from her mental harangue, she slips into a restless sleep.

CHAPTER FIVE

Jackee lurches awake with a start... a mental "start"... since her body doesn't have a flinch or twitch left in it. Her eyes just pop open. The portion of the bed supporting her head and upper body is elevated so she can see into the room.

Phil, tall and athletically slender, is leaning against the foot rail, a strange smile tugging at the corner of his mouth. Blue, wide-set eyes that should be filled with compassion instead send a momentary chill slithering down her spine.

"Hi, baby. Sleeping, weren't you? How're you doing? Oh, shit! There's no way you can tell me, is there?"

Can he really be this insensitive? What's with that smirk?

"Anyway, you'll be coming home soon as the rooms are ready." He perches on the side of the bed.

"I'm building a suite from the maid's quarters. Paying a big premium for 'em to work extra innings. Gonna make you as comfortable as possible. You've already met the live-in nurse and the therapist I've hired. Both highly recommended. The guy's an ex-boxer, a real Appalachian hick, but they say he works magic."

She blinks once. She'd thought of them earlier. The man is gigantic, craggy-featured with shoulders a yard wide, like some fabled Gothic warrior. Probably pretty good looking once. The mahogany-skinned woman is tiny as an elf... an unlikely pair.

He sat, somber amber eyes holding hers, as the little nurse studied her charts. Jackee caught snatches during their whispered huddle: "... not your usual... no recovery... but this is different."

She sensed gentleness in this fierce-looking giant's battered face, as he took her hand, explaining, in a soft Southern drawl, who they were and promising to return. Her husband apparently arranged exactly that.

"I'm fixing up two apartments over the garage," Phil says. "The nurse's room will connect to yours, and Charlene and the big lug'll have separate digs over the cars. You can't believe how complicated it was, getting water and sewer connections out there.

"Gotta sign on a new coach to care for the kids, too, with you on the sidelines. One big team, making life as easy for you as we can."

Jackee fights back tears.

He still seems to care, taking charge of our lives. He's been so preoccupied with his job these last few years.

She was always proud of his success at North Chicago Printing. He didn't need to work. Daddy left them more money than they could ever spend. She had berated herself at her anger when Phil's job kept him away from home so many evenings. They *were* grooming him as the company's next president.

But after that horrible mishap last summer, almost losing his entire family, he was back home, loving and supportive. Even now, with her locked in this silent Hell, he's taking care of everything. It isn't going to be a picnic, and a lot of guys would bail out. She blinks back resurgent tears, and he smiles again.

"The boys wanted to come, but I decided against it. Seeing you like this might be too upsetting. There'll be plenty of time to acclimate them when you get home."

My sons! He's never brought them, even once. Why? They need to know I'm still thinking of them. Her eyes brim again, beseeching him to change his mind.

"Well, I gotta go," he blurts, tugging at his collar. "They say you're able to leave, but the house won't be ready for a few more days. I'm pulling out all of the stops, Jackee. If you could only talk... Maybe the therapist or nurse can figure something out. I may not be back for a day or so. I got a big project at work, and I need some quiet time to get it done."

He slid from his seat at the edge of the bed, and brushes a few loose strands of golden hair from her still bandaged cheek. His fingers trace the lines of her jaw and neck. They disappearing from her sight, but she knows where they have gone. He was always especially fond of her full, firm breasts, but they can no longer bring either of them any pleasure.

Nothing! I feel absolutely nothing, except this stupid sense of floating in warm water. What wonderful goose-bumps his touch used to bring.

A pall of depression swamps her. Phil can't know how sad he made her. There is no way to show her love for her boys...or her husband. This painful moment makes that crystal clear.

My life has ended. I just didn't have the good sense to die. How can I fight, Daddy? remembering her earlier dream. *There's nothing left to fight with. Nothing to do but think.*

Think, think, think! It's enough to drive me crazy.

Phil brushes droplets from the corners of her emerald eyes.

"Jesus, Jacks. Things never seem to work out like they're supposed to. I never thought this is how we'd end up. I'm really sorry."

Not your fault, darling. Just one Hell of a rotten break. I've been mostly lucky all my life. What a way to even the score!

He bends down, kissing her on the forehead. Lightly, she supposes.

Mmmm. Musk after-shave. Daddy's favorite, too.

Tears bloom again in the corner of her eyes.

Damn, the little things we're often too busy to notice. Her eyes narrow, expelling the droplets to slide leisurely down her cheeks. *Something else there, though. A smell? No, something else. Something...a sense of...of what? Something foreboding?*

She shakes it off.

What an imagination.

She finds his ocean-blue eyes with hers. Despite a smile they seem somehow cold, without real compassion. A corner of his mouth twitches up, almost a grin, as he pats her hand.

"Gotta go. See you again, real soon. I'll send your love to the boys." Then he is gone.

Jackee sighs. She's alone. She'll *always* be alone now, trapped in her own head.

How will I ever cope? It's not fair!

All I can do is think.

Think!

Think!

Think!

CHAPTER SIX

A white ambulance, buffeted by angry winds, turns into the cobblestone drive of a sprawling, stone and cedar-walled ranch house.

The November afternoon is crisp and bright. The Sun, a frozen disc of twenty-four karat gold, slides slowly toward the horizon. Its parting fire singes the distant, snow-filled cumulus clouds with streaks of mauve, magenta and indigo, bringing promises of winter's first attack.

A cluster of maples vainly spread stark, leafless fingers against the coming onslaught, as the cold sphere of fire plays peek-a-boo with the thickening gray-white blanket in the West.

The house, in the village of Glencoe, overlooks a small wooded park. Twice a week during the season, professionals meticulously maintain the acre of ornamental landscaping. The myriad flower beds, however, were solely Jackee's domains...until now.

The ambulance navigates the circular drive, easing to a gentle stop. Carved oak entrance doors swing open, sprouting two little blonde heads, peeking pensively around the jamb. Nine-year-old Malcolm has his mother's startling green eyes, contrasting younger Bryan's violet blues. They wait, huddled against the growing cold, gaping at the long, white vehicle.

"That's what they take dead people in." Bryan whispers, wide-eyed.

"No, silly," Mal replies. "Those are black. The white ones are for sick people, like Mommy. We gotta help take care of her, Bry, Daddy's busy at work, so it gonna be up to us."

"Okay Mommy knows we'll always love her, doesn't she?"

"Sure." Malcolm turns, making way for an ageless, dusky-skinned woman, struggling into a thick wool sweater. She is closely followed by a huge man, wearing a pea coat.

Kevin Martin carries middle-age well. His rugged round face is somehow gentle, in spite of many seams and scars, the legacy of his boxing career. Thick, bushy ridges, shading surprisingly soft, intelligent amber eyes, frame a bent, twice broken nose. A blue woolen knit cap covers most of his mahogany crew cut, and the tips of his ears. While no longer in fighting trim, he hasn't gone to flab. At six-foot-four and 242 pounds, he's heavily built, with broad shoulders, corded biceps and huge hands that are as gentle now as they once were punishing.

Phil, wearing a red and green ski jacket, scrambles out of the opening rear doors as Kevin and the nurse, Maria, arrive. The two boys strain to peek inside from their perch on the black slate stoop, but can only see gloomy shadows. The driver slides out the gurney, wheeled legs unfolding, and there is Jackee, covered by a white blanket and strapped down for the ride home.

Kevin takes control of the gurney, leaning over to better see his patient.

"Welcome home, Miz Maren. Bet you're gonna be a lot happier here. We got a lot of work ahead of us. The docs say not to get our hopes up, but that's all we got to go on... hope."

His voice is pleasantly deep and surprisingly clear, despite the Southern patios.

"But, 'enough of that. There're two young'uns here pawing the ground, eager to welcome their mama home." He guides the stretcher to the raised stoop. Her sons crowd around her, assuring their undying love. Emerald eyes shimmering, she chokes back sobs only she hears.

Phil lounges against the door, a smile tickling his lips. Sharp-tipped fingers trip across her mind, bringing a sudden chill unrelated to the brisk wind. She has no sense of cold or heat.

He looks... amused? Why? What's funny about this? Forget it. I'm home. Home at last.

My wonderful sons. Finally, after all these lonely weeks. They seem so happy to see me, even like this. Why did Phil keep them away? I missed them so. How to show I love them? No way to do it. I'd scream... if I could!

She struggles against more tears. Being a crybaby only makes things more difficult.

I'm a Webster, goddammit! We're tougher than that.

Kevin reappears, pushing a shiny new wheelchair, all chrome and soft beige leather. He scoops up her as easily as a child, fastening her into the seat with a harness specially designed to keep her body upright and support her head, allowing her to be moved around with ease.

"Okay, fellas," Kevin says, "let's get your mama outta this cold. Ya can show her the new room your Daddy set up for her." Malcolm and Bryan bound off, heading for the recently redecorated and enlarged maid's quarters where their mother will live.

They take turns displaying the features built in for her: a power-tilt bed, and a massage table for the physical therapy necessary to keep her muscles from atrophy. This will move to a special "gym," the fourth bedroom, where modifications are not yet completed.

A small black refrigerator hums quietly in one corner. A two-door cabinet above stores supplies, mainly the canned nutrient, fed her twice daily through her nasal tube. Several complicated-looking chrome and plastic medical machines line one wall: monitors of her health and physical condition.

A doorway leads to Maria's connecting bedroom. She'll be close by, day or night. Two tan leather chairs and a small chocolate corduroy sofa are placed where Jackee, with the bed tilted up, can see any guests. A small glass coffee table sits bereft of magazines.

After reviewing her new digs, they head for the den. Kevin pauses by the glass-paneled and mahogany French doors, opening to her garden... barren now in the face of winter's hurrying approach. That's where she had lost herself over the years, working in therapeutic solitude, nurturing an eclectic variety of flowers and shrubs.

Dry leaves spin in frantic circles, hurrying across the landscape, borne on blustery winds.

Not the only things dead around here, but at least they can still wiggle and skip, and do the shimmy. So desolate and colorless now. Just like my future.

"Well, how d'ya like it?" Phil followed them into the den. "I spent a bundle getting this ballpark ready. You've got everything here you'll need, and Maria's right next door."

She sighs... or at least thinks she did. *I've just traded one hospital room for this fancier one.* Despite her resolve, moisture again fills her eyes.

This is what's left for me. Can I survive like this?

The vivid dream of twelve days earlier flashes in her head. Daddy, cheering her on.

How can I fight? I can't affect anything, stuck inside my head, only watching. Her malachite eyes glisten with moisture.

What will happen to my sons? So strange that Phil was never really close to them. An athletic father, with two boys to mold, seldom taking an interest... throwing a ball, or teaching them to bat. Now they need a mother. Maybe he's right. Find a governess... someone who might really care.

Her thoughts only deepen the bog of despair, slowly drawing her down into utter hopelessness.

CHAPTER SEVEN

Kevin gently scoops her from the massage table, settling her in her chair, fiddling with the straps to keep her upright. The ease and care with which he lifts her gives a momentary sense of soaring, setting the surface of her dark little pond rippling.

They just completed ninety minutes of therapy, working all of her large muscles through contractions and extensions, and rotating her joints, including her head and neck. He finished with a firm massage, none of which she felt.

How depressing. I always loved a massage.

"That's it for this morning. We'll have another go this afternoon. Gonna work up to longer sessions, but your body's been inactive for so long, we gotta take it easy at first. Ya feel any of this?"

Two blinks.

Nothing intrudes on the weightless, completely disembodied, floating sensation of her new, maddening existence.

Eerie and depressing to see his huge hands on me with absolutely no sense of their touch.

"No, huh? Well, that's what the docs said to expect, but they've been wrong before. Problem is, since ya can't talk, we can only guess at your wants and needs." He gazes at her, pulling at an ear lobe.

"Let's see if we can figure a way to communicate. Gotta have some idea what's going on in that pretty head." He perches on a chair in front of her, his dark eyes searching hers.

"Don't happen to know any Morse Code, do ya?"

Two blinks.

"I'm not surprised. Know what it is though?"

One blink.

"Good. You're kinda doing it, blinking for 'yes' and 'no.' Tell ya what. We're gonna develop our own eye-blink 'Jackee Code,' and expand our vocabulary. I'll work out some simple things, and we'll learn 'em together. We'll teach Maria and your family, too. Okay?"

One blink, with suddenly teary eyes.

Thank God for this wonderful man. I'm lucky Phil found him. At least Phil's sticking it out, in spite of this tragedy.

Kevin spins her chair, wheeling her into the den, settling her by the French doors. The setting sun scatters long, ragged shadows across the bleak creeping-bent lawn, turned straw yellow by the onset of winter. A small stand of barren trees behind the house shimmer in the waning light.

"I'll give ya some quite time while I work on our new code. Okay?"

One blink. *Quiet time? I'll have a life full of that, won't I?*

She stares absently at the stark landscape, thinking of her parents and how young they were when they died.

Are all the Websters cursed?

Memories of Mama swim into her head as she slips into a restless sleep.

She stood in a large, bright white room, holding Daddy's hand. A once pretty woman, now terribly wasted away, lay on the bed, ash-blonde hair spread on the pillow like a silver halo. Her mother's merry gray eyes are closed, her often smiling lips still.

A bottle of clear liquid hangs near the bed, plastic tubing trailing from it to a bandage on her arm. It's very quiet...the only barely audible sound is Mama's soft, shallow breathing from inside the clear plastic canopy. Tears trickle down Daddy's tanned cheeks.

"Mama has gone into a deep sleep." His voice quavers, choked and hoarse.

"It protects her from the bad disease in her, Countess. She's resting for her trip to see God."

She looks up at him, and he squeezes her hand softly. "Mama isn't coming home, darling. She's going to live with God. There'll be no more pain. She'll be there, waiting until it's our time to join her. Be happy for her." But he doesn't look at all happy, and neither is she.

"Mama! Mama! Don't go." Jackee pulls away and falls on the bed, taking her mother's skeletal, pale hand.

"I love you, Mama. I'll be a good girl. You'll be happier at home, Mama. Please don't go!"

"She can't hear you, Countess. Mama is in a deep, peaceful sleep and can't hear anything.

"She can't hear you... can't hear you... can't hear you..."

The words ring in her head as she jerks awake.

She can't hear you.

Her eyes flutter, clearing the cobwebs of sleep, the dream still fresh, an exact memory of the last time she saw Mama. She blinks away fresh tears.

Damned crybaby!

Was it true Mama couldn't hear me? Was her coma really so different from me?

Except for my eyes, they might think I'm in a coma, but they've got machines telling them my brain is still a busy little beaver. Did they have those gadgets twenty-five years ago? Probably not.

Oh, Mama, there was so much I wanted to tell you, if only I had thought you could hear me.

She closes her eyes.

Be brave. You're a Webster, dammit.

She glances at the wall clock above the fireplace. Maria is due with her "evening meal."

How utterly degrading, being fed, diapered and cleaned like a baby. Only I'm taking my meal through a tube instead of a nippled baby bottle. But that's what it takes to keep me alive.

Then Kevin will be along for more therapy and some class work. My husband really mined me a gem with that giant!

Despite Phil's outward support, it's Kevin, not her husband, helping her deal with the isolation. Maybe Daddy hadn't missed the mark with Phil after all, but it doesn't matter now.

I'm a sorry lump... a drain on everyone. How did this happen? There's something else... something I should know, hovering just at the edge of my mind, but I can't quite snag it.

Something important I need to understand.

Too tired to ponder it now. Why do I get so sleepy, doing nothing but think? Well, tomorrow's another day. One of hundreds... maybe thousands... with nothing to do but think.

Think. Think. Think.

Gotta learn to manage somehow.

She dozes in her chair. Maria arrives with her evening meal, but lets her sleep. She can feed her later.

She certainly isn't going anywhere in the meantime.

Chapter Eight

"Good morning," Maria peers in from the doorway, seeing Jackee's eyes are open.

"We're up with the birds today, aren't we? Well, it's never too early to get a start on the day. I'll get your bath and we'll change that smelly diaper. You relax, and I'll be right back."

No need to rush. I'm getting damned good at relaxing. God! I'm like an infant...dirty diapers and bottle-feeding. It could be worse, I guess, but I can't imagine how.

Maria's cheerful little "We this" and "We that" doesn't bother her much anymore.

Jackee glances at the calendar, hanging next to the big clock.

So this is it. Mid-December. Home nearly four weeks, and we've got our routine. Never anything new to look forward to. How long can I possibly survive in this frustrating little Hell?

She's grown accustomed to the eerie, floating sensation in still water, now her sole existence, but if Kevin hadn't taught her to "talk" with her eyelids, she'd have already gone mad.

Maria, a sunny smile on her face, wheels in a cart with a large basin for her morning sponge bath. The smell of her earlier bowel movement isn't pleasant. Her liquid diet doesn't produce much solid waste, but its pungent aroma makes up for what it lacks in volume. Urine passes through a permanent catheter into sealed reservoirs, stored under both her bed and wheelchair. Always compulsively clean, lack of control over bodily functions disgusts her.

What a mess. I'm a stone around everybody's neck. Should have died. Simpler and less agonizing for everyone. This isn't living, anyhow.

"Okay. Here we go." Maria strips off her nightgown.

"I'll clean you up. Then we'll finish our bath."

The soiled diaper deposed of, Jackee, lying on her stomach, hears the sponge, dipping in and out of the basin.

A sponge bath can be so pleasant, even sensual, but there are no tingles...no goose bumps...nothing. Don't know if she's washing my back or my toes.

Tears creep into the corners of her eyes.

Life's so empty...a permanent vacuum. Can't have even the smallest pleasures.

Maria turns her over and begins on her front. Not much over five-feet and one hundred pounds, the little mahogany-skinned woman is amazingly strong. Jackee closes her eyes and imagines the warm water, softly flowing over her.

She forces herself to relax... mentally, of course...and imagine something more pleasant. Not like Phil's erotic touch that set her skin on fire, but never brought her that mystical experience her friends all talked about...an orgasm. Her thoughts drift aimlessly.

"Alrighty." Jackee's eyes snap open. Done already? She lost all sense of time.

"We're all dressed for the day. Ready for breakfast? Kevin will be here soon, and we don't want you working on an empty stomach." Maria retrieves a large can from the refrigerator.

"Looks like enough left for a full meal." She pours the brownish liquid into a measuring cup.

"Ah, just right."

She pauses as she attaches a funnel-like device to the end of her nasal tube.

"Hmmm. This thing doesn't look quite right," she says, fussing with the valve. Finally, everything arranged to her satisfaction, the nurse begins emptying the nourishing liquid into the clear plastic tube, going up her nose to the back of her throat, down her gullet, and through the sphincter muscle, carrying the fluid directly to Jackee's stomach.

Maria stops halfway through the process, her caramel-colored brow deeply creased, the corners of her thin, straight-lipped mouth twitching downward.

"This is going much too slowly. Must be some sort of restriction. We may have to replace the tube later. Don't worry, hon. Just a little longer to finish."

Ten minutes later they're done and Maria is gone, leaving Jackee with thoughts of things that keep going wrong. She dozes briefly, awaiting the new man in her life, out for his morning run before beginning her therapy.

CHAPTER NINE

Jackee awakens at the sound of Kevin opening the door. For a big man, he moves softly, but she always hears him coming. Heightened hearing seems one of nature's compensations for her loss of so many other facilities, a dubious benefit at best. Does she hear more clearly, or just listens better? Regardless, very little of what goes on anywhere in the house gets past her.

"How's my girl doing this morning?"

His craggy face creases in a lopsided smile. His warm camaraderie fills her. Despite her inability to move or speak, he is coming to know her.

"Now that breakfast settled some, we'll get started on therapy. Then, if ya want, I'll read ya the paper. See what's in the news."

She blinks once. His tender concern warms her. Someone who cares how she feels and what she thinks. It ought to be Phil instead of this big bear.

"I like when ya smile at me with your eyes. Funny that I know you're smiling, but I do."

Another single blink.

Somehow he senses my moods. Amazing to find any reason to feel even remotely happy, but it's all relative.

He settles her in the wheel chair, her body strangely alive with tiny tingles as he takes her so easily into his powerful arms. Impossible, but still it is there. Her normally calm pool ripples and sloshes.

Only my imagination, but that's all I have left now...imagination.

She feels her very safest when he holds her. A fondness is growing toward him that probably isn't unusual in a patient/therapist relationship.

This gnarled, gentle giant is so full of real compassion, his battered, fist-scarred face no longer intimating. Phil, at his very best, was never as tender. Just different personalities.

Kevin wheels her into the den.

"I'll be back. I heard someone coming up the drive." She, too, hear the crunch of tires on snow.

A second winter storm had swept down from the North during the night. The grounds sparkle, a crystalline white rolling blanket, pristine and beautiful under the cold brilliance of the Sun, just peeking past a battery of cottony clouds.

This was probably my favorite place in the house, but now it's become the center of my world.

Viewing her silent garden, hiding beneath the snow, and the barren woods beyond, she sighs. This is the start of every day, somehow infusing her with a need to survive. And later, seeing her boys playing in the snow will swell her heart with happiness.

How does something so simple push joy through so much misery? What's in store for them, with me like this?

She has no answers, but there are many questions to consider. Some of those are still undiscovered.

She blinks, hearing someone enter the room.

"Well, Jackee, yer looking mighty thoughtful." Kevin turns her chair away from the French doors.

How can he know that, just from my eyes?

"I don't want to disturb whatever's running around in that pretty head, but it's time for therapy. Can't fall behind, and I've got some personal business to do. But first, ya got a visitor."

"Who?" she signs.

A tall, thin boy of about fifteen appears in the doorway. Carefully plastered-down black wavy hair frames a swarthy, pock-marked face. He's wearing his only buttoned sport shirt, and his one good pair of cargo pants. Restrained affection glows in his dark brown eyes.

"Miss Jackee?" He shifts nervously from foot to foot, his hands clasped behind his back.

"Miguel," she blinks. The boy's brow wrinkles, and he looks to Kevin.

"She talks by blinking. Your name is Miguel?"

The nut-brown head nods, his eyes bright with moisture.

"She hoped ya'd come to see her," Kevin says.

"I couldn't get no one... *anyone*... to bring me, 'til now." He speaks slowly, with careful pronunciation, just as she taught him.

"I wanted to come to the hospital. My uncle said he would drive, but Mister Maren said... he said not to. He said she couldn't see me no... anymore."

"But ya came anyhow?"

"Yes. Miss Jackee, she's... she's been everything to me. She taught me I was smart... that I was as important as anyone. I was flunking out. Running with bad kids. Now I keep my nose clean. I'm... I'm second in my class. Maybe I can even go to college, if I can get a scholarship. No one in my family ever even finished high school." Tiny rivulets trickle down his cheeks.

Jackee's eyes speed into staccato blinking. Kevin nods.

"She says she's proud of ya, and ya should come any time ya can. She asks if ya'd give her a hug."

Miguel Gomez steps hesitantly forward, kneeling beside her chair. Sobbing softly, he wraps his arms around his mentor, resting his head on her lap. Funny it's he needing comforting more than she. Who else will help him direct his life? He gets little from his family and only bad influences from his peers. Her eyes fill with tears.

One more thing I can't attend to. Somehow, I have to keep him on the right road. She begins blinking a lengthy message to Kevin.

"Miguel?" he says.

"Yessir?" He stands, knuckling his eyes. "I'm sorry. I shouldn't have..."

"That's okay, son. It's hard to see someone ya love like this." The boy nods.

"Jackee says she'll set up a college trust fund for ya. Work hard and keep up your grades, and college'll be paid for."

"She'll what...? Oh, Dios mio, I will! College! I promise, I will. I want you to be proud of me." Jackee's eyes flutter.

"She *is* proud of ya. Now, I need to take her for therapy, son. Ya come and see her any time. It gives her something to look forward to."

"Thank you, sir. I'll try." He knuckles his eyes and shakes Kevin's hand, turning to leave, then pauses, looking back.

"I do love you, Miss Jackee. I'd be in a gang, maybe even dead by now, if it wasn't... if it *weren't* for you." He hurries away. Kevin wheels her to the newly converted exercise room.

"Don't know why I'm surprised," he mutters.

"Yer some terrific lady, worrying about others, when you got more'n enough on your own plate."

CHAPTER TEN

The newly constructed "gym" sports a padded, leather-covered massage table, and a cabinet full of ointments and solutions Kevin will knead into her body. There are several pieces of workout equipment, and a complete free-weight system.

Kevin uses the bench press, with weights to 200 pounds, four times a week. A stair-climber is there for aerobic workouts to compliment his four-mile run every morning. A body as large and powerful as his needs a lot of exercise to keep fit. Phil is also a regular visitor, using the aerobic equipment and lesser weights.

Positioning Jackee on the table, Kevin removes her sweat suit and placed a clean, white towel over her breasts. Her only remaining clothing is a pair of white, cotton panties... and of course, a diaper.

He works with professional detachment. Although she sees little of what he does, without the slightest sense of his touch, she still trembles deliciously... in her mind. She instinctively knows when his hands are working near erotic places.

What an imagination. Just wishful thinking.

The massage starts with her neck and face, working down to her ribs, the abdomen, hips, and finally her long, still shapely legs, and feet. After a thorough warm-up, he begins flexing and moving every limb, as well as her neck and head. Even fingers and toes are cycled repeatedly through a range of motion, doing the work Jackee can no longer do for herself. Conditioning is imperative to her survival. If her already thinned body deteriorates, she'll be more susceptible to disease. An active brain needs a relatively healthy vehicle to keep it alive.

An hour of manipulation is followed by another rub down, loosening and stretching muscles to avoid cramping, before moisturizing emollients are applied.

Twice weekly Kevin weighs himself on the electronic scale, and then, with Jackee in his arms, re-weighs the two of them together. Her weight, plus the circumferences of various body parts are transferred to charts for her doctor's review each month. They discuss her progress, suggesting any changes in the routine that seem warranted.

Jackee lost a considerable amount of weight in the hospital, so her medical team is trying, somewhat successfully, to fatten her up. Dr. Berg, her internist, instructed Kevin to boost the caloric content of her meals by about 10%, trying to speed up her weight gain.

"Well, that's it for this morning." Kevin repositions her in her chair.

"Wanna go back to the den and see what's happening in the World since yesterday?"

She blinks once.

A moment later, she is settled in front of the glass doors. An untarnished white sea of snow rolls in cottony brilliance across the yard, swelling and receding over the landscape, its surface broken only by a single set of rabbit tracks. Leafless maples and oaks paint stark skeletons, silhouetted against the nearly cloudless sky.

"It's gonna be real cold for the next few days, so the snow should stick around. Pretty, ain't it?"

One blink.

"Like Winter best, or Summer? One for Summer, two for Winter." Whenever possible, he asks questions Jackee can answer with a "yes" or "no," saving her time and effort.

She blinks once, then twice.

"What? Oh, ya like 'em both the same?"

One blink.

"Well, I ain't too crazy about winter, being from 'Bama. Don't get much of it there. But, I'm here now, so we can enjoy the seasons together."

Jackee studies him for a moment. A small mental shiver tickles her spine.

What'll I do if he leaves? He's my primary link to sanity. Doesn't he have other clients? Phil's idea of caring for me seems consigning someone else do it. This big guy's the only one really keeping me in the game.

My sons are great, but they're only little boys. Life'll be pretty damned bleak without Kevin Martin around.

Seeing him watching, she begins a lengthy message.

"U not here f'ever. Yes?"

"Not here...what? Oh, forever?"

One Blink.

He shakes his head, taking her hands in his. Her eyes scrutinize his.

"Look, this ain't my typical job. We both know it's bigger 'n that. I never back off a good fight. Got no place more important to be than right here.

"I'll stay long as ya can stand me. I may need a little time off occasionally, but if ya want me, I'm here permanently. What d'ya say?"

She blinks a teary response.

"Yes. Yes. Happy!"

"Good. Me, too. Ya and the boys are real special to me. So don't worry none. I'm here until ya tell me to leave."

He grins impishly. "Don't know how, but I kinda recognize a smile in those lovely green eyes."

She blinks once.

How can he observe joy when there's no visible change in my face? Impossible? Maybe, but he somehow senses my emotions. Kinda spooky.

Kevin sighs, not unhappily, and picks up the *Tribune*.

"Now, let's see what's interesting in the paper today."

CHAPTER ELEVEN

Jackee is "talking" with her sons when Kevin returns from his morning run. The boys carry most of the load, largely about their day at school and how bitterly cold it is outside.

"Hi," Kevin says. "How're ya guys doing?"

He sits on the sofa where he can clearly watch her eyelids. Little Bryan crawls onto his lap, and both boys begin babbling together about the day's adventures. He gently ruffles the little man's yellow hair.

It's wonderful how they've taken to him. Ought to be Phil, but he hasn't spent much time with them since this disaster.

When they talked themselves out, Kevin picks up Mal, placing him on his other knee.

"Ya guys like fishing?" he asks.

"Oh, yeah!" Mal says. "We all went on a big boat on Lake Michigan with Grandpa, right before he... he went to visit Grandma in Heaven. It was real fun. I caught the biggest... Ironhead, I think... of the season. The Captain told me. It's the one on the wall in my room."

"Steelhead, ya mean, son. Yep, that's a beaut. I bet he weighed a good twelve pounds. Gave ya a tough fight, did he?"

"Boy, I'll say!" Bryan pitches in. "He jumped three times, real high. Daddy had to hold Mal up, but he fought him all alone, didn't you Mal."

"Sure did," says the older boy, puffing out his chest. "All by myself. I guess it took hours. Mommy caught a big...lake trout? Yeah, a lake trout. She said she would, and then she did! Mommy did things like that sometimes. It's real funny."

"I bet," the big man says. "Well, how 'bout we do some fishing up at the Chain-O-Lakes next season. Ya caught those big fish on a charter boat, didn't ya?"

Malcolm nods. "Yeah, a real big boat. The captain even let me drive a little."

"Musta been fun, but I'm guessing they supplied all the tackle. Ya got any of your own?"

The boys look at each other and shake their heads, dejection creasing their smooth faces.

"Not to worry. I'll get ya some proper rods and reels, and when we get a nice day, I'll teach ya how to use them." The momentary smiles on their faces wither, as Phil enters the room.

"What's this about fishing?" He asks, eyebrows arched, looking first at Kevin, then his wife. Only Jackee heard him arrive.

"You'll be playing in some other ball park by then, won't you, Kevin."

"No, sir. I talked to Jackee 'bout that today. She wants me to stay, permanently. I'm happy to help any other way I can. Most boys like fishing, and you're pretty busy, so I figured I'd fill in. Didn't think ya'd mind, long as they were happy."

"Well, you're wrong! Nothing's happening in this ballpark without my say-so. If Jackee wants you caring for her, that's fine. She should be comfortable, or happy, or whatever the Hell she feels. But the boys are *my* responsibility, not a hired lackey's. And it's about time you gave my wife some respect. She's *Mrs. Maren* to you. You're her servant, not her friend."

What a thing to say! Jackee's jaw would have dropped, were it able.

This man has done nothing but give of himself in the short time he's been here. What's gotten into Phil? I won't stand for it.

She tries to signal her anger, but no one is watching. The big therapist stares at Phil, his face strangely blank.

"I agree, first names are usually reserved for friends," Kevin says softly. He turns to Jackee, eyebrows raised.

"Do I qualify as your friend?"

She blinks "yes."

"Do ya mind if I call ya 'Jackee'?"

Two blinks. Kevin crouches, taking her limp hand in his, smiling gently. He glances fleetingly at Phil, before returning to her wonderfully expressive green eyes.

"Let's put it another way. Do ya *want* me to call ya 'Jackee'?"

She blinked a response.

"Mommy said, 'Yes. You best friend,' "little Malcolm interprets." Kevin's our friend, too, aren't you Kevin? We like you a lot."

The boy has no inkling of the skirmish being fought in front of him.

"Why, thank ya, son. I'm real fond of both of ya, too. Is that all, Mister Maren?"

Use of Phil's formal name makes it obvious Kevin doesn't group him with those he considers friends. Phil shakes his head and shrugs.

"Well, if that's what she wants, I suppose it's okay You're here for her, so you can play it her way, now that you've developed some sort of communication. Don't get in *my* way, and everything will be fine."

"Yes sir. I don't want to be a bother to ya. Just do my best to keep Jackee healthy as I can, both body 'n mind. I'm sure that's what ya want."

Phil regards the big man thoughtfully. A gauntlet had clearly been thrown at his feet.

"Right." He's brisk now, all business. "But that's *it*. You're to care for Jackee, not entertain my sons. That's *my* job, or that of the governess I'm going to bring in. If they're going fishing, *I'll* take them. You stay out of my family's life. Got it?"

"But Jackee wanted..."

"I don't give a damn *what* Jackee wants, unless it's for her personal care. You're working for *me*, Martin. Understand that. If you can't do what I ask, I'll get someone else. It won't matter much to her, anyway, in this sorry state."

Good God! How spiteful. Mental hackles ridged her back.

Would he say that if he really loved me? Am I'm only an inconvenience? Things sure aren't what I'd expect between us, and I'm getting a strong vibe that's not something new. But to treat his sons so callously. That's just cruel! She caught his mocking azure eyes with hers.

Please, Phil. Please!

"Mommy is saying 'please' with her eyes," Malcolm pipes up. "Kevin's only trying to help, daddy. You're busy at work all the time. Fishing was so much fun that time with Grandpa."

Phil strokes his son's golden locks as he looks at Jackee. She senses he's suddenly strangle uneasy. Shifting from foot to foot, he studies Kevin, head bowed submissively. Shaking his head dismissively, a smug smile steals across Phil face. His small shrug is the picture of nonchalance.

"Oh, all right. He can take you, if it's what you really want. Now off to bed. Both of you."

He stares at Jackee as their sons leave, his face hardening, lips pressed into a narrow slit. Acid bitterness seems to fill her mouth, even though in a corner of her fear-paralyzed mind, she knows it's only imagined.

She cowers in her chair, trembling

"Remember," his voice softly ominous, "don't make any other plans without checking with me first. I'm in charge here, not Kevin Martin. Not you either, Jacks. Me! *I'm* running this house. The governess *I* choose will see to the kids. I've got it all planned out." He turns abruptly and stalked off, a vacuum of frozen silence spinning in his wake.

Jackee's cringe morphs into seething rage, overshadowing fear.

Why such animosity? Such blatant distain. Can I cling to any hope he still loves me, in spite of...of this fiasco? Did he ever, for that matter? Why would he so carelessly threaten my life... my very existence... if he cared at all?

Kevin handled the whole thing very well. Thank you, God, for this man. I feel so much safer, knowing he's going to be here.

Always! The thought settles her.

Phil better not try to change that. What will I do if he forces Kevin to leave? Got to involve Arthur Osborn, if necessary. He controls the trusts. That'll get Phil's attention.

How far will he go to get his own way? How much will he really risk?

Those questions frighten her. Phil might stop her from seeing Osborn, so it may be up to Kevin.

What's gotten into him? Has my accident turned him so nasty? Or just brought the real Phil into the light? I wonder if I ever really knew him?

She sighs, looking at Kevin, a quizzical smile twitching at his lips. Warmth infuses her.

Kevin! Kevin! What a guy. You're only here to care for my body, yet you've done so much more. You're the one most concerned with my emotional well-being. You taught me to "talk," and help maintain my sanity. I can't image life without you.

Amazing! I never thought of myself as a snob. Still, all the guys I dated between Phil... and Phil... were clean-cut and attractive, from fine old families. Well, wealthy ones, anyway.

I'd probably never have even talked to him, with his poor South drawl, even if his face weren't so fight-damaged then. Might have even been ruggedly good-looking in his youth, but I still wouldn't have looked at him twice. He's from a totally different world.

How foolishly shallow! Here's a real man... strong, sensitive, self-educated. He's tender in ways Phil never was. I hadn't realized exactly how different they are, until now.

What if I'd met Kevin Martin twelve years ago, somehow realizing who he really is under that scary physical shell? I think Daddy would have liked... and trusted him.

Kevin, seeing Jackee apparently lost in thought, awaits signs she is done. Finally, she raises her eyes and "smiles," calm and in control again.

"Having some thoughts about that tirade, were ya?"

One blink.

"Anything ya want to talk about?"

"Yes. U."

"Me? Hope that's good."

"Yes. U R best."

"Me? Like in Best Friend?" He shrugs and smiles.

She senses his fierce desire to hang in there, despite his boss's growing antagonism. Her fondness for this unusual guy is mutating into something more than friendship.

"Yes. U best." Warmth infuses her, the remainder of her anxiety slipping away. This gentle giant, along with her sons, are the very center of what remain of her life. Phil, immersed in his job, isn't home much. Maybe that's best, in light of that afternoon's angry outburst.

"I'm mighty flattered. Not used to having a beautiful lady think of me as a best friend. And you're the most beautiful lady I've ever known, inside and out."

She blushes, or at least thinks she does. His grin is impish.

"We'll start a mutual admiration society." He grins again. She smiles with her eyes.

"Well now, want me to start reading *Gone with the Wind,* or do ya want to watch some TV? One for the book, two for TV."

She blinks once, so he moves her to face his armchair, and begins to read.

"Scarlett O'Hara was not beautiful..."

CHAPTER TWELVE

Damn! Maybe Kevin was right.

Jackee sighs, listening to them eat.

It's lonely here, all by myself. Maybe I should sit with the family during dinner.

No. That's got to be so uncomfortable for them. It certainly would be devastating for me. Just hearing them eat is agonizing!

Life now is as much an aural game as visual, interpreting exactly who is doing what by the sounds they make. Unable to turn her head or move around to investigate a noise, she is forced to listen more carefully. No other way to learn what is going on around her. Otherwise, she is restricted to what she can see directly in front of her, and what she can smell.

She seems to have developed "Bionic Ears," seldom missing a single sound within the house. She records noises and odors with new interest. Figuring them out is the challenge. Time passes more quickly playing this game, distracting her... at least momentarily...from the intense frustration of her sensationless existence. Eating is a painful exception.

I loved mealtime, with all of us together, discussing events of the day. Even when Phil worked late, it was quality time with the boys, recapping their day at school, or at play. Sitting there now, helplessly, while they eat and talk around me...God, it's more than I can bear.

Charlene's serving the main course...roasted chicken and sweet potatoes. The odors are distinct. Then the unmistakable sounds of Phil cutting the bird into pieces with a serrated shears.

"A wing, Daddy. I want a wing." Bryan begs for his favorite piece of any fowl.

"All right. All right. I've cut one off for you. Relax."

Phil will appropriate the breasts. Luckily, Malcolm loves the thigh and leg, because his father doesn't like sharing the white meat. Bryan gets both wings, and maybe part of a leg.

Kevin and Charlene will share another chicken in the kitchen. He will probably eat half the bird, and perhaps the leg quarter from the other side. Charlene will only take half of a breast. Like a good Irish lass, she'll fill up on potatoes.

What a freckle-faced treasure. She came to them through an employment service on a one-year housekeeper's visa and quickly became like part of the family. Her fondness for Mal and Bry...and they for her... transcended a mere job.

Jackee procured a permanent Green Card for her, and subsequently arranged for her brother, Sean, to immigrate as an auto mechanic at the Jaguar dealer in Wilmette. Charlene will be eligible for U.S. citizenship next year, and is already studying for that test.

Finished with dinner, the clatter tells of her sons stacking dishes and carrying them to the kitchen. Phil prefers they leave that for the hired help, but Jackee insisted the boys learn to be considerate gentlemen. They are still doing the chores their mother assigned them, much more the product of her influence than Phil's. He rarely involved himself in their rearing.

He's so different from Daddy. First my little brother, Charlie, died, and then Mama, only six years later. Only the two of us then. He put so much love and effort into raising me. Nothing was too good for his little Countess, but I never felt really spoiled.

Daddy tried hard to do it right, but he was so inexperienced. I guess that's one way he and Phil are a lot alike, never needing to be involved in rearing the family, until Fate mixed in. The difference is, Phil seems unprepared to take any real interest.

Dear Daddy! I miss you so! Would things have gone so terribly wrong if you were here? Tears trickle from her eyes.

I'm the last of the living Websters, and look at me, barely living at all.

She sighs. Things certainly aren't what they first seemed.

Why has Phil suddenly turned so nasty? He seemed to actually enjoy menacing me. Would he treat someone he loved like this? I think not. I've been such a fool.

Kevin will try to protect me, but why should he even have to? This is only a job, after all, and Phil can fire him at any time. I'd better tell Kevin to contact Arthur Osborn if I'm not able, if Phil gets out of hand.

Arthur's an astute judge of character, and never seemed very fond of my husband. I suppose he saw Phil more clearly than I ever did. Nothing would surprise me now. That scares me, because it makes no sense. Kevin might end up in the middle, if I'm threatened.

She visualizes Phil's reaction to that. It scares her even more.

Numbed by the press of her thoughts, she sits dully, closing her eyes.

Kevin peeks in, and seeing Jackee apparently napping, wheels her to her room. Therapy is finished for the day. He settles in a chair, watching her, almost as if standing guard.

Rising quietly, he approaches the bed.

"Sleep soundly, my sweet," he murmurs. "I'm watching out for ya. Gotta be careful, though. Not give Phil any excuse to fire me, now he's discovered I'm not a country hick." He lightly brushes a strand of hair from her face, before turning to leave.

She sighs. *At least there's one man in my life who cares,* and drifts off, at peace.

Chapter Thirteen

"There. Comfy, now?"

Jackee blinks once.

Comfy? I wouldn't know if my foot were on fire.

Maria plumps the pillows, arranging her in a half-reclined position. Extra bolsters are wedged against each of her sides to keep her upright.

"Need anything else?"

Two blinks... "No."

"Alrighty. Then we're done for the evening. Kevin'll be back later to read to you, if you want. I'll be next door, if you need me." The petite woman bounces out of the room.

Jesus, where does she get all that energy? And so what if she is next door? I've got no way to call her.

Kevin tried connecting a whistle-like device to her nostril, but it doesn't work. She is limited to "demand breathing," and is unable to exhale with any added force, no matter how hard she tries.

It doesn't matter. I've lived... if you can call it that...eight weeks of this stupid, empty existence, floating in that imaginary pond, and for what? I may as well be in a coma, or even dead.

Just like Mama.

Just like Daddy.

Dear Daddy. Was your coma...or Mama's...anything like this? Could you hear and understand what was going on around you?

Reluctantly, she unwraps the dark tapestry of those entombed memories, needing to see them in the stark light of her current existence. There are still things to be explained. She remembers that terrible time...

◆❖◆

Something was wrong. Terribly wrong!

She just *knew* it.

She fidgeted in her seat, waiting for her father to emerge from the doctor's office. Daddy, who rarely had a cold, did not look well. The headaches were wearing him down. She was surprised he asked her to drive him to this appointment, as if needing the company.

"Mrs. Maren?" She blinked, pulling herself from her musing. The neurologist stood in the doorway to his office.

"Your father would like to talk to you." He gestured, holding the door open. Ice fused her spine, immobilizing her legs. This was *not* good. Struggling shakily to her feet, she took two deep breaths, and strode into the room. Whatever it was, Daddy wanted support, not pity or hysteria. How bad could it be? He wasn't even sixty-five.

Chester Webster stood, taking her hands, squeezing gently.

"Bad news, Countess."

"Oh, God." Her emerald eyes tear, her lower lip trapped between her teeth.

"It seems I have a brain tumor." His hazel eyes held hers.

"Oh, Daddy!" She staggered, her resolve evaporating. Only his strong grasp kept her from the floor. Biting her lip, she struggled for balance. She should be the one leaned upon. He needed strength from her, not panic

"Is it... is it... malignant?"

"I'm afraid so," the doctor said, "and growing rapidly."

"Can't you do something?" Her knees were jelly.

"Unfortunately, it's inoperable," Chester said.

"These things can sneak up on you. By the time Chester was experiencing regular headaches, it was already well established."

"How... how long?" she asked.

"No way to know for sure." The physician paused, massaging the bridge of his nose. He glanced at her father, who gave a small nod.

"Probably five or six months. Chester said you would insist on knowing."

"Time enough to tie up loose ends," Chester said. "I have a Living Will, Jackee. Promise to not delay things...when... when the time comes."

She nodded, taking him into her arms, her face nestled in the crook of his neck. Tears trickled across her cheeks. He hugged her, caressing her back.

A huge emotional vacuum loomed for her without him. Although always busy as one of Chicago's premier bankers, he invariably made time for his Countess, even before Mama died. He was at every ballet recital...every horse show... all her charity galas.

She learned responsibility and compassion through his actions. His very being was deeply interwoven into the fabric of her life, but never as a critic. He enthusiastically supported everything she did... everything she was...with the one possible exception of her marriage to Phil.

Jackee sucked in a deep breath, clenching her teeth. This was her time to lend support. Repay him in small measure for all he'd done for her. He was so brave. She would face this with the same courage. They would *live* these last weeks together, not hunkered down in an emotionally frozen bunker, awaiting the end.

"Well, Daddy, it looks like we'll be seeing a lot of each other." She dabbed her eyes with a tissue and blew her nose.

"I'll bring the boys on the week-ends, and you'll come for dinner during the week. We'll plan some nice activities. I'll take care of everything."

"That's not necessary, Countess. You have your own life to live... your own family."

"*You* are my family. I want your grandsons to have fond memories of this time with you, not brooding or silence. Plenty of opportunity for that later."

"How can you do this? You're so busy with your chairmanship at the United Way, and your church fund-raiser. Isn't that only three months away?"

"I've got good assistants. They'll have to do without me for a while. Seeing to... to our time together is far more important. We'll take that fishing trip on the lake. The boys will love that."

"You can't just disrupt your life, my dear. What about that little Puerto Rican boy you're mentoring? You've changed that kid's life."

"I'll work it out. I'll bring Miguel along, too. Meeting you will be good for him. I'm weaning the 'Barrio' out of him, and I don't want him slipping back."

"And Phil?" He left no doubt as to his attitude toward her husband.

"I don't know. He's very busy at work. *You* are my priority."

"All right. I guess I'm in your hands, my dear. Nowhere I'd rather be, under the circumstances."

They spent every possible moment together, just as she promised. Jackee put on hold the myriad social obligations she had sought as the wealthy daughter of Chester Webster. She mined a rarely needed store of inner strength, planning her father's last days on earth, intent on making as many happy memories as possible. She filled his schedule with family activities, but couldn't stem the naked terror, creeping over every wall she erected against it. She couldn't imagine life without Daddy.

Chester Webster died almost exactly five months after being diagnosed with cancer. True to her word, no extraordinary efforts were made to delay his passing. His last four days were spent in a near-death sleep.

She was like a little girl again, watching over him, just as she had with Mama, over twenty years before. Her eyes filled at the acid-etched memories of praying at his side, only accompanied by the shallow rasp of his breathing. Phil never came, but she didn't care. This was between her and Daddy.

There was that one special moment of quiet supplication, near the end.

"Oh, Daddy," she had whispered, taking his hand. "I'm going to miss you so much. You were always there for me, being two parents at once after Mama died. If I had a problem, you'd fix it." She had hoped there *was* another life, and he'd be with Mama again, certainly in Heaven.

"Who else will help me, guide me? You *can't* leave me, Daddy, do you hear? Oh, please hear me!"

Jackee sat, stunned, as his hand slowly tightened on hers. His voice seemed to whisper in her mind, "I'll be there, Countess. I'll always be nearby, if you need me." Through tear-flooded eyes, she saw his previously limp hand, curled firmly around hers. It *wasn't* her imagination! Slowly, his hand relaxed, and the moment was gone. Chester Webster died two days later.

Five days after the funeral, his Last Will and Testament was read in Arthur Osborn's quite, mahogany paneled office. The Marens were the only existing family there, along with her father's two long-time employees, Inga and Marie.

There were charitable bequests and comfortable trusts established for his two faithful servants. They would live without financial concerns for the rest of their lives. Even the stoic German, Inga, broke down and cried. The rest of his enormous estate was put into trusts for his only living child, Jackee, and his two grandsons, with Arthur Osborn as Executor and Trustee.

Phil exploded with an acrimonious barrage. He hadn't received a legacy of his own. The maid and the cook did better! Jackee never understood his anger. They had the trust income, more money than they could possibly spend, but he had stalked off, firing off acrid accusations. Jackee and the attorney stared at each other in disbelief.

"I can't understand why he thought he should get an individual bequest," Osborn said. "I've never seen a man leave anything to a son-in-law while his daughter was still alive. His child and her descendants always get everything, usually in trusts such as these. But the whole family shares in the benefits. Very odd behavior. Just what I might..."

He looked at Jackee and shook his head, but didn't finish. She never understood why... until now.

Visualizing Phil's actions that afternoon, they radiated in a new light.

He eventually cooled down, becoming more affectionate than he'd been in years. He continued managing our funds, and Arthur didn't object as long as I approved. After all, Phil is the V.P. of Finance at North Chicago, so who better to do it?

But looking back, he actually pandered to Daddy for years, even before his illness. Was that only an attempt to gain favor? It brings me back to the same persistent question...did he ever really care about me, or was it always the money?

I might write off his attack on Kevin as unthinking if Phil weren't far too bright not to realize his threats are hurtful. Was it intentional? Certainly not what I'd expect from someone who wants the best for me.

Daddy never said so, but I'm coming to realize now why he never really approved of Phil. He even told me before he died, that he made some small changes to his will. To better "protect" the children and me. I never knew from what. Think I'll invite Mr. Osborn out, to find out exactly what those were.

Drained from reminiscing, she closes her eyes, drifting into a restless sleep.

Chapter Fourteen

Jackee blinks, awakening from a brief nap at the sound of someone entering the room. Her big clock says Nine PM, a little early for Kevin to be saying good night. It's Phil, however, who moves into view.

"Ah, you're awake. Didn't want to bother you if you were sleeping."

"I up," she signs, doubting he understands.

"Yeah, whatever." *More fodder for how little he cares, never bothering to learn my new way of talking. One more thing to wonder about.*

"Anyway, I wanted to tell you some good news. We got off on that tangent this afternoon, and I forgot."

He watches her, a speculative look in his eyes, the shadow of a smile dancing across his lips.

"I've hired a governess for the boys. Believe it or not, it's my secretary, Rhonda. Seems she loves kids. I tried to talk her out of it, because she's the best gal I've ever had. But she really wants the job, and at least I know whom I'll be bringing into the house. We'll fix up the guest room for her.

"She'll start as soon I can get Martha back from Howard. She's not Rhonda, but she knows the job.

"So, the kids'll be well taken care of. I know you worry about that, so you can rest easy."

He leans over, brushing her forehead with a perfunctory kiss before turning to leave, unaware that his nearly silent little chuckle, uttered under his breath, is clearly heard by his wife.

I wonder what he thinks is so damned amusing?

CHAPTER FIFTEEN

Clean. Pristine. Unblemished.

Jackee gazes at the immaculate sea of white. Naked oaks and maples spread thick black arms and spidery fingers against cloudless, ice blue skies. The thermometer hovered near zero for several days. While only a little over an inch of snow fell, there isn't the slightest hint of thaw. Only a few bird and rabbit tracks scar the otherwise untarnished crystalline blanket.

Clean, Pristine, Unblemished, she sighs again.

I was so foolish in believing that about our marriage. Innocent me, expecting the American Dream: a wonderful husband, a beautiful home, and two great children.

Now he's flaunting this beauty, supposedly coming to care for the kids. The need is there, no question, but what's with his choice?

Rhonda Armstrong has a successful career and must have brains to go with her looks. Becoming nanny for two children she barely knows is a step backward, no matter how much he pays.

Something else going on. Maybe the reason for all those late night out, working? Yeah, working at what? I wonder.

Gotta find a way to protect my sons, especially if Phil has other plans. I'm not important...nothing more than a shell now anyway. The boys need love and happiness, and that rarely comes from Phil. I'd gladly give up what little is left for me to see to that. All Daddy's wealth can do now is keep me alive and comfortable.

Comfortable! What a laugh. I live inside my imagination, so what's comfortable? Still, in spite of everything, I get these strange "feelings"... like physical responses... even though I know it's only in my mind.

The thump of two pairs of little feet, scampering through the foyer pulls her from her thoughts. She was so engrossed, she didn't hear the school bus. They're late, she realizes, glancing at the clock. What detained them in this frigid weather? Hangers scraped and clattered on the hall closet rod, and then, full of laughter and giggles, they spill into the den to see their mother.

"Hi, Mom," her oldest is grinning. He's getting so tall, looking a lot like his father; yellow-blonde hair, twinkling blue eyes over a straight little nose, full-lipped mouth fond of smiling, and a prominent manly chin. *He's going to be a lady killer someday.*

"Hi, Mommy," Bryan echoes. A smaller, green-eyed, softer fac-simile of his big brother, he's bubbling with his customary exuber-ance. No one is more full of life than the smallest Maren.

They're growing like weeds.

"Hi. U fun?" Jackee signals.

"Oh yeah." Malcolm's face is flushed. "After the bus dropped us, we started a snowball fight. But it's so cold you can't pack the snow. Ya gotta squeeze it for like a minute, and when you throw it, it still flies apart. It was great."

"Yeah. Real fun," her seven-year-old adds. "We couldn't throw 'em for anything. So when Mal wasn't looking, I put some down his collar." He dissolves into gales of laughter.

"Wise guy. I caught him and washed his face with snow," Mal puts his arm around his little brother with a playful squeeze. Bryan grins. They sense she is smiling back, basking the tenderness of it. She's bathed by the unconditional warm brightness of their love.

"Love U. Come. Kiss."

They swarm over her with hugs and kisses. Mal stands with his arms around her, head resting on her shoulder. She knows they are still cold by the rosy hue of their faces, but will never again experi-ence their chilly little bodies, pressed tightly against hers. Lost forever is their knowing weight on her lap, snuggled close for warmth and affection. There's no longer any way to share their joy, or comfort them in sadness.

She is alone.

Alone, no matter who is around.

Always alone.

Locked in this miserable cell, devoid of all sensation.

Alone!

She floats, suspended in this imaginary pool, an existence of non-existence.

I so miss that warmth and peace, with these two happy little guys in my arms. Malcolm lifts his head, the adoration in his eyes tempered by sadness.

I love Mommy so much, he says.

"We love you so much, Mom," Mal say again. She looks at him quizzically.

Strange that he repeated himself.

"We don't have anyone to talk to about things. It's hard for you, 'cause your eye-words are so slow. Dad said that lady from his office is coming to take care of us. He says you won't ever get better, so you can't do it anymore. Is that right?" Anxiety clouds his face.

We don't want anybody else but you, Mommy. Please get better!

What the Hell... ? She is looking directly at her son, hearing his last words, but he never opened his mouth! The skin on the back of her neck seems to prickle. She stares at him, trying to clear her thoughts. Something strange...

"Yes," she blinks. "No. I..." She stops signing, groaning internally, mentally "gritting" her teeth.

Damn! Too damned frustrating, spelling this out. If only I could talk to them. She studies her nine-year-old, moisture accumulating in the corners of her eyes.

I wish you'd get Kevin, Mal. I just can't do this. He'll explain everything easier than me. If only he could...

"Okay. I'll go see if he's in his room. Bry, you stay with Mommy." Her eyes flare wide.

What in God's.....

"Sure," Bryan puffs out his chest at his important new assignment. Malcolm hesitates after only a few steps, looking confused.

"Can you *talk* again, Mommy? I thought I heard...Nah! I'm just so used to your eye words, but it sure felt like I heard you. Funny, huh?"

He hurries away.

CHAPTER SIXTEEN

Oh my God, what was that? Jackee's eyes franticly trace her son's departure.

Did he actually hear my thoughts? Her skin crawls (only in her imagination?) with goose bumps, her heart hammering, her lagoon roiling into a miniature, storm-tossed sea.

Somehow, he heard me!

Jesus! Is it possible? Can I actually talk to them again! Her mind races back and forth, searching her memory for answers.

Was that the first time I aimed a thought directly at someone? Usually, I think about *people. Why talk to someone who can't hear you? How I've floundered, signing with my eyes, when I might actually speak to them. Is that what Daddy was telling me in my dream?*

How fantastic! Her inner body trembles. *Can Kevin hear me, too!*

Please God, make this work. I need this! I really, really *need this.*

Malcolm prances into the den, with Kevin Martin only a few seconds behind.

"Hi, Jackee. This here young sheriff put the arm on me. Say I'm wanted for questioning. What's up?" He squats in front of her.

I'm fine. She holds her breath, her eyes fastened on his, words spilling through her mind. *Kevin.* She pauses. *Please God, make this work!* Gulping a deep, mental breath, she hurries on. *If you can hear me, please explain to the boys about Rhonda coming here. They don't understand.* Her eyes plumb his for, searching for recognition.

"Well?" the big man asks, his shaggy eyebrows raised.

Kevin! Damn it! Can't you hear me?

You are *talking, aren't you, Mommy? Why do I hear you in my head, when you can't talk out loud?* Malcolm put his hand on her arm.

"I can hear you, too, Mommy," Bryan whispers in her ear.

Shhh, Bry. She is suddenly uneasy. An inner sense screams "danger."

Don't tell anybody. It'll be our secret. Only you, Mal and me. We can talk, and no one else will know! Don't even tell Daddy. Okay?

Okay, Mommy, both boys words echo in her head. *It's our big secret.* Their mental voices sound exactly like their physical ones. She would be shaking with excitement, if it were possible. Instead, disappointment floods her.

Damn it! Why be surprised? Life's been chock full of frustrations lately. It's pretty obvious Phil isn't the loving spouse I expected. If that's true, might his knowledge of this be dangerous to me?

Gotta think it through before I tell anyone, especially Phil. Even confiding in Kevin might be dangerous. Her chest throbbed to the thunder of her heart.

At least my sons can hear me! I'm not so alone anymore, but I gotta stay calm. Can't let the boys sense my tension.

Her eyes find her oldest son's. She steadies her breathing, relaxing her mind.

Isn't this exciting? Now, Mal, I'm going to blink you to ask Kevin the question about Miss Armstrong. We have to pretend to use my eye-words when others are around. Okay?

Sure, Mommy. This is great, isn't it?

You bet. A secret's always fun. Wait for me to blink, and then ask Kevin.

Her new friend waits patiently, an expectant, whimsical look on his craggy face.

"I fine," she signs, answering his earlier question. "Ask." she blinks to her son.

Now, Mal.

"Okay Mal, what's up?" Kevin hunkers down in front of the small boy.

The nine-year-old repeats the questions he had asked his mother. Kevin looks thoughtful for a moment, then turns to her.

"Ya want me to say what I think, which ain't necessarily the party line?"

She blinks once. *I'm getting tired, so I'll let Kevin tell you everything.*

She watches as her two sons turn their attention to the big therapist. Now that they can "talk," she can explain it herself, but

Kevin is there, expecting to help out. And she wants to hear his views on how it will affect them all.

"Okay guys, here is how I see it. This may be a bit confusing.

"First off, ya know how your Mommy is now. Sad thing is, the doctors say she ain't gonna get any better. Ya have to accept that. She loves ya just as much as ever, and I know ya feel the same toward her." Two small blonde heads bob in agreement.

"My job's to care for her, and to help any other way I can. I'm not going anywhere, if I can help it. So ya can count on me. But your Daddy's still responsible for ya, and he makes the decisions. If your Mommy wants to disagree about something, I'll do it for her. But it'll be tough for her to have much of a say about what's going on. Only the real important stuff. Understand?"

Both boy nod again.

"Now, about Miz Armstrong. Your Daddy says she's gonna be your nanny, but I don't rightly know how much she'll actually be involved. Maybe a little. Maybe a lot. Maybe none. We'll see."

He pauses, looking at Jackee, thoughtful for a moment. Her emerald eyes glisten with unshed tears. He shrugs slightly, moisture glazing his own eyes.

"But, your Mommy's gonna be here, and so'll I. Maria, too, so you'll always have us to rely on. Any questions?"

Tiny rivulets roll down Jackee's cheeks.

I guess that puts everything in perspective, doesn't it.

"Where's Miss Rhonda gonna sleep, Kevin?" the seven-year-old asks.

"In the guest room, your Daddy says."

They look at each other, then at Kevin, before turning to their mother, hugging and kissing her. Tears flowing unabated, she yearns to cuddle them in her arms, giving and seeking comfort. Never again! She struggles to shield them from the forlorn bitterness raging in her head.

This isn't living. It's barely even existing.

"Well, she can come," Mal announces. "We don't care! You're our Mommy."

That's right. She fights roiling emotions. *No one else can ever be your real Mommy. But Rhonda is coming, so we've got to make the best of it. Be nice to her if she treats you well.*

Malcolm looks at his mother and nods, standing a little straighter. As the oldest, he has to take charge of his brother.

Tears coursing across her cheeks, she blinks a reply for Kevin's benefit.

"Yes. Love U both."

"Okay guys. Ya go play for a while. I gotta talk to your Mom." The brothers leave, hand in hand, a little wiser. She senses their jubilation at being able to talk to their mother again.

"I know that might'a been tough on ya," Kevin says, his voice husky. "But I gotta say, this gal coming here just don't smell right. It's not my place to say anything, but I don't want to see ya hurt."

"Thanks. Phil Okay" He doesn't need to know of her growing qualms.

"I hope so. Ya got plenty enough on your plate without problems from him. I got this bad habit of speaking my mind. Hope I didn't offend ya. It really ain't my place."

"U fine. U say U think. I like."

I'm not putting him the middle again by admitting my own fears. Damn, what a letdown. What good is this thing if it only works with kids? I got all worked up for nothing.

She raises her eyes to the big therapist.

"Ya *want* me to say whatever I think?"

She blinks once.

"Even if it's something ya might not want to hear?"

"Yes."

"Okay. Obviously, I don't cotton to your husband much, but ya picked him. I doubt ya'd marry a guy because he's handsome. Must have been some chemistry there.

"Well, I'm rattling on, so I'd better shut up."

"U say good."

"Glad ya think so. Need anything before I go back to studying?" Two blinks.

"Okay. See ya around bed time."

One blink. She fights more tears.

Damned crybaby.

My life's so full of frustration. Nothing's worked out like it should. Nothing! I'm trapped in here, ruled by a man I'm having serious doubts about.

Suddenly, my boys can hear me, but no one else does. What damned good is that? Well, there is something there! Maybe with practice, I'll learn to expand it. Got nothing but time.

Kevin had hung a mirror near the French doors. Sitting in her favorite spot, as she is now, she can see anyone passing the doorway or entering the room. She watches him depart, her emotions once more under tight rein. She thinks again about what just happened.

That big guy sure understands people. I guess he should. That's the MBA he's studying for at Northwestern: Human Behavior.

What will it be like when Rhonda gets here? I never got to know her. Only saw her twice at Phil's office. She certainly is a beauty.

Kevin's concerns parallel hers, but she'll give Rhonda the benefit of the doubt. Presume her intentions are legit, until proven otherwise.

Of course, Phil's handsome, charming, and has full use of our trusts. An ideal target for a conniving vixen. Especially with his wife effectively out of the way. Did that figure into Rhonda's desire for this job?

Regardless, Jackee will have little to say about this, or anything else, for that matter. Phil made it plain he is in charge.

Fate has really managed to screw up my life.

Chapter Seventeen

She blinks awake, her eyes luminescent emeralds in the dim light.

What time is it? Glowing hands on the big clock tell the tale.

One-fifteen, and Phil still isn't home. Four of the last five nights, coming in after Midnight.

Her newly acute hearing wakens her, marking his late returns, a fact of which he is probably unaware...if he even cares.

This can't be his job. Gotta be another woman. The gorgeous Ms. Armstrong? Seems pretty likely, with her about to move in. Wonder how many late nights there'll be after that?

I guess it's not unreasonable for him to take a mistress, with me like this. He always wanted sex, and we weren't doing it much the last few years. Not that I wasn't willing. I enjoyed making love, even though I never experienced an orgasm. It still felt wonderful, and I was giving my husband satisfaction. That was enough for me.

But why his need to sneak around now? Who'd blame him, under the circumstances? Well, maybe the Chairman of his company, the old prig... but nobody else, not even me.

So why hide it?

Unless it's nothing new!

He was coming in late long before I fell into my personal little Hell. Working late, or dinner meetings with the Chairman, he said. They're grooming him as the next president.

Or was that only a smoke screen? Was he out catting around, even then? He even missed my last birthday dinner. Always had an excuse, and I never pressed him. How stupid and trusting, but why would I expect him to lie? No one did that in my family.

Kevin, in his own quiet way, was saying something isn't right. It's one thing to take a mistress now, but if he's been seeing her for over a year... ?

Jeez, was he cheating on me even before I wrecked the car?

What a scary accident. That detective was more than just curious.

God, what terrible memories.

She had steadfastly refused to allow her mind to dwell on the accident or the events leading up her present state, but now her desire to know the truth was stronger than her fear of the past.

Jackee caught a glimpse of her reflection in a door glass as they hurried her into the Emergency Ward. How ghastly she looked.

Her left cheekbone was smashed, swelling her eye closed. The air bag broke her nose and impaled her lips on her teeth, condemning her to a liquid diet for six days. Her left arm was fractured, while her distended tongue and swollen lips made her sound drunk when she grunted out a few words. She was stiff and sore for weeks afterwards, but there were no life-threatening injuries.

A Skokie detective visited her in the hospital that evening, and again later at home. Apparently, the left brake-line fittings were loose, which allowed fluid to escape, and caused them to fail. Hard braking created a sharp swerve right. If that had happened on Eden's Highway, the Mercedes would have flipped, surely killing everyone. The officer ask if she had any enemies, which seemed ridiculous. Phil just had the brake serviced a few days before. The shop may have done shoddy work, but certainly not on purpose. Phil filed a negligence lawsuit, but the officer still seemed skeptical.

The detective looked hard at her. "Miss Maren, this type of thing rarely happens by accident. If you remember something, anything... even from someone you think is highly unlikely... please call me." he said.

Jackee dismissed his concerns as typical police attitudes, always looking for a crime. Though she felt he had his suspicions of whom he meant by 'highly unlikely'. Cops always looked at the spouse first.

She healed, fussed over by her husband, who actually took time away from work to see to her needs. Hoping a positive side-effect of that scary disaster was the repair of the chasm that was slowly growing between she and Phil, Jackee recovered with surprisingly few serious effects.

A short, thick scar covered a depressed area over her left cheekbone. Frequent headaches were the product of chewing on the right side. Breathing through her battered nose was labored, causing a dry mouth and sore throat every morning. Her doctors wanted to await the full reduction of swelling to see if corrective surgery were required.

Nearly five months passed before she re-entered the hospital (primarily due to Phil's insistent urging) to repair her cheekbone, remove the scar and correct the septum of her nose. Simple procedures done under general anesthesia, but she was very nervous. Hospitals had only bitter memories for her.

Phil took the day off to see her through this first surgery of her adult life, which would have been avoided, despite the ugly scar, except for the difficulty in breathing. Each morning was worse than the last. Phil was supportive and encouraging, chiding her for her fears.

She went into surgery at Nine AM, a vibrant and beautiful young woman. By Eleven that morning she was potentially more beautiful, but never again vibrant.

♦ ❖ ♦

Now here she is...immobile, dependent and silent.

Reliant on a man who no longer seems to care.

Did he ever? That question keeps nagging me. We married after his family business...and most of their wealth...evaporated, and his father had died so suddenly. Was I just his ticket to the lifestyle he was accustomed to? It sure seemed like love to me.

Rivulets spill over cheeks no longer round and full with the beauty of youth, but she has no sense of them trickling across her face. The police dropped the investigation, finding no hard evidence of foul play, and she never gave it another thought...until now.

I'm so trusting. Why didn't I ever question his behavior? He was probably cheating on me right along. The surgical accident just makes it easy to bring the affair into the open.

All those convenient accidents!

First the car, then the surgery. If he were having an affair, those made things awfully easy for him. Full control of our trusts and a gorgeous girlfriend! If he is unfaithful, Fate couldn't deal him a better hand, even if he scripted it himself.

Scripted it himself?

What a scary idea. Gotta think about this when I'm not so tired.

Eyes close, her thoughts drifting, but before dropping back to sleep, she hears the rumble of his Corvette, then the quiet opening and closing of the front door. He doesn't raise the garage door so not to awaken Kevin, but that no longer hides his late arrival from Jackee.

She glances at the clock.

Two A.M. There's gotta be more to this than work. I'll think about it tomorrow. Just like Scarlett. There's a world full of tomorrows to think. Only think. Can't let it drive me mad.

Gotta hang on somehow. Got Kevin to count on, and now I can talk to the boys. Two lines to continued sanity, thank God.

Maybe something more will develop. I'll have to wait and see. I've got nothing but time.

Chapter Eighteen

Think! Think! Think!

She lay in bed, awaiting the start of her day.

Thinking. That's what's left to me. Stretching and flexing my mind.

Considering others, weighing new ideas, and planning future events. A thin line separates her from madness.

Who am I kidding? It's blatant fantasy. An exercise in futility!

She has to move, talk and interact to have any effect. Life needs expectations, things forever denied her. She used to think she made a difference. Not anymore. She exists with no purpose. What can she achieve like this?

A waste of energy.

A waste of resources.

A waste of time!

Kevin will do whatever she asks, but she can imagine no tasks for him. She can talk to her sons, but they are too little to do much, other than love her...one of her few remaining treasures.

How did this happen?

Eyes focused inward, she struggles to conjure up elusive memories, trying to stitch together the details.

The culprit is anesthesia, interacting with tranquilizers.

Why weren't those two Valium listed on my admittance forms? Did I even fill them out? I was so muddled, nervous about surgery so soon after the accident.

Let's see. We arrived at Admitting, and an orderly took me to my room. Phil went off...

Suddenly, a wellspring of images bubble up, spilling memories across her mind.

As they wheeled her away, Phil stayed behind to check her in.

He registered me, and never listed the tranquilizers I took that morning. Did he forget, or...

My God, did he try to kill me? Did he know tranquilizers and anesthesia...?

Whoa! That's one scary leap. Why would he want me dead?

Hmmm. Or, why not, if he were already having an affair with Rhonda? He encourage...no, insisted...I take those two Valium that morning! And where did he even get them? I never used tranquilizers. To calm me down, he said. Well, I'm permanently calm now.

Damn! First the car accident, right after he fixed the brakes. The police never found any criminal evidence. But if he were already cheating on me...and the millions in my estate... ?

How could he stoop to cause the accident? He'd risk killing his sons. Oh! But he didn't know they'd be with me that time. I was supposed to drop them at home first, but I was running late. Can he really be that callous...wanting me dead? God, how terrifying.

Malachite eyes glisten wetly. Nothing in life prepared her for such ultimate wickedness, especially from one who is supposed to love you. It's beyond comprehension.

Wow, that's a lot of unfounded supposition. That this whole thing was intentional? Trying to get me out of the way for the money...and, maybe Rhonda. If that were true...I thought I was in love a beast.

Or am I just desperately searching for a villain...other than plain bad luck? Despite everything, I survived, mired in this eternal Hell. Like a science-fiction movie: "The Brain with No Body." The Brain should have super-human powers, wreaking revenge on its tormentors before expiring as the old castle burns down around them.

Wow, a grade-B horror movie! Still, something strange is happening. I can "talk" with the boys, and I'm so much more aware of things around me. As if I sense others thoughts. Maybe even their emotions.

She closes her eyes, sifting through kaleidoscopic images. It's all so confusing.

Kevin's coming to know me... the old me... so much better than he should. People talk about "reading emotions in the eyes," but that includes facial expressions and body language. I have absolutely none, yet he intuits mine. Seems impossible...unless I'm projecting those things he can somehow read?

Jeez, what wishful thinking. Hoping I'll develop some exotic power. Maybe a way to deal with Phil, who's apparently not the loving husband I'd imagined. And his chippie, too, once she's in the house?

Only two day until R-day... Rhonda's last Friday at work, and her first day in the house... with Jackee's husband, children... and her.

If my guess is right, they'll probably be screwing right in my old bedroom. Will I hear that, too? Enough! Recriminations won't get me anywhere. What's done is done. Better prepare for what's yet to come... and that's Rhonda.

How will things change, once she's here? Kevin'll protect me as best he can, but I'm still so helpless. Phil's running the ship, and there's nothing I can do but sit on deck and watch.

Damn!

This is not what I expected out of life!

As bad as things are, can they possibly get worse?

Chapter Nineteen

The three of them cluster around her, peering down with serious faces.

I'm a butterfly, trapped in a glass slide.

Maria and Kevin examine her nasal tube, with Phil hanging over their shoulders.

What the Hell is he doing here? He doesn't give a damn whether my tube is working or not. He makes me nervous.

"It's not taking the liquid properly," Maria says, looking at Kevin.

"Well, this end looks okay. Must be a restriction inside. No reason not to change it, is there?"

"No, I guess not. I've inserted them many times." The nurse looks at her patient and smiles.

"Nothing to worry about, my dear. We're going to ease this old tube out and slide another one in. Usually, this is done under anesthesia, but in your case that might be an unnecessary risk. Give us two blinks if you should feel anything, and we'll stop. But, you never feel anything, do you?"

"No," she blinks.

"That's so sad, but helpful now. Here we go."

Kevin steadies her head as the nurse slowly withdraws two feet of discolored plastic tubing. Jackee mentally braces herself, but there's only the acrid smell of bile as the last of the slimy serpent slips from her nostril. Phil turns away, apparently revolted by the procedure.

"There's the culprit, Maria. See that kink. Tube musta twisted a little each time ya fed her."

"I think you're right, Kevin. I'll have to be extra careful. Never had a patient on the tube for so long."

"I bet." He leans over, brushing back her hair.

"Everything okay?"

One blink

"Ya feel anything?"

Two blinks.

"Good. Let's get the new one in so we can get on with the morning's therapy."

"Here it is, guys." Phil reappears at the bed, holding the glistening new tube with a piece of cotton, his hand tremoring.

"Untouched by human hands."

Maria, hands encased in surgical gloves, takes the flexible plastic, nodding absently.

"I'm outta here." Phil wipes his forehead with mock relief. "This is more than my tender stomach can take."

He pecks her on the cheek, his plastic smile piercing her with momentary chill. Tiny beads of perspiration dot his brow.

Edgy, Phil? I'd be surprised if you really give a damn about my well-being. There's a funny odor about this. It's almost as if I can smell something... bad... on him, like a dog, smelling fear.

Oh, what an imagination.

Maria prepares the tube and Jackee closes her eyes, relaxing her mind as if it were her body, as the insertion begins. Phil's presence plagues her. It doesn't fit with what she is coming to suspect, and that's scary. She can't shake the senses of something exuding from him.

Something... what? Sinister?

Is something going on? Something bad for me?

That last look was so... so wicked.

Oh, get a grip! I'm looking for trolls under every rock. What can he do, with Kevin here?

Chapter Twenty

"Malcolm, why aren't you dressed? You'll miss the bus."

"I don't feel good, Daddy." He looks down, withering under the heat of his father's scowl. "My stomach hurts, and I had a watery poop."

"Does he have a temperature?" Phil asks, turning to Charlene.

"He shouldn't miss school for a little upset stomach. I don't want him home... I mean, he's not really sick, is he?"

"No, sir." She affectionately ruffles the boy's blonde hair, feeling his forehead.

"But his face *is* flushed. Malcolm never misses school unless he's really ill. Miss Jackee would keep him home if..."

"I don't give a rat's ass what *she'd* do. Dress him, and send him off."

"He's already missed the bus, sir. Someone will have to be driving him."

"Can you do it?" Phil glances at his watch. "I should be getting to work."

"I can't leave the missus alone, sir."

"Alone? Oh yeah. King Kong's away this morning. What about Maria?" He paces impatiently around the room.

"You sent her to get supplies. She should be back any minute."

"Yeah, I forgot. Today's your day off, isn't it Charlene?"

"Aye, sir. 'Tis that. My brother is coming... Ah, speaking of the devil, he's here now," hearing two short beeps from the driveway.

"Fine. Get Mal dressed and you can drop him at school on your way out."

"But, the missus? I was going to wait..."

"Not necessary. I'll stick around until Maria gets back. Get your day started sooner."

"If you're sure it's all right..." She glances at the den, clearly uneasy leaving Jackee before the return of at least one of her professional caretakers.

"It's not a problem. Get moving. I don't want the kid to miss any classes."

Charlene touches the boy's forehead, kneeling in front of him.

"How about it, young sir. Are you well enough to get ready? There's no fever on your brow. Maybe you'll be feeling better at school with your friends."

Mal sighs, looking at the entrance to the study, where his mother is sitting.

Should I go, Mommy? I guess I'm okay He knows she can hear his silent question.

If you feel up to it. Your father doesn't want an argument. If you feel ill later, see the nurse. She'll get you home, if it's necessary.

"Okay" He smiles shyly at Charlene. "I'll get dressed." He hurries off.

Phil says, "I appreciate you taking him, Charlene."

"You're sure you don't mind waiting..."

"No. You go on. There's nothing pressing for me at work today."

"All right, sir. I'll just tell Sean the plans. If you will, ask the young master to come out to the car as soon as he's ready."

"Right. You go ahead. He'll be right behind you."

◆❖◆

The house is still except for Phil quietly shuffling papers in his study. Mal made his belated departure less than five minutes before.

Something's fishy. No use bucking Phil if his mind's made up, but this is uncharacteristic concern for Mal's education. I can almost sense tension on him.

His chair scrapes on the oak parquet floor, his briefcase latches snapping closed. A moment later, he materializes in her room, silently appraising her.

"Everything all right, my darling wife?" His strong mouth twitches sardonically. "That new tube bothering you any?"

"No."

"Guess you wouldn't know. But sometimes a new thing is worse than its replacement."

What's going on? And that strange odor on him? Faint, but familiar. Can't place it.

"Well, gotta go. Important meeting this morning, and I'm already late."

What meeting? You said there was nothing pressing. Don't leaving yet. I haven't been alone since the accident.

"Maria'll be back any minute." He wheels her to her bedroom. "Already overdue. I can't wait any longer." He lifts her onto her bed, cranking down the headrest.

Don't do this. I hate lying flat. I can't see anything.

"U said U wait," she blinks hurriedly as he starts to leave.

"Shit! You know I don't understand that eye-blink garbage. Anyway, I'm outta here. Take care of yourself, darlin'." He hurries away, chuckling softly.

He's up to something. A visceral fear claws at her. *Somehow, I'm in danger! But, what can he possibly do if he not even here?*

Chapter Twenty-One

Something is wrong!

There is no pain, no discomfort, no feeling... but Jackee *knows* something is wrong. This strange new sense tells her things she shouldn't perceive.

Something isn't working right, and there is no one there to tell.

Goddamn Phil! The bastard left me just when I might really need him. It's the first time I've been totally alone since the surgery.

What a lousy coincidence if something bad...

Or is it? Can I really be that unlucky? Has that louse managed something dangerous for me? Christ, how paranoid! What could he possibly...

She gasps, suddenly struggling to breathe.

That smell!

The acrid sting of bile, slowly swamping her nasal passages, ignited a fire in her brain. Tears blur her eyes. Drawing even a single breath is suddenly a distressing task.

Reality rears up like an angry dragon....

Stomach acid!

Somehow its corrosive bath is sneaking around her feeding tube and into her esophagus, mingling with her breath, searing her senses. She'd heard how painful that could be. The only advantage to her current state...no pain. But why this difficulty in breathing? Lying flat on her back probably made things worse, but...

OhmyGod! Arlene Callahan! She "shudders" at that terrifying memory.

An undiagnosed diabetic, her college sorority sister hadn't felt well one afternoon. She went to her room for a nap, suffered a diabetic seizure, convulsed, and threw up. Unable to move, she lay breathing acid fumes from her own bile. Her lungs were so badly damaged, she needed a respirator for the rest of her short life.

Can that happen to me? My God! Did Phil cause this? Somehow I know...

She wheezes, light-headed. The virulent stench makes even a shallow breath labored.

Oh, God! Oh, God! Smothered by my own body. Where the Hell's Maria? Been gone way too long. Phil sent her to the...

Oh, that bastard! Said he didn't know she was gone, but he sent her. Damn him! Did he deliberately empty the house, even sending poor Malcolm to school?

But how can he possibly...?

She tries inhaling short, shallow breaths, but has difficulty controlling her tempo.

Hard to concentrate. Can't breathe. My brain's frying. Gotta stay calm. Panic's the enemy. Think, damn it!

Why was Phil here when they changed my tube? To sabotage it? He handed it to... Oh, God!

Eyes watering, her thoughts scatter like dandelion spores in a breeze. Clenching down, she struggles for control.

Why would he do this now? I'm not in the way of anything he wants.

Ohhh!

Lightning bolts streak through her brain. Even short little gasps of breaths are a struggle. She needs help, fast.

Maria! Goddammit, what's taking you so long?

Panting, she fights her breath... a Catch 22. She needs clean oxygen, but might hyperventilate with quick, shallow breaths, passing out.

Then she'd really be in trouble!

Help! HELP! Someone help me.

Head spinning, she projects her thoughts.

But there is no one there who can hear.

Chapter Twenty-Two

Malcolm had terrible cramps and continual chills.

He shuffled down the hallway, his pink hall pass clutched in one hand. He shuddered.

Golly, I'm cold.

He paused in front of the doorway, *NURSE* emblazoned in plain black letters on frosted glass. Daddy would be real mad if he went home early, but he felt so lousy.

He pushed through the door. Two other kids were sitting on a bench. Slouching down on the unpadded oak seat, he wrapped his arms around himself to try to quell his shivering.

A few moments later, the inner door opened and a freckle-faced girl with blazing red hair came out, holding a yellow Home Pass. The generously proportioned nurse followed, a crisp vision of white starch and silver blonde hair.

"I called your mom, Jenna. She'll be here by the time you get outside. Drink lots of fluids. This three day flu is going around."

She turned, studying the three students perched anxiously on the bench. Her arm shot out, a flaming red-nailed finger stabbing accusingly at Malcolm.

"You." Perfect teeth flashed behind bow-shaped lips. "You look *terrible*, young man."

"Let me feel you head." She drew him close. He trembled at her rose-smelling warmth.

"My God, you're burning up. You're getting two aspirin and then I'm calling your mother. She should never have let you come to school like this!"

"She can't come. She's in a wheelchair. Maybe my dad is still home."

◆❖◆

Malcolm sat in a chair, aspirins taken, a thermometer stuck under his tongue. Nurse Gould hurried back from phoning his house.

"Nobody home, it seems."

"Maybe Daddy went to work. They're not supposed to leave Mommy alone."

Was Mommy okay?

The nurse nodded and withdrew the small glass tube from his mouth.

"Jesus! 103.5. You're on fire, kiddo. If I call a taxi, can you get in the house?"

"I have a key."

"Will there be any money for you to pay, or must I do it for you?

"Daddy keeps some in the kitchen, in case Charlene goes shopping. I can use that."

"Good. You certainly are an efficient young man. I call Yellow Cab. Do you feel well enough to wait on the bench inside the front door?"

"I guess. Do you know what's wrong with me, ma'am?"

"Looks like the flu. You'll be fine again in three or four days, but when you get home, I want you to go right to bed. Will there be an adult there soon?"

"Maria, mom's nurse. Should have been there."

"Fine. When she come home, have her call me at this number, and I'll tell her what I've done for you so far. In the meantime, have a big glass of apple juice and go right to bed."

"Yes, ma'am."

CHAPTER TWENTY-THREE

Things are deteriorating fast.

Jackee gasps, struggling unsuccessfully for a clean, cool breath. The acrid foulness is overpowering. Panting, she tries again.

Ohhh! My brain's on fire! I may die if help doesn't arrive soon. Where's Maria? Been away for hours.

God, I'm smothering. Can Mal hear me from so far away? Better try, before it's too late.

She concentrates, corralling what little strength she has left.

Malcolm! Mal, come home. Mommy needs you. I'm sick, Mal. Help me!

She listens, unsuccessfully trying to hold her breath, hoping to clear her befuddled mind, but there is no answer. A foggy vision materializes in her head... her son, reaching out, calling for her, clutched in the restraining arms of her husband, a wicked sneer contorting his handsome face.

The illusion wavered, like the broken surface of a glass-calm lake, and Phil morphs into a tall, buxom blonde, clad in shimmering white. Malcolm, looking terribly ill, is cradled in her gentle embrace.

I'm hallucinating!

Shaking her thoughts free, she concentrates on surviving, struggling to slow her breathing, trying to somehow sneak fresh air around the deadly fumes.

Uuhh, uuhh! No good! So foul. Must be some air there. Just not enough.

She slowly fades toward a dark pit of semi-consciousness.

Gonna die! My own useless body's killing me. Phil and his bitch'll get everything. Who'll care for the boys? Not that callous bastard.

Gotta hang on. Can't leave the boys alone!

Breathe, dammit, breath! So bitter, but some oxygen there. Maybe enough to keep me going.

Can't die! Not now!

Too much to do.

She spirals down, her usually peaceful lake now a black whirlpool, sucking her under the caustic foam of her own making.

Fight! Gotta fight. Can't quit now.

Oh, God, I can't end like this.

Not like this.

Mal may be my only hope, but I'm may be too weak for him to hear me.

Mal! Mal, I need you.

She fades, her energy slipping away.

Mal sat on the bench, flushed and clammy, shuddering uncontrollably. The nurse came by twice, checking on him. He grinned at the attention.

His smile faded as he thought of his mother.

Why did daddy leave her alone? Maria should have been there. Something was wrong. He sensed it.

He tried to call to her, but fever had sapped his ability to focus.

Where's the taxi? It was only a ten-minute ride home. They had to hurry. He felt it in his bones.

Mommy needed him. Where's that taxi?

Hurry!

Please hurry!

CHAPTER TWENTY-FOUR

She wallows in the surf of her mind, resolutely clinging to consciousness, flotsam on the acidic tide washing over her. Little oxygen is making it past the caustic barrier to her fouled lungs, but she's determined not to surrender.

What happened to Maria? Phil sent everyone away, leaving me alone to die!

How paranoid. How could he arrange this? But I think he's tried to kill me before, with the surgical accident. And now this?

He wants me dead. Can't accommodate him. Won't do it. Gotta hang on.

Someone will come. Bring me fresh, delicious oxygen. Gotta stick it out.

A new breath buries her brain in flames. Her eyes are blurry pools.

Oh God, it's useless. I'm dying!

Her senses reel in free-fall, but some blurry thing tickles her disoriented mind.

Malcolm's coming. Coming to save me. Doesn't know to hurry. Won't get here in time.

In her growing delirium, she calls out again, only a faint whisper now, as she continues fading into pre-terminal stupor.

Mal! Malcolm! The last of her strength fades. *Hurry! Mommy needs you.*

Too Late. Too late.

She slips away, reluctantly giving in toward the cold grasp of Death.

CHAPTER TWENTY-FIVE

Mal! Malcolm!

He sensed it, feebly ticking at his mind.

"Hurry, sir. Mommy needs me. Hurry, please!"

Mommy, are you okay? No answer. A rush of black panic washed over him. Why didn't she answer?

"I thought you was the sick one, kid."

"I've only got the flu. Something's wrong with Mommy. I can feel it."

"Ah, what an imagination. The nurse said there wasn't nobody home. Why would ya think your mom was sick?"

"I just know it. Please hurry."

"Yeah, sure. Kids! Uh-oh, what's this?" The taxi braked to a stop behind a line of motionless cars. Flashing red and blue lights were barely visible about a quarter of a mile ahead.

"Must be an accident. Sorry, kid. Looks like we're gonna be tied up for a while."

"We're almost there, aren't we? My street's just past those cars."

"Right, but looks like all of Dundee's blocked off right now. They'll probably start working cars past, a little at a time. Nothing we can do but wait."

Two minutes passed, but they hadn't moved. Mal fidgeted on the seat, his own maladies forgotten. Something was wrong with Mommy. Something very bad. He couldn't sit there, doing nothing.

Hesitantly, he opened the car door, stepping out. His head hurt, and he was all sweaty, legs wobbling like a newborn calf's.

"Hey, were ya goin'?" Artie Green swiveled in his seat when he heard the door latch pop.

"I gotta get home. I know my mom's in trouble. It's not far. I'll run by the side of the road."

"Can't let ya do that, kid. You're real sick. Look, ya can hardly stand."

Artie was a stout, homely man, with a mouth full of bad teeth, so he rarely smiled. He had a nasty look about him, but was in reality a soft touch, especially for kids. He jumped out of his cab, snagging Malcolm by the arm.

"Please, sir. My Mom! I gotta go."

"No way, kid. Ya could get kilt, running down this highway. I'm responsible."

"But, my Mommy. She can't move or talk or anything. She needs help, bad."

"How d'ya *know* that, kid?"

"I just *do*! We... we sorta communicate. Please!"

"What d'ya mean, 'communicate'?"

"She can't talk, but I sorta hear her in my head. Please, sir. I gotta go!"

Artie groaned, shoving Malcolm back through the open door.

"Shit! Get in the cab. We'll go."

"But all the cars...?"

"Just get in the damned car!"

They climbed in, slamming their doors.

"I'll probably lose my damned permit," Artie grumbled, as he pulled out of line and started down the narrow shoulder, the taxi pitching and tilting as they went.

He lowered his window. An old Chevy pick-up and a new BMW were wrapped around each other, nestled in the culvert. No one seemed hurt.

"Got me an emergency," he yelled, edging by. "Real sick kid here." The cop waved furiously, but Artie never slowed. The officer was writing in a notebook. Probably his license number. He was in deep shit now. This better be worth it.

They entered Mal's street.

There was his house.

Mom! Mom! Are you okay?

No response, but he was more than close enough to trade thoughts with her. Why didn't she answer? He coughed, then shivered, his head on fire, but the darned flu would have to wait.

Something *was* terribly wrong with Mommy.

As they pulled into the drive, he saw something clamped to the passenger side of the front seat of the taxi. Something instinctively he knew Mommy needed.

CHAPTER TWENTY-SIX

Can't draw a single breath. Not even one sour, lung-searing, mind-stunning little gasp. No one is coming.

She descends beyond delirium, and strangely, recognized she is there. There is no pain. No inferno in her head. Because she is...

Dead!

A surprising end to a life all too short and so recently filled with disappointments.

No memories flash before her eyes. There *is* a bright light at the end of a tunnel, beckoning her, but no sense of peace.

Instead of joyous calm, she's rift with bitterness, more angry than she'd ever been when alive.

It's not my time, damn it. I still have things to do here.

She floats free of that motionless prison, rising above the bed. Her gaunt, pale body lay stretched out on the sheets below.

Not breathing. Not the slightest rise and fall of her chest.

I'm white as chalk. Dead. No time to make a difference. Did that bastard do this to me?

She has no tears. A corpse doesn't cry.

Will a seraph come to escort her to Heaven? Mama and Daddy would be waiting.

A large, ugly creature suddenly rushed out of the shadows.

Angels are beautiful, but this is a demon from Hell. Never dreamed I'd be going there.

A silvery rock in the devil's hand slams mercilessly into her face.

Everything dissolves to black.

CHAPTER TWENTY-SEVEN

Her thoughts, though sleepy, are still crystal clear. She spirals slowly downward, an effortless passage greased by a cushion of cool, soft air. Far below, her little lagoon, her quiet place for so many weeks since the surgery, tranquil again, beckons. The caustic, vile odors are gone. There are no smells without breath. Immured by a numbing lethargy, she accepts the final truth.

It's over.

Finally, peace. If I were alive, I'd be angry. Even furious. Still so much to do, even like this. Somehow provide my children the love and care my husband will never give.

Root out his real involvement with my death. Maybe seek retribution. All gone now. No chance to hunt down facts, find a way to meet out punishment, because...

I'm dead!

So, there is an afterlife for the soul.

A place to think.

Her feathery descent ends as she slips quietly into the warm, calm lagoon, floating once again in her dark little sea of nothingness, gentle ripples dissipating in never-ending circles. All returning to glassy stillness.

Can this be Heaven? Or am I damned to some nether world until things can be set right on Earth?

She is too languid to care. She was a regular churchgoer, giving her time to make things better for the less fortunate, trying to make a difference in the world. A soul who certainly ought to be with God. It looks like He has other plans.

Even in death, things aren't going right. Why aren't her parents there to greet her? She's free to ascend, her spirit unchained from that inanimate shell. Why haven't they...?

Ohhh!

She senses a strange pressure on her chest, as clean, pure air surges through her. Cleansed for the journey to Heaven?

Finally! But, where's the glorious tunnel of light everyone talks about?

There! There it is!

Brightly lit, spiraling down from above. The pathway to God.
She even hears his voice.

"Come on. Come back to me, sweetheart. Come on."

She giggles. *I never suspected God might sound like a Puerto Rican.*

◆ ❖ ◆

Juan Calverra, the EMT, straddles the supine blonde, left hand over the right, arms locked, pressing rhythmically on the center of her chest. A commandeered desk lamp lights her face, as they searched for signs of life.

"Come on. Come back to me, sweetheart," he cajoled. "Come on."

Abdul Salaam, his partner, steadies her head, a huge black hand gently pinches her nostrils while he slowly pumps the rubber ball, forcing air in and out of her tortured lungs.

It was Artie Green who gave her a chance. At little Malcolm's hysterical insistence, the cabby, a long-time sufferer of emphysema, grabs his portable oxygen bottle and mask and follows the boy into the house. The kid seems so sure, and he still has to collect his fee.

Not finding his mother in the den, the boy drags the man to her bedroom. Bursting through the door, Artie sees a chalky-faced blonde woman lying on the bed, white as death.

"Holy shit." Rushing forward, he jams the clear oxygen mask onto her face, opening the valve before snatching her up and placing her on the firmer, thick-pile carpeting.

"Call 911, kid! I'm gonna try some CPR." Malcolm races for the phone, as Artie pulls the mask away for an instant, listening close to her mouth, and then nose.

"Shit! She ain't breathing."

Straddling her hips, the mask back in place, he begins the rhythmic press and release motions on her breastbone, working her lungs.

"Boy, she's some beauty," he mutters. "How the Hell do I get into these things?"

Fire-Rescue arrives in four minutes. The little boy is jumping up and down on the driveway, screaming at them to hurry.

Scurrying into the house, they discover the taxi driver hunkered over Jackee, doing a credible job of CPR, his oxygen mask strapped over her face. Maria, who also just arrives, follows close behind.

The nurse quickly kneels, reaching under the clear mask.

"Let me get this damned thing out of the way."

She withdraws the recently installed feeding tube to provide a better seal for Artie Green's oxygen mask while the paramedics set-up their own CPR paraphernalia.

With nothing more to do, she frantically beeps Kevin before finally noticing little Malcolm standing in a corner, shivering and pale.

"You're pretty sick, aren't you?"

He nods. She feels his head.

"Wow, you've got a furnace going there."

She hurries him off to bed, promising to keep him posted every five minutes on his mother's progress.

Chapter Twenty-Eight

Her usually serene pond stutters and sloshes, angry little wave-lets slapping at her, as acrimonious sounds besiege her solitude.

Isn't there tranquility, even in death?

She lurches as the glowing tunnel to Heaven tilts sharply, spinning away, casting her adrift.

Oh God, what have I done? Why don't you want me?

The last of the pathway to eternal peace dims, disappearing far above. Only a blazing light remains.

She hangs in a strange limbo, uncertain what to do, or where to go. Heaven seems closed to her. Is she damned to Hell? How can that be? If the pathway were gone, why is there still so much light? And why is her head hammered by so many discordant voices?

Her eyes, stung by the penetrating brilliance, flutter open, startled by many faces hovering close by. She's inundated by a barrage of emotions flowing at her.

Never thought death might be so hectic.

"Hot damn! She's back!" The Latin-accented voice of God is that of a pencil-mustached, olive-skinned face directly over hers.

"We've got you going again, lady. Everything's gonna be okay"

He slips a clear plastic mask, glowing slivery in the lamp-light, over her nose and mouth.

Oxygen. How wonderful.

He stands, turning to a large, grinning black man, exchanging boisterous high-fives.

Not God after all. Fire-Rescue paramedics? Which means I'm...

...Alive!

Oh, thank God!

Still alive!

So many people, all talking at once.

Mommy!

Malcolm appears magically at her side. Maria snags his arm, restraining him.

"Hang on, young man. We don't want you giving your mom the flu, or whatever you're down with."

Malcolm stands back, showering her with thrown kisses.

"Oh, Mommy. We were so worried. I *knew* there was something wrong."

I called to you, Mal. Did you hear me?

My name, maybe. "I just had a feeling you were in trouble," he says aloud.

Thank you, darling. You saved my life.

Not me.

The little boy jumps up and darts into the crowd, reappearing moments later, a large, homely, and very reluctant man in tow.

"This is Mr. Green, Mommy. *He* saved your life, until the paramedics came."

Her eyes flutter irregularly.

"She says 'Thank You.' She wants to reward you somehow."

The cabby blinks in surprise. "She told you that with her eyes?"

"That's how she talks."

"Jeez! Well, thank you, ma'am. Really weren't nothin'. The kid here figured you needed the oxygen. Persistent little guy. Lucky I carry it with me. Lucky, too, I guess, that I just took a course in CPR. Who'd figure I'd be usin' it so quick."

His gap-toothed grin isn't a pretty sight. She chuckles sleepily to herself.

First thing Mr. Green gets is a complete dental makeover. Implants, if necessary. Little enough to trade for my life.

She sighs happily at the sound of approaching thunder, the heavy tread of running feet. A moment later, Kevin Martin bursts into the room, his deep voice rough with anger and frustration.

"What the Hell's going on here? What *happened*, Maria?"

Kneeling next to Jackee, taking her pulse, the nurse is visibly shaking.

"I don't know, Kevin. Looks like a bad case of acid reflux." Her voice cracks. "Don't know how it got past the tube, but it did. Lots of it. Wouldn't be so serious if she could swallow, or even just sit up." She gestures at the level bed.

"I left it tilted up, as usual. Don't know how it got flat like that."

Thanks to Phil for that. Was it intentional? Trying to kill me again?

"Stomach acid must have begun filling her esophagus. Probably started inhaling the fumes. I only hope it didn't damage her lungs." She avoids the agitated therapist's eyes.

"How long before ya caught it?" He's down next to her now, hand on her forehead.

"Malcolm found her. I... I was out of the house."

She rings her hands, face flushed, studiously examining the pattern in the carpeting.

"You weren't *here*?"

"Nobody was here, I guess."

"How the Hell... ?"

"I don't *know*. Mr. Maren sent me for supplies, even though I told him it could wait 'til next week. He was here with Charlene when I left."

"It was Charlene's day off," Malcolm says, his voice strained and thin.

"Her brother came, and they drove me to school on her way home."

"What're you doing out of bed, our little hero?" The nurse places a hand on his forehead.

"Still got a whopping fever. You need more aspirin."

"Daddy was supposed to wait here for you, Maria."

"What did ya say, son?" Kevin kneels next to the pale, shivering boy.

"Daddy said he'd stay with Mommy 'til Maria came back."

"Terrific! Ask the fox to baby-sit the chickens."

"What *are* you talking about, Kevin. He's her husband, for God's sakes."

"Nothing to worry your head about, kiddo. Let's see to our patient, and we'll straighten everything else out later."

"We should get her to the hospital," the black medic says. "This lady had no vital signs when we got here. She was clinically dead for maybe five minutes."

"Jesus!" Kevin growled. "What a fiasco." Maria groans, eyes wet.

"Hey, cut it out. Wasn't your fault. We both know who's responsible for this."

I suspect more purposefully responsible than even you imaging, Kevin.

"Ya think there any permanent damage?"

He places a huge hand on her shoulder, squeezing gently, offering silent support.

"Maybe her esophagus and lungs, if acid vapor burned them."

She dabbed her eyes with a small tissue. Kevin curses softly, kneeling beside Jackee, studying her keenly, gently stroking her head, fighting down tears.

"I'm gonna remove this oxygen mask for thirty seconds," he say. "See how you're breathing on your own. If everything's okay, blink once. If you're having trouble, blink twice."

Her lids close once, the emerald eyes exuding trust. He shivers, then reaches down, carefully removing the face mask, watching her intently for any sign of difficulty. Her nostrils flare slightly with every breath.

Nearly a half-minute drags by before she blinked once.

"Everything's okay?"

"Yes."

So tired. Just want to sleep.

"Think you should go to the hospital for a check-up?"

"No. Do here."

"Don't trust those places much anymore, do ya?"

"No."

"Don't blame ya, under the circumstances. I'll get Dr. Berg to come over later. Okay?"

"Yes."

"Good. Meantime, we're gonna figure out what happened, and see it don't happen again."

CHAPTER TWENTY-NINE

Jackee lay in bed, upper body elevated to about forty degrees and propped in place by supporting pillows, still wearing an oxygen mask. The cool, clean air soothed what, for a sentient being, would be a very painful esophagus. She struggled against sleep while monitoring Kevin and the doctor in the next room

"Well, Doc, how is she?" She visualized a pensive Kevin, looming over the smaller gray-haired man as he returned various instruments to his copious black bag.

"About as good as can be expected. I tested her lung capacity as best I can. I'd guess it's been reduced by maybe ten percent. Even that may regenerate. It isn't life-threatening, and she doesn't need oxygen for any movement, other than your physical therapy."

"What *about* physical therapy?"

"Shouldn't be a problem. Go easy for a few days and see how she does. I've inserted a new tube and given her a mild sedative. She needs a good night's sleep, but everything seems fine under the circumstances. She's a remarkably tough lady."

"I don't understand what went wrong." Jackee recognizes tears in Maria's voice. "I've done that procedure many of times without a problem."

"The fault wasn't yours, my dear. It was the tube."

"What d'ya mean, Doc?" Kevin asked.

"The new tube Maria inserted had dozens of tiny pin holes all along the last foot or so. Acid and acid vapor escaped above the stomach sphincter. Strangest defect I've ever seen."

"Damn it! Could it have been intentional?"

"Yes, I suppose, but who would want to do something like that?"

"Who knows? I'll have that tube checked out later." But Kevin curt response indicates he has a pretty good idea who might want Jackee dead. So does she.

Nothing would surprise me anymore.

The doctor and Kevin return to her room. The big man kneels beside her bed, taking her hand, the muscles of his jaw clenched.

"How're ya doing?"

"Tired," she blinks.

"That's the sedative. Lucky the little guy came home early," Kevin says.

My little hero.

"Yes. Another five minutes would have probably been too late," Dr. Berg says.

"He's pretty sick, too. Got quite a fever."

"The three day flu. His temp's down to 101. See he gets plenty of fluids and aspirin every four hours until the fever breaks and he'll be fine."

Kevin, nods, still at Jackee's side, her hand protectively in his.

She is slipping slowly into a sedative-induced fog, listening to them recriminate about things over which they had no control. She's breathing easily, the acid fumes in her lungs apparently extinguished. Her mind, though logy, is clear.

What a nightmare!

She sighs, languidly embracing the approaching mantle of sleep...dark and soothing. The doctor left, but Kevin and Maria still hover nearby.

Need a good night's rest. Gotta be sharp. Rhonda's coming.

Their voices, cloaked in the shadows of drowsiness, impinge on thoughts.

"What the Hell happened," Kevin asks the nurse. "How could ya leave her alone?"

"Christ, Kevin! It was only a thirty minute errand, and Mr. Maren and Charlene were here." Angry tears flood Maria's cocoa brown eyes.

"Thirty minutes? Ya were gone over *two hours!*"

"Yeah, well I ran out of gas on Dundee Road, right in the middle of nowhere."

"What?"

"It's really strange, because I'm sure I had nearly a half tank yesterday."

"D'ya think there's a leak?"

"I don't know. I'm no mechanic. I looked under the car, but didn't see anything. Anyway, it's full now. I'll check again tomorrow. I was so damned mad, I almost broke my foot, kicking the damned car. I've *never* left a patient stranded before."

"Look, kiddo, you're the most reliable nurse I know. Stuff happens. Let's see it don't happen again."

Jackee, pulling the last black folds of sleep over her, grasps a final, curious thought, before drifting off.

That's what I smelled on Phil this morning.

Gasoline!

The last thing she sensed was someone easing out the rear of his house. She heard the creek of the metal door, and felt... somehow... the heat of the incinerator. Then a soft plop of a bag dropping in, and the *pssst* of several squirts of charcoal lighter fluid.

Whoosh!

Her eyes jerk open, as she intuits flames blazing out, its tongue caressing a face. She pictures Phil lurching back, dropping the lid with a noisy clang, cutting off the questing inferno. The air around her, one hundred feet away, is filled with a strange, burnt smell.

Jesus, that was close. Wonder if he dirtied his pants?

She listens to the roar of the fire, and sighs. Damning evidence is probably turning into no evidence at all.

Slipping back into the warm embrace of her quiet little lake, she realizes she doesn't care. She has other, more important tasks to face.

Staying alive is at the top of her list.

CHAPTER THIRTY

Jackee struggles out of the gentle arms of sedative-induced slumber. Kevin is quietly rummaged around her room.

She glances at the big clock on the wall: Midnight.

"Where in the Hell is that lousy tube?" He mumbles. "Ain't in the trash or under the bed. Gotta be here somewhere." He looked at Maria, who is aiding in the hunt.

"I remember Dr. Berg examining the end, clucking to himself like an angry chicken," she whispered. "I don't know where he put it after that."

They gave up the search of her room, and Jackee slipped back into the arms of the Sandman, knowing the fruitlessness of their efforts.

Kevin called the doctor at home, first thing in the morning. After a short apology for the early intrusion, he asked about the whereabouts of that pesky plastic tubing. Jackee is pretty sure she has the answer to that.

"I'm not sure where it is. I may have put it in the trash can when... No, I remember. Mr. Maren arrived, understandably very upset, and asked to see it. I presume it went into the trash after that."

I know my hearing is unbelievable, but how do I hear what's being said on the other end of the phone?

"Damn! I wish ya hadn't..."

"What?"

"Never mind. Thanks, doc."

"How's our patient sleeping?"

"Peacefully, thank God. I think she may come through this okay"

Kevin hangs up, and groaned.

This had to be Phil. He was there. Even handed Maria the tube. Then burned the evidence last night. Not enough I'm trapped in this Hell, but the bastard wants me dead. He's bringing his mistress here, and he wants me out of the way.

And our sons? What about them?

"Gotta be Phil." Kevin's mumbled words echo her thoughts.

"Well, he'll have to climb over me, and I'm a pretty big hill. If he tries something like this again, I'll... I'll kill the bastard!"

Jackee trembles at that comment.

Kevin isn't a fool. He values life, and won't stupidly put his own in jeopardy. But he obviously draws the line at Phil putting Jackee's life in danger.

These are commitments you make for someone you love, not just a patient. Even ones you've become friends with.

It'd be nice to be loved... but unrealistic. I'll have to put it perspective for him.

CHAPTER THIRTY-ONE

D-day. Or really, R-Day.

Jackee gazes absently at the snow-blanketed yard.

Rhonda's arriving today, a one-woman invasion.

Thirty hours ago I was dead. No prospects left. But here I am, with this new challenge, and I'm glad to be alive, even if only like this. Gotta see if I can still make a difference.

No question about it. Phil tried to kill me! Kevin looked for the faulty tube, but it disappeared. Hubby's singed eyebrows confirm what I heard that night. Pretty much guarantees this frozen Hell I'm in wasn't an accident, either.

The bastard tried to kill me twice! And now Rhonda's coming here to live.

Phil and Rhonda missed dinner. Charlene, who put extra effort into a special meal, was distraught. Characteristically, Phil didn't bother calling to say they would be late.

I wonder if Rhonda's a little uneasy about being here with me? She can't believe I'm still innocent to their affair, but why would she care? Phil sure doesn't, and there's little I can do to cause them trouble.

With Kevin here, Rhonda won't bother me either, provided she doesn't try to wrap the big, sweet guy around her little finger. I hope he's smarter than that.

Good old Kevin. Busy, busy, busy, all day to keep me from thinking about tonight.

Therapy was waived for the day in deference to her recent brush with death, but there is no sign of any difficulty breathing.

He took her on an extended walk around the neighborhood instead, reviewing myriad Christmas decorations, out in full force. He prattled on non-stop, trying to distract her from dwelling on Rhonda and Phil together in *her* house.

He must suspect I know their lovers. I only hope she doesn't make things tougher by being a bitch. What'll she do around here, with the boys in school?

Phil added some new workout equipment to the treatment room.

She can't keep a shape like that without some effort. I should have done more, too. I'd gotten so involved with our sons and my social obligations, I never made time. Wouldn't have changed anything, if he were already cheating, but I should have done it for myself.

Where are they, anyhow?

As if in reply, she hears two cars pulling into the drive, one growling the low, throaty rumble of a powerful engine. Kevin pokes his head through the doorway.

"They're here. Would ya believe she's driving one of those classic E-type Jag sport cars. Sure can't afford *that* on a secretary's pay."

What a surprise. More proof he's been keeping her, probably with money from the trusts.

The louse!

"Ya try to keep calm. I know this is aggravating, but let's make the best of it. I'm hopeful this gal ain't a bad sort. We'll know 'bout that pretty soon. She may be just as uncomfortable as ya, so don't go burning holes in her with those green lasers of yours. Everybody's gonna be lot happier if we can get along."

His concerns fill her with warmth.

He wants to avoid any confrontation, but I'm not nearly so certain Rhonda's not "a bad sort." She's stolen my husband. I only hope she leaves me in peace.

I wonder if she were in on Phil's plots? Even an instigator? First the anesthetic "accident," and then yesterday's blatant fiasco. The smell of gasoline on him makes that one pretty obvious.

Can't bear it if he did this and gets away with it. Never been vindictive, but no one else suspects him...except maybe Kevin.

It's up to me to see he's punished. But, how the Hell can I do that?

I'm useless!

Phil and Rhonda scuffle through the front door under obviously heavy burdens, proceeding down the galley way, past her den, to the guest bedroom. Kevin fidgets at her side, holding her lifeless hand, offering silent support.

"Might as well give 'em a hand. He must have borrowed a station wagon to carry all her stuff. Quicker this is over, the better."

She blinks once, and he leaves the room.

The three of them continue going in and out, transporting Rhonda's possessions into the guest room. Her sons creep into the den, Bryan crawling onto her lap, hooking an arm over the chair back, resting his head on her shoulder. Her heart swells to bursting at their unconditional love.

"Is it Miss Armstrong?" Mal, looking wan, keeps his distance, perching on a chair.

"Is she moving in tonight?"

Yes. She's come here to live.

"She's moving into the guest room?"

Yes, for now.

Tiny tears wet the corners of her eyes.

"Should we call her Miss Armstrong, or Miss Rhonda, or what?"

You ask her what she wants you to call her.

"Shouldn't we ask Daddy? Maybe he knows," Mal asks.

No, ask her.

Rhonda's response might give Jackee a clue as her real expectations.

"Okay. Can we ask her now?" asks Bryan.

No. They're busy. Ask her in the morning. You guys go to bed now.

"Do we have to?" They are plainly disappointed.

"We thought we should... sorta welcome her to our house, or something."

She glowed with warmth at their thoughtfulness. They are *her* sons, infused with Webster traditions. Neither Phil nor Rhonda can change that. She fills her answer with love.

That's a nice idea, but Mal's still too sick. Do it in the morning. Okay?

"All right, Mommy. We love you the most." Bryan gives her a big hug, and Mal throws a kiss. They leave, passing Kevin on the way back to his patient.

God, I love those two little guys. Talking to them is one of the happiest things left to me.

But if I can do that, why can't I do more?

CHAPTER THIRTY-TWO

"Well, that's it," Kevin says, entering the den. "That gal's got plenty of clothes and shoes and stuff. I suppose she'll be mostly setting up tomorrow.

"Anyway, I doubt they'll come in here tonight. Want to go to bed now?"

"No. 30 later." Her dark green eyes sparkle with lingering tears. He dabs them away with a tissue.

"Okay. Want company?"

She blinks twice.

"Okay. Keep calm, if ya can. He's got a lot of balls bringing his mistress in here, but there's nothing we can do about it."

"I okay Not mad. Curious." Blinking words has become as natural as talking, sending abbreviated messages with speed and ease. Kevin reads them just as quickly.

"All right. I'll see if they need any more help. Then I'll be in my room. Promised Mark Howe I'd go over his progress reports. See ya in about thirty minutes."

He pauses at the entrance. Her eyes follow him in the wall mirror. The room is dimly lit, as she prefers it in the evening, but there is no mistaking her focus.

She senses him shiver slightly, and she's flooded with a sudden premonition that something strange is about to begin. Not just the mistress living together with the unwilling wife. No, something much more... frightening? Was that the right emotion? She isn't sure.

Rhonda, surely Phil's mistress, is moving in.

A guy might do a lot for the love of a beautiful woman... and my family's fortune. I'm certain now Phil's made attempts on my life, and he may try again.

Kevin will surely try to stop him, one way or another. He can't very well throttle the man, unless he was caught in the act, and that seems unlikely.

Might Kevin try to engineer an "accident" for Phil? I've had more than my share of them. Why not Phil? Can't allow him to put himself into jeopardy for me.

Gotta be some other way.

Her eyes return to the mirror. She clears her mind, settling into a patient calmness.

CHAPTER THIRTY-THREE

Jackee sits alertly, awaiting her arrival.

I know she'll come. She's won't just pop in here without checking me out.

Kevin reappears in the doorway, a mother hen worrying over its chick.

Damn it, stop hovering over me. Nothing more you can do you haven't already done. It's her I'm waiting for.

He shrugs and leaves.

This is the beginning, and Rhonda's got the edge. My one-man team...my Paladin...Kevin, will guard me as best he can. The real test is between Rhonda and me, though she may not know it. I hope not. I'll need every advantage I can get.

Problem is, I've no plan. Not a single idea of what, if anything, I might achieve.

She watches the mirror, waiting for the redhead to show herself, filled with a strange certainty some avenue will present itself. What that might be, considering her current ineptitude, is a total mystery.

Patience and watchfulness. That'll be my credo. I've survived three brushes with death. Not about to give up this worthless shell yet. Daddy told me I'm stronger than I know. She'll learn I'm still alive, and not to be regarded lightly.

The house is quiet in these late evening hours. Maria appears, taking her pulse and blood pressure, probably at Kevin's bidding.

Wonderful, cautious Kevin. I feel so safe with him here, despite my last close call. I won't use him for vengeance, though. Rhonda's the master manipulator, not me.

Besides, shoving Kevin into the breach might bring him danger, and that's not acceptable. He may play a part somehow, but not because of his size and strength. I need to create something that will haunt Phil forever.

Question is, how do I do that?

Engrossed in thought, she was taken by surprise by a quiet movement in the hallway. Her eyes find the mirror just as Rhonda moves silently into the open doorway, leaning against the jamb, arms crossed in front of her.

She hovers motionless, her hazel eyes meeting Jackee's green ones in the reflection, locked in a silent confrontation. The moment dragged by on turtle's feet. Rhonda finally breaks the link, surveying the room for a few seconds, then again finding those emerald orbs, still seeking hers in the mirror.

Rhonda smiles softly, then turns to leave, uttering one hushed word.

"Tomorrow."

Yes, tomorrow our quiet war begins. Will she even know it's being waged? Does she realize how well I actually understand what's going on?

A few moments later, Kevin returns to put her to bed.

"Do ya need anything, before I head for my room?"

"No. Sleep now."

Tomorrow. It all begins tomorrow!

Chapter Thirty-Four

Peeking in from the doorway, Kevin sees Jackee's eyes are open.

"Well, good morning. Up kind of early today, huh?" he says, stepping inside.

"Heard U," she signs.

"Yeah, there's no sneaking up on ya. Just checking in before my morning run. Ya feeling okay?"

"Yes."

"No trouble breathing?"

He laid fingers on her throat, checking her pulse, clearly still concerned.

"No."

"Head's clear? Nothing foggy or confused or anything?"

"I fine. Ready to skip rope."

"Huh? I don't..."

"In head, K. Skip in head."

"Oh, you're joshing me, huh? Still got a sense of humor, even after... well, you know. Can't help fretting, though, and..."

"Is done. I fine now. No worry."

"Can't help it, but ya checked out pretty good, thank God. So, I'll be back in about an hour. Ya need anything?"

"No. Nice day?" she blinks.

"Yeah, beautiful. It's warmed up a good bit. Maybe we'll take that walk I promised ya."

"Good."

He tilts the bed higher, adjusting her pillows. Her hair makes a golden halo for her head

"See you when I get back." He hurries from her room.

Three day have passed since she died and been reborn, thanks to Malcolm, bouncing back with little noticeable ill effects.

She "trembles," certain Phil sabotaged her new tube. The roar of flames and the clang of the incinerator, like the Bell of Doom, had seemed a sedative-induced nightmare.

Later that evening, his singed eyebrows and the missing old tube told an unmistakable tale of evidence going up in smoke. No other reason for him to dump trash, a chore Charlene always handles. He is unfamiliar with how it works and was careless.

Still hard to accept he's actually tried to kill me! She blinks away tears.

But why? All the money is his to use, and his sweetie is camped inside my front door. He has everything, and it's still not enough!

How terrifying! And it's pretty obvious to me, at least, this wasn't the bastard's first attempt.

So, now what? Will he try again? Can't tell Kevin. That could be dangerous for him, and he may already suspect on his own.

I'm trapped, forced to wait and watch, but what can I do to protect myself?

I'm so damned helpless!

CHAPTER THIRTY-FIVE

Dear sweet Kevin. Is this the classical therapist transference I studied in Psyche class?

I don't think so.

What an unusual blend of masculine strength and feminine sensitivity. Face it Jackee, you're falling for him. And why not?

Nice to be treated with care and understanding. Not the charade Phil must have been living for... how long? Years, maybe.

If I were able, I might run off with the guy... or better yet, boot Phil and his chippy out on their asses. Then the boys would have a real father image.

That happy fantasy evaporates, blown away by the wind of reality.

What a joke! No way to kick-start this dead machine. The engine's fried, and only the computer and the headlight still work. Can't fix the rest.

Now that I'm sure Phil did this to me...put me in this Hell...I keep wondering if Rhonda were involved? Even if she were, nothing I can do about it. I never suspected he didn't love me.

What a fool!

He has to pay... to really suffer for what he's done. Banish him to some Hell of his own, roasting over... She blinks.

Revenge?

Wow! I've never lusted for revenge in my entire life. But things have changed. Never had a reason before. Still, it's useless! What can I do, like this?

Nothing, damn it!

Nothing!

She blinks again, flushed with anger.

Quit that!

Websters don't give up, no matter what the odds.

Daddy said I can do anything I put my mind to.

Chapter Thirty-Six

Kevin settles her on the massage table, the first time since her recent close call. She sees his manipulation of her arms and legs as though watching a movie. Sensationless floating is her sole existence. Thoughts drift to Phil and his attempt (or *attempts?*) on her life.

How crass, bringing his mistress into our house. To flaunt her like that!

She struggles against anger growing in her belly, spreading in scorching waves throughout her consciousness.

Bitterness is useless. Gotta stay in control. Finding some way to make him pay might give life meaning again.

"Ya sleep okay?" Kevin roll's her onto her back.

She blinks once.

"Good. I gotta admit, you're taking Rhonda being here pretty calmly. Not sure I could've, if it were me."

"I okay."

"Yeah. Well, I worry some about Phil. There was something fishy about that damned tube. I don't trust that man."

Jackee smiles at him with her eyes.

If he only knew!

"I okay. He not hurt me."

Hopefully he'll be too nervous to try again.

"Hope you're right. I'm gonna be extra careful, just in case."

"Oughta be near fifty today. We can mosey on down to that little strip mall, and ya can look around some of the shops, if ya want."

She blinks once.

Won't involve him with my suspicions. He's got his own. Knowing mine can only make him more fearful of ever leaving me alone again.

I wonder what dear hubby's cooking up next? It won't be divorce. That'd cost him access to Daddy's fortune. That'll never happen.

Enough black thoughts. They'll only put me in a funk. It'll be nice to visit even the few stores at that mall...to get out with some sunshine and fresh air.

Thank God I can still sense odors. A sunny, cold winter day smells so clean.

So, it's hi-ho, hi-ho, off to the stores we'll go.

She chuckles in her head where only she can hear them.

What a perfect Snow White I'd be... except for the damned wheelchair. Of course, Kevin doesn't exactly qualify as anybody's version of a dwarf.

She drifts off into a mindless fantasy world of fair maidens, heroes and demons.

Not so different, really, from where she is living.

Chapter Thirty-Seven

Therapy done for the morning, and dressed in a warm-up, Kevin wheels her to the den so she can view the yard.

Clearly warming up, snow held captive by near zero temperatures for nearly a week is finally in full retreat. Things are so beautiful when blanketed by a few inches of clean white powder, accenting the uneven terrain. Warm weather quickly transforms everything into a dingy brown morass, but it is temporary. There'll be plenty of new snow to come.

Not even Christmas yet, and one of the things we can always count on in Chicago is plenty of winter. Cold in the winter and hot in the summer, and if you don't like it, just wait a moment and it'll change. A common Chicagoan quip about their unreliable climate.

Looking out the windows, her mind drifts aimlessly, until Maria cleans her up and dresses her for her afternoon expedition.

Just after One PM, Kevin wheels her out the front door and down the drive, heading for Dundee Road. It's a half-hour walk to the little eight-unit mall, but as promised, the day is beautiful and sunny. She's with her now favorite man, infused with a sense of contentment. Life actually seems worth living.

They tour all the stores. Kevin buys an ice cream cone, and she's a little jealous.

"This is my biggest weakness," he says, "ice cream. I love it, especially chocolate with fudge or nuts. And it loves me. That's one reason I run every morning. It's that or fat." He laughs heartily.

Settling on a bench, he talks about little, unimportant things, sensing she doesn't want a serious thought on her mind at that moment. Eventually, he spins the tale of his youth, and how he got into boxing.

"I was big from the get-go. Over ten pounds when I was born. They put me straight into a regular crib. Hour later, I'd crawled from one end to the other.

"I was always kinda quiet. Wouldn't hurt a mouse. I'd catch 'em in the house and drop 'em in a field, a mile away. Kids at school didn't chance fooling with me much. In kindergarten, I was big as most Second Graders.

"Had my first fight when I was eleven. Some Eighth Graders were picking on my older brother. We were poor sharecropper's kids, going to the Town school, and they thought they was better'n us. My brother was kinda scrawny, believe it or not."

He chuckles, eyes fastened on distant memories. He shrugs, looking at her, and grins.

"Anyway, I barreled in. Whupped 'em both, getting a bloody nose in the process. One of the teachers saw the whole thing, and kept me outta trouble.

"He was coaching a boxing club and asked me if I wanted to learn to do it right. They were mostly Seventh and Eighth Graders, but we were pretty much the same size, so it was okay. No one bothered my brother after that, either.

"I fought my way to being school champ when I was twelve. Coach put me in a local junior meet, the youngest there by three years, but he said he thought I had a real future, maybe another Great White Hope."

"U like box?"

"Like it? Yeah, I enjoyed developing the physical skill and coordination. I liked outclassing the other kids as much as out punching 'em. Always was quick and light on my feet, despite my size. Had good hand-eye coordination, too.

"Hoeing fields by hand, and chopping wood makes for strong shoulders and arms, and a lean, hard gut. Nobody hurt me much, no matter how hard they hit. I got a head of stone, I guess." He chuckles again, rubbing his jaw.

"Anyway, I developed some good skills, along with some powerful punching.

"I entered a bunch of local meets in the next few years. Won them all, mostly by knockouts, even with the 16-ounce gloves. Enjoyed everything, except for hurting the other guy, but that's part of boxing. Coach said if I kept up my training and did well in some bigger meets, I had a shot at the Olympics in four years. Then I could turn pro and make more money than I ever dreamed of. Maybe even be the heavyweight champ of the World."

"U go Ol'mp'cs?"

"Yep. Won the gold medal, too. Fought a big Cuban in the finals. One of the few guys ever hit hard enough to really hurt me." He touched his nose.

"Broke my snout, but I knocked him out in the third round. Biggest thrill of my life, standing on that platform singing the Star Spangled Banner, with that piece of gold hanging around my neck. I was right proud.

"After that, fighting lost some of its magic. It *was* mighty exciting to get thousands of dollars for usually ten or twelve minutes work. Nobody I was fighting lasted four rounds with me. I put 'em on the floor in a hurry, but I was starting to feel real guilty, hurting all those guys. No permanent damage, though, so I justified it. I was saving the money to get pappy off that damned farm."

Jackee studies the craggy planes of his face, fascinated by how someone born to poverty had struggled to get ahead, against all the odds.

Life was so different for me. Daddy never just gave me things. He made me learn the value of doing it myself, but being Chester Webster's daughter gave me a big head start.

"As I worked my way up the ranks, the fighters got better, and I started taking more punishment. Still didn't usually hurt much, but it surely did rearrange my face." His hand went to his bent nose again.

"Still knocked out most everybody I fought. At twenty-five, I was number two contender for the Heavy Weight crown, but the champ kept ducking me. Finally, we had an agreement for me to fight Carlos Arenas, the top contender. The champ'd fight the winner within the year.

"Arenas was damned good. Another big, tough Cuban. Won most of his fights by knockouts, too. We mixed it up good for five rounds, but then I got lucky. I dazed him with a left hook early in the sixth, and then hit him with a five punch combo in the head and body before he finally went down." Kevin looks away for a moment.

"He never got up." His voice cracks. "At least not in the ring."

Remembered despair crumples his face. He sits silent for several moments, hooded eyes filled with anguish, then shakes himself, as if shedding the memory, and sighs.

"I felt so bad, I quit boxing. Had a contract to fight the Champ, but he tore that up in a hurry. Probably happy his two toughest opponents were gone.

"My manager was mighty hot. First he threatened to sue, then be begged me to at least wait until after the title fight. But I couldn't stomach it no more. Fighting for the crown would have been worth a couple million dollars if I'd won, but I'm not so sure I woulda, my head being where it was at the time."

"Yes. Must want it." She understands desire, now that she lusts to destroy Phil.

"Right. All I wanted was to help Arenas get better. My trainer, Mike Murphy, got me into physical therapy training. Didn't have much higher education, so I started with school and the P.T. courses. Worked on a garbage truck in the early mornings to help pay my way. Smelled bad, but the money was good."

His nose wrinkles. She's captivated by how the memories are photographed on his face.

"I visited Arenas every chance I got. He was in a coma for eleven weeks. The docs said he'd never recover enough to lead a useful life. Too much brain damage. I told him to pay 'em no mind. We were going to get him up and around. I wouldn't take 'no' for an answer. Took more'n a year, but he made it. Now he's a physical therapist, just like me."

"U sad U boxed?"

How easily he talks with me. I can't remember my last serious conversation with Phil.

"Not really. Didn't like inflicting pain, but they were trying to hurt me, too. It got me outta 'Bama, and paid for my education. Who'd think I'd be studying for a master's degree? Me, a poor sharecropper's kid.

"Being a therapist pays good, and I've got nearly enough saved to shake pappy loose from that damned piece of overworked dirt they call a farm. Give him some peace in his last years. Guess I've helped ten people for everyone I hurt, so I'm comfortable with that. My only regret is never losing this poor-South drawl. It's kinda embarrassing."

"U fine. Good man. I like much."

"Well, thanks. That means a lot to me. I think you're pretty special, too. But I suspect ya know that. I sorta sense things about ya, and ya seem to do the same with me." He grinned. "Maybe we knew each other in another life."

Or we have a different connection in this one. Somehow, I seem to get inside his head.

He looks at the fiery ball, squatting just above the tree-lined horizon.

"Near sunset. We oughta start home. Been having such a good talk, the time got away from me. Never told anyone my whole story before. Guess I wanted ya to know all about me."

"I glad. Like to know all. Glad U on my side."

"Thanks. I'm glad to be there. We better get going, though. It'll be neigh dark by the time we get back. Maria'll chew me out."

They start off, arriving at the house at dusk. As Kevin guessed, Maria and Charlene both are worried and a bit angry they were gone so long, but relent when Jackee "tells" them how much she enjoyed that afternoon.

CHAPTER THIRTY-EIGHT

Jackee wakes the next morning, refreshed by a sound night's sleep. Getting out of the house has lifted a pall of loneliness.

Her camaraderie with Kevin infuses her with warmth, a euphoria that may not last with Phil and Rhonda around. It's something unpleasant she'll have to deal with.

No question they're lovers. I hear them doing it last night, and they're at it again right now. I hope I'm the only one who hears them.

"Uh, uhh, uuhhh." The redhead's rhythmic chant rings in her head, along with a lower undercurrent of Phil grunting. They are both approaching orgasm.

"Huhhhhh-uuhh," Rhonda moans. The sound of the other woman's intense release peppers her. Phil's guttural sounds continue unabated.

"Uh, uhh, uuhhh." Rhonda is surging toward another climax, as Phil seeks his own orgasm.

Jackee's quiet pool riffles. Hot, tingly sensations...surely only imagined...swamp her, accelerating her heart as their intensity increases.

God, how wonderful!

Her body seems suddenly alive, no longer suspended in weightless, floating nothingness.

How is this happening?

"Huhhhhh-uuhh."

Rhonda's second climax, and still they're not finished. Jackee's damp with perspiration as sounds of continued passion reverberate in her head, setting her heart galloping.

"Arrgahh!

"Huhh-huhhhhh-uuhh!" Finally, completion for both! Jackee pants, gasping for air. Her diminished capacities aren't prepared for such an erotic tour.

What the Hell was that? They're screwing like a pair of minks, and I get all stirred up, clear across the house. How do I feel their excitement? This telepathy thing?

Will I be cursed to hear every damned sound? Some things are better left unknown. They're sure not trying to hide their affair.

He's such a callous bastard, but I really don't know what to expect from her. It'd be easy to blame Rhonda for everything, but I know better. She may have put out bait, but if he weren't looking, she'd never have gotten her lovely red hooks into him.

No, it's all on Phil's shoulders.

How could I have married such a louse? Not to mention an attempted murderer!

Maria interrupts her thoughts with breakfast and her outfit for the day.

Chapter Thirty-Nine

Alone!
You are alone. Murmuring softly.
Forever alone. Hissing quietly.

Whispering cruelly, the winter wind sucks at her soul. Desolate, she whimpers in dismal harmony with the French doors, groaning against fresh gusts, drawing futilely at their panes.

Jackee stares numbly at the barren landscape as windows rattle, moaning soulfully. A few remaining dry, brown leaves skitter across the patio, doing the hoochee koochee, given life and energy by the crisp northerly gale, soughing around the house, scratching for entry.

Winter is marshaling itself for its second major offensive of the season, but the specter of heavy snow isn't what depresses her.

No errands to run, no places to go. Bad weather is not what keeps me housebound. Kevin will take me for walks when we get a sunny day, but those will be rare.

Then the real author of her despair...that insistent sound...that metronome beat...insinuates itself...

Creak... creak... creak.

Damn! They're at it again.

She struggles to shield her mind, unwilling to listen, but unable to stop. She can't generate any distraction powerful enough to mask that noise.

Creak..creak..creak.

Bedsprings, settling into to a familiar cadence, as the moaning and murmuring bombard her at a staccato pace. Squeals and urgent mutterings are overridden by a chanted "Uh, uhh, uuhhh," ramping up to a long, emphatic, "Huhhhhh-uuhh!"

Quickly, the whole aural vignette begins again, the decibel level jacked up a few notches. Rhonda is having one of her multi-orgasmic episodes, while Phil builds toward his own climax.

How the Hell does the bitch do that?

Jackee is inexplicably breathless, her heart racing with a strange excitement their sexual escapades somehow stir in her. for five weeks her sole sensation revolved around floating weightlessly in a dark, quiet pond.

Then Rhonda arrives, and Jackee's inundated by waves of erotic stimuli, slowly at first, but with growing intensity.

The mirrored surface of her black lagoon ripples, small wavelets escalating to a heavy roil, swamping her with surging waves of erotic arousal. Electric-like bolts charge dead nerves, her heart hammering mercilessly at her breast, her skin afire with what are surely imagined goose bumps. A slippery wetness (also imagined?) flows between her thighs.

Both terribly exciting and cruelly frustrating, she reluctantly cherishes their intensity, even if only as a fantasy. She feels *alive* again, rift with sensations far beyond anything she's ever experienced, even before the accident. In some strange way, she's tapped into Rhonda's carnal soul, swept along as the redhead plunges through climax after climax.

This is too much! I've never had an orgasm, and it's not about to happen now. They're supposed to require a lot of time and clitoral stimulation, but that bitch has two or three every time they hit the bed. That's something I never got from Phil. One more place he fell short.

This is their second time today. Lucky the boys are at Phil's mother's. I doubt he'd stop because our sons were home. He's so damned arrogant, now that I'm so... so useless.

Useless!

That's it exactly! Just an observer. No input. No say in anything. Only listen and watch, while he brings his tramp into my house. Household manager and governess to the boys. What a transparent charade!

I'm surprised he hasn't already moved her into his bedroom. How long will this last? They're humping like dogs in heat almost every evening.

Their callousness infuriates her, despite the pseudo-physical pleasure she's somehow sucked into. All efforts to insulate herself fail miserably. Each episode engulfs her more and more, drowning her in heated arousal she shouldn't feel.

And for what? for nothing, that's what! No way to relieve this wonderful tension, all this artificial excitement. So like him to leave me hung out to dry, unsatisfied and angry.

Of course, he has no idea what's happening, and maybe that's best.

She had laboriously blinked her frustration to Kevin. Although unable to trade thoughts with him as she does with her sons, he still seems to sense anger, glittering brightly in her eyes.

"I know," he replies. "I try to distract the boys. They're a little young to understand what's going on. Funny thing is... don't hate me for this... but I kinda like Rhonda. She mighta gone after another gal's man, but she's looking for security, and Phil's her ticket.

"She might not realize how completely ya understand what's happening. Your *husband's* the real louse." Jackee eyes smile agreement.

"If he's gonna do this, he shouldn't be so open about it."

"Rhonda's a beauty, but I don't think she'd hold a candle to ya, if ya were up and around. You're one very special lady." He drops his gaze, blushing.

Her eyes twinkle with affection for this gentle man, studiously examining the tops of his shoes, his face glowing a light shade of crimson.

It's nice he likes me. I hope this is becoming more than just another billet. Too bad I can't tell him how strongly I've come to feel, but that might drive a wedge between us.

Friendship or not, this is still only his job.

"Well, time for therapy. Might get your mind off less pleasant things. We'll weigh you again today. Gotta get you as chubby as we can."

Chapter Forty

Jackee lay propped up in bed, ruminating.

Strange. Nothing works except my eyes, but after therapy, I'm very tired, same as if I'd worked out on my own. No difference for me between sitting and lying down, but I'm more awake when I sit, and sleep easier in bed. Thirty-five years of old habits are hard to change.

Kevin weighs and measures her after her "workout," checking various dimensions from head to toe, quietly muttering under his breath.

"Damn. Lost another two pounds! This gotta stop."

Thank God someone worries about me. He treats me so much better, more respectfully, than Phil ever did.

Her eyes glisten with moisture.

I wasted my youth on that self-serving bastard, instead of finding a man like Kevin Martin, who might love me, not my trust funds. Don't know what Phil felt in the beginning, but no question why he's here now. When did that change, or was it always just the money?

Strangely, she "tingles" when Kevin fingers brush her breasts and belly, taking measurements. She seems to tremble, her breath coming in short little gasps, when he gives a massage. Somehow she "feels" his touch.

Of course, she has no tactile response, no sense of his hands on her. Yet, a stirring will grow between her legs, where there can *be* no stirring, her heart doing a rapid jig.

It all started with her strange carnal arousal, blooming from Phil and Rhonda's escapades.

I've heard of men who lost a limb and still swore that they could feel their toes or fingers itch. The power of the mind. She chuckles sleepily.

Sexual arousal is becoming my itch.

Weary from mental gyrations, she closes her eyes.

Jackee awakens at Maria's arrival to prepare her "dinner." The lovebirds are back from tennis, showering. She still marvels at hearing them, clear across the house.

Rhonda must be serving up some mighty steamy appetizers over there. I'm all tingly, and the old heart's tapping a merry jig. They really are some pair, probably better suited sexually than Phil and I ever were.

She shakes her mind clear, blanketing as best she can the unwelcome and frustrating stimuli, turning her thoughts to her sons, who won't be home until Nine.

She aches for their presence, the weight of affection. Though she can't feel their hugs and kisses, she still "feels" them in her head. Their love, warm and comforting, pours out to her from their minds.

Mal. Bry. She reached for them, knowing they are probably too far away to hear. She's desperate for a distraction from the heated sensations tumbling around her. There is no response.

Maria finishes with her meal. "Eating" requires nothing more than her being there. Thankfully, Kevin arrives shortly after Maria packs away her supplies. The new tube, carefully inspected by everyone before insertion, is working perfectly.

He wheels her to the Family Room where she can view the garden and watch the birds and squirrels. She hears footsteps coming down the hall, the two lovers heading for the dining room. She gets a brief glimpse of them in her mirror as they passed by, arms around each other.

The blatant bastard. He doesn't give a damn about how open they are.

Kevin hunkers down in front of her.

"Ya need anything?"

"No. Sit. Look."

"Okay. If it's okay, I'm gonna visit an old patient in Highland Park. Be gone two, maybe three hours. Maria'll keep an eye on ya, and I'll be back in time to put ya in bed. That all right?"

She blinks her approval and he hurries off, leaving her with her thoughts and no one to talk with. Mal and Bryan won't be home from her mother-in-law's for a while, and Phil and Rhonda, solely engrossed in each other, have no interest in entertaining her. Just as well. That'd be more than she can stomach just now.

The brisk winter wind renews its attack on the windowpanes, still singing its plaintiff song...

You're alone. Alone for the rest of your life.

Alone!

Unshed tears fill her eyes.

Damn it! I'm only thirty-five and locked in this prison for life. Solitary confinement and full restraints. No parole; no reprieve. Phil's my warden, and Rhonda's the cellblock boss.

Kevin thinks Rhonda's " okay," but I know better. She's devious, manipulative, and certainly not short on intellect. She wants it all.

The hardest thing to swallow is Phil trying to kill her...more than once! She's brimming with a bitter taste new for her...hate! He wanted her dead, but she ended up trapped in this Hell instead. She rarely lusted for anything throughout her life, but now she craves absolute retribution.

Can't let him get away with attempted murder. Him and his chippy. Daddy never trusted him, and did what he could to protect me before he died. Phil may have some real surprises coming, but that's only a beginning. I need to find a way to really punish him!

Finished with dinner, Phil and Rhonda amble into his study. The clink of glasses suggest an after dinner brandy. Despite herself, she listens to their giggling and murmuring, and a little breathless squeal. The air crackles around her, flooding her with unlikely warmth.

What an imagination! I can feel nothing.

Yet somehow the heat on her skin, the moist press of his mouth against her lips, is all there. Impossible stirrings mushroom, sending her heart on hummingbird wings.

No way to explain this, but the angrier she gets, the more fully she seems to share their passion, increasing in intensity with every experience. Her heart fluttering, skin ablaze, she "shudders," sensing again implausible moisture between her legs.

She struggles for breath, her dead body engulfed in flames. Then things begin to cool, the thumping in her breast slowing, ragged waves in her little lagoon receding to ripples, finally settling again to a glassy calm. Surfacing from that sensual morass, she realizes the lovers stopped their sexual play.

God! *I've never experienced anything like that before.*

Tired and weak, she drifts aimlessly, totally spent.

CHAPTER FORTY-ONE

Kevin returns just as Phil's mother drops off Mal and Bry, all arriving in the den together.

The boys kiss her and chatter about their visit to the Field Museum, carrying on a vocal conversation, while she answers with her mind. Finished dissecting their day, they kiss and hug her again, and then leave her with Kevin.

"How'r ya making out?"

"Okay."

"They bother ya while I was gone?"

"No. Yes." *It'd be so much easier if we could talk, like with the boys. Long messages are so frustrating.* Tonight she tries.

"I angry. They love. I feel. No good."

"Damn, and I was away. Ya feeling any better? Can I do anything?"

He misunderstands. She sighs, too tired to fight for clarity.

"I okay. Sleep."

So what if he knows? He can't change anything. If that happens, it'll be solely up to me.

Kevin wheels her to her room, lifting her as carefully as a fragile glass figurine, settling her gently on the bed. He fusses with the bedding, covering her with a tartan flannel blanket. A huge hand gently brushes golden strands of hair from her face. He studies her, as if sensing and understanding her turmoil.

"I know, Jackee. This ain't fair. Gonna be tougher than ever with Rhonda here, and them so open about their affair. At least ya got one real friend here.

"No, make that three," he laughs, as her sons materialize, crawling onto her bed to cuddle and kiss her good night. Malcolm seems especially happy, now that his flu is gone. After they leave, she looks at him.

"Thank U." Her eyes fill with warmth.

He grins, nods, and then leaves her for the night.

I suppose I could use Mal to relay my frustrations, but these are things he won't understand. And, who know how Phil might react, if he learns I can communicate with my sons.

All of this...talking to the boys, sensing the lovers' passion...it's all some sort of telepathy.

Can I develop it into a useful tool to use against Phil, or am I only consigned to eavesdropping? I desperately need something to give me an edge.

So tired. I'll work on it tomorrow.

She drifts off into a world of turbulent dreams.

Chapter Forty-Two

Oh, God! I'm dying.

Jackee bolts from a restless sleep, heart racing, her breath hissing in short gasps, her body seemingly consumed by flames.

Please, no! Not again! I'm not ready.

Fully awake now, surrounded by the dim shadows of her bedroom, she blinks, realizing the end of life isn't really eminent.

Creaking bedsprings and soft, passionate whimpers filter into her consciousness.

Damn the horny bastards, they're doing it again!

Her dark lagoon pitches and sloshes. She gasps, "quivering" as an erotic fire sweeps over her, swamped with sensations she's never before experienced.

How the Hell does this happen?

God, to be whole again! To have real feelings.

She struggles to clear her head, but the more their ardor engulfs her, the more impossible it is to break free.

Damn! It's their sex, not mine. I want nothing from that murdering bastard. As usual, he's leaving me cold and frustrated.

I refuse to be aroused by them. It's wrong!

She struggles to block the inferno of passion, visualizing herself a child, lying chilled in the snow, arms and legs sweeping back and forth, creating a snow angel. Shivering at the recalled cold, the erotic heat dissipates. Her thumping heart slows, the illusory quivering and tremors blown away. Her breathing finally slowing, she is again afloat in her pool of sensory nothingness, its rippled surface gently calming.

Steeling herself, she listens for them, but there's nothing.

Strange to be done so quickly. She hears their voices but they are without sounds of passion, and quickly cease.

She glances at the dimly lit dial of the big clock on the wall.

Eleven o'clock. I only slept about an hour. I was dreaming of... what? Slowly it comes back to her in bits and pieces.

Daddy was by my bed, and Kevin, too, looking even larger than life. The vision slid slowly into focus. He father took her hand and caressed her cheek.

"Countess! Look what they've done to you. But you *can* survive this. Don't give in. You can find the way, if you try. You're much stronger than you know. Stronger..."

It was then she awakened to the drumbeat of her heart, her body consumed by erotic flames she can't possibly feel.

All only in my mind, but still so real.

She blinks away tears.

What does it mean? Is Daddy still watching over me?

The door opens to the nearly silent tread of Kevin, coming to her bedside. Despite the dim light, she sees his eyes, filled with concern and tenderness.

"Ya okay?" He adjusts her pillows. "I had this strange feeling ya needed me."

"I okay"

"Can I do anything?"

Two blinks: "No."

"Ya know ya can ask me anything... anything at all, no matter what?"

One blink, a smile twinkling in her eyes.

"Want to talk some? I don't mind. It's not late."

Two blinks, and then the sign for "sleep."

"Okay. See ya in the morning. Supposed to be nice tomorrow, so if ya want, we can go to Old Orchard. See what's on sale in the big stores after the holidays. Maybe ya want to buy the boys something. Sound good?"

"Yes. Happy."

What a wonderful guy. One of the finest men I've ever known. Not counting Daddy, of course.

Kevin pauses at the door looking back, grinning and shaking his head.

"It's strange. We only communicate through your eyes, but I seem to know if your happy or sad or angry. Not an easy way to get to know ya, but it's like we got empathy for each other. I sense ya feel it, too. Never happened to me before. I've spent so many years caring for people, but I've never had time to actually..." His voice trails away, eyes dropping, his head making a little impatient shake. He looks at her again, making an almost inaudible sigh.

"Yer like a special friend I've known for years. Somehow I've learned who you are, through those wonderful green eyes." A large hand strokes his chin, his eyes glistening with moisture.

"I'll always be here for ya... your protector."

Like in my dream!

"I'll keep ya safe as I can. I swear no one will ever hurt you again." His voice cracks, and there are definitely tears there now.

Does he mean Phil? Can he know the truth? She blinks a message, but he can't read it from the doorway. Moving to her bedside, he sees her eyes, too, are wet. He dries her cheeks with a tissue.

I can't tell him how I've managed to fall in love with him. He'd be embarrassed, thinking his friendship was misunderstood. I only want him to know how much I value his support. I'm so exhausted, but I hope he'll understand.

She began her message again.

"U special friend. Most important. Thanks. Need U here."

Towering above her, taking one of her fragile pale hands into his giant paw, he caresses it gently.

"I'm glad. The feeling's mutual." He grins, topaz eyes glistening wetly.

"Yes. Life better with U, even like this."

"Well, you're gonna swell my head, ya keep this up. But all this gabbing musta wore ya out, so I'll let ya get back to sleep. We're gonna have a big day tomorrow."

She blinks once. He adjusts her pillow and blankets, again brushing a few stray strands of hair from her face, continuing to putter, as if unwilling to leave. Does he have something else to say? He stands back, and she sees something in his eyes, something he's struggling with but can't get out.

"What," she asks.

"Nothing." His voice strangely hoarse. "Just checking things. See ya in the morning." He hurries from the room, leaving her to her thoughts.

How strange to fall for such an unlikely guy. The shrinks can talk all day about transference, but I'm in love with a very special man. Got nothing to do with how he looks. No one would ever understand, if we'd found each other...before.

It doesn't matter. No way to share the sentiment, even if he felt the same, so I need to be careful. He already senses something, and it's making him uncomfortable. Better to just accept his friendship for what it is. Thank the Lord he's here to watch over me.

She drifts off drowsily, wondering what happened to the two lovebirds. No more sexual energy pinging at her.

Strange for them to finish so quickly... and quietly.

Chapter Forty-Three

Half way across the house, Jackee's "bionic" ears picks up Phil and Rhonda, as they settle in for the night. Although they spoke softly, the door closed, it seems as if she's right outside their room.

"You look beat, Phil," the redhead says

"Yeah? We'll, my plate is getting too full at work. Too many projects, and you're not there to help."

"Isn't Martha cutting it? She's usually very efficient."

"Yeah, she fine. I just take everything so seriously. I don't want them thinking they made a mistake, cutting Derek from the squad."

"You're kidding? He was half dead. We did them a major favor by exposing him."

"He did it to himself," Phil chuckled. "He fucked up even the simplest projects. You just arranged for management to discover his incompetence."

"Yeah, and when they asked how any work was getting done, I confided to them it was you, 'covering' for your boss. My hero!"

Jackee tingles, sensing his lips brushing her forehead.

"Wonder why I bother sometimes. With the money I've been liberating from the Webster trusts every year, I really don't need the headache. I wouldn't know where else to put the cash if I hadn't set up that Cayman Island account. Smartest thing I ever did. It's like Switzerland—very private."

"Quit complaining. You enjoy the challenge and the power. You'll be elected President of North Chicago soon. With Derek Charles gone, you're definitely the front-runner."

"I know. Just venting. But my load at the office has doubled since I'm chairing the New Plant Committee." His hand ventured across Rhonda's breasts, igniting tiny lightning bolts across Jackee's otherwise dead body.

"I knew *something* was bugging you," her voice husky. "It's been cutting into our love life." She pressed her fingers against his lips before he could respond.

"I'm not complaining. You're still wonderful! Just a little less often than usual. I guess I'll have to be a little more creative. Time to chase your troubles away."

A small groan of pleasure from Phil. *None of the thousand dollar hooker I used to see can hold a candle to this satanic angel I've fallen in love with.*

Jackee blinks.

What the Hell? He certainly didn't say that aloud. I must have read his thoughts. This telepathy, or whatever, is stronger than I imagined.

Goddam him! Stealing from my trusts! That thieving bastard! The blonde's anger suppresses the tsunami of erotic sensations flooding over her from the master bedroom.

Why? I relied on him to handle our finances, and he was free to buy whatever he wanted. Why feather another nest, unless he's planning on leaving. But he'll never walk away from my money. So he tried to kill me instead?

Unbelievable!

What a fool, to marry such an unprincipled louse! Undermining his boss to get his job. Cheating on me. Thousand dollar hooker, for God's sake.

This must have been going on for years. To think I'd actually loved that Cretan.

Infidelity is moot, at this point. Who can I even tell about his thievery? Certainly not Arthur Osborn, or even Kevin. Got no hard facts, and who'd believe I'm listening to his thoughts, as well as their voices, clear across the house?

Her heat cools as she considers what just occurred.

That's something new...and pretty damned exciting! Or was this "gift" always there?

A recent dream remembering riding Apache as a teenager spilled through her head...an Open Jumper show in Lake forest. She was the fourth of the six riders qualifying for a timed jump-off. The course was shortened to eight fences: tall walls, oxers and towering spreads. A professional rider had just gone clean, at a very fast time.

"Okay, boy." She patted Apache. "Let's do it with style."

She grimaced at her hollow bravado. The horn trumpeted, signaling the beginning of her round. Circling once to give him a look at the first fence, she took a big breath, and turned the horse in, moving forward in her seat, preparing for the jump... a big, artificial stone wall.

"Okay, go, boy. Go!" The horse surged forward, fearlessly charging the fence. Everything seemed sharply magnified, etched in black and white.

"Now," she whispered aloud, bending forward, knees pressing his sides, grabbing his mane for support. He collected himself, arching into the air, clearing the fence with ease.

Left. A pair of three-stride in-and-outs. They pivoted sharply, gaining pace.

Time. We need speed.

As they flowed effortlessly over the course, she retreated into a "zone," a tunnel of concentration, seeing each obstacle in clear relief, the horse responding confidently to the instructions coming from her hands and legs.

They cleared the last fence, hurtling past the finish line without a single fault, when she first became aware of the roar of the crowd. Buoyed with exhilaration, she and the horse were one.

Only then, rising out of her crouch, had she realized her eyes had been *closed* throughout the entire round!

How could that be? She had seen everything so plainly!

That's how it was then, and at many other successful horse shows. Was she seeing the jumps through Apache's eyes?

Strange. The lady who bought him after I quit riding, could never get him to jump worth a damn. Was I inside his head, without even knowing it? I can "talk" to my sons. Was Apache getting his instructions from my mind, as well as my legs?

Maybe I hear Phil like that...and Kevin? Is he sensing my thoughts without actually hearing the words? Is that what my dream was all about?

Telepathy.

Maybe the reason my mind survived that operation? And again, the other day? Because I wouldn't let go? I never did things like that... like a telepath... on purpose, but I never knew to try. If I really have that power, that might change things.

Gotta see what develops. Maybe find a way to actually talk to Kevin. If he could hear me, or feel the sense of my thoughts...wow, how exciting. I'm so damned frustrated. But something's there, if I can only figure it out. Something to store away for future use.

Maybe my time will come, after all.

She closes her eyes, tired but strangely elated, awaiting the dark shadow of sleep.

Finally, there may be a way...

Her thoughts stagger to an erratic halt, leaving her staring blankly into space.

Boy! Never thought thinking was so much hard work.

Green eyes flutter closed as she drifts into her first dreamless sleep of the past forty-eight hours.

CHAPTER FORTY-FOUR

What an exciting day!

They drove to the huge Old Orchard Mall, only her second trip away from the immediate neighborhood since the surgical "accident."

Murmurs, elbows in ribs and outright gawkers watched as Kevin wheeled her through the upscale shops. Shoppers were fascinated as the thin, beautiful blonde communicated with the fearsome-looking giant by merely blinking her eyes. Two men even recognized Kevin, asking for his autograph.

Jackee dictated their route, directing Kevin to make the purchases: presents for the boys, an elegant silver tea set for Claire Maren, Phil's mother, who was providing her grandsons some much needed woman's love, and a lovely robin-egg blue silk skirt and blouse for herself. If they are going out, she wants to look nice. Her old clothes hang on her like sacks... very large sacks.

It's wonderful to be out, making decisions, being with a man who is happy strolling the Mall with me.

I feel better than I have in weeks.

Phil was always about doing his things. I was such an innocent. I see things differently now, but it's a little late, with me stuck in this shell. He's running the show whether I like it or not, but I refuse to let it depress me.

Returning home, Kevin settles her in front of the French doors. Her gardens are barren, the lawn still sporting a few patches of dingy snow, all muddy and soft until the next freeze. Spring is still months away.

"I gotta run a few errands and buy supplies. Shouldn't be too long."

"Okay. I rest."

Amazing. I did nothing but blink my eyes and think about what to buy, and I'm bone tired.

She gazes blankly out the window.

Will there ever be anything more to life than this? Even an invalid needs something to look forward to.

Her eyelids flutter closed.

◆❖◆

Awakening slowly, she feels his presence, even before opening her eyes. Phil hovers close by, watching her, his face a dark mask in the shadows. She "shivers," suddenly chilled.

We're alone. Will he try again? What's that in his hand?

"Ah, sleeping beauty awakens."

He's carrying nothing more threatening than a book, but still she can't relax. He reeks of animus.

Do I really smell that, or just more imagination?

"I hear you and the Hulk took a little shopping trip today. That's gonna stop. No more spending without my permission. You're costing a fortune as it is. A hopeless waste of assets. Everything'd be easier if you'd give in and die."

It's Daddy's money, you bastard, and I'm not giving up so easily.

"Ain't her care's paid for by her trusts?" Kevin's deep voice rumbles from the doorway.

Phil turns, scowling, as the therapist, back from his errands, stalks into the room.

Thank God. Phil won't try anything with him here.

"Mr. Osborn told me that, so she seems to be paying for her own care. Ain't that right?"

Phil glares silently at the larger man, now facing him.

"Mister Osborn likes that I'm keeping Jackee's body fit. Her mind's already mighty healthy. She's got the potential for a lot of years, and I intend to help her fulfill it."

Phil glances at Jackee, his face strangely blank. Finally, he shrugs.

"I don't give a damn. I'm not living my life around her pitiful needs. Just keep out of my way, Martin. The Trusts may be paying, but I hired you, and I can as easily fire you. Osborn has nothing to say about it. Understand?"

"Yes, and I appreciate ya letting me do my job, sir." No hint of sarcasm there.

Phil glances back and forth between his wife and the gentle giant who has assumed the added role of her champion. He nods curtly and strides from the room.

She "smiles" at Kevin, her eyes filled with love.

That was a dangerous stand, but he won't sit quietly if my well-being is at stake. He's become important to me in ways he doesn't even know.

Phil better not try to force him to leave. Without Kevin here, who'll protect me?

"I'm sorry if that stressed ya." He settles in front of her. "A bit of a Mexican stand-off. I'm hoping we can all live amicably, but if he tries to fire me, I *will* see Osborn. I think he'll have the last say on things.

"It's unpleasant, with him so open 'bout his affair with Rhonda. We'll have to live with that, as long as he don't interfere none with your care."

He hesitates, obviously struggling with something.

"What?"

"Look, I'm guessing ya realize that thing with your tube was no accident. I'm not gonna to stand around and let that man put you in danger again. I'll do whatever it takes to stop him, even if it means..."

"No. Dangerous 4 U. He not try again."

"I'm not worried about me. He's not gonna hurt ya anymore."

"Do nothing!"

A hard stare, willing her words, as well as blinking them.

"Take care me. Do nothing Phil."

"I only want to see you're safe, is all. This ain't just a job anymore."

Something in his face... his manner... said his feelings may have grown beyond just friendship.

How wonderful to be loved by this sweet giant, just as I've come to adore him.

"Thanks. U good friend. Important to me, leave P. alone."

"Yeah, but if he tries something, I'll..." He stops, raked by green fire from her eyes.

"He not try again. U do nothing. Nothing! Understand?"

Kevin seems about to say something else but stops. He nods, looking strangely uncomfortable.

She can't let him jeopardize his life for her. Other plans are forming in her head. He must be convinced not to do anything physical, if Phil threatens her again. Protect her, but no violence.

He sighs, turning to leave, just as Maria arrives. Jackee glances at the clock.

Six o'clock. Time for another feeding, just like the zoo. How I hate that troublesome feeding tube.

Kevin had removed every low mirror she might see herself in. The clear plastic tube and the clip sprouting from her nostril makes her look like a freak.

She was always a bit self-conscious, no matter how many people extolled her beauty.

CHAPTER FORTY-FIVE

Phil and Rhonda left for the movies after dinner, and the boys are studying in their rooms. Kevin comes into the den, crouching on his haunches to better see her face.

"One of my old patients had a minor reinjury. Knows I'm unavailable but asked if maybe I'd come over and design a treatment program for his new trainer. I'd only be a few hours. Mind if I go?

Two blinks. *He'll probably be back before the two lovebirds.*

"Okay. I'll make it quick as I can. Ya want to stay here or go back to bed? One for here, two for bed."

One blink.

"Okay. Need anything before I leave?"

Two blinks.

"Right. This guy's come a long ways. Don't want him to slip back. See ya soon."

One blink.

He leaves, and she is alone. Staring idly out the window, her mind wanders aimlessly.

She naps, awakening when her sons come to say good night.

They're so at ease with me, especially now that we can "talk." Still keeping that a secret, especially from Phil. The less known by my apparent enemies, the better.

The two boys are far less relaxed around their father, especially since he's sending them to military school in southern Wisconsin for the next term.

The miserable bastard! He knows how much they mean to me. What does he gain be being so damned spiteful?

She had fought to keep them home, with Kevin as interpreter.

"She wants to know why you're sending your sons away to school next term?" Kevin asked.

"Because I want to. All the reason I need. They're only in the way here. It's better for everybody."

"Not 4 me," she signed.

"She loves those boys, sir. Sending them away is bad for her morale."

"Then you'll have to find another way to boost her spirits, won't you, Martin? I really don't give a damn, and I won't be inconvenienced just to make life easier for you."

"Fite 4 me." Her eyes were fraught with panic and frustration. He nodded and sighed.

"Ain't Rhonda supposed to care for them. Why is she here, if you're sending them away?" Putting the lie to that farce, once and for all.

"Racine Academy is a top school. They'll get a good education and learn some discipline. I don't know why I'm even discussing this with you."

Phil was incensed, not used to being argued with. Certainly not by a hick like Kevin Martin.

"Glencoe schools best," Jackee signed. Kevin relayed it to Phil, adding his own thoughts.

"And your sons are the best behaved, most polite boys I know. Seems to me Jackee's taught 'em plenty of discipline."

"I know what she wants, but it's not her choice. I...and *only* I... make the rules now, not a woman who can't do anything but blink her eyes. They're going away to school. There's no way you or Jackee can stop it."

Rivulets of tears slid down Jackee's gaunt cheeks.

He's finally out in the open. The last of the kid gloves are gone.

He bore on, removing any doubt over where he stood.

"Things are gonna change, starting with Rhonda moving into my bedroom today."

He looked at Jackee with open distaste.

"After you die, we'll be married, and I'll finally have what I've missed from the beginning. If that bothers you, die now, and end your suffering. Ours, too."

He glared at her before stalking out of the room.

Kevin took a step after him, huge fists balled, and then turned toward her, fury distorting his face. She felt beaten. Then, slowly, green fire blossomed in her eyes. He stepped back, shaken by their intensity.

"I hate Phil. Get even. Promise."

He looked at her, clearly uncertain if she wanted him to get even for her, or if she expected to do it herself.

Two emerald lasers found his eyes, and he wondered no longer.

CHAPTER FORTY-SIX

With Phil off at work, Rhonda is in the house with little to do. Jackee is conflicted by the redhead's effort to befriend Mal and Bryan when they are still at home, but she really appears to like them.

They spend hours talking and playing games, getting to know each other before Phil sends them away.

Rhonda shows considerable skill at gaining their trust, and even friendship, providing female input Jackee can longer give. Not necessarily the way Jackee would, but a lot better than nothing at all.

Jackee was surprised at Rhonda's emphatic position against Phil shipping them off to military school. Jackee heard them arguing as clearly as if she were sitting outside their bedroom door.

"Why are you doing this?" Rhonda had asked. "They're no bother to anyone. Certainly not to me. Isn't it better for them to be near their mother, despite her condition."

"I couldn't care less about keeping the blonde bitch happy. And I won't inhibit how I act in my own house, you know, with us being a couple, because it might bother them."

"That's no reason, Phil. They seem to have accepted...and even like... me.

"You're using them as pawns against Jackee, despite the fact you're in complete control."

"Yeah? Maybe, but this is how it's gonna be."

Jackee could almost sense the look Rhonda gave her husband, but that's where it ended.

CHAPTER FORTY-SEVEN

Jackee sits securely strapped in her chair, the neck-brace supporting her head, hands crossed in her lap, rehashing those painful memories. Malcolm and Bryan arrive, and are draped lovingly around her when Charlene comes to take them to bed. They deliver kisses and hugs, unfelt but cherished just the same. Soon they'll be gone, and she'll be denied even that.

She is alone again. Kevin won't be back for at least an hour.

Phil and Rhonda arrive, giggling and talking animatedly about the movie. She listens with half an ear to their rehash of several lurid sex scenes while they collect two brandies before sidling into the den, arm in arm, studiously ignoring Jackee.

They perch on the sofa, his arm circling her waist, her head on his shoulder, gazing at the tranquility of the garden, starkly barren but artistically lit for the evening.

He tilts her chin, kissing her softly, as her hand caresses his neck and ear. Heat blisters Jackee's dead lips, sending nervous little wavelets across her tranquil lagoon of nothingness. His hand drops to first brush and then cup Rhonda's breast through the soft cashmere, his fingers tweaking the nipple, bringing it immediately erect.

Jackee's pulse surges to a raucous din in her ears, her mental body trembling. The lovers intertwined, Phil's roaming hands and searching lips spread molten furrows across Jackee's normally nerveless flesh. She quivers, gasping for breath, nerve-endings afire, screaming an ecstasy she'd never before experienced.

Oh God, I hate the bastard, but this feels so...wonderful!

Rhonda's beige sweater is shed, and he's struggling with the button of her skirt.

"Phil, we shouldn't," her voice husky. "Not here. It's not right."

Jackee is transfixed, gasping for breath.

"Forget her. She's a dead lump. Let's show her how to really make love."

He nuzzles her breasts, sucking the nipples, as he pulls down her skirt and panties in one swoop. Rhonda arches back, whimpering, eyes closed, hands in his hair, his serpent's tongue darting between her lips. Jackee is ablaze, engulfed by a forest fire of lust.

Phil's clothes are quickly gone. Her red nails lightly rake his chest and back, as Jackee is sucked into the depths of sensual oblivion.

Then, in a corner of her mind, anger blooms.

This is wrong. She gasps, fighting for control. *I don't care how incredible it feels. Bad enough having her in the house, but screwing the bitch right in front of me is inhuman!*

And how the Hell am I so completely hooked into this?

Still riding the skirts of Rhonda's passion, her fury overshadows excitement. When Phil looms over the squirming redhead, about to penetrate, Jackee explodes.

Stop! she screams, though no one can hear. *Stop! You can't do this! Not in front of me! This is wrong! All wrong!*

Rhonda wriggles around on the couch, trying to sit up.

"What?" Phil hisses, his voice clouded by passion.

"Stop. I can't do this. It's wrong. All wrong!"

Jackee and Phil are equally stunned. The redhead echoed Jackee's silent plea, almost word for word.

Phil glares at her.

"What's this? You cool off last night, right in the middle of things, and now you can't make it because she's watching?"

"I... I don't know. It's weird." Her voice choked, she reaches for her sweater. "You know I want you, but there's this little nagging voice saying, 'Stop. Don't do this. It's wrong.' "

"You got a *conscience*, Red? And last night?"

"I was so turned on. Then I went... went cold, like someone threw a bucket of ice water on me. I was shivering, and just wanted to sleep." She sits, the sweater draped across her breasts, confusion lining her face.

Bewildered, Jackee watches them, the heat gone...the last vestiges of arousal swept away by the redhead's distress.

What's going on? I can talk with my sons, but that's it. Am I projecting feelings to Rhonda, rather than words? Or is she reading my mind instead?

Memories whirled dizzily back and forth, like a computer sifting information, exploring past experiences.

It must be me! In my dream, Daddy said I'm stronger than I know. Maybe it makes some kind of sense.

Maybe it was me, in Apache's head, making him jump so well. And that time we went fishing with Daddy. I said a big fish would bite, and there he was, a lake trout. Am I some sort of telepathic freak?

Then why can't I talk to everyone like I do with the boys?

I must be wired in somehow with Rhonda, too, whenever she's turned on. If I can do this, maybe I'll finally be able to talk to Kevin.

Engrossed in thought, she barely noticed the bickering lovers leave, Phil angry and Rhonda sullenly petulant.

Good. A little fighting in Paradise is only fair. Even up the score a bit

CHAPTER FORTY-EIGHT

Awaiting Kevin's return, her head buzzes with new possibilities, now that she knows to try. When he finally arrives, she yells at the top of her mental lungs, *Kevin, you big lug, hurry up and get in here. I need you.*

"Hey, Jackee, I'm coming. Are ya okay?"

Her heart skips.

He heard me! My God, he heard me!

Her eyes sparkle as Kevin appears in the doorway.

"I got back quick as I could. I shouldn't have been gone so long, but they wouldn't let me go. Ya okay?"

Damn! Was his answer only a coincidence? He's gotta hear me!

"Yes. Listen." she blinks.

"I don't hear anything special."

One blink, and a hard stare.

"Okay, Okay. I'm listening, but what am I supposed to hear."

Kevin, I love you! No response. She tries again. He cocks his head, but shows no recognition.

Damn it! Flunked again! Why can't he hear me? I must contact people differently. If I even reach them at all. This thing is so damned selective.

Tiny tears well up in her eyes.

I hoped if I told you how I felt, you'd... but you can't hear me. Only my sons, and maybe Rhonda. Oh, damn. Talk to me, Kevin. Tell me how important I am to you.

He looks at her quizzically, a hand brushing her wheat-colored hair back, his thumb gently rubbing the tears from her eyes.

"I'm sorry I was gone so long. You're so important to me."

Startled, her eyes fly wide.

"Don't look so surprised. I told ya nothing's going to get in the way of this job. I just had an urge to tell ya again. Okay?"

"Yes." *Another coincidence?*

"All right then, time for sleep. Wanna tell me what I was supposed to hear?" He settles her on her bed

"Nothing. Is okay"

What's there to say? Nothing that'll make any sense to him. Can't sleep, though. Too much to ponder.

Somehow, Rhonda picked up my thoughts last night, and again this evening. Now maybe Kevin, too. Like coming from their own head, rather than from me.

If that's true, that may open doors I never imagined.

Finished arranging her on the bed, the big man stands back, smiling softly. Time for one final test before he leaves

Say, "See you in the morning, my friend."

She'd hold her breath if she could, but her pulse is racing.

If this really works...

He leans over, kissing her gently (she supposes) on the forehead

"See ya in the morning, my friend."

Wow! I did it! Maybe I can get into their heads...plant thoughts they'll think are their own. Wonder if it's like hypnotism, where I can't make them think or do things they would normally reject. Got see how this plays out.

Will this be the advantage I need? That's the famous sixty-four dollar question.

Maybe, just maybe, there's a way now to get revenge on Phil. Punish the bastard for damning me to this motionless Hell.

for trying to kill me!

This is going to take some work. Gotta discover what I'm really capable of.

She lay awake for hours, mulling over the evening's events, already making plans, but there was no clear direction where to begin.

The path is there, though.

A way to get even.

I know it!

CHAPTER FORTY-NINE

Nothing very encouraging has turned up.

The calendar on her wall tells the tale. They are well into the New Year, but her unique abilities haven't provided much more control of her life or the things around her.

And control seems a major issue.

The boys are at military school, and I can't do anything about that.

Phil and Rhonda are settled in like newlyweds, screwing incessantly. Gotta block out all that weird stimulation or it'll drive me crazy, and I can barely control that.

Then there's Kevin. How would he react if he knew I've fallen in love with him? More need for control. Nothing to be gained by telling him, and I won't jeopardize our relationship on a foolish whim.

God, how neat to actually be loved by such a tender, caring man! That'll never happen, especially now.

She gazes out the French doors, oblivious to the view, and "sighs."

So, what's with these telepathic powers? So far, not much. Seems strongest when people are aroused or excited. Maybe it's triggered by adrenaline. Is there something there I can use to punish Phil? Hope there's more to it than just sex.

Nearly a month has slid by since her first inkling of some unusual mental gift, but she still has no real idea of its strength or limits. Whatever, she is unwillingly sucked into Rhonda's carnal heat more and more.

It blasts across her like a Sirocco wind, roiling the otherwise calm surface of her imaginary little lake into a tempest. Fiery waves slosh over her, spiking her heart, robbing her of breath, sending bolts of erotic lightning through her, as she angrily fights to stay emotionally afloat until they finish.

I'm stranded in here, with no way to control them or what they're doing to me.

She struggles helplessly to rebuff the tides of stimulation inundating her.

Thankfully, they usually keep their passion in the bedroom, distance making her task a bit easier.

CHAPTER FIFTY

With the boys at military school, Rhonda turned her attention to Kevin, often keeping him company while he gave Jackee therapy. They would talk later over coffee in the breakfast room, sharing stories about their mutual, poor-Southern backgrounds. Jackee got valuable insight into Rhonda when she overheard the tale of her youth one day, as the settled at the table.

"When I was ten, we moved from squalor in the Kentucky hill-country to squalor in Chicago's Little Appalachia."

As Jackee listened, she inhaled the aroma of strong coffee and heard spoons clink against cups.

"I've got two older sisters and a brother. Mom was a waitress. Never made enough for more than the bare necessities. Pop was typical Appalachia white trash, drinking and caroused in the country bars, spending pretty much whatever she earned. Beat her regularly, and raped my sisters."

"A tough way to grow up," Kevin said.

"You don't know the half of it!" A clear tremor in her voice and a momentary pause, filled with tension, before continuing.

"He was killed in a knife fight when I was eleven. Luckily, he hadn't gotten around to me, yet. When I heard he was dead, I cried... from relief, not sadness. He'd already knocked-up my oldest sister. It probably sounds terrible, but his death was a real load off all our backs."

"I can understand that," Kevin said.

Sitting in the den, out of sight, Jackee somehow sensed unshed tears lingering in her eyes.

"Did your sister have the baby?"

"Yeah. Mom didn't hold with abortion, and incest wasn't un-common with them... you know, Kentucky hill folk." Her words dripped with remorse.

"My niece is totally retarded." Sadness shifted to exasperation.

"Interesting ya refer to 'them,' not 'us.' Ya really set yourself apart, haven't ya?"

"I guess. Always knew I was different. I fantasized someone left me at their door when I was a baby. Some high class folk whose daughter had a little bastard they wanted to get rid of."

"Do ya still believe that?"

"Nope." Resignation laced her voice. "I look too much like Mom, only not so worn out and beat up. She must have been a real pretty little girl.

"I'm their kid all right.

"After Pop died, the first guy I had to fight off was my brother. Taking over for dad, I guess. Tried to take me in a vacant field out back when I was twelve. Big mistake." Her voice went flat and hard.

"What happened?"

"I kicked him in the balls and landed a roundhouse right on his nose, that's what. A quick end to any ideas his little sister would be an easy lay."

"Musta been some good genes there somewhere." Kevin was chuckling. "Yer bright, despite such a dysfunctional environment."

"Thanks. Yeah, I guess I was the only one in the family with any real desire to do something with my life. Bound and determined to get out of the shit-hole we lived in. Hoping Prince Charming would ride in one day and carry me off. Unfortunately, he never showed, so it was up to me to go out and find him."

"Ya had a plan?"

"Yep. I put this determined little nose to the grindstone, and did damned well in school. My English teacher was impressed with a little backwoods girl trying to shake off the Kentucky dirt. Started tutoring me twice a week after school to improve my speech, even after I'd moved on to high school. By tenth grade, I'd pretty well shed my poor-South accent."

"Wish I'd been that lucky. I still sound like a country bumpkin."

"It's just dialect, Kev. Anybody spending time with you can see how smart and interesting you are. Phil's the only one who won't admit it."

"Why thank you, ma'am. That's the nicest buttering up job I've heard in a long time."

They laughed, plainly at ease with each other.

"Anyway, I figured my best chance was a white-collar job. You know, meet a better sorta guy, and hopefully catch a good husband. So, I took typing and shorthand in high school. Got an afternoon job at the local burger stand. Knew I'd need a treasure chest for more training. I wanted a career that would put me where I could meet the right guy."

"That's a lot of planning for a teen-ager."

"Always thinking ahead, and I was discovering how easily I could... you know... manipulate others... men mostly... into doing what I wanted." Heat flushed Jackee's face. Was Rhonda actually embarrassed? A sigh, and she continued.

"I bloomed early. That was a big help in getting guys to do things for me. Even my teachers weren't out of reach. You'd be surprised how hard some of them chased me."

"Not really," Kevin said. "Lots of mature guys get hot over a beautiful teenager, especially if her body-language says she might be available. It's the kinda thing I'm studying for my masters. Be interested in how far ya were willing to go, but it is kinda personal."

"It's strange, because I've never admitted any of this to anyone. Not exactly the kinda thing I oughta be proud of, but it's easy talking with you.

"We're a lot alike, using our special skills to dig out of poverty. You with your strength and athletic ability, and me with my looks."

"And brains. Beauty will only take ya so far without some smarts. I suspect ya got a lot more of that than most people expect in someone so beautiful. I got to admit, ya had me pretty well fooled for a while."

Rhonda burst out laughing. Somehow, Jackee saw the sly wink and friendly little punch to his shoulder.

How do I know these things?

"Don't give me away," Rhonda said. "You might ruin my reputation as a bimbo."

"My lips are sealed." He chuckled softly.

Why am I surprised at how both clever and smart she is? Jackee thought.

"I *wasn't* really free with my favors though, which wasn't easy, because I already had very strong urges. I handled that... myself... if you know what I mean. I needed a good reason to be with a guy." The blonde sensed strain in the long pause, then a silent sigh.

"There was the problem of birth control," she continued. "Didn't like what pregnancy did to my mom and sisters, so I had my tubes tied as soon as I could find a doctor who would do it... uh, off the books, if you know what I mean. Never told mom."

Kevin whistled softly.

A drastic step for someone so young, Jackee thought *and quite calculating. Pretty dangerous, too, using some back-alley quack.*

"I vowed never to sleep with any man I didn't love," Rhonda continued, " unless it promised something useful in return. That'd be different. That was *Business!*"

He grunted, and Jackee was thoroughly surprised by her candor.

"Look, you of all people should understand. I don't even know why I'm telling you this. It's not exactly flattering."

"Sometimes we do things out of necessity that we're not proud of," he said. "It can haunt us for years. It can be a catharsis to get it off our chest. That's what therapy's all about."

"Yeah, I guess. And like I said, you *are* easy to talk to. First person I've met who's not so damned judgmental. Anyway, that's how I got into secretarial school. Couldn't afford it, even with a part-time job, but my high school business teacher couldn't keep his hands off me."

"Did that bother ya?"

"You kidding? He actually thought the whole thing was *his* idea. He'd do anything to ease his conscience. Recommended me to a local business school for a "hard luck" scholarship. I got it, based on his glowing account of my abilities, which by the way, wasn't exaggerated. I was damned good. I did like the guy, too, so we had an innocent little affair. He was my first, even though I was already sixteen. I certainly loved the sex." Another pause, and Jackee's mind seemed drawn into a faraway, wistful memory.

"So I established my goal: find a wealthy guy to take care of me. I was dreamer enough to hope for a man I could love, who'd make my future secure. Give me everything I wanted, both physically and financially. I was lucky enough to find Phil, who fit that to a "T.""

"But he was another man's wife. That didn't bother ya?"

"No one forced him to come after me. It's pretty obvious he wasn't happy in his marriage. This unlucky thing that happened to Jackee only made a move easier for him."

Jackee "heard" Kevin's breath catch in his throat, his heart skipping over itself, as Rhonda, stood, stretching her nubile body, luscious curves well defined against the taut, thin material of her workout suit..

"So, here I am. I don't mind being a kept woman for a time. Despite your best efforts, I'm betting Jackee won't live that long. I know that'd be sad for you, and I'm sorry, because I like you.

"I see how much you care for her. My being here doesn't change anything. You're doing your best to keep her alive, and that's that. Phil and I are really out of that picture."

Jackee heard Kevin sigh, sensing melancholy, and wondered if Rhonda's prediction might come true much too soon.

◆❖◆

Remembering that conversation, Jackee realizes how surprisingly impressed she was with Phil's mistress. This exquisite young woman is charming and has more brains than even Phil gives her credit for. She's confident of her rare beauty, yet has a relaxed, non-challenging nature that makes her easy to like, probably by both sexes.

I wonder how devious she really is? Hard to believe she never offered Phil any encouragement. Is she just entrenching herself here, or is she honestly trying to make the best of the situation?

My guess is clever connivance, and Kevin's being taken in. That's okay, though, because it might fit in with an interesting idea I've had... a neat way to take away everything that son-of-a-bitch husband of mine wants.

Kevin wouldn't be human if he didn't become a little infatuated. She wanders around the house barely dressed in cut-offs and a half tank top that hardly covered anything.

When sitting anything other than fully upright, a hint of her pubis and much of her lovely breasts are plainly visible. No man can help but be turned on.

Jackee was unhappy her boys might see her like that, but Rhonda changes into something more modest whenever she spends time with them.

Kevin's a different story. How can I be jealous? Any man would be attracted, and I've got no tools to compete with her. Rhonda turns him on, but he's committed to me.

It seems, maybe because of this telepathy, he's somehow come to know me.

He'll never let Rhonda come between us.

Unless I let him.

CHAPTER FIFTY-ONE

Rhonda lounges around the breakfast room, reading the paper and sipping espresso until mid-morning, before beginning a daily workout regime. Their exercise room has all the bells and whistles.

Forty-five vigorous minutes on the stair-climber is followed by half-hour on the rowing machine. She works with the strength equipment and smaller free weights three or four times a week, before capping off each session with a hundred sit-ups. Twenty minutes of stretching completes the routine. The redhead's gorgeous, trim body is no accident. Jackee reluctantly admires her dedication. All this sweaty work usually coincides with Jackee's daily physical therapy.

Dinner time is approaching, and Rhonda is restlessly stalking the hallway like a sleek, copper-tressed panther. Jackee idly stares out the den windows, struggling to keep the other woman's prowling from fracturing her euphoria.

Thoughts drift to her sons. She receives adorable letters from Wisconsin twice a week, brimming with news of their small adventures. She misses them terribly.

Thank God for Kevin, my anchor to sanity.

His honest friendship, plus this new obsession to punish Phil (*Murderer!*), are two steel columns supporting a fierce will to prevail, beyond all expectations. Something strangely new for a woman whose competitive fervor never went beyond jumping Apache, and that more for love of the horse than winning ribbons.

She sighs. Kevin is downtown, partying with an old high school chum from Alabama, agreeing to go only after repeated urging and a stern look. She is no longer surprised he can determine her emotions solely through her eyes, recognizing the difference between stern, anger and happy. After several futile telepathic attempts at contacting him, she quit trying.

Nor would she plumb his mind. He's entitled to the privacy of his own thoughts, unless "The Plan" required it. Phil will be punished, whatever it takes, using whomever she has to, including

Kevin, if necessary. She rejects any sense of guilt from a lifetime of morality that might jeopardize her fierce desire for ultimate retribution.

Rhonda's restless meandering brings her to the entrance of the den, interrupting her musing. The edges of the woman's emotions tumble into Jackee's head, heated and chaotic. The redhead hesitates, then slips in, momentarily perching on the arm of a leather easy chair, only to bounce up to resume prowling. The air crackles like an electric cloud from the sensuous aura enveloping her.

"Where the Hell's Phil? I'm so horny, I might jump him before he even gets in the door." Hands on hips, an ingenuous smile illuminating her perfect face, she studies Jackee.

This gorgeous creature is manipulating everyone in the house...except me. No need to buffalo me. Still, her love for Phil seems genuine. Or is it just lust? She's certainly wired up tonight.

Jackee's "deprivation" pool shimmers and ripples, stirred by the Santa Ana winds of the redhead's arousal.

"This terrific hunk in my exercise class really came on to me today. Asked me to develop a personalized workout program for him."

To fill her time during week-days, she'd taken a three-day-a-week position at a fitness center as an aerobics instructor. From what Jackee picked up, her classes were heavily attended...by men.

Why tell me?

"I'd show him a new routine, and he manage to cop a feel or two. Then he plants this thick, hard cock right between my buns. Didn't do him any good, but boy am I turned on.

"If Phil doesn't get home soon, I'll have to do this myself." She stalks across the room, her palms cruise up and down curved thighs, barely covered by a tight, short black skirt.

Jackee watches, incredulously.

Do I really need to know this? That's girlfriend talk, and we're anything but that!

The rumble of Phil's Corvette spins Rhonda around, and grinning mischievously she races for the front door.

"Hi, gorgeous." His voice muffled by attacking lips. "Hey. Whoa! Let me get out of my coat. God, you look terrific."

"Oh, baby, I missed you all day. I need you, now!"

"Easy, Red. Not here. This marble is hard as a rock," he chuckles, "and it's not exactly private."

"Jackee's the only one around. Charlene and Maria are in their rooms. Oh, Phil, I'm so on fire!"

"Slow up, babe. Let's have a drink and relax. We've got the whole evening."

His comments are again slurred by passionate kisses. A small grunt, as he hoists her in his arms. Jackee's skin prickles with imagined goose bumps, electric tentacles surging throughout a body that should feel *nothing*.

Ripples became wavelets in her dark pond. The bouquet of their passion fills her senses. They slip into the den a few moments later, Rhonda cradled in his arms. He half-reclines on the sofa, the redhead snuggled on his lap, cognac-filled glasses discarded on the coffee table.

Jackee pants, short of breath, overwhelmed by growing waves crashing over her.

Damn them! Why come in here? To torment me?

The lovers lock in a fiery embrace, hands roaming freely, her cut-off tank top quickly discarded as he hungrily attacks her breasts with his mouth.

"God, I can never get enough of these," he pants, lavishly visiting one, than the other.

Although furious at their insensitivity, Jackee is totally unprepared for the hurricane of sexual heat thundering over her, lashing her already roiling lagoon. Fire erupts in her own breasts, a molten cascade scorching her with an inferno she knows she should *not* feel.

Yet here she is, skin quivering, heart trying to pound its way into her throat. A throbbing, wonderful intensity blooms between her legs, her breath coming in ragged gasps. Snatched up by the onslaught of Rhonda's raging passion, she is unable to stop them... or herself!

Phil's shirt is gone, as Rhonda fumbles with his pants while he strips away her skirt. Linking his hands under her hips, he snatches her up, burying his mouth and face in the trimmed coppery silk of her pubis.

Oh, God! What is... Jesus! I never felt... Ohmygod!

Jackee's motionless body "trembles," as Rhonda, wailing softly, arches her back, thrusting against his lips.

Kinetic little explosions strafe Jackee's senses, bringing tears of awe. She's swept up, surfing a totally unfamiliar crest of pleasure. In a corner of her mind, she knows this time she doesn't *want* them

George A. Bernstein

to stop. Sucked in by the vortex of Rhonda's libido, she is on for the entire ride!

It's... not...fair! He's never... made me... feel like this! Why didn't he... do this to me?

She is flotsam, spinning crazily in a whirlpool of sensations. Phil's hand and mouth explore every erogenous zone, lingering here, scurrying there. To Jackee, it's *she* they are consuming.

Rhonda, hazel eyes wild and red hair askew, slithers on top, slathering him with her mouth. Jackee gags, struggling for air. What Rhonda tastes, Jackee tastes. Sensations on the redhead's lips and tongue are in the blonde's mouth.

The lovers squirm into a reverse position. Jackee shudders, drawing a sharp breath as his skillful tongue probes, tweaking and sucking Rhonda's tiny pleasure button, swamping the blonde with unbearable tension. Wave after heated wave immolates her with a veritable cyclone of passion. She can't wait any longer.

Oh, fuck me! Fuck me, she wails.

"Oh, fuck me Phil! Fuck me now!" Rhonda pants. Jackee gasps, barely able to breathe, as he lifts the writhing woman onto his lap, slowly sliding inside of "them." The two women, drenched with sweat, are deluged by mindless urgency. Murmurs and soft moans fill the air as two bodies slap together in an ever-increasing tempo. Jackee's senses are blistered, her dead body "quivering," as she struggles for breath. The lovers drive on, surging and receding with greater and greater urgency. Phil's hands and mouth roam everywhere, bringing them to the edge of Nirvana. Rhonda arches back, thrusting herself sharply against him, shrieking. Jackee's silent howl echoes in her own head.

They crash (all three of them), plummeting into shuddering orgasms, racked again and again by pulses of mind-bending release.

Jackee collapses (physically, of course, she had not moved a millimeter), gasping for breath, her eyes wet pools. Rhonda slumps against him, moaning softly while his fingers and tongue continue their teasing exploration.

As Rhonda's ardor slithers into a soft afterglow, Jackee slides down from this Mount Everest of pleasure. Phil's touch, no longer sensual, fades and the stillness of the dark waters washes up around her.

"Wow, Babe," Phil whispers to the still panting woman, plastered against him.

"That was really frenzied! I sure ain't complaining, but what got into you today?"

"I... I don't know. I got so horny, waiting for you. Once we got going... Jeez, it was almost like there was another me... a *different* me... making love to you. Really weird, but it was probably the best ever. Absolutely blew my mind." She grins impishly.

"No two or three orgasms this time. Just one mammoth bell-ringer. Christ!" She shivers.

"Want to go again?" He strokes her side, teasing her nipple with his tongue.

"Not now. I'm whacked out. Maybe later." She looks at Jackee, chilling suddenly with a flash of conscience.

"We shouldn't torture her like this. She's never had an orgasm, you said? That's punishment enough for anyone."

Phil laughs, pulling her closer, nuzzling her neck.

You're wrong about that, guys. These are tears of pure joy. Don't know how it happened, but that was my first orgasm. What a doozy! What's really amazing is, while I don't have a single quiver or twitch in me, it's like I'm thrashing and heaving and pumping and slithering and altogether going wild. Such an uncontrolled frenzy!

Can't be only imagination, so somehow it's tied to Rhonda. I sure want it to happen again... soon! So many years, not realizing what I was missing.

All those years, Phil denied me any physical pleasure, and then cheated on me with someone else! What a rat. I'll have to think about what he really deserves later. Right now, I need a nap. I'm drained.

"Right now, I need a nap." Rhonda levers herself from the couch, stretching her magnificent body.

"I'm drained!"

Rhonda and Phil had a late dinner. Things were returning to normalcy, with plans for the move to the new factory finally completed. He was finally getting home at more regular hours.

Those late nights at work were an uncomfortable reminder to Rhonda of the evenings *they* had spent together before Jackee's "disability."

CHAPTER FIFTY-TWO

The still surface of Jackee's mind shimmers, little ripples lapping against her senses, surging quickly into small wavelets, churned by a fresh, hot wind, soughing through the valleys of her mind.

They're doing it again!

Her dead body miraculously alive, imagined prickles erupting across her breasts and down her belly, igniting a delicious, impossible tingling. Only the cacophony of her heart and quickening breath are real, but that doesn't matter, because...

They're doing it again!

A wonderful, if unlikely physical awakening seizes her. Flushed with glorious heat, sizzling electric pulses storm her nerve-endings, igniting her entire body. for the barest time, she is a sentient, sensual woman. Phil ignored Jackee for years, so why shouldn't she gain what little pleasure he can provide now?

Her pulse throbbing, skin ablaze, she gasps for breath, flooded by Rhonda's amorous flame. Phil's fingers skip, caress and probe, erupting goose bumps. His mouth and tongue explore her belly, lick and ear, suck then nip a nipple.

Eyes closed, Jackee gulps as he enters, his heat and weight immolating her. She and Rhonda are one, writhing, panting, plunging, their legs tangled with his. Long fingernails rake his back, as he thrusts deeper and deeper.

Jackee "quivers," strung taut, struggling for control as he surges rhythmically against them. Never breaking stride, he arches up on his forearms, his tongue venturing around her ear and across her eyes before consuming questing lips. Their arms and legs band him in a sweat-slickened prison, as shock waves thunder through them, an orgasmic tsunami, radiating to every corner of their being. Their wet, velvety clamp spasms around his manhood, drawing out the last of his juices.

But *she* was only there in Rhonda's head. Physically, she lay motionless and alone.

A-a-r-h-a-g-h-h! A feral shout ricochets across her mind.

"A-a-r-h-a-g-h-h!" echoes from across the house.

They surge against him with one last powerful thrust before slumping back, exhausted. Jackee sprawled, drenched, her acid-scorched lungs begging for oxygen. Slowly, the howling winds dwindle, thundering waves recede, sloshes gently, becoming still again, the last little ripples fading away. Ragged breathing finally subsiding, she slides back into the nothingness that frames her everyday existence. Sensations gripping her only moments before melt into a mere but wonderful memory.

God, it only gets better and better. Not sure I can survive anything more exciting. I've never experienced anything like this, even in our earliest years together. A few times I hovered on the brink, never quite getting there, but it was nothing like this.

Of course, it's Rhonda, not me. I'm a tag along on these wonderful, heart-stopping journeys!

Their voices trickle across her mind.

"Wow, that was unbelievable" Phil says. "Never thought our sex could get any better, but you're proving there's always room for improvement."

"God, that was the best." She was still panting softly.

"Not sure I can survive anything more exciting." Again, mimicking Jackee's thoughts.

"Oow! Jesus, baby, you've scratched me to ribbons. I'm gonna have to glove you next time." His chuckle bore no anger.

"I'm so sorry! I've *never* done that before. It's like...some strange wild thing takes over. It's the best sex ever, but it's sorta scary. I'm not used to losing control."

Rhonda *is* clearly uneasy. Jackee knows sex usually gets her "off" two or three times before Phil climaxes, and then she's ready to go again. But now, with Jackee riding shotgun, she's having only one orgasm... a really mind cruncher... and then falls asleep, exhausted, even during the day.

The motionless blonde agrees, the sex *is* mind-blowing!

But even more than this incredible pleasure, I discovered something exciting here for me. Something else I can use.

Exhausted, she, too, drops into a dreamless slumber.

CHAPTER FIFTY-THREE

Jackee gazes at the garden, blanketed by over a foot of new snow. It's Saturday, and Phil is home, sharing a late breakfast with Rhonda. They made exquisite love early that morning... all three of them. A wry chuckle echoes in her head.

What a shock if they knew I'm right there with them, maybe even contributing to the action.

She's shared sex with them for nearly two weeks, and was no longer harboring guilt. She was conflicted at first, despite the incredible physical pleasure. This is the only sentient experience in her meager existence, but isn't she wrong to embrace it? Its author *is* the soulless bastard who tried to kill her... more than once.

At first, these voyages to Nirvana were almost scary...and terribly exciting. Each one increased in intensity, leaving her gloriously wrung out... and hating herself for reveling in their fulfillment.

Hard to believe I'm only telepathically involved. It feels so real. So incredibly physical! Phil made love to me for years, but never created anything remotely resembling this.

Those mind-bending orgasms! Never had even one in all that time. God, what I've been missing! Too bad it's my hateful husband stirring the pot.

Most exciting though is, the more stimulated they are, the easier I reach their minds. Don't know why, but my strange ability is getting more potent every day.

Can I do more... maybe even exert some control? It's hard to quantify, like exercising. Suddenly, one day you can lift a previously immovable weight. Gonna have to challenge myself with more difficult tasks.

Dwelling on endless possibilities saps her energy. Her eyes flutter closed, slipping off into chaotic dreams.

◆❖◆

Jackee awakens, finding Kevin squatting beside her.

"Everything okay? Ya need anything?" He adjusts her in the seat, checking the straps.

"No, I fine." His nearness floods her with peace and content-ment never felt in all her years with Phil.

How strange that this unlikely giant is my first true love. My feelings for Phil were based on a mountain of lies. Too late now. No chance this guy... forget it.

She smiles through her eyes, knowing now why he senses her whispered affection. He blushes, glancing away.

"Ya turn me to jelly when ya look at me like that." He brushes a hand across his eyes.

"Look. If ya don't mind, I'd like to visit with Mark Howe. See how he's doing."

He picks up a hand from her lap, stroking it gently as he talks.

How thin and fragile it looks. I'm still losing weight, I guess. He's meeting with Dr. Berg, so he must be worried. No need for him to realize I know.

"Go. I okay" Her heart flutters.

I so want to tell him how much I've come to love him, but how would he react? Why make him so uncomfortable he might leave? I can't bear the risk.

To her surprise, he leans down, kissing her tenderly on the cheek, cupping her face gently in his hand, a tear glistening in the corner of his eye. Eyes wide, she watches him leave.

Is it possible? I could search his thoughts, but that's a promise I'm not about to break. No purpose in knowing, anyhow.

Damn!

Life's not fair!

CHAPTER FIFTY-FOUR

Rhonda strolled into the den a few minutes after Kevin's departure, wearing a sensational one-piece black workout suit, open to the waist in back and plunged in a sharp "V" nearly as low in front. Jackee sighs.

I should hate the bitch, but I can't help appreciating her assets.

Rhonda settles in front of the television, idly flipping through the channels, toweling off a light sheen of perspiration. Phil shows up a few moments later, clad in bikini shorts and a sweat-dampened tank top. They'd been working out.

Damn. Even though I despise the bastard, he's still sexy, especially now that I'm smack in the middle of their wonderful love-making.

Wouldn't he be shocked if he knew he was doing both of us.

Visions of their last episode quicken her heart, blowing ripples across her still waters of her mind, igniting what must be an imaginary ache between her legs. Liquid green eyes study Rhonda for a reaction, but she seems engrossed in the TV.

Damn it, woman, don't just sit there. You're the hot one. Go get him!

Rhonda glances at Phil, who is searching for something to read, and then returns to the television. Panting softly, skin damp with newly discover passion, Jackee loses herself in fantasy.

Look at him, barely dressed, all tanned and sweaty. Last thing I'd do is watch TV. If I were you, I'd sidle up behind him. Tease those magnificent boobs across his back. Caress him with those perfect nails. Pull close, blow in an ear and...

She pauses, blinking, as the redhead looks at Phil again, licks her lips and slides out of her chair, moving up behind him. Dead nerves flare as Rhonda lightly rakes his sides with her beautifully manicured fingers, swaying back and forth, her now erect nipples barely caressing his back. Phil leans into her, dropping a hand to stroke her thigh. Jackee, panting with mushrooming lust, continues the fantasy...

... and now slip a hand under his shirt, teasing his chest and belly...

Rhonda pursues the seduction as if taking directions. Jackee senses her vague uneasiness at the power behind these demanding impulses.

The redhead hesitates, considering the unthinkable...resisting her sexual urges. No chance! Her own ardor, exacerbated by Jackee's unabated goading, engulfs her.

Kiss the back of his neck. Lick an ear, breath on it. Hook a leg around his thigh, working your body against him.

Jackee, so lost she can hardly think, watches breathlessly as Rhonda plays out her flight of whimsy. The blonde relinquishes control, releasing her senses to be swept along by a tidal wave of the redhead's passion. The raging inferno of their combined desires is in full charge.

Phil sweeps his lover into his arms. She's a wild animal, aflame with the consuming lust Jackee has kindled. Her flimsy top peels back, his lips and tongue torturing her skin. His fingers, running on electric little feet, charge every erogenous nerve ending. She gives a small atavistic snarl, ripping off his shirt.

Jackee spins out of control, submerged in their ardor. Mentally, her head is back, breasts thrust in his face, crying out with exquisite pleasure.

"Aaahhhhhh!" Rhonda groans, head thrown back. She snatches away Phil's shorts, her hands and tongue attacking him everywhere. Sliding down, she takes him in her mouth. Jackee gags and Rhonda pauses, readjusting herself and starts again. Years of modesty and restraint are vanquished for the inert blonde.

Jackee's lagoon, now a wild river, bear her flame like a raft hurtling rapids after rapids, each more exciting and dangerous than the last. She writhes and heaves, strokes and licks... all solely within her motionless shell.

We're ready. Can't wait any longer. We're ready now!

Through blurred vision, she sees the woman stand as Phil drags her toward the sofa.

The armless chair. Do it on the chair, facing him so he can suck our tits.

Rhonda pushes Phil into the chair beside the couch, quickly mounting him while he buries his face between two incredible mounds of flesh. Wrapping him with her long legs, she thrusts against him. Her feminine but muscular body, slick with perspiration, attacks his with skill and fervor, surging back and forth, back and forth, lost in an erotic frenzy.

The blonde battles for breath. feral lust draws her into the center of Rhonda's wantonness, sensations so fierce it's almost too wonderful to bear.

Jackee's erotic little raft dashes along a canyon of searing passion, plummeting down, down, down through endless plumes of sensual spray, spinning into an oblivion of shuddering release. She gasps at the explosion bursting through her, consumed by its flames, thrust beyond anything she'd ever known...ever even imagined, totally spent.

Jackee struggles for breath, crawling back from the incredible miasma swirling around her. Eyes still closed, her pulse retreats toward normalcy.

Damn, my butt hurts!

She laughs bitterly, knowing it was Rhonda's she senses. The phone lines to her own are permanently disconnected.

Opening her eyes, she sucks in a breath with a sharp hiss.

What the Hell... .

A bare shoulder looms inches from her face. Glancing past sweat drenched skin, her heart tumbles. There *she* sits, in her wheelchair, fifteen feet away, green eyes wide, filled with terror.

A panic-filled wail splits her head. The room spins, her stomach heaving with the taste of bile. Closing her eyes, "shaking" her head, she fights down rising gorge. Despite wildly confused senses, somehow she can feel him inside her, semi-hard. A convulsive shudder chills her like a splash of icy water, and all tactile awareness bleeds away like a punctured tire.

Seconds later, she's floating again, motionless and void of any sensation.

Slitting her eyes, she sees Rhonda on Phil's lap, whimpering softly.

My God! What was that? An illusion? A desperate fantasy to be a real person again? I'm right there with them, sharing all Rhonda's wonderful, intense sensations. But this time, something else happened... something more.

I controlled the action! Rhonda responded as if taking orders!

"Hey, beautiful," Phil whispers. Jackee raises her eyes.

"My God. What a wild time! Who would have thought you could improve on perfection?"

He tilts her chin, kissing her softly, his thumb banishing moisture from her hazel eyes.

"Hey, why tears?"

"I...I don't know." Her voice cracks, that of a scared little girl.

"The loving is unbelievable, but something else comes over me. Like voices telling me what to do... and how to do it. I don't know, I got so turned on, I lost control again."

She was squeezing his arms hard enough to leave bruises.

"I *never* lose control! Not until lately, anyhow."

"Is that so bad. What a fabulous ride that was!"

"No. It's that same weird thing. Like I'm two people. When I opened my eyes... Jesus! It was... well, I saw *us*, you and me, sitting here from across the room. I screamed, but there was no sound. I thought I was going to faint. Then I was here again, in your arms. Oh, Phil, I was so scared. Don't ever let me go again!" She shudders.

"Easy, babe, easy. You were right here the whole time. With all that passion, maybe you were hallucinating. It was only an illusion."

"But it seemed so *real*!

Jesus! That's what I saw. If it's my telepathy, things are getting very interesting. Gotta think about it later. I'm whacked. Need to nap.

The last thing she sees before closing her eyes is Phil carrying a whimpering Rhonda toward their bedroom.

"I'm whacked," she says.

"I need a nap."

CHAPTER FIFTY-FIVE

Jackee lay awake in the darkened room. Their ménage a trios had wiped her out, and she had dozed in the den much of the afternoon. Now in the middle of the night, when she should be asleep, her eyes are open, her brain clicking in high gear, reviewing her amazing day.

We're a powerful sexual threesome but they didn't know that, and I intend to keep it that way. I'm hooked on the incredible high of their lovemaking, like a damned junkie, but there's more...so much more!

Somehow he's touching my skin, his tongue in my mouth, his beautiful, hard thing inside of me. But this time was different. I instigated everything, and seemed so much more a part of things, as if I were actually in his arms.

Can I do that again? Can I ever do it at all without Rhonda's fiery libido? So many questions, and no real answers... yet. Gotta be patient. Experiment. See where this leads.

This may be my roadway to vengeance. Can't get hopes too high until I know more.

Meanwhile, I'm reluctantly enjoying all this wonderful sex. Kinda pissed the bastard never did any of this for me. I don't have Rhonda's libido, but if he really cared, he would have worked harder to fill my needs, instead of just his.

Well, I'm getting my fill now.

Jackee closes her eyes, but sleep doesn't come. Charged by questions yet to be answered, something occurs to her.

Why wait? If I can control the action, why not at Three A.M.? It'll be a real test of how much power I really have.

Thinking how to begin, the surface of her once still lagoon ripples. Already panting, she is filled with delicious expectations. Her heart trips over itself as she floats the hand of her consciousness out to Rhonda's slumbering mind.

Can she actually touch such peacefully resting thoughts? She'll soon know.

Good! There are threads of her dream.

She plucks them up gently, working her way to its very core.

Ah, a passionate fantasy. Perfect!

Rhonda. Wake up. We're still so hot from the afternoon's wonderful sex. We need to do it again!

The bed creaks. Straining to listen through Rhonda's ears, she hears Phil mutter.

"What! What's going on. Oh, baby, it's Three A.M."

"God, Phil, I'm so hot. I need you, darling. I *need* you!"

"Well, tomorrow *is* Sunday..." The rest is reduced to muffled muttering. The fire of their embrace singe her lips, setting her heart galloping.

Their heat sweep over her, one crashing, erotic breaker after another, whipping her pool into a sensual froth. She fights to keep her head above that glorious foam, but the two lovers' passions, once ignited, rage quickly out of her control.

I want to feel him in me. She senses a weak, frightened response.

I want him! I want to hold him, she shouts.

Again, wavering resistance, stronger this time, but not enough against Jackee's intensity. Then she is *there* with Rhonda, sitting across his lap, his erection buried deep inside of them. Rhonda plunges against him, rising and falling, rocking side to side, forward and back. His busy fingers and devilish tongue drive them toward a wonderful madness.

Unable to hold back any longer, they all cum with a shuddering release, Rhonda's head thrown back, squealing aloud in concert with Jackee's silent cry of ecstasy, as he explodes inside of them. She sees him...feels him... touches him. Then in the recess of her mind, she senses a silent but powerful shriek...

"N-o-o-o-o."

Jackee spins away through psychic space. Rhonda, strengthened by terror, yanks herself back to reality.

Jackee lies covered with perspiration, gasping for breath and comprehension.

What was that? Wishful thinking?

A banshee wail and racking sobs echo across the otherwise quiet house, telling her otherwise. When it comes to sex, she seems able to influence Rhonda's actions beyond all expectations.

She again awaits sleep, wondering what else she might do? And to whom?

If she ever discovers I'm there with her, can she learn to re-sist? Gotta be more careful. Can't give myself away.

Her last waking memory is the persistent sounds of Rhonda whimpering, filled with terror, while Phil softly comforts her.

CHAPTER FIFTY-SIX

Dark rings of sleeplessness shadow Rhonda's hazel eyes the next morning.

Jackee, who had fallen into a deep, dreamless slumber, is lazily content, but seeing the redhead's distress, she sighs.

This wonderful sex is so damned addictive. It's a whole new World for me, but I'd better ease up on active participation. Wonder if I'd be this hooked if I weren't locked in this supposedly dead shell? Fucking the bastard who's trying to kill me.

Besides, it's Rhonda's fire that light me up, not mine, so who knows? Far safer than any drug addiction. Anyhow, while it's incredibly exciting, I need more. It doesn't help me punish Phil, but maybe it's opened a door to other possibilities.

If I can get inside Rhonda, and listen to hers and Phil's thoughts...maybe even influence their actions...what else can I do?

Gotta keep experimenting. Quantify my power but don't cause Rhonda to feel threatened again.

I'm still not sure exactly what happened yesterday. Gotta understand it all, if I'm to succeed. Both times it seemed so real, as if I'm right inside her for those few incredible moments. Then I slipped away, as soon as things cool down. It scared her half to death.

Can't keep that up. A panicked Rhonda doesn't fit into my new plan.

Better let things get back to normal. Plenty of time to probe later. Learn if my strengths... and limits... are sufficient to do what I need to get Phil.

Unwittingly, Rhonda is right in the middle of Jackee's developing scheme for retribution.

I won't shed any tears if Rhonda's sacrificed. She did steal my husband and certainly has her eye on my trusts. Would Phil have tried to kill me if he hadn't fallen for her?

Doesn't matter now.

I know what I want to do...a karma for Phil he'll never expect...and no one is going to get in my way.

I just hope everything works out as I'm envisioning.

Time will tell.

CHAPTER FIFTY-SEVEN

Weeks slide by, her life falling into a new and erotic routine, as the three of them share wonderful sex. Jackee occasionally pitches in to meet her new lusty needs, jealous she was never capable of such pleasure, but never again let her involvement get out of hand.

Rhonda embraced this new level of erotica, relishing by far the best sex of her life. But as wonderful as the love-making was, after a few weeks of sating a previously unknown thirst, sex was cast into a supporting role, secondary to her main goal: the destruction of her cheating, murderous husband.

Kevin lengthened her twice-daily therapy sessions in an effort to stem some slight, but persistent weight loss. The paradox was, while he was maintaining muscle, he might also be burning calories she could not afford to waste...a classic Catch 22. He clearly committed every fiber of his being into her rehabilitation, but he rarely competed against so dire a final result.

Rhonda is a different and intriguing puzzle for Jackee, in addition to their erotic connection. She was showing more than a friendly interest in that big, battered, hulk: Kevin Martin. All very confusing to him, but right in line with the blonde's maturing plan.

Spring has arrived in force, and Kevin grabbed every opportunity to venture out, taking Jackee the beach, malls, and nearby parks. She relishes these small adventures.

She knows he worries about her weight loss, but the wasting away of her body had recently stalled. Added supplements were prescribed for her liquid diet, trying to regain some of the lost weight, but with marginal success.

Jackee is too immersed in her machinations to worry about that. She'd leave that to Kevin.

The total destruction of Phil is her total focus.

CHAPTER FIFTY-EIGHT

Jackee steadfastly resolved to avoid tampering with Kevin's mind or listening for his thoughts, but her needs are changing, and so are the rules. Rhonda, with little to do when she isn't working at the spa, seems intent on developing more than a casual relationship with the big man.

Her workouts, luscious physique erotically displayed in scanty outfits, frequently coincide with Jackee's therapy sessions, where she'd engage Kevin in gentle banter. To his credit, the therapist kept things friendly but reserved, resisting her sensuality with amiable firmness.

Jackee's Plan, however, requires something different.

Wouldn't they be surprised if they knew what I have in store for them?

Resolved not to directly enter his mind, she instead "whispers" in his ear.

Don't reject Rhonda. The words caress his subconscious. *It's only a little innocent teasing, a harmless flirtation.*

Squelching his resistance is a concession to the needs of her blossoming scheme. Engineering this seemingly innocuous liaison is keystone to its success, and not something to be rushed.

I seem able to influence Rhonda at will. She's easily reached when we have sex, but I can also plant suggestions when she's calm, or even asleep.

She encourages Rhonda's growing interest in Kevin, and being a mortal man, he can't avoid responding. Still, Jackee has reservations.

Despite her scheme's need to manipulate them toward a single goal, she is still seriously bothered by the moral implications of meddling with their psyches.

What right do I have to tamper with Rhonda, just because she's the usurper here? Or Kevin, because it fits into my plan? Never thought I'd ever be so consumed by something as tawdry as revenge, but does that justify interfering with their lives?

Sure, I'm doing it for the "right" reason... but isn't that the excuse of all tyrants? I'm determined to destroy Phil, but I can't get around the fact I'll be using people...people I care for, like Kevin, and even Rhonda, who's no longer only a distant and meddlesome name.

Well, I'm only doing things that shouldn't cause them harm. Maybe even reap them some long-term benefits...if all goes well. I don't possess any other tools. It's my only chance to succeed.

Misgivings justified and resolutely set aside, Jackee continues directing the little play she is writing and producing, although the final act is still not clearly in sight.

She steadfastly avoids listening to Kevin's mind. He deserves privacy. Sometimes she absorbs a sense of his thoughts, projected more on an emotional than verbal level. Agitation or arousal is still required to actually enter most heads, with Rhonda the sole exception. That's probably because they share so much sexual synergism during their erotic co-adventures. Rhonda, the focus of her burgeoning plot, is the primary recipient of her efforts.

So now, time for a little trip.

Resting in bed, the house still, Jackee closes her eyes, floating on the surface of her quiet lagoon.

Hi ho, hi ho, it's off to work we go. Up, up, and away!

Her consciousness breaks free from the gentle grasp of the water below, rising away from the restraints of her useless shell. She sees herself, motionless on the bed below, her hair a golden halo on the pillow.

God, I'm so thin! Can't worry about it. That's Kevin's job. On with the mission. No need to travel very far.

Seconds later, her ethereal self hovers before a shimmering door, glistening with silvery light. Struggling again with moral dilemma, she hesitates.

Damn it! This is the only thing left for me. I refuse to sit back and let them have their way, destroying my life...planning my death.

Stiffening her resolve, she caresses the slick, quivering surface in front of her.

Open. She pictures Ali Baba standing before the sealed cave. "Open Sesame" would be a little too corny.

This portal pulses, drawing outward like the aperture of some great camera lens. It's not her first visit. Drifting forward on a vaporous cloud, she shivers at the familiar static tingling always assailing her here. There is the wide hallway, lined with animate doors of all sizes and shades. On her left a red oval-shaped passage oscillates slowly, emitting a warm, magnetic pull.

No time for that today.

She'll lose her way amongst all those wonderful carnal sensations, and with only the two of them home, it will be a waste.

Pressing on, she finds the steely gray gateway into the computer's main frame. It opens freely at her familiar presence. She drifts noiselessly into a place strewn with disparate objects, some floating, others hanging, motionless. She pauses, gazing up at the huge iridescent screen. Few things are actively in motion, drifting up to collide with its shiny surface.

A nearly somnolent is Rhonda's watching television.

Jackee's "hand" gently strokes its glistening exterior, gaining its attention.

"Keep the boys home," she whispers. "Glencoe has better schools. They need to be near their mother while she's still alive. It's important they like you."

These are things to which Rhonda is already receptive. With the end of the school term, Malcolm and Bryan's return is near.

With the boys home, she'll try to win them over. She'll marry Phil when I'm gone, and their acceptance would make her a solid member of the family. Exactly what I want.

Gotta strengthen her resolve to confront Phil. It's so easy. She's not even aware I'm here.

The day's mission completed, Jackee flows back the way she came, slowly, silently, careful not to disturb objects, in apparent disarray, scattered across her path.

She scrupulously avoids doing any damage while in this private little chamber:

Rhonda's mind.

CHAPTER FIFTY-NINE

The two lovers had their first full-blown argument about the little boys in late May. The three of them in the family room, Jackee was an avid eavesdropper.

"Look! They're my kids, and what I say goes." This was a conversation Phil plainly didn't like.

"Frankly, I'm not crazy about them being here, judging us. It's for their own good. What can they possible gain by being near that motionless lump? They're going to eight weeks of summer camp and then back to Wisconsin for the Fall term, and that's *that*!"

"Hold on a minute!" She stamps her foot, face flushed, hands planted aggressively on her hips. This is obviously very important to her, and it's plain she isn't going to back down now. She clearly intends to set some ground rules...establish she's not just along for the ride.

"Let's clear things up, so I know exactly how I stand. Am I someone you plan on spending your life with, or only a convenient mistress?"

"Oh, c'mon, baby. I can't live without you. But what's *that* got to do with this?"

"*Everything*! Tell a mistress, 'This is it. Take it or leave it,' and she can walk or she can stay. But if I'm to be your wife someday, I want a say on decisions that affect me.

"They may be *your* kids, but they'll be *my* family, and I'll be responsible for raising them. I don't want them 'judging us,' as you put it. I need to earn their respect and, hopefully, their affection. I can work on that if they're home.

"I don't want them hating me because they thought I didn't want them around while their mother was still alive."

Jackee listens as Rhonda spouts all the ideas she was cultivating, a bit awe-struck at her intensity. Plainly, Rhonda's own thoughts parallel Jackee's, even if for different reasons.

Phil looks surprised by her vehement outburst. He opens his mouth twice but no words come out. Then he grins, pulling the somewhat reluctant woman into his arms.

"Hey, gorgeous, you've really given this some thought. You're more than a crazed sex-pot, after all." She smiles, unable to maintain a scowl in the face of his gentle teasing.

"Look, I hadn't thought of it that way," he says, "and it makes sense. If that's what you want, then we'll do it your way. You're the one who'll be stuck with them."

"I'd like that. Jackee did a great job raising them. Now I want them to learn to trust me."

"Okay. It's your call. Maybe I'll make some time to throw the ball around with 'em, too. Do some father things, for a change. Might even be fun."

Arms circling him, her head tilting back, she smiles, nibbling at his ear.

"Good! After all, isn't their care what you hired me for?"

Phil chuckles. "I suppose. That, and all the extra perks."

"You mean all this wonderful sex," she whispers throatily.

"Yes. Especially that," he picks her up, carrying her to the sofa, where they make slow, passionate love.

All three of them.

Malcolm and Bryan arrive home two weeks later to the exciting news there will be no more military academy. They'll finish school in Glencoe, and Rhonda will do her best to fill in for their mother. Only four weeks of Summer Camp. The rest of their vacation will be spent as a family. Kevin will even take them on the promised fishing trip to the Chain-O-Lakes.

Both boys give Rhonda big hugs and shy kisses, thank their father rather formally (knowing in their hearts these are not his decisions), and then run to their mother whom they hug and kiss with unrestrained devotion.

Rhonda smiles thinly, apparently jealous. A small shake of her head sets russet locks swirling, as she spins on her heel and stalks from the room.

CHAPTER SIXTY

You need time alone with Kevin.
Take the summer off from the Spa, Jackee whispers to her.
Develop a friendship... maybe even more than friendship. He's a challenge for you.

The idea isn't that outrageous. Kevin understands Rhonda... the things that drive her... a lot better than Phil. That's strangely comfortable for her. He's gentle, intelligent and without judgment. Jackee is encouraging a change in perception of him from a battered country hick into an alluring task.

Tasting her thoughts, the blonde realizes Rhonda first wanted to deflect his affection from Jackee, offended he might care for that immobile shell more than her. Now, with Jackee's prodding, she wants him... physically *craves* him... impossible as that might seem. A crazy idea, but the very thought of making it with someone so large makes her... and Jackee... very wet.

And seducing him may be dangerous to her future.

That makes Rhonda even wetter!

She links arms during their walks, their bodies in teasing contact. His arousal is unavoidable. He is, after all, a mere mortal.

She has no inkling Jackee hovers in her head, murmuring encouragement, titillating her subconscious with erotic fantasies. Rhonda's own carnal desires require only a modest push.

Phil is spared any direct meddling. Jackee has no desire to change him. Her plan... her crusade for his ultimate damnation... will succeed through her influence on others.

She's orchestrating things toward that end, but is paying a potentially deadly price. The mental energy expended is whittling away her meager reserves, but she will willingly accept her fate... even death... to achieve success.

As Jackee's power grows, she discovers new skills. While floating inside Rhonda's mind, curious to see what makes the girl tick, she opened several "doors" leading from the hallways of her semiconsciousness.

There is the room of Early Memories, a sad, tension-filled cubi-cle, tightly bound by strands of emotional steel. She senses growing tension whenever she is there, so she doesn't linger.

Another is the Map Room, littered with the younger woman plans, past and present, some discarded, others actively in pro-gress. Although intensely curious, sharp pangs of guilt drive her out without studying these. Even Rhonda is entitled to private dreams and aspiration, despite the fact they may involve Jackee's future.

Continuing to prowl, fascinated by the complexities of this un-usual woman, Jackee muses to herself.

Rhonda might enjoy herself here if she were more involved in the daily routine. People might like her for who she is, not how she looks. Jackee chuckles, realizing she is describing herself.

Too bad adopting the boys is probably fired by personal gain, rather than being a real mother to them.

That afternoon, she hears Rhonda trading stories with Maria about their backgrounds. Later, she brainstormed with Kevin on ideas for his Master's Thesis. What a surprise.

She's doing some of the things I thought about while cruising around in her head. Seems like such a change. Is it my influence?

Jackee can't ignore her own guilt. She's never forced an opinion on anyone, but The Plan requires Rhonda and Kevin to venture down a certain path. Rhonda seems to accept her roll, while a reluctant Kevin resists his. She has to meddle for things to go smoothly.

Amazing how I can shape their attitudes. Is that brainwash-ing?

The very word... something done at Guantanamo or Islamic torture camps... gives her chills.

I can't shake the guilt over screwing with their minds. Do I have another choice? It doesn't matter! I'll do whatever necessary to crucify that murderous bastard and make a better life for my boys.

So vane, to think I can really make a difference. What if things don't go as I plan? I do have the tools to teach them their "lines," but how much real control do I have?

Brainwashing? She shudders.

I suppose it is. Hopefully, Rhonda will be better for it. I don't intend to change Kevin. Only influence him a smidgen.

She sighs, mentally shaking her head.

God, what self-indulgent crap! No excuse makes this right...but I'll do it anyhow. Gotta utterly crush Phil, and this my only chance. If Phil tried to kill me...get me out of his way...how might he make Mal and Bry suffer when I'm gone? Anything is better than him!

Rhonda must change, and Kevin has to accept things he might otherwise reject. They say the end justified the means, but who would have thought I would ever embrace that dictum?

Well, they're in for a surprise.

Her conscience roughly shoved aside, Jackee continues subtly plying the redhead, constantly alert for any sign the woman senses her presence. So far, there is only what she considers positive changes, clearly noted by Kevin, something he voiced last week.

"Ya know," he had said, "sometimes I think you're a lot like Jackee, if she were up and around. You're really not such a hard case, after all."

"I used to be." She smiles. The three of them are in the back yard.

"I guess living here has changed me. You know," she turns, standing very close to him, "if I weren't involved with Phil and his kids, I'd have no trouble falling for you, and the Hell with all the money. You're the nicest, most honest guy I've ever known."

Kevin blushes. "I gotta admit ya turned out a lot different than I expected. Either ya changed, or I misjudged ya. Not sure which, but ya could have most any guy. Why would ya be interested in a beat-up old country boy like me?"

"You're not any guy, and you're not beat up inside, where it really counts."

She stands on her toes, pulling his face down for a tender, yet sensual kiss. Ham-sized hands on her waist gently disengage her, his eyes wide.

"What're ya doing'?"

"Can't you tell?"

"I can tell, all right. Just can't figure why? You're Phil's woman. Why mess with me?"

"I told you. I think you're special. Can't you accept that?"

He shakes his head.

"No. you're a beautiful gal, with plenty of smarts, who could have any guy ya wanted, but ya hooked Phil. I'm not in his league.

"While I like ya well enough, I'm not interested in being a diversion 'cause you're bored. I got other things to do."

Hands on hips, lips pouting, her liquid-gold eyes sweep over him. Then she smiles.

"You're wrong, Kev. I meant what I said. There's a strange pull between us that's got nothing to do with appearance. But a girl can never be too careful, so maybe I *am* looking for back-up." Her grin is mischievous. Kevin chuckles.

"What's this, a little dose of honesty?"

"Maybe. The honest thing is, you *do* turn me on!"

Her arm snakes around his neck, and she kisses him hard, her tongue darting against his lips, burrowing for entry, her sensuous curves, tight against him. He lingers against her heat, tasting the sweetness of her mouth, before struggling for separation. She is quite strong, and his efforts aren't convincing.

When she finally draws back, her eyes are as filled with surprise as his.

"That's more like it." Her voice husky.

Kevin stepped back, his tongue trailing across his lips, as if still savoring her taste.

◆ ❖ ◆

Jackee sighs, relishing the wonder of the kiss and the touch of their bodies, still amazed how completely she shares Rhonda's erotic sensations.

How marvelous! It's going so well, but all this manipulation is exhausting. Why is Kevin still so reluctant? He seems to like her.

"It's obvious how much you care for your patient," Rhonda says.

"I hope there's some room left in that big heart for me. I may need it someday."

He chuckles again. "Always there for a lady in need."

She smiles, taking his arm in hers. Jackee's eyes shine wetly from this first romantic contact with her new love.

They stroll back to where she sits, as Jackee opens her "phone line" to Rhonda's musing.

You fool. Seducing Kevin has no positive bearing on my future. What's come over me? Sentiment getting in the way of judgment? If I'm not careful, I might become a nice person.

How boring! That's Jackee, not Rhonda Armstrong!

Well, it's time to pitch Phil about adopting the boys.

Strange. Becoming their new mother seems almost as important as having a say in those lovely trusts.

Jackee smiles.

This part of The Plan is trotting along, right on schedule.

Chapter Sixty-One

Jackee lay in bed, rehashing her scheme, now fully blossomed in her head. Each step dovetails with the next, leading to her ultimate goal. Is there a real chance for success?

Thanks to her psychic ears, she heard Kevin talking to her doctor.

"Can't figure it out," he had said. "I thought we had this whipped, but she's losing weight again. More therapy's only gonna burn calories. If we don't come up with something else soon, she'll run out of steam in a year, two at the most. Can I see ya early next week?" His choked voice said everything. Despite Kevin's single-minded dedication, she was going to die... soon.

She gained some much-needed weight while she explored her new psychic sexuality, a time when she was happy and at peace. Now she's back at work on her mission of retribution. Her careful guidance of the two major pawns in her game is eating away at her.

Won't know my limits without more experimenting. A risky gamble, especially now I've learned there's a time limit.

Maybe only a year left, and mental acuity will surely suffer first.

Time to target a final date. Six months isn't too soon. If I can do it all by then, my death won't matter. Living in this perpetual void is getting boring, despite the great sex.

Gotta be careful, though. Too much overt testing might spook Rhonda, or worse, alert her into resisting me. That could ruin everything. forget morality. Nothing else will matter in the end, because I'll be long gone by then.

So far, Rhonda is assimilating Jackee's directions with little resistance. At first, it was necessary to linger in her subconscious, continually dictating to the undercurrent of thought. When Jackee left, Rhonda tended to lapse into her old self. But after each visit, Jackee left a little more of herself behind. One thing she doesn't want to alter is Rhonda's sexuality. Her own inability was a shameful waste. The two women melded into one terrific sex partner.

No more room for doubts. *My scheme's as complete as it's gonna get. Gotta be confident I can pull this off. Make my louse of a husband suffer for the rest of his life and ensure the boys will be taken care of.*

Dear God, please give me the time and strength to do what I must.

CHAPTER SIXTY-TWO

Luckily, my hearing is better than a robin's.

Jackee watches two red-breasted birds hunting worms, a sure sign Summer has arrived. Cocking their heads, they listen for their prey, pecking into the ground, drawing the wiggly meal to the surface.

If I hadn't heard Kevin talking with Dr. Berg, I might never have discovered how near the end was. Can't delay any longer. Gotta go with my timetable, whether I'm ready or not.

She "shivers" at the realization that schemes of Revenge could have been left half done. She would die a very angry woman if Phil got off Scott free.

Dwindling days left her with several complicated tasks yet to be completed, a challenging mental juggling act. Has she thought of everything? One loose string can unwrap the entire bundle. for the umpteenth time, she reviews the major spokes of the wheel, grinding slowly toward Phil's comeuppance.

Rhonda is a continuing work-in-progress, but it's getting easier every day. We've shared so much, my presence seems natural to her. I've tinkered with her basic nature much more than I ever intended, but I'm so comfortable in there. We're like sisters.

In spite of a still troubled conscience, altering certain things about Phil's mistress is a major cog in her plan. In the end, that's all the justification she needs.

Developing this little affair between Kevin and Rhonda isn't as easy as I expected. He's holding back, maybe not trusting her motives. Gotta convince him she's not just taking advantage of my misfortune. Hopefully, the physical attraction will do the rest.

Rhonda appears not have been involved in planning her "accidents," from what I've seen of her thoughts.

Good thing, because this romantic connection is the core of my scheme.

Metamorphosing under Jackee's tutelage, Rhonda's own attraction to Kevin is growing, but Jackee needs to pick up the pace to meet her new timetable. It's utterly debilitating work.

Next on the docket is the redhead's pitch to Phil about adopting his sons. Despite a transparent desire to get her hands on the trust funds, she really seems to like the boys.

Bringing all the strings together at once is critical. I'll work that out with Mr. Osborn. Thank God for Daddy's attorney.

Have to keep honing my abilities. Learn exactly how much I can actually do... and, frighteningly, what I cannot! No guarantees I can even pull any of this off, but this is it. No time to come up with anything else. Got no other alternatives, anyway! Even if I can't do it all, most should work. That'll have to do.

I'll either succeed or not, but I don't intend to fail!

Jackee gently manipulates the lives of three people, each unaware they are pawns in her desperate game. It's early August. She has four and a half months until her preselected "D" day: December twenty-fourth: Christmas Eve.

A day for giving and receiving gifts.

How appropriate!

CHAPTER SIXTY-THREE

Breakfast completed, she pensively awaits her secret love, replaying in her head Kevin's overheard conference call with Dr. Berg and a small council of nutritionist and experts on muscle atrophy from the previous evening.

"Regular therapy has firmed her body," he said, "but she's still slowly melting away."

"We're feeding her more than enough calories to sustain her condition," the nutritionist insisted. "It's as if she were exercising, burning fuel that she can't afford to use. But there is no way she can move, is there?"

"Thinking," the doctor said. "Mental strain can burn lots of calories. Is she in any kind of emotional turmoil, Kevin?"

"She oughta be, in her condition, especially married to that..." He paused "...but no, she doesn't seem to be. Things were going pretty good for a while there, and she even gained some weight. Something does seem to be occupying her thoughts, but I don't see any real distress. Regardless, she's losing weight again. If it's from thinking, that's really all she's got left in life."

In the end, no one suggested any new answers.

"We can't feed her anymore," said the nutritionist. "I'm afraid that would overload her fragile digestive system."

"You'll have to continue with her therapy, and hope your efforts will reverse this deadly cycle. If not..." No need to finish.

Kevin pushes into her room, right on cue, pulling her from her memory of that recent call.

"Time for therapy. Ready?" he asks, still troubled in the aftermath of his call.

"Yes."

He lifts her onto the massage table and starts removing her clothes.

Rhonda, heart-stopping in a tight-fitting, backless magenta body suit, her alabaster skin glistening with a light sheen of sweat, is just finishing her own routine. She gives Kevin a saucy grin.

"Hi, big guy. My, don't you look sexy." He's dressed as usual; boxer cut-offs and a sleeveless T-shirt, displaying his heavily corded arms.

"Me?" He raised his eyebrows. "Can't quite picture me as sexy. That's your department, and ya do look pretty terrific."

"Why, thank you." She places a hand on his rippling biceps.

Seizing the opportunity, Jackee floats into the woman's consciousness, the familiar doors opening easily at her presence.

He's so strong, but gentle. Those muscles really turn me on. A little touching, a little teasing. I wonder what it would be like...

Rhonda steps closer to Kevin, fingertips trailing down his arm, her tawny eyes warm and inviting.

Kevin's attempt to back away is stymied by Jackee's massage table. Rhonda moves in, her nubile body hovering within inches of his, one hand tantalizing his side, the other sliding teasingly along his arm.

Despite his struggle for control, her touch and damp-musk smell ignites an erection. Here is maybe the most beautiful woman on Earth making a pass at *him*. Jackee hovers at the edge of his consciousness, surprised at his reluctance, but unwilling to actually enter his mind to discover his thoughts. She "whispers" to him.

There's nothing wrong with this. Let yourself go. It's okay to find a little romance, if you can. Jackee would approve.

She senses his liking Rhonda... and physically wanting her... fills him with guilt. She is, after all, the interloper. She murmurs in his ear of beauty, passion and a common Southern heritage. That, and his own libido weaken his resolve.

Rhonda slides closer, molten golden eyes holding his, her breasts and thighs grazing him with the barest touch.

"Y'know, Kev, sexy doesn't always mean handsome, and vice-versa. Big muscles can be exciting, especially if the guy carrying them around is as nice and tenderhearted as you. You sure do turn me on!" Stretching up on tiptoes, sliding into full contact, her arm circling his neck, she kisses him. Her parted lips are both soft and demanding, as her tongue searches for his.

Momentarily lost, his hands encircle her waist, drawing closer, savoring her heat, her smell, their tongue fencing. Erect nipples, straining against thin Lycra, seem to pierce his chest. Her hips molded against his and the hardness there, scorch him. Fully ablaze, the air sucked from his lungs, he presses against her, relishing the sensory explosion. Slowly, panting for breath, he stands back, hands on slim waist, brown eyes wide, filled with surprise... and maybe a little fear.

"We... we can't do this. It ain't right, especially in front of Jackee. You're Phil's woman. I think ya really love him. Why jeopardize that?"

"Maybe so." She pants, breathless. Long fingernails trace the line of his cheek, the curve of his lips, her smile winsome.

"But know this. I'm not playing with you. If it weren't for Phil, I'd be on you like a red-tick hound, and the Hell with the fact that neither of us is ever likely to be wealthy on our own. A crazy idea for me, because I've always believed it was as easy to fall in love with a rich guy as a poor one. Anyway, you're better off without me. I may not be as nice as you think." She snuggles her face against his chest, their arms lightly around each other, her voice a whisper.

"Funny," he says, staring off, still trying to control his galloping heart, "I was thinking just the opposite. But, ya should be with a guy that'll take care of ya, financially. I'm not the jealous type, but as unlikely as it is, if we were ever together, I'd always be wondering when ya would find someone more fitting."

Rhonda grins, shaking her head.

"You'd never have anything to fear. We're a lot more alike than anybody would ever guess. You *understand* me so well and, believe it or not, that's very comfortable. Life would be a lot less complicated around you."

She stretches up, kissing him lightly on the lips. A playful pat on his rump and she gathers her things, giving him a sidelong glance, a strange smile dancing on her lips.

Jackee slides out of Rhonda's mind, glowing with warmth. Not fair that this is the only way to share his love, and he'll never even know it's her as much as Rhonda he held in his arms.

Good thing, too. What a shock that would be!

Kevin watches Rhonda sensuous departure, his tongue flickering over his lips. He makes a soft sucking sound, puckering his cheeks.

Jackee shivers, waiting for him to return to her therapy, still tingling from the sensual touch of this man she's come to love. Things are really cooking, and neither one has any inkling she is encouraging them. She needs a nap. Scampering so quickly back and forth between their minds, feeding their passion, is exhausting.

Can't sleep yet. I need to talk to him before we leave here. Give him a push in the right direction.

Chapter Sixty-Four

Therapy finished and settled back in her special chair, she watches him towel off.

"Well, that's it for the day." He crouches in front of her. "Need anything?"

"Yes. Talk"

"Okay. I'll get a chair." Grim faced, his anxious energy bombards her. No need to sample his thoughts to sense shame over his weakness with Rhonda. He will never do anything intentionally to upset her.

He settles where he can easily see her eyes, and jumps right in, trying to make things easier.

"Sorry about what happened with Rhonda. She's hard to resist, and I *do* like her, in spite of why she's here. But, it's just not right, her and me."

"No. R. okay," she signs.

"U and R. okay. R. good. P. bad."

"Ya like her, despite everything? But this thing today was meaningless. Nothing can ever happen between us. It's only flirting."

"No." So weary. Lengthy discussions are draining. Her eyes hold his for a silent moment before continuing.

"I die soon. U and R. good."

He lurches backward, collapsing the folding chair and landing flat on his butt. Worth a laugh at any other time.

"What? No, Jackee, it's not..."

"Yes. Yes," she interrupts, emerald eyes flaring.

"Hear U fone. Know. Is okay I no good." Exhausted but determined, she pushes on.

"P. bad. U and R. good." She closes her eyes, drawing back to rest.

Kevin is shaken. Shoulders sagging, he sighs.

"Okay. Ya look tired, so let me do the talking. Answer with a 'yes' or 'no.' Okay?"

She opens her eyes and blinks once.

"So, ya heard me talking to the Doc? I don't know how ya do that. Anyway, he didn't want me to say anything, but I guess I'm relieved it's out. Ya got a right to know. Want me to tell Phil?"

"No. Later."

"Okay, but I think Rhonda suspects. She's been doing some reading and knows if weight loss continues, ya eventually..." Tears flood his eyes. He takes a couple of deep breaths.

"It's hard for me to say!"

"How long?"

"Maybe...maybe ten or fifteen months." His voice chokes as he squeezes out the terrible reality.

"A lot depends on your rate of atrophy or if ya contract some kinda virus. That's my main worry, the weaker ya get. We'll be watching for that." Rubbing the moisture from his eyes, he studies her, full of wonder.

"Okay I no good. U and R. good."

"Don't make any sense. Why ya think there's any chance Rhonda and I might ever get together (a catch in his voice)... afterwards? Seem impossible, with Phil in the picture. She's just flirting for something to do, don't ya think?"

"Things change. U and R. good, if chance comes." Her green eyes bore into his, and silent encouragement whispers in his mind. Maybe Jackee knows what she is talking about. Incredible. A woman like Rhonda, interested in a big lug like him! His face flushes at the memory of her pressed against him.

"Well, ya understand women better'n me." He pauses, a sudden doubt tickling his thoughts.

"This ain't just to spite Phil, is it? Just for revenge?"

Clever man! But that's only going to be a side effect.

"No. U and R. good."

"Okay, Okay. Ya think if something happened after...after... Damn! I can't spit it out. But, you're okay with it. Right?"

"Yes. B4 good, too."

"What? B4? Oh, before? Don't want me to wait, if... ? Wow! I don't think I could..."

"Yes. Yes. B4 good, too." Her liquid green eyes flare.

"All right. All right. I understand. You're one terrific lady."

Unshed tears pool again in the corner of his eyes.

"Pushy, but terrific. I guess that's one of the reasons I've learned ta... ta care for ya so much. Rhonda's a Hell of a great gal, much to my surprise, and a lot smarter than most people suspect.

"So, if something ever develops, as doubtful as that seems, I promise I won't pass it up"

"Good. T'nks."

"Thanks? Nothing to thank *me* for. It'll never happen, but I'd be the lucky one, wouldn't I? But, I'd rather..." He stops, his eyes flooded again.

"That all for now, boss?" He laughs, blinking the moisture away.

"Yes."

"Ya gotta be real tired after all this talking. Want to take a nap, or sit in the den? 'Yes' for bed, and 'No' for den."

One blink, so he wheels her to her room, settling her in bed and dimming the lights.

Chapter Sixty-Five

They just finished their morning therapy. Kevin settles Jackee in her chair, and squats next to her.

"Everything okay?"

"Yes."

"Good. I got an idea I want to talk to ya about."

Her emerald eyes find his, sending an avalanche of tiny goose bumps down his spine.

He blinks, then takes her hand in his.

"Ya remember last winter I talked to the boys about fishing."

"Yes. P. angry."

"Right, but we straightened that out. Thing is, we never did it. Now they'll be going back to school in a couple of weeks, so I thought maybe we should go."

"Yes. Good."

"The four of us."

"Me? How?"

"Sure. We can rent a pontoon boat on Channel Lake. Best to go mid-week, when it's not so crowded. Not the greatest boat for fishing, but I think it's more important to do this with ya and the boys. We'll still catch some fish. There's some big ones in there, too, since they stocked muskellunge, but they're pretty rare."

"Is safe?"

"Oh sure. The boats almost like a motorized raft. Plenty of room for your chair. We can pack a lunch. The boys can swim some. Make a whole day of it. What d'ya think?"

"Like it. Fun for boys. Boat big?"

"Yeah. They can handle ten, twelve people easy."

"Good. Ask R."

"What?" Kevin's bushy brows arch.

"Ask R. come, too. Good for boys."

"Jeez, I don't know..."

"Yes. I want." Her eyes say there is no use arguing. He sighs.

"Okay, but she may not want to go."

"U ask. She go."

"Whatever ya say, boss." He chuckles. "I got some tackle, and I can get the rest from a friend. Next Tuesday okay?"

"Yes. U tell boys."

"Okay. I'll talk to 'em this afternoon. Rhonda, too. Then I'll call the marina and reserve the boat."

"Good. Long drive?"

"About an hour. I figure we'll leave about Seven. Get a good jump on the day. We'll be home in plenty of time for dinner."

"Maria?"

"Why don't we give her the day off? I can take care of every-thing. If Rhonda comes, it'll be a snap. Ya get a one day reprieve from therapy, too." He grins mischievously.

"Can hardly wait." There's a smile in her eyes. He wheels her to the den for some quite time alone.

Interesting coincidence. I took Mal and Bry fishing with Dad-dy when we learned he was dying. Now the story is repeating itself, with me the one about to leave.

I want this to be a good memory for them.

Chapter Sixty-Six

The next afternoon, Jackee touched Rhonda's mind, and found her already excited about the trip. She saw it as a great opportunity to bond with the little boys—and Kevin. Probably wanted to show him she was a real woman. Someone to have fun with. Not just a sexpot. No intervention for Jackee required

"What are the boys so excited about?" Phil asked, as they prepared to leave for dinner.

"They're going fishing with Kevin."

"Fishing? When?"

"Next Tuesday. Jackee's going, too."

Not going to tell him you're invited? Interesting. He was leaving for his office very early now, for some quiet time to work on New Plant projections. He may never know she was joining them.

"Really. How are they gonna get her on the boat? With that big chair, she could fall over and drown. Wouldn't that be lucky!"

"Phil! Your sons will be there too, you know. Besides, Kevin says Channel Lake Marina has a pontoon boat. Those are very stable. Plenty of room for her chair."

"Channel Lake Marina, huh? I think we rented from them once when I was a kid. I kinda remember their equipment wasn't in the best shape."

"Kevin knows what he's doing. This may be the last good outing for the boys with their mother." Jackee couldn't see the gleam in his eye, but sensed something was going on in that devious head.

"Hopefully!"

The blonde shuddered at the animus in his voice.

Why am I being so paranoid? What can he do to me, fifty miles away?

The front door closed behind them, leaving her with her thoughts and questions.

Nothing was even simple with Phil.

CHAPTER SIXTY-SEVEN

Rhonda pulled her Jag convertible into the parking lot just as Kevin was getting Jackee situated on the boat. Kevin grinned as she sauntered up, dressed in denim cut-offs and a man's buttoned sport shirt, bare midriff with the tails knotted around her waist.

"Wasn't sure ya were coming," he says.

"Wouldn't miss it, but I had to get Phil off to work first." She holds up a wicker basket. "Brought some fried chicken, yummy biscuits and slaw."

"Okay. It never hurts to have extra when were all day on the water. Mal, why don't ya take that and store it with the other food."

"Sure, Kevin." He pockets his wireless PDA computer. Internet chess would take a back seat to fishing today.

"That's a pretty big boat," Rhonda says. "That a cabin in front?"

"Yeah. Only a cuddy-cabin and a head, but room to change into a swim suit for later, if ya want."

"I'm wearing it under these." She pats her shorts. "If the boys weren't here," she whispers, one finger tracing the line of his jaw, "I'd do some topless sunbathing. That'll probably have to wait until we do this alone."

"forget it." His voice goes husky at those erotic images. "Yer still off limits.. Remember?"

"Yeah, but you're a very special guy, you big hunk. Who knows what could happen?"

"Nothing's gonna happen. Come on, let's finish loading up. There's some live bait in those two minnow buckets. I need to finish securing Jackee's chair. Don't want her rolling off the deck." She nods, skipping off the boat to retrieve the two metal pails and some extra rods and reels. Malcolm and Bryan don orange life vests, the older boy offering one to Rhonda when she reboards.

"Here. Everybody's got to wear one. It's the law."

"Okay, sweetheart." She ruffles his blonde hair. "Don't want to get a ticket, do we?" They giggle.

"All right," Kevin says. "We're ready to go. Deck hands, man the lines." Malcolm runs to the bow, Bryan and Rhonda to the stern. The mooring ropes are cast free, thrown up on the dock. With the hundred-horsepower outboard motor at idle, they slip away from the dock.

"Ya grab seats. It's a short run to a good, weedy bay I know. Lots of pan fish, some bass, and maybe even a pike or musky. Hold on."

The powerful engine spools up and the twenty-four foot boat surged ahead. Pontoon boats didn't really get up on plane, but this one skims along at a pretty good speed. They'll be fishing in fifteen minutes.

CHAPTER SIXTY-EIGHT

Jackee, her face shaded by a large-brimmed sun-hat and polarized glasses protecting her eyes, watches Kevin and Rhonda setting out the lines. The redhead plainly has some experience at fishing.

I'm glad she came. It'll give her a chance to bond with the boys, and maybe make some progress with Kevin. She really seems to be enjoying herself.

"I got one! I got one," Bry yelled, reeling madly as the light spinning rod bobs and jerks. A moment later, a small, colorful fish is flopping on the deck.

"That's a keeper." Kevin pats his head. "A nice eight-inch bluegill. Very good eating." Bryan beams, watching Kevin drop the fish in the live well, while Rhonda rebaits his hook with a small, red worm.

Quite a girl. Not afraid of worms. She's a lot more from Kevin's world than Phil's.

Malcolm tries to be the cool older brother when he catches the next fish. His disappointment is obvious when it's too small to keep.

Rhonda squeals gleefully when her bobber disappears fifteen minutes later. A largemouth bass had inhaled her little shiner minnow. After a brief tussle and two jumps, the fourteen-inch fish is wiggling on the deck.

"That's a nice keeper." Kevin is all smiles. "The bass don't taste as good as pan fish, though. Mind if we turn him loose?'

"Not at all. Let him grow up and give someone else a thrill. This is fun."

"Nothing like a day of fishing to chase your trouble away," the big man says, watching her hook another minnow just behind the dorsal fin.

"Yer pretty good at this."

"I used to be a country girl, remember. Did a fair amount of fishing in Kentucky."

He chuckles, shaking his head.

Jackee relaxes, closing her eyes. *Wish I can feel the Sun on my back... the breeze on my face.*

At least I can smell the lake. She savors the excited chatter of her sons... the friendly banter between Kevin and Rhonda.

What a truly beautiful day!

◆ ❖ ◆

They lunch on a beach sprinkled with picnic tables and two charcoal pits. Kevin lights a fire, and the boys roast marshmallows. Rhonda shows them how to make smores with chocolate bars.

Jackee's next meal isn't scheduled until the evening, but she has pangs of what must be psychic hunger, watching them wolf down their fried chicken, sandwiches and large glasses of iced tea. She always loved picnicking at the beach.

Back on the boat, Kevin starts the engine.

"Is that okay?" Rhonda touches his arm. "It sounded a little labored."

"These big engines get a little tight sometimes. Shouldn't be a problem. I got another spot ta try at the far end of the lake. A bit of a run, but it might be worth it. Been a few musky caught there this year."

"There sunfish there, too? We need action to keep the boys interested."

"Sure. Smart thinking. The pan fish are why the musky are there."

"Great. Can I go for a swim? It's getting hot."

"There's a nice beach on the way. We'll stop there first. Everybody'll enjoy a dip."

CHAPTER SIXTY-NINE

An hour later, they motor away from the beach, heading for Kevin's special bay. He leans against the helm, barefoot and in boxer swim trunks, letting the Sun and the air dry him. The two boys, having changed back into long pants and shirts as protection against the Sun, sit in deck chairs, playing Internet games with Malcolm's PDA. Rhonda lounges across the bow, stretched out on a large towel.

The stunning redhead wears a rather simple two-piece swim-suit. Nothing too erotic, but even this innocuous outfit doesn't diminish her incredible sexuality. Despite his resolve, Kevin is seriously turned on.

Jackee senses those tumultuous emotions spilling out of him.

Good. Today has shown him...and me, for that matter...she's more than a gorgeous sex goddess. Keep building The Plan! I'm making some serious headway.

Twenty minutes later they are anchored inside the mouth of a large bay, thirty feet away from a sprawling bed of lily pads and pickerel reeds. Kevin baits two sturdier casting rods, one with a six-inch golden shiner, and the other with a similar-sized black sucker. Red and white bobbers will suspend the little fish about 30 inches below the surface. The rods placed in holders, he assigns the one with the shiner to Bryan, and the other to Malcolm.

"If ya see that float go under, ya wait until I tell you. It can take a fish a while to actually start swallowing a large bait. Meantime, ya can use these lighter rods and see if we can't catch some more dinner."

With all the lines set, Kevin produces a portable radio.

"Let's see if I can get a weather report. That western sky's start-ing to look a little menacing." He fiddles with the switch and knobs, but gets only light static.

"Damn! The batteries are 'bout dead. I just replaced 'em yes-terday." He fishes in one pocket, then another, a scowl darkening his face.

"Where the Hell's my cell phone? It should...oh, damn it. I musta left it on the charger in my room. What an idiot..."

"Take it easy, Kev. I've got mine, and you got the boats two-way radio."

"Yeah, better try the marina on the ship-ta-shore. They gotta have any weather advisories."

Jackee watches Kevin fuss with the radios. She smells the air, filled with moisture. A storm *is* coming. Will it hit...?

Oh, oh. Strange, feral emotions spill into her head. She shivers at its intensity

Danger! Something is...oh, God! We're being stalked. She sensed sly, fierce intent. *Some deadly thing is sneaking up on us. Someone mean and vicious.* A chill skitters down her back. *Has Phil hired yet another assassin?*

How can I warn them? Must be a lunatic! Any minute he'll...

Oh, Jeez. She chuckles, her fear spilling away, and glances at her sons.

Bry!

Hi, mommy. I'm having so much fun. I wish you...

Shh. Reel in that little rod and pick up the one with the big minnow.

But, I'm catching...

There's a big fish about to eat that minnow Bry. Hurry! The evil thing she sensed was a predator, probably a pike or musky, stalking the golden shiner, not them. She was shaken by the wicked emptiness of that wild mind.

"Oh, boy!" Bryan shouts, reeling frantically on the small spinning reel.

"What's up, Bry," Rhonda asks.

"I'm gonna catch a big fish!" His voice shrill, he looks at the redhead, thrusting his little rod at her. She takes it, eyebrows raised, as the boy grabs the heavier casting rod.

"What's going on?" Kevin says. "Bryan giving up so soon?"

"He thinks something is after his shiner."

"Well, it might have to wait. All I'm getting on the ship-ta-shore is static, and it looks like we're in for a storm. Gonna have to bug out any minute now."

"But I'm gonna catch a big fish! A musky!"

Here he comes, baby. Don't yank on the rod until I tell you.

"Look, Bry. There's nothing bothering that....Oh, oh." The red and white float begins to dance and skitter in circles.

"Something's got that shiner nervous. Gotta be pretty big or...ooops, there she goes!" The bobber plunges out of sight, making a soft "pop" as it disappears.

"Okay, easy now." Kevin pulls some slack line off the reel.

"We don't want him to feel anything. I'll tell you when to set the hook. This can take a while before he starts to swallow that shiner."

He glances up at the fast approaching thunderheads, billowing across the sky, swallowing the Sun. Lightning bolts, one after another, pierce the black mass, filling the air with the rumbling thunder of a Panzer attack and the sharp odor of ozone. Kevin shrugs and fastens his attention on Bryan's float, still visible six-inches below the surface.

Bryan, listen to me, not Kevin. The fish has already eaten that bait. Start reeling fast, and when you feel something heavy, yank the rod up hard as you can. Do it now!

"Okay." the boy hisses through gritted teeth, cranking as fast as he can.

"Hey! Not yet, it's too..." The line snubs tight.

Now, Bry! Now! Jackee is as excited as her son, who hauls back as hard as he can. The stiff rod-tip yanks down, pitching the boy forward. Kevin snatches him under the arm as the water exploded, a silvery missile hurtling into the air, head shaking, gills rattling.

"Wow! A big musky. I gotcha, kid. Hang on." The reel sings, line peeling off as the fish runs for deep water.

"Keep the rod tip up and bent. Reel fast any time ya can gain line. You're in for a fight. Tell me if ya need any help."

"No! I got 'em! I got 'em! This is *my* musky!"

"Sure looks that way, son." Kevin chuckles. "Yer lucky he seems well hooked." He glances again at a roiling black mass, hurtling down at them from the northern sky. Lightning flash after flash pierce the sky and the air is filled with a rolling rumble, like stampeding buffalo. He looks at Rhonda and Malcolm.

"Put away everything loose. Rhonda, can ya start the engine? We're gotta be ready to bug out as soon as we land this fish."

"Sure. Mal, you stow the lunch and loose chairs in the cabin. I'll get the engine running."

Kevin supports the little boy as he stubbornly fights one of the toughest battlers caught in fresh water. The three-and-a-half foot long fish leaps again, swirling on the surface and charges to boat.

"Reel, son! Reel fast as ya can. Mal, ya get the anchor up so he can't tangle the line on it. Rhonda, get that engine started!"

"I'm trying! I'm trying! It won't seem to turn over." The air reverberates with an earsplitting crash, as a bolt of electricity shatters a tree on the nearby shore.

Jesus, that was close! This might become dangerous.

Jackee speaks to her son. *You fight him hard, honey. There's a bad storm coming, but we'll stick it out until you land that fish, if we can.*

"I got him, Mom," Bry whispers. "He's not gonna get away from me."

Kevin signals Rhonda, still fussing with the motor's controls.

"Here, ya help Bryan. Let me see if I can get her running." They quickly change places. He races to the helm, fiddling with the controls and the ignition key. A gust of cold wind whips across the bay, stirring small white caps. They pitch and roll, water sloshing up on the deck. A pontoon boat is a stable platform, but with the anchor up, they are drifting, picking up speed at the urging of a fierce wind.

"The damned battery's just about dead! I can't believe it. Nothing's working on this stinking boat."

Rhonda jumps when another lightning bolt splits a tall fir tree, fifty-feet away. Its summer-dried foliage burst into flames.

"What about the fish, Kevin? Should we cut him off?"

"No! No!" Bryan shrieks. "My big fish! Mine!" The silvery torpedo is taking line again.

"Don't worry, son. No reason to cut him loose if we're not going anywhere." He touches her shoulder. "I'm gonna check on Jackee. Oughta get her into the cabin, but the way we're pitching around, I'm afraid to move her." He digs a yellow plastic slicker out of his duffel bag.

"This oughta keep her dry, anyhow."

Jackee watches the frantic activity: Bryan fighting the big fish, with Rhonda's support; Malcolm scurrying around, clearing the decks of anything loose; and Kevin, desperately trying to get them under way. The whole thing is strangely exhilarating to a woman condemned to a life of boring inactivity. Kevin appears at her side, covering her with the parka and checking her straps and the chair's lashing to deck cleats.

"Scared?"

"No." Her eyes are sparkling emeralds. "Having fun."

"Are ya, now? Quite a change from sitting around the house."

"Yes. Wish I feel wind."

"Yeah, but I wish there were less of it. This could get dangerous."

"Not afraid. Safe with you here."

"Thanks for the vote of confidence."

Another slash of electricity hurtles overhead, followed instantly
by a kettledrum roll of thunder. The air reeks of ozone. That was
close! He turns to Rhonda and the boy.

"How's it coming?"

"The fish isn't giving up." She looks at him, grinning. "But neither is Bryan."

"Here, let me take him. You and Mal get into your rain gear.
That storms gonna hit us any second. We're gonna be at it mercy,
with no engine."

They switch places, and she helps Mal don his parka, and then
got hers. The wind ripping through them made even that difficult.
Kevin drapes another poncho over Bryan's head and back. The boy
isn't parting with his rod for even a minute to slip into it.

"You might want to put on your other clothes, too. It's gonna
get cold." Nodding, she hurries to the cabin, returning quickly with
her shorts and shirt. Rain is coming now, hurtling almost parallel
to the water.

"You got your cell phone?" he asks. "We gotta get help, somehow."

"Yeah. Good idea." She fishes it out of her pocket.

"Try the marina. The number is painted on the side of the cabin." He adjusts his grip on the little boy.

"Ya getting tired, son?"

"No. I'm gonna get this fish, Kevin! I'm gonna get him." His
voice drops to a whisper. "I want to put him on my wall. He's bigger
than Mal's steelhead!"

Kevin can't help smiling at sibling rivalry. He glances at Rhonda. Shielding the phone from the rain with her body, fighting for
balance on the pitching boat, she dials the number.

CHAPTER SEVENTY

Huddled in her chair, Jackee's senses are awash with something new and terrible. The frantic struggles of the fish are inundating her mind! She has never experienced anything so savage, and yet so simple...so incredibly void of thought. Anger, fear, but nothing remotely resembling reason. Chills course through her, her thoughts trapped with this wild creature.

The rain slams against them, the boat heaving and sluing with the howling wind and roiling waters. Lighting lights the sky, followed instantly by a reverberating boom, the strike missing them by scarce feet.

Suddenly, a rending squeal, as the boat lurches to a shuddering stop. The upwind side heaves high in the air, than slams down, bringing Kevin to his knees.

"Yow!" Rhonda, leaning against the cabin door, screams. Her balance lost, stumbling across the deck, she crashes against the gunnel, pitching over the side.

Kevin dives, catching her ankle, dragging Bryan after him. Miraculously, the little boy lands on his seat, still clutching his rod. Malcolm scrambles across the deck, wrapping his arms around his brother.

"Can you hold him, Mal," Kevin groans, his shoulder muscled bunch, trying to hang on the both Rhonda and the boy.

"I got him. Pull Rhonda in." Kevin sees they are safely sitting on the deck, and let loose. He slides along the deck, grabbing the girl first at the thigh, then around the waist, lifting her back into the boat.

"Ohhh," She moans. "That hurt."

"Ya okay? That was a close one."

"Yeah, I guess. Knocked the wind out of me when I hit the railing. I...ohh, *shit!*"

"What?"

"I lost the cell phone. What happened back there?

"Musta hit a rock bar. Whatever, we're drifting again. We're in trouble if we don't get some help soon. The starboard pontoon may be taking on water."

"We gonna sink, Kevin?"

"I sure hope not. Probably get beached first. And Bryan won't give up on that fish."

"I don't think I blame him." Rhonda chuckles, in spite of aching ribs.

"Me either. Some guys fish for years and never catch a good musky. If he lands it, with this storm and all, it'll be a memory of a lifetime. If we manage to survive this!"

Didn't realize things were so bad. The angry sky was continually filled with fire. *Everybody looks wet and haggard. I'd probably be miserable, too, if I felt anything.*

I'd better see if I can end this. She looks at her son.

Mal, get ready. The fish is going to come in now. She reaches for that atavistic brain, sending soothing thoughts. Slowly the fear subsided, the anger cooling.

"Kevin," the boy shrieks over the wind. "He's tired. I think I got him."

The big man scrambles across the deck, snatching the large landing net from its lashing. The boat, pitching and heaving, makes standing difficult. A moment later, balanced on his knees, Kevin scoops up the huge fish. It lay struggling in the rubber mesh of the net.

"Wow. This guy weighs a good twenty pounds." He hefts the fish high for all to see.

"Way to go, Bry! What a beauty!" Rhonda claps her hands.

"He fought so bravely," Kevin shouts over the howling wind. "Let's turn him loose."

"No, no! I want to mount him!"

"Rhonda, grab the camera. We'll get a photo, measure and weigh him, and then release him. Taxidermists don't use the real fish anymore. They make a fiberglass reproduction."

"Will it still be my fish."

"Yeah, exactly. But we gotta do this quick. We're about to get beached on that rocky shoreline, and we're gonna be scrambling for our lives."

Rhonda limps back, camera in hand, while Kevin measures the fish.

"forty-four inches, and fat, too. Let's see. Twenty-inch in the girth" He slides the scales hook under its jaw.

"About twenty-four pounds. A real trophy, buddy. A lot of people never catch a musky. Come here and hold him." Sitting on the deck, Kevin hefted the fish, with Bryan on his lap, holding a fin. Rhonda shot three photos.

"Okay. We gotta get him back, quick." Kevin leans over the pitching gunnel, holding the fish in the water.

Time to wake up.

Jackee fires energizing thoughts into the dulled mind. The big fish shudders, twists, and flips a watery good-bye with his tail.

"Boy, he recovered fast. That's good. Now everybody grab your stuff, and get ready to abandon ship. We got maybe a minute before we hit that shore."

He materializes at Jackee's side. "I'm gonna undo your straps but ya gotta stay in the chair until we stop. I'll carry ya ashore, then come back for the chair. Ya doing okay?"

"Yes. See boys safe."

"Rhonda's got them. I gotta take care of you." He turns to the others. "Sit down and hang on, guys. Here we go."

Drifting sideways at a surprisingly rapid pace, pitching and bobbing, driven before blustery winds, they lurch to a stop with startling abruptness. Malcolm tumbled, spilling over the side and onto the beach. Rhonda leaps after him, landing lightly and drags him away from heaving pontoon.

"Bryan, get off the boat. I got your mom. Be careful. This deck is real slick."

The pelting rain is now mixed with stinging, pea-sized hail. The sky is blackened everywhere, lightning erupting all around them, six or seven bolts a minute. Another tree bursts into flames, fifty yards up the shore, a veritable Roman candle.

Kevin lurches to his feet, dancing left, then right, the deck turned into a rollercoaster by the surging waves, slamming into the side of the boat, drenching them with spray

He snatches at Jackee in her chair, still securely lashed to the deck, steadying himself before managing to hoist her free. Staggering backward under the assault of an extra-large wave breaking over the railing, he flounders, catches his balance, and stumbles to the shore-side gunnel.

He glances at the fragile body in his arms. Her green eyes, searching his, seemed filled with trust...and fear. He isn't going to let her down now! But getting off this boat in one piece isn't going to be easy.

Kevin drops into a partial crouch, sensing the deck's action beneath his feet, searching for the right instant to vault free of the violently pitching craft. Surprisingly, the deck dropped sharply just as he pushed off. His feet skidded out from under him, his right foot catching the railing, pitching him headfirst over the side.

Jackee, still clutched close to his breast, is about to cushion his 240 pounds, landing on the riprap-covered shore.

CHAPTER SEVENTY-ONE

Kevin sails through the air head first, the rock-strewn beach rushing up to meet him. Twisting violently, he manages a partial roll, curling himself around the woman in his arms, landing hard on his left shoulder, rolling over, the back of his head smacking down on the riprap. Somehow, he managed to thrust his body under Jackee, partially cushioning her from the jarring impact.

"Uuuhhh!" He laid on the slippery wet stones, stunned, his blonde patient draped across his chest, waves slapping against them. His legs quiver, twitch, and then are still.

"Kevin!" Rhonda is quickly at his side, feeling the pulse at his neck.

Strong. Probably just dazed. Grabbing him under the arms, she tries to slide him away from the water. The surging hulk of their craft looms menacingly close.

"Mommy!" Bryan joins her, tugging at his arm.

"Quick, Bry. We gotta drag them away from the boat."

Heaving together, they are still unable budge the pair.

"I'm going to move your mom. Try to keep that boat off Kevin, Bry, but don't get hurt. The way it's pitching around could be dangerous."

She scoops up the blonde, amazed at how light she is. Little more than skin and bones. She staggers ten feet inland, before laying her on the wet sand. Jackee's eyes find hers.

"You'll be okay here. I gotta try to move Kevin." The blonde blinks once. Rhonda turns back to Kevin, filled with adrenaline and renewed energy.

"Give me a hand, Bry. We gotta get him away from those pontoons."

Rising under the force of a large wave, the silver and red aluminum hull heaves up and slams down, pounding the beach like a pile driver, inching closer to the groggy man's legs.

Grabbing him under the arms, heels dug in, she lifts and heaves, with little Bryan, arms around her waist, adding his weight.

Unremitting waves march the hull farther on shore, a strong surge rearing the menacing float for another attack on Kevin's legs. Rhonda darts into the surf, grabbing at his ankles.

"Rhonda!" Bryan screams.

A dark shadow looms above her. Ducking, she slips, falling face down in the surf, as the pontoon crashes down, spray and sand stinging her face. Spitting sand, she rolls away, looking up. The overhanging deck would have brained her without Bryan's warning.

"What are we gonna do?" Bryan crawls to her side, tears streaking his rain-drenched face.

"Gotta move his feet, or they'll be crushed." The battering hull tramps closer, one thundering step at a time. Two or three more strides and it will consume him. The overhanging deck was a daunting problem.

"I'm gonna try to time it, Bry. You yell when it's about to fall. Okay?"

"You'll...you'll get killed!"

"Not if we work together. Only got a few seconds before it gets to Kevin. We gotta save him. Can you be brave for me?" He nods, his face twisted with fear.

Awaiting her chance, Rhonda darts forward just as the pontoon crashes down, arriving at the stunned man as the hull begins to rise. Grabbing his ankles, her feet skid out from under her, landing hard on her rump, legs splayed.

"Look out!"

Rhonda rolls over, twisting her legs away just as the pontoon bangs down. A second slower and she might have lost her feet.

Struggling to her knees, she snatches his ankles, hauling them far enough sidewise to avoid the next impact, but the force of the blow sends her sprawling, stinging her face with sand and spray. Scrambling back to her knees, she grimaces at a sharp pain in her leg. Glancing down, there's blood mingling with the foamy surf.

"What the Hell am I doing," she muttered. "I'm gonna get killed trying to rescue this big lunk. Since when am I a hero?"

Gritting her teeth, she scrambles back to Kevin, again catching his ankles. Sitting, she digs her feet into the sand and pulls. The boat is on an upward cycle. If she doesn't move him now....

"Yowww!" A monster wave breached the hull, knocking her flat, filling her mouth with water. She slid half under the boat, tangled with Kevin's legs, as deck reached the top of its arc, pausing momentarily before rushing down, about to crush them both.

Fueled by adrenaline, she executes barrel-roll, somehow managing to hang onto Kevin's legs, dragging them after her. The boat slams down, smashing the sand in the exact spot they lay an instant before. Rhonda spins away, sitting up, shaking uncontrollably, sobbing.

"Jesus! Jesus God! Oh, Christ, that was... I coulda... oh, God!"

"Rhonda! Rhonda!" Bryan rushes to her, wrapping his arms around her neck. He, too, is crying.

Lying on the sand, fifteen feet from pandemonium, Jackee squints through the rain, now mixed with tiny hail.

Gotta calm her down. Get control. May be up to me to save us.

"Kevin's clear for the minute, Bry, but we still gotta move him farther away," Rhonda says.

"You're bleeding!"

"Yeah, but it's only a bad scratch. Be brave now. I need your help." He nods, wiping his eyes.

She staggers to her feet, looking at Kevin, still unconscious on the beach, and only two feet clear of those punishing pontoons, irresistibly marching closer with every wave. She wipes rain and sand from her eyes, and groans.

"How am I gonna move that big lug?" Limping back, a rivulet of red trickling from mid-thigh, she again goes after his ankles. Easier to lift and a better grip to tow him away.

"No! Look out!" Bryan grabs her arm, pointing. Pulling on his feet is swiveling his head under the boat.

"Christ! That's no good! Thanks, Bry."

Quickly switching ends, hands under his arms, she struggles to haul him away from danger.

"Goddammit! All those workouts and weight-training, and I still can't move him." Maybe it was a release of adrenaline, but she's suddenly infused with strength she's never known. Heels dug in, leaning and lifting, with Bryan dragging at one of his arms, they manage to gain five feet of separation from those massive pontoon, still punishing the beach under the onslaught of heavy waves.

Kevin moans, shaking his head and blinking. He rolls to his side, rising on an elbow.

"I'm...I'm okay" Groaning, he struggles to sit up, rubbing the back of his head.

"Oh, boy! That was close." He winces at the growing lump he finds there.

"You landed really hard," she says. "You scared the Hell out of me."

"Rhonda saved your life, Kevin." Bryan hugs him, eyes wet, but not from rain. "She pulled you right out from under that boat."

"Wow, thanks. Just seeing a few stars now, and had the wind knocked outta me."

They all give a start at a loud crack, lightning striking some-where very close by. The wind-whipped deluge isn't abating. Kevin suddenly lurches around, eyes going a little wild.

"Jackee?"

"Right behind you. Had to move her to get to you."

"Thanks again." He struggles to his knees. "Yer a good guy to have in an emergency."

He crawls to his patient. A crooked streak of electricity bursts from the black blanket hanging low above them, striking the shoreline, vaporizing a cloud of steam. Kevin's hands and feet tingle from a mild discharge. He looks at Rhonda again

"Damn! She's soaked. Where's Mal? We gotta get off this open beach. We're sitting ducks here."

"He was a little stunned when he flipped out of the boat. I put him under that tree for some cover."

She helps Kevin lumber unsteadily to his feet. He winces in ob-vious pain, Jackee in his grasp.

"That's not safe, with all this lightning. We gotta find a better place to sit this out."

"Right." She limps away. Kevin shifts Jackee in his arms and turns to the younger boy.

"C'mon Bryan. Let's move."

He hadn't hobbled more than twenty steps when a flaming bolt hurtles out of an inky cloud, spearing their boat, launching it two feet out of the water and up on the beach like so much driftwood.

"Wow, great timing," he mumbles. Blinking to clear his vision, he looks at his patient, cradled in his arms.

"What a fiasco. Ya okay? You're soaked." Rainwater drenches her face and hair, and is obviously making its way inside her slicker.

"I fine. Feel nothing." Her green eyes are wide, filled with trust. His heart swells. She's safe, at least for the moment, but that might change in a hurry if they don't get help soon. Exposure can turn to pneumonia in no time, especially in her weakened state.

Rhonda catches up with them, little Malcolm cradled in her arms.

"What's with the boy? I thought ya said he was only shaken up?"

"I don't know. He must have landed harder than I thought. Got a pretty good knot on his forehead, but his pulse and breathing seem good."

"Might have a concussion. We'll check him over, once we settle somewhere safer. Damn! How did I let this happen." Kevin stumbles, catching his balance, a sharp stab of pain clearly photographed on his face. Rhonda touches his arm.

"You checked the weather?"

"Yeah. No forecast of anything like this."

"Sometimes freak summer storms pop up unexpectedly, don't they?"

"I guess. No excuse for everything else that went bad, though. Two radios and the engine battery? Talk about bad luck coming in threes!" He stumbles again, grimacing.

"That was a hard fall, Kev. You coulda separated your shoulder." He shakes his head.

"I'm pretty hard to hurt. Lot of boxers found that out over the years."

"You're one amazing guy, Kevin Martin. No wonder I find you so exciting."

"I'd prefer some other kind of excitement. We're in real trouble here. Right now, we gotta get some protection. Ya take care of the boys, will ya? I gotta look after Jackee."

"Sure. C'mon, Bryan. Let's find some cover." With Malcolm in her arms, and Bryan hanging on to her belt, she trudges across wet sand, buffeted by fierce winds and buckshot rain, looking for somewhere to hide from the elements.

"Wow! What a storm," Kevin yells. "Don't go near any big trees. Those willow bushes there'll be our best bet. Not much cover, but they shouldn't attract lightning. Come on. Let's keep moving."

He pushes through a crease in the willow thicket, crouching down under overhanging branches and a canopy of long, slender leaves, shielding Jackee's body from the celestial onslaught with his own.

Rhonda burrows under another bush twenty feet away, its tangled branches clawing at her, catching her slicker and snagging her feet. Finding an open hollow, she places Malcolm on a sandy spot, sliding his small knapsack under his head, and tucking his slicker around him. Bryan, eyes as big as quarters, sits holding his brother's hand.

Rhonda catches Kevin's eye, giving a wry little smile, and shrugs. He shakes his head slightly, dispelling demons, and turns back to protecting Jackee. Hail peppers his back and head. Icy water trickles down his neck.

He glances again at Rhonda and the boys, hunkered together, offering them whatever shelter she can muster. Jackee sees red-head strip off her own rain parka and arrange in on willow branches above unconscious Malcolm. Bryan jumps up, draping himself across her back, protecting her as best he can from the piercing onslaught of frozen rain.

What a miserable and dangerous way to end what had been a beautiful and exciting day. Kevin's doing the best he can to keep us safe.

Kevin folds Jacked deeper in his arms, screening her from the elements.

I must be so damned wet. If I suffer exposure...

She doesn't want to think about that!

CHAPTER SEVENTY-TWO

The storm rages on, lighting assaulting them, four or five strikes a minute, igniting several nearby firs. Despite the downpour, the trees, heavy with pitch, burst into monstrous torches.

Kevin nervously scans their willow thicket refuge. If that's hit...

As if some demon read his mind, lightning lights up a larger willow tree two hundred feet down the shore. Flames shoot along its multiple branches, down into the tangled mass of underbrush. Ultra-flammable twigs ignite, exploding with white-hot heat, erupting across the top of the brush, leaping from bush to bush, racing toward them at incredible speed.

Nothing burns quicker or hotter than willow.

"Quick! Quick!" Kevin shouts. "Get out of this brush. Back to the beach. Hurry!"

Rhonda lifted her head, seeing a ball of fire streaking toward her.

"Run, Bry, run!" Grabbing Malcolm, she plucks her parka off the limbs, trying to retreat the way she came. Bryan darts through a tiny opening and onto the beach, but she can't break through the mass of interlocking twigs. The slender, flexible branches formed an impenetrable mat.

Meanwhile, the blazing inferno, now less than a hundred feet away, streaks toward her, consuming everything in its path.

"Rhonda! Hurry! Hurry!" Bryan jumps up, waving his arms. Kevin lay Jackie down and limps toward her, but there's no time.

"Oh, Jesus," she cries, dropping to her knees.

Lay on your back. Slide under the bush! Yeah! She rolls over, the roar of the flames assaulting her as she slides under the willows, pushing as fast as she can.

I'll never make it holding Malcolm. If I left him....No! I can do this. Gotta save us both.

Her head pushes free of the bushes. A few more kicks...but the fire is only feet away. One mighty shove, and she tucks her knees, rolling like a log, barely clearing the deadly furnace.

A loud *whoosh,* as a blanket of heat speeds past, singing hairs on the back of her neck. Kevin lurches to her side, dropping heavily to his knees, dragging them further away.

"Shit! That was close!" she whimpers, tears blended with rain. "We coulda...we coulda been..."

"Don't think about it. Brave thing ya did, saving that boy. Some woulda left him to save their own hide." He cradles her in his arms, sitting in the sand, rocking softly.

"Jesus, I've never seen a storm like this," he says.

"What's...what's gonna happen to us, Kevin?" She sobs, gasping for breath.

"First, we gotta survive. Then figure how to get some help. We don't get rescued pretty quick, Jackee's in big trouble." He glances at his patient, little Bryan hunkering over her, shielding her as best he can from the raging elements.

Jackee looks at her son.

Gotta stay calm. Can't show my own fear. She smiles at him with her eyes.

You've been very brave, Bry.

"I'm scared, Mommy."

I know, but everything'll be okay now, sweetie. Be strong and do whatever Kevin asks of you.

She is joined by Kevin, while Rhonda and Bryan, wet and shivering, hover together for shelter, lying flat on the sand. Nearly forty minutes pass before the storm finally dissipates, winding down to a light sprinkle and ashen skies. Kevin struggles to sit up, Jackee again clutched in his arms.

"Hang on." Rhonda staggers up. "I'll see if there are any cushions left on the boat to lay her on. Your arms gotta be killing you." She turns to Bryan.

"Watch your brother, sweetie. I'll be right back." Still limping, she jogs over to what is left of their beached craft. She stops, hands on hips, shaking her head.

"Wow! Kev, you gotta see this!" He limps over, still cradling Jackee in his powerful arms. The tilted hulk that, just an hour before was their floating palace, sits askew on the beach.

"Jesus," he mutters. Kneeling, he gently lays Jackee on a sandy patch, hoping she isn't injured. She feels nothing, but the shock of that fall may have done some internal damage. Placing his rolled up poncho under her head, he turned to the boat.

"What a mess! We're never getting outta here on this." The center deck is sheared open for half its length, with the starboard pontoon reduced to a hardened pool of melted aluminum. The motor's cowling was blown away and the engine block looks fused. All the electronics are fried beyond repair.

"Won't they be out looking for us?" Rhonda rests an icy hand on his bare arm.

"Hope so. Boy, you're freezing." He takes her into his arms, pressing his body against hers, running his hands up and down her back.

"Mmmmm. Feels good."

"Only trying to warm ya up. Get your blood flowing again."

"Oh, it's flowing, all right." Tiny kisses pepper the base of his neck.

"Cut it out. We got serious problems here. We're wet, cold, and out of contact with the world. I'm worried about Jackee and Mal. She could have internal injuries from that fall, or even catch pneumonia, and he's surely got at least a mild concussion."

"Can you light a fire? Lucky the gas tank didn't blow when that bolt hit."

"Yeah, I can use that. Those willows will dry out in a gas fire, and burn hot enough to get some bigger pieces going."

"If you can make some smoke, think somebody will spot us?"

"Maybe, but I'm sure everyone's off the lake, and we drifted way back into this bay, where almost nobody comes. It could be hours."

"What're we gonna to do?" Tension edges into her voice.

"Relax. I'll get a fire started, try to rig some shelter, dry out...and pray. I gotta see if there's some clothes for Jackee in the cabin. She's soaked."

CHAPTER SEVENTY-THREE

Jackee listens to them discuss their predicament as they dress her in a dry outfit from the still intact cabin.

Kevin's not the only one worried. Gotta get through this, but I'm so tired. Giving Rhonda the extra strength to pull Kevin from under that boat, and then helping her find a way out of that firetrap without leaving Mal behind. That was the toughest. She was getting ready to abandon him to saver herself.

Gotta find some way to get help. Be damned if I won't complete my plan. Last thing I need now is a bout with pneumonia!

How did I get so unlucky to have so many things go wrong today? Was it Phil again, somehow sabotaging the boat? But how could he know of the storms? Is he so heartless, not to even care what happens to his sons, just to be rid of me?

She looks at Bryan sitting next to his brother. *He's so proud of his big musky, but now he's scared. He'd probably rather be playing Internet games with....*

Oh, how stupid of me!

Her sons will come to the rescue again!

Bryan, come here. Mal will be okay for a moment.

Coming Mommy. Are you okay? He wipes tears from his eyes, trying to look brave.

Of course, my champion fisherman. You did a wonderful job today. I'm proud of you.

The boy beams, a smile edging onto his face as he settles next to his mother.

Can you play games on the Internet with Mal's little computer?

"Sure, mommy."

And send Instant Messages to your friends?

"Mal does. I don't know how to do IM's. Why?"

Show it to Kevin.

"I don't have it, Mom. It's in Mal's backpack, I think."

Where's that?

"I don't know. I... Oh, oh."

"What?"

"Rhonda used it for his pillow in the bushes. I bet it's burned up."

Go get it, Bry. Maybe it survived. We need that computer!

He jumps up, racing over to the charred remains of what was once their shelter. Crawling along, he searches for the backpack. It's hard to tell exactly where they had been, and black ash covered the sand. It was right about....

"Hey, Bry, what're ya doing."

"Looking for Mal's back pack."

"Careful, son. Might still be pretty hot in there. The pack's probably toast, anyhow."

"Gotta find...there it is, I think." Squirming on his belly, he slithers partly under blackened branches, catching a strap, which disintegrates into black powder. Pushing deeper, black ash showering his face, he gets a hand on the bag. It was coming apart as he pulls it out.

"Found it, huh?" Kevin stands over him. "Looking for something special?"

Bryan nods, rummaging through the remains of the badly burned bag. Grinning, he draws out his treasure, showing Kevin Mal's little wireless PDA.

"Bryan, you're a hero. Why I didn't think of that?" He turns it over in his hands.

"The casing is scorched, but it looks okay. Let's hope it's still working. Can ya put me in contact with one of Mal's friends? Send 'em a message?"

"I never did it, Kevin. Mal only let me play games, once he was on line. Can you figure it out?"

"Lemme see it. I've never used one of these before." He pushes the Power button but nothing happens. Flipping it over, he pops the back open.

"I wonder if the batteries... No, here it is. Damn! This wire burned up. Looks like it connects the battery."

"It won't work, Kevin?" Rhonda limps over.

"Not unless I find a way to fix this wire."

"Maybe we can find something on the boat."

"Good idea. The cabin didn't seem badly damaged. Might be something there we can use."

A few minutes later he's back with a length of lamp cord. Using a piece of broken glass, he strips the insulation off of a six inches piece. Now, how to make the connection? No way to solder them, so he'd have to try twisting them together. Unfortunately, his thick fingers are not made for such delicate work.

"Damn, I just can't get in there."

"Let me try," Bryan says. "My fingers are little, and Mal and I wired some toys last Christmas. You show me what to do."

"Good idea. Here, look. Wrap one end around that little terminal by the batteries."

It takes three tries, but the boy finally achieves a shaky connection.

"Now, the hard part. Ya gotta gently twist this end around that little stub of wire. There's not much to work with, and it might be brittle, so be very careful."

Bryan makes a small loop of the lamp wire, but the cold rain numbs his fingers. He tries to hook the little stub of lead wire, but can't control his shaking hand. Finally success on the fourth attempt.

"Careful, son" Kevin says. "Tie it around...Damn!" A tiny tremor while tying the splice snaps off the little wire from the PDA.

"Oh, Kevin! I ruined it! I ruined it!" Tears well, spilling across frosted cheeks.

"Not your fault, son. It was too brittle from the fire. Maybe we can still get it going." Kevin studies the wiring, Rhonda looking over his shoulder.

"It's never gonna work, Kevin," she says. "What're we gonna do?"

"Fix this damned thing somehow, and get some help quick, or Jackee's gonna catch pneumonia."

He pokes at the broken wires. Gotta be some way to make a connection. Something to replace solder.

"Bry, ya got any gum?"

"Yeah, I think so."

"Good. Start chewing."

A few minutes later, and after several fumbled attempts, Kevin manages to splice the wire in place with two sticky wads of gum.

"Not very secure, but hopefully it'll work."

Turning it over, he pushes the "Power" button. A small beep, and the screen lights up.

"Well, I got it going, but got no idea how to use it. Rhonda?"

"Me either, Kevin. This is a lot newer model than mine. I convinced Phil to buy him one with all the bells and whistles. I got no idea how it works."

"Can't be too hard. Let me play with it." Perching on the sand, the redhead looking over his shoulder, they study the little computer.

Bryan, ask Kevin to put Mal next to me. I'll see if I can talk to him.

"He's unconscious, Mommy," he whispers.

I know, but maybe I can reach him. Hurry."

"Kevin, can you move Mal near Mommy? Then I can watch them both."

"I'll do it," Rhonda said.

"Good idea, son. Meanwhile, I'll see if I can figure this thing out."

A moment later, Malcolm is stretched out next to his mother, covered with his yellow slicker for warmth. Jackee isolates herself from the sounds of Kevin and Rhonda, working with Mal's PDA, reaching gently the boy's mind, searching for any tendrils of thought or dreams. There! Something incoherent swirling out of this head.

Mal, can you hear me?

Uhhh.

Mal, I know you're sleepy, but you've got to hear me. Focus on my voice. It's very important.

Uhhh. Uhhhh.

Bry, you hold his head on your lap, and listen hard, so if I can talk to him, you'll hear what we need to know.

Bryan gently cradles his brother's head, smoothing his yellow hair. Jackee clears her head, centering her thoughts, focusing on Malcolm's somnolent mind.

Malcolm, we need your help. I know your head hurts, and you're sleepy, but I can tell you'll be okay. You don't have to wake up. Just let Mommy in so we can see how to use your PDA. It's urgent, Mal.

She probes gently, seeking an opening. Finally, a small crack, a quiet little fissure in the tumultuous barrage swirling in his head. Narrowing her thoughts, she slides in, shuddering at a sudden sensory assault. Momentarily blinded by a kaleidoscopic whirlpool of light and crackling flashes, she recoils, losing her foothold, flung away...ejected, as if falling off a wildly spinning merry-go-round.

He's hurt and frightened. It's amazing how much goes on in an unconscious mind.

She centers herself, pulling all her psychic power in to one "finger," gently stroking his panicked mind.

Easy, son. Relax, no one will hurt you. Everything will be fine in a little while. Relax. We need your help.

She senses the fusillade of tension and fear easing, the fiery detonations in his head receding. Weaving carefully through a maze of imagery, she is finally able to gently lay her "finger" on the core of his thoughts. A salvo of visions flash by, as if surfing TV channels, making her dizzy.

Malcolm, try to control yourself. We need information.

Huh? Weak, but is it cognitive? Fast-forward mental video continues unabated. Her head spinning, she is losing orientation. If this doesn't stop, she'll have to leave again.

Slow down, son. You're safe. You have to concentrate.

Huh? Ohhh. He was struggling to focus, but his visions keep swirling around her, sweeping her up in their intensity. She is totally confused and has to get out.

Jackee gasps for breath, her mind hovering just outside his. Kevin, hearing her struggle, is quickly at her side.

"Ya okay?"

"Yes."

"Sounded like ya were breathing kinda hard there."

"A dream. I okay."

"Ya sure?"

"Yes. I fine. You work PDA. Bryan trying 2 remember how."

"Good, 'cause we're not having much luck." He settles next to her, close to the fire, Rhonda huddled close, and goes back to work.

Back in control, her breathing normal, Jackee tentatively reaches again for Malcolm's troubled mind. She's tired and unsure how much more she can take. Maybe she should try "whispering" in his ear.

Mal, we need to know how you send Instant Messages on your PDA. No need to talk. Can you visualize it for us?

Mom....mommy?

Yes, darling. You're okay. Just resting after bumping your head. But we need your help now. Please, let me in, and picture how to send messages on your PDA.

O...O...Kay. Her vision swims, as if peering through turbid water, and then there is Mal, sitting cross-legged, playing with his little computer. She slides closer, "looking" over his shoulder, as little fingers fly over the tiny keyboard. She projects her vision to her younger son.

Do you have it, Bry?

"I...I think so," he whispers.

Good. Go tell Kevin you figured it out. Hurry.

"Okay." He settles his brother's head on the knapsack, smoothing his hair, and hurries away.

She can barely make him out talking to Kevin, as they hunkered over the little computer. Bryan is back in a minute.

"It didn't work. Maybe I didn't get it right.

Sit down. We'll try again. Mal?

Mommy?

Yes, sweetie. We need to see how to send messages again.

Okay I think I'm feeling better now. She visualizes him again, sitting with the little computer on his lap, his fingers leaping across the keys.

Slower, son. Do it very slowly, so Bry can understand. The boy in the vision looks up, smiling, and turns back to the PDA, his fingers moving almost in slow motion.

Bry. Concentrate hard. You have to get it right.

Okay, Mommy. I'll try.

She absorbs what Mal is doing, projecting it to her younger son.

Do you see how to do it, Bry?

Yeah, I think I got it.

Okay, try to show Kevin again.

CHAPTER SEVENTY-FOUR

"No one's responded, Bry. Now what? Can we try someone else?

"Most of Mal's friends are still at sleep-away camp until this week-end. Sammy's almost always on his computer. They play chess a lot."

Kevin glances at his watch.

"Diner time. Maybe they're eating."

"Try him again," Rhonda says. "Maybe he'll hear the message alert and come to look."

"Okay. How long are these batteries good for?"

"I don't know. We used it off and on all day."

"Great! Well, I'll give it a shot. All we can do is hope for the best."

◆❖◆

"Sammy, did you wash your hands?"

"I forgot, mom."

"Well, go do it. And put on a clean shirt."

Sammy ran to his room, stripping off his favorite, scruffy T-shirt. Hands washed, he was pulling on something more presentable, when his computer beep at him. Another Instant Message. He glanced at his door, then ran over and hit a key, bringing the screen back to life.

It was, as he hoped, a message from Mal, his best friend.

Darn! This will only take a second. I'll tell him I'll text him after dinner. He clicked "accept," his eyes going wide as he skimmed the words.

"Wow!" He raced for the dining room.

"Dad! Dad! It's a message from Mal. He..."

"Sam! I told you no messages now. You're going to get grounded if you can't listen."

"But...."

"No 'buts.' Sit down and eat your dinner. I'll deal with you about this later."

"But, dad..."

"Enough! Keep this up and I'll take away that damned computer."

"Dad, it's..."

"Sammy!"

"... it's important. They're in trouble!"

"Now, this is too much. I ... Trouble? Who's in trouble."

"That's what I'm trying to tell you. Malcolm, his mother and brother. They need our help."

"That's ridiculous! His mother is locked in a wheelchair at home. God knows, they have plenty of help."

"But they're *not* home! They're on Channel Lake, stranded by a storm!"

"What!" Robert Allen gave his son a stern look. If this were some sort of game...

"They went fishing. They all went fishing. Their boat is broken down or something."

"Unbelievable! Why didn't they call for help there?"

"I don't know. They're using Mal's PDA."

"Jesus! Are we ever going to have dinner." Bob Allen stood. "C'mon, show me. This better be good, or you're in big trouble, young man."

"Hurry, daddy, hurry!" Sammy towed his father by the hand. He sat at his son's desk, frowning.

"So, where's this important message, young man?"

"It...it was there a minute ago, dad. Really, it said..."

"Cut it out, Sam. Couldn't be that important. It says here they're off line."

"But Dad..."

"Enough of this foolishness. Down to dinner. We'll arrange your punishment later."

"But..."

"Enough, I said." He stood. "Let's go."

◆ ❖ ◆

"What happened, Kevin? Sammy answered, and then the screen went blank."

"I don't know, son. I just..." He turned the device over.

"Oh, damn! The wire's loose." He pushed the loose end back in place, packing the gum around it. Pushing the "Power" button, the PDA beeped.

"Got it working. Hope they're still on line."

Kevin's fingers were punching the buttons as fast as he could.

They were just out the door when Sammy's computer sang to him.

"It's Mal again, Dad, I know it." He raced back to his computer, clicking on "accept."

"That's it, young man. I'm taking this computer away..."

"Dad, here read it. I told you, they're in trouble."

"This is ridiculous. We're going to dinner." Grabbing his son by the arm, dragging him toward the door, glancing at the screen as he passed. Pausing, he took a step backward, releasing his grip on Sammy's arm. Sitting at the desk, he read the message.

"Unbelievable!" He typed quickly, read the response, which stopped in the middle. They were off-line again. He grabbed the phone. It was answered on the first ring.

"911. What is your emergency?"

"We need the sheriff. There are five people stranded and in trouble on Channel Lake. I can give you some general directions on where to look."

CHAPTER SEVENTY-FIVE

Kevin kneels next to Jackee, adjusting her position on the sand and checking her pulse. He moved her closer to the fire, and erected a heat reflector from a piece of the aluminum hull, which is effectively drying her out and keeping her warm. The skies are clearing and the last of the drizzle ended ten minutes before

Over an hour has passed since his brief e-mail exchange with Sammy's dad, but no rescue boat has arrived. Malcolm's PDA quit just as Kevin was sending their location. The battery had finally died, and he may not have gotten through.

Rhonda and Bryan hunker near the fire where Malcolm is spread out, covered by a yellow slicker.

Jackee watches Kevin fuss over her, adjusting her head on a boat cushion and listening to her breathe. He's done everything he can, and they are in fate's hands now. She tries to access her own condition, but when you feel nothing, it's not easy. No apparent problems breathing, but that can change if they don't get help soon. No tolerance for that now, with the Plan so near fruition. She *has* to survive long enough to see Phil get his comeuppance.

She senses Malcolm's awakening mind. He's groggy, but seemed otherwise okay He'll surely have a headache, but that'll....

Something....? She strains to listen.

Yes! A motor. A rescue boat, searching for them? She reaches for her youngest son.

Bryan! He crawls to her side.

Tell Kevin you hear a boat. Maybe he can signal somehow. He jumps up.

"A boat, Kevin. I hear a boat." The big man rises, stepping away from the crackling fire, cocking his head.

"I don't hear...Wait. There it is. Good work, son." He grabs an arm full of wet, leafy willow branches he'd stashed close by, tossing them on the fire. He lifts Jackee, moving her further from the flames, then runs back, snatching up a soda can filled with gasoline.

"Stay clear, everyone," he says, tossing the can on the fire.

Whoosh! BOOM! The small bomb ignites with a loud report, hurtling flames twenty feet high, followed by a smoky cloud, billowing into the sky.

"You think this will work?" Rhonda asks.

"I sure hope so. This bays pretty long, so they're quite a bit away. This stuff should create a lot of smoke, though"

"What if they don't see it? Will they keep looking at this end of the lake?"

"They gotta know we're missing, even if Sammy's dad never got our message."

They look toward the open lake, hoping for help. The fire is burning hot, the wet willows sending up their distress call, but the top of the dark column of smoke is torn off by still-brisk winds. Will it rise high enough for the searchers to see?

Jackee reaches out, feeling for their rescuers' minds, already past the mouth of the bay, unaware of their location. Exhausted, she struggles to focus her power. Sensing a bare trickle of their energy, she sends thoughts, hoping they will register as their own.

That bay we just passed. Maybe we should poke around. Could be someone trapped back there.

The sounds of their motor never slows, and what little contact she forged evaporates.

Damn, they're leaving. What else can I do? Another boat may not come this way again for hours.

"They're not coming, Kevin! Make more smoke."

"No uses. They won't see it. Damn."

Jackee closes her eyes, weary, as the hum of the distant engine fades into silence. She should have been strong enough to reach them. Maybe she *is* getting ill. No way to tell, lying in this void. Her breathing doesn't seem labored, but...

Wait! Her psychic ears "twitch." Is that...?

Yes! The engine-noise is there again, getting stronger. They're coming back.

Jackee draws on her concentration, pulling all her remaining energy into focus.

That bay. Let's look back there. Maybe someone's...

The boat sounds strengthen, audible slapping of waves diminishing as it enters calmer water.

Thank God. They're coming.

Bryan! Her son kneels, taking her hand, eyes searching hers.

Tell Kevin you think they're coming back. Make more smoke.

The boy jumps up, running to where Kevin and Rhonda sit, talking. The big man leaps to his feet, quickly tossed another bundle of wet willows on the fire.

A moment later, a Lake County Sheriff's launch cruises into view, planing across the riffled water, heading right at them. The officer at the helm waves.

"They found us," Rhonda stands, waving back. Tears course over her cheeks. "Thank God." She turns, throwing her arms around the big man, kissing him.

Tilting his head back, their eyes lock. They melted against each other, and what started as a celebration quickly morphs into something much more passionate...with Jackee right in the middle, savoring the heat

"We're saved, Kev," Rhonda whispers huskily. "Saved."

"Yeah." His fingers caress her cheek, his eyes filled with wonder.

A quick head shake as he steps away.

"Let's hope it ain't too late for Jackee."

Bryan runs to his mother. "You did it, Mommy. You called them."

Kevin turns, head cocked, then smiles smugly, giving a knowing nod toward the blonde.

She smiles at him with her eyes, and winks. She, too, hopes it isn't too late.

And now it seems the cat may be out of the bag.

I do believe the big, sweet lug as finally caught on.

Chapter Seventy-Six

Kevin winces at the knife-like stab in his left shoulder as he totes Jackee off the sheriff's rescue launch. One of the deputies brings her chair. It's miraculously undamaged, the rubber-lined wheels insulating it from the lightning's blast.

"We're gonna have to have a little straight talk, once we get settled back home," he mutters to her, as he secures her in her chair.

She blinks once, and he understands now how he recognizes the smile in her eyes.

An EMS is enjoying examining Rhonda. Her badly scrapped shin is taped, her ribs bruised but unbroken. The cut on her thigh is shallow. It needed cleaning, but not stitches.

Malcolm was awake by the time the rescuers arrived at their beach. His head felt like bongo drums, and he's still wobbly on his feet. Rhonda lends her hand for support. Other than a walnut-size lump on his right temple, he's suffering only minor scrapes and a runny nose.

Bryan's Medal of Honor is his blistered left thumb, from pressing on the spool of line just as his trophy fish made a speedy run. He's proudly showing everyone the digital photos.

Besides a prominent bump on the back of his head, Kevin is nicked and cut, with scraped knees and a mildly sprained left shoulder, but he hardly notices. His attention is focused on Jackee, the only one without contusions. Exposure is the main concern, but he did an excellent job of protecting her. He absorbed the full impact of the hard fall, saving her from injury, and had managed to keep her reasonably warm and dry.

They quickly loaded up, heading home in the van, with Rhonda following in her Jag. Jackee is numb. Her thoughts wander over the day's adventures.

What a day! It started so beautifully, and almost ended so terribly. Little Malcolm saved me again, although this time he didn't know he was doing it. Getting to be a regular thing with him. And

Bryan is so proud of his fish. Sometimes, good things come from bad situations.

Such a string of bad luck. Two radios dying, and then the boat's battery! Was it was all only coincidence. Could Phil have somehow done this? He wouldn't jeopardize Rhonda....

Wait a minute! He didn't know she was coming! Still, how could he manage sabotage everything? The radio said the storm was a freak, unexpected thing. He couldn't know it was developing.

Well, it doesn't matter now. The Plan is almost complete. Gonna schedule the final act next week. Glad we survived so I can finish this.

Eyes closed, she listens to her sons' excited chatter, their recent danger now an adventure, growing in the telling.

Mal seems pretty fully recovered, and Bryan has his fish and blistered thumb to show all his friends.

A scary situation, but all in all, things didn't turn out as badly as they might have.

She drifts toward sleep, dreaming of jumping Apache...and the big musky.

She shivers at the memory of that savage, empty mind.

Never want to do that again.

People are tough enough.

CHAPTER SEVENTY-SEVEN

Two days since that too-exciting fishing trip and things are back to "normal," whatever that is. Rhonda and Kevin entered into a silent understanding not to tell Phil she was with them on the fishing trip. She blamed the cut leg, shin and bruised ribs on a workout accident. She was worried the two little boys might say something, not knowing Jackee had sworn them to silence.

Most of Kevin's earlier resistance to Rhonda's advances is evaporating after all they shared on the lake...especially that kiss! The numerous erotic skirmishes Jackee engineered between them over the past several weeks has clearly made inroads.

He is a principled guy, but he really doesn't care she's committed to another man whom he obviously dislikes. Protecting each other during their near-disaster is a strong bond. Rhonda was pretty spectacular in an emergency...especially when the blonde helped.

The redhead is a lot more than just a beautiful gal.

Jackee savors those erotic contacts, the only ones she may ever have with this man she has come to adore. Despite the pleasant arousal, building a lasting friendship between these two is as important as developing a sexual relationship. The fishing trip helped in a way she never expected. Kevin is falling for a woman much more like Jackee than either of them knows... a necessary part of The Plan. But pleasure at her success is continually tempered by an unavoidable lingering moral discontent at playing God.

What's the real harm? I'm encouraging what might be a natural attraction, especially since our fishing trip. Rhonda's so comfortable with him. Life with my husband may be charged and exciting, but never relaxing. No reason to feel guilty.

Her conscience once again conveniently assuaged, she refuses to be daunted by the structure of thirty-five years of ethics.

Her eyes are drawn to Kevin, entering her bedroom, closing the door behind him. He drags over a chair, settling next to the bed, taking one pale hand in his.

"It's time we have that talk I mentioned when we got off the lake."

"Yes," she blinked.

He wants answers, and he deserves most of the truth. Not all, but most...

CHAPTER SEVENTY-EIGHT

"Back on the lake, when the Sherriff's boat arrived, Bryan said, 'you called them.' I've been wondering about stuff...how you hear everything, and how...how I can kinda sense what you're thinking. Can you...kinda talk to people with your thoughts?"

"Only sons."

"But how..."

"Talk sons. Hear minds others."

"Ya can hear our thoughts?"

"Yes. Most R and P. Never listen U."

"But then how d'ya call them?" He sits back, eyebrows raised.

"Can listen; suggest; they hear own voice. Not always work."

"So ya can plant ideas they think are their own. Wow!" He shakes his head, confusion photographed on his craggy face.

"Do little. Only if important." *I don't want him thinking I'm playing God.*

"Yeah? So what else?" He fidgeted in his chair.

How much more can I tell him? What can I chance...Oh, Hell, who can I trust more than Kevin?

"I feel, too."

"Feel? What d'ya mean, 'feel?' Like emotions?"

"Mostly R. Like U kiss R." Her eyes plumb his, twinkling like faceted emeralds.

"Ya...ya felt our kiss at the lake? Like you're in Rhonda's head, feeling what she feels?"

"Yes. Liked it."

"Jesus!" He springs up, turns, and shuffles around in a tight circle, working his injured left shoulder.

"I shouldn't get lured into doing that with her. Not because she's Phil's woman, but 'cause...'cause..."

"U luv me," she blinked.

"Yeah, because I..." he paused, mouth frozen in mid-word. "You know...?"

"Yes. And..." Her turn to hesitate, before plunging on.

"I luv U." Fourteen magical blinks of her eyes.

"You love me?" He dropped into the chair like a wet sack, arms dangling.

"Yes. Many months."

"Unbelievable!" He shakes his head, dropping it into his hands, elbows braced against his knees. "To love and be loved by ya, and there's no way... no way to..."

"Yes!" *What hadn't I thought of this before? This will work out better than I planned.*

"U kiss R; touch R; love R. Is same as me."

"Yer kidding? Ya'll be in Rhonda's head, feeling everything she feels?"

"Yes! Maybe better." She holds his gaze. "I luv U. She maybe too"

"Wow!" He can't help grinning. "A three-some with the two most gorgeous women in the world. Every man's dream!"

"Yes." The blonde chuckles at the irony. "But she not know I there. Only U, me. Can't tell her. Not tell anyone. Scare them."

How exciting. So much more than I ever bargained for. But also very dangerous, should Phil or Rhonda ever learn my secret.

Kevin's grin slowly evaporated, replace by a wrinkled, somber brow.

"Let's face it. This is fantasy. No way we're doing anything more'n flirting, kissing, and maybe some touching. It's plenty hot, but I'm never gonna crawl into the sack with that beautiful redhead. Why would she jeopardize her future with Phil on a fling with a country hick like me?"

"Maybe she marry P money, but luvs U in heart. U more like her than P."

"Loves me? Don't seem likely." He shakes his head. "Like, respect, maybe. But Love? I doubt it."

"Try. See after I gone. Things change." She's amazed she's not exhausted after so much interaction. She's so excited, adrenaline must be keeping her pumped up.

I'll sleep like a baby tonight. Gotta keep it going right now.

"I dunno. How can it happen...?"

"Give chance. R wants, too."

"Ya really think so?" He stares at her. "Yer not gonna influence her somehow. Push her into doing something..."

"No. I just on 4 happy ride, if you there." *A little white lie, 'cause she may need a bit of coaxing, but it's what Rhonda really wants, too.*

George A. Bernstein

"Well, we'll see. Knowing you're there... well, that's added incentive."

"Good. I eager, too."

Kevin lurches to his feet, dragging the chair back to its place near the sofa. He turns, staring at her, lips pursed, his brow knit with wrinkles. Crossing his arms across his massive chest, he slouches against the doorframe.

"Boy, this is a lot to consider. I never imagined ya might love me, too." His brown eyes plumbed hers, and he shakes his head, as if dispelling demons.

"Now we got Rhonda somehow in the middle, and I got feelings for her too, 'specially after all we shared in that melee. She's turned out to be a pretty special gal. I... I like her too much to use her, just to feel like I'm being with you. Don't seem right, no matter how much I want it."

"Is okay. U luv R 4 R. I lucky to share with her."

"Yeah? Well it's all spittin' in the wind. She's got a plan, and Phil's it... not me. I'd be the monkey wrench, and she's too smart for that."

"We'll see." *This is a whole new road to travel that I never thought of 'til now. An exciting prospect.*

Now I've got a more important challenge for Rhonda... discussing with the little boys their adoption. Something that will, necessarily, focus them on the reality of my impending death. Got to get her off the dime and talking to Phil... soon.

CHAPTER SEVENTY-NINE

Rhonda sits on the floor with Bryan and Malcolm in the den, two days later. Jackee has been "prepping" the redhead and now hovers nearby, watching.

"Listen, guys. We need to talk." They sprawl on the floor, facing Rhonda, who's dressed down for this occasion, in jeans and a denim shirt.

"This isn't easy." Nervousness suddenly dissolves, replaced by confidence.

"We've gotten to know each other real well, right?" They nod.

"I take care of you, help you with school, and even go fishing with you." They all giggle. "Yeah, that was some adventure, wasn't it?" Two small heads bob again. She runs her fingers over Mal's blonde locks. The shadow of the bruise lingers on his forehead. He smiles.

"I think you guys are great, and I know you like me, too. If I had sons, I'd want them to be just like you. In fact, I feel like you *are* my sons." They sit very still, eyes suddenly serious.

"Now, here's the tough part. You know how your mama is now. It doesn't look like she's getting any better. You can see how thin she's become, no matter how hard Kevin tries, and he's doing the very best anyone can.

"The sad fact is, if that keeps up, she'll get weaker, and that means she's more likely to get sick. Even though her mind's working good, her body's not doing so well. If she catches any little virus she could... she could die." She blinks moisture from her eyes, a look of surprise creasing her lovely face.

Bryan, barely old enough to understand the concept of death, begins to cry softly. Malcolm has tears in his eyes, but manages some control. A protective arm around his little brother, he looks at her with saddened eyes.

God, they're taking this so well. Jackee refocuses on the woman's mind.

"It's so sad, but it's important to face the truth. But, *I'm* always going to be here. Your daddy and I will get married after your mama... you know...

"I'll take care of you, just like I've been doing. Just like your mama. So I'd like to become your real mama. We can do that with our laws. It's called adoption. I'm sure you've heard of it. That way the law will say I *am* your mother, and I'm responsible to take good care of you." Bryan knuckles away his tears, looking first at his brother and then at Jackee.

"I know it won't be the same as your first Mommy. No one can ever replace her, and I won't try. I only want to carry on for her after she is gone. You know, keep us a family. What d'ya think?" She opens her arms to them, uncharacteristically choked with emotion.

They glance at their mother, as if awaiting her approval. Rhonda sees Malcolm mouthing silent words. They both nod, as if responding to some soundless conversation.

Eyes wet, they crawl into the warm comfort of the young redhead's grasp. All three sit there, crying silently. Rhonda is suddenly filled with an exciting idea. She glances at Jackee.

"Hey, let's ask your Mommy what she thinks. She can answer with her eyes." So they do, and Jackee blinks her approval. The boys swarm over their mother, hugging and kissing, pledging their everlasting love. Jackee's eyes find Rhonda's, blinking a message. Mal, realizing she doesn't understand, interprets for her.

"Mommy says, 'Thanks.'"

Wow, that went well. Another cornerstone laid, pretty much on schedule. Rhonda did well with the little cues I fed her. The only thing more important than punishing Phil is providing the boys with loving care. I think the redhead'll be a far better mom than I ever expected...a lucky bonus.

She had sent the two boys encouragement as Rhonda talked. *It will be all right. Rhonda is a good lady, and she'll take care of you, just like I would. Be brave for me.* She's so proud of how they handled this.

They're probably too young to fully understand death. They saw what it meant with Daddy, though. They'll cope somehow, with Rhonda's help.

While steering the "The Plan" down its scripted road, Jackee still joins in their lovemaking, reveling in her newly awaked sensuality. She occasionally starts and sometimes even cautiously directs their passionate encounters, partly as further tests of her expanding powers, and occasionally because she just enjoys being the initiator. Unfortunately, the effort is wearing on her, sapping some of her precious reserves, so she's begun rationing her participation.

She was a passive participant all her life, and is ecstatic to be in control for a change. If it were only Kevin, instead of her hateful husband.

Everything is going along fine, but underneath her confidence lingers concern for the things that can go wrong.

So many things!

Murphy's Law is surely lingering nearby.

Can't consider it. That's courting defeat. I'm playing this game presuming everything will fall into place, just as I plan. If not, I may fail, but that's not acceptable.

Phil will be punished!

Nothing's going to stop me.

Not now.

Not after I'm sacrificing my very life for this!

CHAPTER EIGHTY

Scarlet and yellow leaves spin and twist before a soft breeze, doing a dervish dance. This is one of those beautiful Indian Summer days that occasionally grace the fall...sunny and warm. Sitting in her den, the weather is not on Jackee's mind.

Less than two months until "D Day." Gotta get it done. I'm running out of gas. Dying doesn't scare me anymore. This life is useless. Only hope I've got the time and energy to survive long enough to finish. Time to bring up the curtain on the final act.

So much has happened since first discovering her strange mental gift. Can't falter now, with all the groundwork laid. Her job with Rhonda is about as complete as it will get. Little more to do with the limited time and energy she has left.

Rhonda and Kevin are a clandestine twosome. The confused redhead is infatuated, if not already in love with the gentle therapist, and he no longer resists his own enchantment with her. Their tense adventure on Channel Lake was added glue to their attraction.

Poor Kevin, feeling so guilty he's betraying me by falling for the interloper. Why? I'm dying, so his obligations to me will end. He needs continuing reassurance.

Things went so well when Rhonda talked to the boys about their adoption. Maybe her interest in the kids *is* a positive result from her dysfunctional childhood. Jackee hopes so.

She has done all she can. Any more meddling may be dangerous. People are a lot more pliable when they don't know they are being manipulated. She hopes everything is in place when the time comes, and hasn't overestimated her ability.

Dear God, please allow me enough time to finish.

She is lost in thought, staring into space, when Kevin enters.

"Jackee, Mr. Osborn's here." The attorney enters, taking her hand.

Kevin places a chair in front of his patient. "Sit here, sir, so she can see ya more easily. Ya know we've developed a kind of Morse Code with her eyes?" The attorney nods, settling in the chair.

"She'll talk and I'll translate. If ya want to verify anything, just ask. One blink is 'yes,' and two are 'no.' It's easier if I offer her options when I get the gist of her thoughts. Long conversations tire her. I know some of what she wants to tell ya, so that'll help speed things along. Ready Jackee?"

Jackee blinks once, and then her eyelids flutter in an irregular pattern, pausing briefly every few winks. Arthur Osborn is mesmerized, watching the still beautiful but very thin daughter of his deceased best friend, "talk" to the huge man sitting next to him. Finally, she stops, looking directly into his eyes.

"What did she say, Mr. Martin?"

"Everybody calls me Kevin, sir." He sighs.

"She said, 'I want a divorce'."

CHAPTER EIGHTY-ONE

"Divorce?" Arthur Osborn's usually placid face creases with surprise.

"Please understand I am not questioning your decision, my dear. In light of his shameless behavior, bringing his mistress openly into your house, well, you should have kicked the philandering rascal out long ago. But why, suddenly, now?"

"I can answer that, and save her some energy," Kevin says. "She's told me what she wants over the past several days. Ya can verify everything when I'm done."

"Is that all right with you, Jackee?" the attorney asks.

She blinked once.

"All right, Kevin, what's this all about?"

"Well, sir, first off, the divorce ain't due to Phil's cheating. Actually, Jackee's come to like Miz Armstrong. Thing is," his voice cracks, "Jackee ain't gonna live much longer."

Osborn exhales a long sigh, his elegant carriage sagging.

"In spite of our best efforts, she's continued to atrophy. That opens her to all kinds of viral infections that could end things pretty quick. I was really worried about her catching pneumonia after that disaster on Channel Lake. We're watching her best we can, but her body'll eventually become too weak to survive. According to her Living Will, she wants to be allowed ta...ta die naturally, once the things she called ya here to discuss are completed."

The big man licks his lips, glancing at his thin, still exquisite patient, who has become the very center of his life. Unshed tears glisten like tiny diamonds in his eyes. He swallows twice before continuing.

"Miz Armstrong's taken a serious interest in adopting Malcolm and Bryan, once she and Mr. Maren are married. Jackee and the boys agree. She's mainly interested in seeing to the welfare of her sons while she's still alive.

"By going ahead with a divorce now, Phil can marry Rhonda, who can then adopt the boys, with Jackee's consent. Then she can... can go, knowing everything's done like she wants."

"Is this true?" The attorney looks at her, battling his own tears. "This is what you want?" He shakes his head, sadness photographed across his continence.

One blink.

"Have you discussed this with Mr. Maren? He'll be very concerned a divorce might affect his inheritance from you and the trusts."

"She understands that, sir. While I don't know the details of what Mr. Webster set up, Jackee told me that the boys' and her trusts should pass on, as provided for by her father before his death. She doubts Phil'll have any problem with that."

"Are you in full agreement with all of that, Jackee?"

The still luminous green eyes blink once.

"All right, then," he sighs. "I'll get things in the works. Have to meet with Phil, of course. He's got to agree to a No Fault divorce. I'll represent you as your Attorney In Fact through your Durable Power of Attorney. The actual adoption will have to be heard in front of a judge. I don't anticipate any problems, if all parties are in agreement. Mr. Maren can hire his own attorney, if he wishes, but I suspect he will not.

"There will be several hearings, but everything should be completed by mid-January."

Jackee blinks twice, and begins a lengthy message. Kevin turns to Osborn, who is awed by how easily they communicate.

"She says, 'No.' Wants it done by Christmas. She hopes everything can happen all on the same day: the divorce, Phil's marriage to Rhonda, and then the adoptions. She knows she's asking a lot, but hopes ya can treat this like her dying wish, and see it's expedited.

"I gotta add my own caution here." Kevin's weathered face cracks like an old block of granite, his voice husky. Water again makes tiny pools of his dark eyes, little rivulets spilling over the craggy surface of his cheeks.

"The way she's declining, she might not last much past then. I know it's her heartfelt wish to see this done before she... passes on."

"I understand," the attorney says, placing his hand on the big man's arm. "You have been of great service to her, Kevin. It's a miracle she can communicate with us at all, thanks to you. It's quite apparent you've become...fond of her. No surprise there. You have obviously discovered her exceptional nature, despite her incapacitates. It will be a great loss for all of us when she... she is gone. I wish there were something else I could do." Her eyes find his.

That'll be provided for you, Arthur, if God allows me enough time, energy and sufficient ability to finish this. I fear we're cutting it very close. Her eyes flutter closed, receding within herself, happily exhausted.

The iron's in the fire.

No turning back.

CHAPTER EIGHTY-TWO

Three days later Osborn calls, Kevin bringing her the speaker phone.

"I talked to your husband this morning at his offices. He had doubts, wondering at the need for all this, but I pointed out that this could be a definite plus for him. Many might view his open arrangement with Miss Armstrong in the same house with an incapacitated wife as quite callous.

"Your blessing of his remarriage to Ms. Armstrong, and her adoption of your sons, would surely help his standing. Nasty rumors can hinder advancement into top corporate circles."

"Jackee asks if he agreed, sir?"

"He wondered if this would affect his inheritance of the Webster estate. I reminded him that everything resides in the three trusts established by Mr. Webster. He asked if there had been any changes since Mister Webster's passing.

"I said 'No.' It would be my duty to inform him if any modifications were made. To do otherwise would be a breach of ethics. Nor were you contemplating any revisions to your will.

"He seemed satisfied, and rejected the need to enumerate the details of the trusts.

"He was pleased all was happening so quickly, and assured me of Ms. Armstrong's agreement. She's apparently excited about becoming the boys' mother.

"I've arranged with Judge Halpern to hear everything in the afternoon of December 24th, as you requested. I guess I've still got some pull.'

"Jackee says 'Thank you," sir. Glad it's all arranged."

"Frankly, I wonder why she's making this so easy for him. The provisions of the trusts shouldn't cause any real problems for the son-of-a-bitch."

"I believe she wants to see the boys settled and well cared for before she goes, sir. She says she's pleased that all went so well.'
Kevin thanked the attorney as they disconnected. Then he wheeled

Jackee into her room for some quiet time before retiring for the night.

Good. Everything's right on schedule.

Just a few things left to do. I'm eager to see if I can pull it all off.

CHAPTER EIGHTY-THREE

Rhonda steps off the stair climber just as Kevin completes Jackee's therapy for the afternoon. Settling the blonde in her chair, he notices how gingerly Rhonda is toweling off.

"The ribs still bothering ya?"

"Some. I'll get over it."

'Yeah, but they took a pretty good whack on that railing. Want to see if I can give ya any relief?"

She glanced at Jackee. "You got free time?'

"Yeah. We're done with therapy for the day." He crouches in front of his patient. "Ya need anything else right now?"

"No. U help R."

"Okay. Where d'ya want to go? One for the den, two for the bedroom."

She blinks once, so he wheels to her place in front of the French doors, where she can watch the myriad fall colors.

"I'll be in my bedroom," the redhead calls. "I think I'll be more comfortable on my bed than that hard therapy table."

"Okay. I'll get my stuff and meet ya there in a couple of minutes. Soon as I get Jackee situated." He turns back to his patient.

"Ya don't mind being alone for a while?"

"No. Thinking."

He nods, and departs. She senses his curiosity over what really does go on in her very active mind.

I know he's thinking about Rhonda, me in her head...us all together, and he's conflicted, This may be the chance we've all three been waiting for...all for different reasons. Let's see if I can help things develop.

She slips her mental bonds, tagging onto the thoughts of Rhonda, who is clearly ambivalent about the big guy's approach. She's eager to feel his hands on her...everywhere!... but uneasy at the ramifications. Jackee projects a vision of *the kiss*, standing on the beach at Channel Lake as the rescue boat approaches. Both the blonde's and redhead's hearts tumble at the memory.

This is more than just a naughty little escapade. He's a guy worthy of real love.

Lodged in the other's head, Jackee is uncertain if that were her thought... or Rhonda's. Regardless, she's there to see and feel whatever Rhonda does. She hopes she won't be disappointed.

CHAPTER EIGHTY-FOUR

When Kevin arrives, carrying a basket of ointments, Rhonda is sprawled on her back across her king-sized bed, still sporting the chocolate brown short shorts and topaz halter top she wore during her workout, her hair a fiery halo on the pillow. His tongue darts across suddenly parched lips, his breath catching in his throat.

"What's bothering ya? The ribs?"

She nods. "The x-rays showed they aren't cracked, but they're still pretty sore. Can you help?"

"I can try. Raise your top up some, so I can get at them. Ya wearing a bra?"

A slow head shake, her golden eyes trapping his, as she lifts the hem of her blouse.

"No funny business now. Just keep 'em covered while I work on this." His fingers lightly trace the large purple bruise, covering nearly a half-square foot of her lower left rib cage.

Pouring a small dollop for oil in one hand, he vigorously rubs his palms together, heating it up. Gently, he works his fingers over and around the injured area of skin, eliciting a small gasp from the supine woman.

Ohhh! Jackee winces with Rhonda, reacting to the pain, and surprisingly, to the eruption of an avalanche of goose bumps.

Oh, God! This is the first time I've actually felt his hands working on me. All these months, seeing but not feeling. I can't wait for what else may happen, but I'm gonna try to let it happen naturally. The less I lead, the better I think it'll be.

"Ohh, that feels good," Rhonda whisper. "Work a little higher, Kev... higher."

"Where? Here?" His hands slide up her ribs, fingers probing for knotted muscles and tender spots. Her arms snake out, fingers interlocking behind his neck. She draws his face under the hem of her top and into the delectable vale between two luscious mounds of flesh, smelling sweetly of fresh perspiration.

"Right there!"

"Rhonda! I said no..."

"I know," her voice husky, "but this is not... funny business. Aahhh!" As his lips, and then tongue develop a will of their own, reflexively exploring an already erect nipple.

Aahhh, echoes the blonde, sitting across the house. *It's me, Kevin. Make love to me... to us. You can love us both, darling.*

The moral battle lost, Kevin strips her of the tank top. Compunction and guilt are swept away at the thought that Jackee promised to be there, too.

Rhonda arches her back as he attacks her perfect breasts with his mouth. Fingers under his shirt lightly rake his broad back and sides with crimson nails, setting his skin afire. She peels away his t-shirt, drawing his face to hers, lips and tongues fencing, setting their hearts... all three of them... into jitterbug mode. Kevin slips an arm under hers shoulders, drawing the smooth heat of her lush flesh against his chest.

Oh God, oh God. I'm on fire. I need this. I really need this.

"Oh, God, Kev," the redhead's voice a throaty whisper. "I need this. I *really* need this."

He nuzzles her arc of her neck, sliding up to tease an ear, as she nips at his. Arching his back, he looks down at her, fumbling with the cord ties of his shorts. Jackee, clinging to the center of Rhonda's passion, is gasping, fraught with anticipation.

Finally, to be with him. To be with the man I really love. Can't leave this world without having made love to him.

"Ahh, Red. What are we doing here?"

"Just what it looks like," she mumbles, her lips and tongue venturing in circles over his lightly furred chest and iron-hard abs. Nimble hands are inside his shorts, sliding them down, long fingers working erotically across his rump. Her head comes up, her lips trapping his, their tongues exploring, his as ardently as hers. Struggling, he gains some separation.

"But why?" his voice a hoarse whisper. "Oh, baby, I want ya. God, how I want ya! I... I..." He shakes his head.

I love you, too, darling, Jackee thinks. *You can say it. Say it, Kevin! I know it's for me. Maybe for both of us.*

"Yer jeopardizing your goals. Ya got everything ya want right here. Why endanger that with a casual fling?" He arcs his neck, avoiding her questing mouth. Glistening golden eyes entrance amber ones, her tongue darting nervously across suddenly dry lips.

"I... I... Oh Christ, Kev. *Yes,* I'm marrying Phil, but... but, I... oh, dammit. I love *you!*"

"But, if you... if I..."

Kevin, just make love to us. Stop talking and do it. I can't wait...

"Just shut up, will you, and make love to me. I can't wait any longer." In a flash, she shed her shorts and his pants are discarded. Strong arms weld them together, their bodies intertwined in electric contact, all reservations blown away by the wind of their passion.

God, he's just as big as I imagined, both women think, as he enters them, Rhonda trapping him with sleek, long legs, and Jackee thrusting her mental body against his.

"Aaaaahhhhh!"

Aaaaahhhhh! Echoes in the blonde's motionless head, her face and body drenched with sweat.

"Sweet Jesus. I can't... I can't... Uuhhh..uuhhh."

Completion rushes upon them, almost before they started, so pent up were their passions.

"I'm so sorry, babe. I've wanted ya for so long, I just couldn't..."

"Me, too, Kev. Me, too. But we're not done. Not by a long shot." She snuggles into his arms, her hands again patrolling his sweat-glistened body. "Not by a very long shot."

They switch ends, their tongues and mouths again teasing each into flaming arousal.

"I love ya, Jackee. God, how I love ya," mumbled so softly that only the inert blonde, clear across the house, hears him.

So lucky to finally find a real man to adore and be adored by. Her eyes are emerald pools, tears trickling across no longer full cheeks. *And this is all I have, with so little time left. So unfair to find true love so late, and with no future. Gotta make the best of what left to me.*

And so they do...the three of them...for two more hours, all before Phil returns for the evening.

Our love is fulfilled as much as it will get. It's time to move into the last act of my play.

CHAPTER EIGHTY-FIVE

Judge Julius Halpern surveys the small crowd filling all the seats in his chambers, and sighs. He glances at his watch. The waning hours of Christmas Eve were clearly weighing on him. He had reluctantly agreed to this late hearing only after Osborn had played on his fond memory of Chester Webster. He looks up as the attorney finishes arranging his papers.

"I would like to thank your honor for taking the time to see us on this holiday eve." He sighs. "I know you are eager to get home to your family. I'll try to be as brief as possible.

"I presume you have had an opportunity to read the briefs I supplied you." The judge nods. Osborn clears his throat and begins.

"We have here Chester Webster's daughter, Jackee. Sadly, she has very little time left with us. She is lawfully wed to this man, Philip Maren. It is Mrs. Maren's dying wish that the following occur here today.

"One: the full and final dissolution of their marriage. Mr. Maren does not contest this, and there appears to be no issue relating to the sharing of property. Mrs. Maren's care will continue to be paid by her trust until her passing.

"Two: the remarriage of Mr. Maren to this young woman, Rhonda Armstrong. We'd like your Honor to perform a civil ceremony immediately after all the divorce papers are properly executed and witnessed.

"Thirdly, upon completion of their marriage, the new Mrs. Maren will adopt Jackee's two sons, Malcolm and Bryan." Osborn gestured toward the two boys, sitting beside their mother.

"As the Attorney in Fact for Mrs. Maren, I am prepared to sign all papers in her behalf, including releases on her sons, to allow for their adoption by the new Mrs. Maren."

The attorney places three stacks of papers on the desk. Removing steel-rimmed glasses, he folds them deliberately, placing them with careful precision in the breast pocket of his navy blue wool suit jacket. He sighs again, massaging the bridge of his aquiline nose, before continuing.

"Mrs. Maren can communicate only through the blinking of her eyes, in a sort of Morse Code. This gentleman, Mr. Kevin Martin, taught her this code and can interpret it, if you wish to question her. One blink stands for "yes," and two blinks are "no." Asking questions that she can respond to in that manner will save time and help keep from tiring her.

"I hope this is all clear. I've tried not to be too verbose, but I want to be sure you fully understand all of the issues before you this afternoon."

"Yes, Arthur. It seems pretty straight forward," the judge says. "Unusual, but straight to the point. May I ask why you chose this particular afternoon?"

"It was Mrs. Maren's request. She wants to make a happy holiday for everyone. Unfortunately, she *is* running out of time more quickly than anyone anticipated. Her primary concern is to see to her sons' future care with a real mother."

"So be it. Mrs. Maren, do you fully understand what Mr. Osborn is proposing?"

Beautiful green eyes blinks once.

"Mr. Osborn has pointed out all the ramifications of these actions, and their irreversibility? You're sure this is what you want?"

She blinks once more. Halpern sighs, clearly saddened by her plight.

"You agree to give up any legal claim to your sons so they can be adopted by the new Mrs. Maren and become legally hers?"

One blink.

"All right. Do the rest of you understand what's going on? You're all in full agreement? If you have any questions, now is the time. Anything?" The judge gazes around the silent room. Then he looks at the two small boys and smiles.

"You boys, Malcolm and Bryan. Do you understand that this lady, Miss Armstrong, will be your daddy's new wife, and also wants to be your Mommy? You will be as much her children then as you are your mother's (indicating Jackee) now. And she will be as responsible for you both, just as if you had come from inside of her. Do you understand?"

"Yes, sir," Malcolm stands, holding Bryan's hand.

"Rhonda's been very nice to us. She's already like another Mommy. We love our Mommy and we'll...we'll miss her." Tears wet his cheeks. "We'll miss her very much." He wipes his eyes on his sleeve.

"No one can ever take her place." He straightens his shoulders. "But she likes Rhonda, and we love her, too. We'll be proud to have her for our second Mommy." Tears bloom in both Jackee's and the redhead's eyes. What a moving speech by the mature little ten-year old.

"Well said, young man. So, it looks like all is in order, and everybody is in agreement. You can precede, Mr. Osborn."

"Thank you, your Honor," Arthur replies, as he started laying out papers in front of his clients and the judge for signatures. An hour later everything is finished, and all documents are signed, witnessed and notarized.

The new Mr. and Mrs. Philip Maren share a long, tender kiss on completing their marriage vows.

Each boy grasps one of Rhonda's hands as the adoption is formalized. Then Rhonda crouches before Jackee, taking one of her nerveless hands in hers.

"I know this wasn't easy for you, but Phil and I falling in love had no real bearing on what's happened to you. I understand your motives for doing this, and I want you to know that I've really come to love your...our sons. I'll care for them just as you would have. If you look down from Heaven...and I know that's where you'll be...I promise you'll be proud of us."

Jackee's eyes blink once, and then flutter a message. Malcolm takes Rhonda's hand, squeezing gently. Rhonda looks at him, eyes questioning.

"Mommy says, 'Thank you. Know you will do best.' I think she's happy."

Rhonda stands, smiling thinly. "I hope so. I really do."

She's jealous I'm still "Mommy" to them.

All the tasks Jackee arranged completed, everyone left the courthouse, each group going its own way. Kevin pauses for a moment to talk to the attorney, handing him a small packet before loading Jackee into the van for the trip to Glencoe. The two boys join them for one last ride with their mother.

The newlyweds leave for a celebration dinner at Maison LaFayette, while Osborn and the judge start for their respective homes.

Got it all done in time. A Merry Christmas for all...exactly as I planned.

CHAPTER EIGHTY-SIX

Got to conserve energy for one last party.

She's become weaker during the last month, and this is the second day she's aware of difficulty breathing. Jackee suspects the onset of pneumonia, maybe a delayed result from their abortive fishing trip.

She told no one.

Lights dimmed, she rests in bed, exhausted.

Thank God it all got done today. Another week may have been too late. Lucky I didn't have to participate much. Wanted to save myself for tonight.

One last party with the cheating bastard before the final act is played out. I only just realized this is how it might end. Just a few things left to tie up in this life.

As Kevin put her in bed, she asks him to stay and talk.

"Ya okay?"

"Yes. Must tell U thing."

"Sure. Go ahead."

"I luv U." Fourteen blinks, filled with magic.

"I...I know. And I love ya, too. Just like we talked about before."

"Yes, but made luv U with R."

"Ya *were* there? Like ya said ya might be?" His eyebrows rising, the hairs on his neck prickling.

"Yes. Every time." There were two reprises after that first erotic encounter, each more passionate than the last.

"Heard U say U luv me. Wonderful."

"Oh Jesus." Tears flood his eyes. He takes her bone-thin hand, kissing it, then holding it to his cheek.

"I've... I've loved ya almost from the first, but I never expected ya to feel the same for a big country ox like me. What good does it do... now?"

"Is okay. Important we know. I happy."

"Me too, my love, but now what am I supposed to do?"

"I gone soon. I know U luv R, too. U and R good."

"That's a laugh. The two women I love most in my life are both married to the same guy!"

"Things change. U and R good." She closes her eyes for a moment.

"I sleep now."

The big man brushes a silky golden wisp of hair from her face, and bending over, kisses her nerveless lips.

"Good night, my love."

"I luv U." Those incredible fourteen happy blinks from smiling eyes.

He leaves, mind swirling with unanswered questions.

CHAPTER EIGHTY-SEVEN

The nearly skeletal blonde dozes, awaiting the return of the new Maren couple. Tonight's amorous odyssey will surely be her last. Thank God Rhonda has unknowingly taught her the beauty of true physical love, and that she was able to share it with the one man they both really adore.

Jackee needs all her failing strength to be a full partner in making something very special from tonight's final erotic voyage.

Their conspiratorial laughter awakens her. Jackee glances at the clock: 11:10.

Good! Got some sleep. I'm fresh and ready to party.

Quelling a sudden case of nerves, she reaches for them.

One last hurrah.

Once in their bedroom, Rhonda's passion needs little stirring. With Jackee ensconced in her subconscious, the redhead begins a languorous striptease, emphasizing the "tease." Every time he reaches for her, she slips away, a ghostly nymph, expertly kindling frustrated arousal. He is quickly hard, panting and desperate to take her, but with Jackee's encouragement, Rhonda is not to be rushed.

Down to bikini panties and an unbuttoned silk blouse that plays peek-a-boo with her breasts, she tantalizes him, a wraith, eluding his grasp. His clothing disappears, one piece at a time, while her fingers, light as butterfly-wing, barely caress his chest. Her voluptuous body hovers near, only to slip away untouched, whipping him to a frenzy.

Panties and blouse discarded, she straddles him, pinning his arms to the bed. Her mouth and tongue venture across his face, teasing his lips, eyes, ears, throat... everything. Erect nipples torment his chest with feathery caresses as he strives to get to them.

Jackee, mentally writhing with flames of ardor, fights for her own control.

Gotta hang on. I only wish I was celebrating this final party with Kevin instead of my murderous husband. But this is it, and I gotta to run the show as long as possible, this one last time.

No longer able to restrain him, Phil breaks free, wild with lust, devouring her in a sensual attack, frantically kissing, stroking and licking, burying his face in the full, lilac-scented swell of her bosom, his tongue a busy voyager. Rhonda gasps for breath, fully ablaze, already on the verge of orgasm, but something holds her back.

Wait! Wait for one really big one, an inner voice cajoles her.

It'll be worth it. Wait! Panting, she fights for control.

Wave after wave of unbridled heat sweep her up in a riptide of erotic sensations. She yanks Phil into a sitting position, slipping onto his lap, her mouth seemingly everywhere at once. Entrapping him with her legs, they begin the ancient dance of love, their synergism, their molding together, a majestic mystery. Undulating, twisting, thrusting, their hands, mouths, tongues, all seeking the path to ecstasy.

They are discovering Nirvana.

The three of them!

With Jackee riding shotgun, Rhonda skillfully drives the coach of their ardor, checking her pace to hold him off, and then increasing it to bring him near, only to tantalizingly deny him again and again. Finally, drowning in sensory overload, Rhonda succumbs, frenetically hurtling her body against his, swamped by their pre-orgasmic throes. Soft growls, whimpers and muttered encouragement's echoed in the room.

Gasping for breath, unable to hold on any longer, Jackee relinquishes her last vestige of control, thrusting herself into the vortex of Rhonda's ecstasy.

Now! she screams at the top of her mental voice.

Now!!

The three of them thrash in a feral frenzy, their bodies slamming together, erupting with wondrous climaxes, their senses spinning dizzily into oblivion.

O-o-o-h-h! the blonde woman, alone in her bed, howls in her mind.

"Oh, Yes! Yes!" softly moans the redhead, clutching Phil tightly in her arms.

How wonderful! Rhonda muses. *This is everything I hoped for. Everything I've dreamed of for so long. It's my house, my money, my family, and the freedom to use it, just as I planned.*

Thank you, Lord, for fulfilling this dream.

Across the house, Jackee lies covered in perspiration, totally spent, the evening's exertions more than her already weakened body can handle.

Kevin discovers her the next morning, dull-eyed and somnolent, devastated to discover she's suffering from the onset of pneumonia. She used up the last of her meager reserves in that final foray into ecstasy.

"How did we miss this?" he laments to Maria and Rhonda, after the doctor leaves.

"C'mon, Kev," Rhonda says. "You know it probably wouldn't have mattered. She must have known she was sick, maybe even that it was pneumonia. Completing her mission yesterday was more important to her than her life. Be grateful she held out long enough to get what she wanted for her sons."

That she was right didn't lessen the pall hanging over him. Jackee is dying, his second love is married to an unprincipled louse, and Kevin is left wandering out in the cold.

Chapter Eighty-Eight

Jackee lingers for six days before fifteen months of silent suffering come to a peaceful end.

Ramparts of slate-gray clouds ominously darken the sky, casting down an icy drizzle. A proper setting for a funeral, with promises of worse to come.

Many mourners defy the weather to attend services at the chapel. Few, however, slog through freezing mud to the graveside. Phil and Rhonda stand silently, their large, colorful golf umbrella strangely out of place. The two boys, in boots and yellow slickers, cling to each other, crying.

Kevin, looking haggard, brought Maria and a tearful Charlene, all huddling together behind the family. Arthur Osborn and several officers from the bank are there, paying tribute to the last of the Websters. Miguel Gomez, shivering in a light jacket, holds a scraggly bunch of yellow flowers, his tears blending with the rain.

Condolences paid, the mourners scurry off to drier environs. Phil starts for the limo, but Rhonda and Kevin linger beside the gaping maw, hungrily waiting to devour the descending casket. Casting a small bouquet of pink roses after it, she turns to him, placing a hand on his heavily jacketed arm. Surprisingly, there are tears in her eyes.

"Don't move out right away, okay?" Her voice is soft, choked. "I really don't want to be home alone. It'd be nice having you around for a while, 'til things get back to normal."

The therapist's eyebrows arch, disappearing under his knit wool cap. This gorgeous woman continues to amaze him. He never expected her to react with such sorrow at the death of the woman she had plotted to supplant. His heart swells at her compassion. How was he cursed...and blessed... to love two such wonderful gals? Both unattainable, except for that brief fling.

"Sure." He smiles sadly, patting her hand. "Got no place special to go, and in no hurry to get there. Could use the company myself." This is surely the end of their amorous escapades.

"Thanks. See you later, then." She squeezes his arm lightly. With her back to her husband, waiting impatiently at the curb, she throws him a kiss. He shivers.

Kevin lingers by the open grave, watching her departure, his heart tumbling in his chest. Is there something else behind that invitation? As if she's waiting for something, and wants him there for... what? To continue their affair? No, that's just not right...no matter how wonderful. And Jackee's no longer there to share it.

He remembers Jackee's words, so often repeated...*insisted* upon... those last few weeks.

"U and R good."

He draws several slow, deep breaths. The cold air chills him, bringing a shiver.

Can't happen again! But how is it she is married to Phil when they'd shared so much together? Oh well, he'll remain at the house for a while, relishing the idea of being near this beautiful and somehow changed woman, whom he has also learned to love.

Miguel Gomez approaches timidly. Kevin smiles through his tears.

"Miguel. It's nice you could come. Jackee would have liked that."

"How could I stay away. I promised to make her proud, but I will miss her so very much.

"So will I, my friend. So will I."

"What am I gonna... going to do now, without her to... to guide me? She changed my life." He spoke slowly, carefully enunciating each word.

"She hasn't stopped, son. Her attorney, Mr. Osborn, will handle your college scholarship. Jackee asked him to take over as your mentor." Kevin squeezes his shoulder reassuringly, handing him Osborn's card. "He wants you to call him next week."

"So you see, she's still taking care of everyone," he says. Miguel nods, his eyes pooling, and pockets the card. They hug, and the boy left.

Kevin kneels at the grave for one final good-bye. What an exceptional gal, seeing to everything before she died. He sighs at the emptiness in his heart.

But he doesn't realize exactly how well Jackee really *is* taking care of everyone.

Especially Phil.

CHAPTER EIGHTY-NINE

"What in the Hell am I doing here."

Phil studied the stark landscape through his car window, unwilling to move. Thick, winter-browned grass, peppered by barren maple and oak trees, spread as far has he could see.

He sighed, stepping out of his Corvette into the cold, sunny day.

Must be kind of pretty in Spring...if you're not superstitious.

"I'm here, so I might as well do it," he muttered. "Don't know why I feel so damned compelled to say 'good-bye'."

Zipping up his jacket against the chilly January wind, he weaved among the headstones, crossing the frozen lawn, crunching under his feet like dry straw. The sound ignited a memory of sauntering through the barn as teenagers, with Jackee brushing down Apache after a successful ride. He smiled softly. Those were good times...but this is better. A lot better.

Two minutes later he was standing in front of her grave. Only three days, so the headstone hadn't been set. There was a marker there, though. A wilted bunch of yellow flowers the Puerto Rican kid had brought sat in a small stone vase. Chin against his chest, hands in the pockets of his heavy jacket, he stood there, smiling softly.

"Well, Jackee, here you are, finally. I gotta give you credit. You were tough. I kept trying to hurry this along, but you always survived.

"I was thinking about our years together, trying to figure it out. I guess I did love you in the beginning, but you were so good... so damned *perfect*. And your father...he treated you like the damned "countess" he called you. You guys loved each other so much! Jesus! What kind of family is that? Maybe I was jealous, but it got to be too much.

"Then the old bastard cut me out of his will! That was when I knew it was the money. The money... and the right kind of woman to share it with.

"So it's finished. You're in the ground, and I'm up here with Rhonda, and all the Webster dough. Just like I planned!

"So, good-bye, Jackee... and good riddance. I paid my dues for twelve years, and things eventually worked out...with some help from me. I've finally got everything I deserve."

Phil turned to leave, filled with relief. This had been a catharsis, clearing his conscience. It was finally over. He could move on, thrusting aside any slight threads of guilt, to the life he had yearned for.

Heading to his car, he saw three men walking briskly toward him. Was that Osborn?

Yeah. What's he doing here?

"Mr. Maren," the attorney called.

"Hi, Arthur. What brings you out here?"

Why hadn't he made an appointment at the office? Uneasiness clawed at Phil's chest when his proffered handshake was ignored. The man didn't like him, but what could the pompous bastard possibly do? With Jackee gone, Phil was bulletproof. His forced smile evaporated under the grim stare of the older man.

"Your secretary told us you were here. We deferred until today out of deference to Jackee, but decided not to wait any longer."

"This couldn't be done at the office? If you want to talk, let's find some place warm. Coffee, maybe?"

Hummingbird wings circled in his stomach. Osborn wouldn't chase him way out here half-cocked. He had something serious in mind. The other two were tough guys, cops or private dicks... not a good omen. A look of disgust creased the attorney face.

"This isn't a social call. As Executor of the Webster estate, I ran a detailed audit of the accounts right after Christmas. Should have done it years ago, but I never expected thievery. I cannot forgive myself for such laggard behavior."

Phil had to force himself to breathe. What did this old dog have in his craw? It'd all be his anyway, once they read the will.

"You did a credible job of hiding the excesses spent from the three trusts over the past several years. Much more than was required to support your family's lifestyle, especially in light of your $250,000 annual salary."

"Hold on." Phil's face flushed. "We... we could spend that money as we saw fit. That was part of the Declaration of Trust."

"*Not* exactly. Trust income is available to meet any *additional* expenses for the expected life-style of the family. That presupposes that you will first live off your salary."

"Yeah. So?"

"With a court order, we have examined your family accounts and find, strangely, that not a single payroll check of yours was ever deposited in any of them since Chester Webster's death. Not one in *four years*, sir!" Osborn paused, raking Phil with a contemptuous stare.

"Nor do family expenses, under *any* legal interpretation, include payments of nearly one hundred thousand dollars a year for a Lake Shore Drive apartment, a Jaguar automobile, and living expenses for your mistress!

"The board of directors of North Chicago have been provided data regarding your past relationship with Miss Armstrong while she was your secretary. They have considerable concern about any improprieties that may have occurred." Frozen vapor from Osborn's breath seemed to frame his words.

Phil glared at the older man.

He's trying to ruin me. Jackee's gone, and this old buzzard's looking for revenge. Phil stamped his feet, but the chill permeating him had little to do with the temperature. Unhappily, the lawyer was apparently just getting wound up.

"This is bullshit!" he snarled. "There's nothing you can do..."

"Quite the contrary, sir. I've just gotten started."

Phil found himself holding his breath again.

"In addition to all that, the Webster trusts were not established so you might fraudulently feather your bank account in the Cayman Islands, to the tune of several hundred thousand dollars per year."

Phil flinched, his gloved hand going to the corner of his left eye, which developed a prominent tick. How could they know? Those were secret accounts, like Switzerland. This was starting to look ugly. Osborn's smile wasn't pleasant.

"These so-called secret accounts, under recent international banking agreements, can be opened to law enforcement agencies of a friendly government if they are the product of criminal activities."

"What the Hell are you talking..."

"Fraud *is* a crime," Osborn interrupted. "You had a fiduciary responsibility to the estate, a trust you blatantly disregarded, to the tune of something well in excess of one million dollars. I intend to see you punished for it." Phil stood in bleak silence, avoiding his eyes. He started to shake, anger flushing him.

"Screw you, Arthur. I'm outta here. See my *new* attorney. I'll get you replaced as executor, too." He pushed past the older man, but was quickly blocked by his two large companions.

Osborn's leonine face cracked with a thin, cold smile.

"We're not quite done."

The dapper lawyer riveted him with his gaze for what seemed an eternity, before finally turning toward his two companions

"These gentlemen are policemen. Lieutenant O'Brien is here on the behalf of the Webster Estate to press charges against you for fraud.

"This other gentleman, Detective Edwards, has more serious matter to discuss with you."

Phil was already spinning into a steep nose-dive. What *else* could they come up with? Even if he ducked jail time, this was sure to cost him his job, and finding a new one wouldn't be easy. The "word" would be out. No need to worry about a job if he were in prison, but fraud *was* white-collar crime. That usually meant light sentences and easy time. He didn't really *need* to work. The trusts provided more income than even he could spend.

The burly detective perched a pair of half-frame glasses on his considerable nose and flipped open a small notebook.

"Mr. Maren," he began, "we've reopened the investigation into the events leading to the incapacitating of your first wife, Jackee Webster Maren. Both the auto accident and then her paralysis stemming from the surgery. The latter seemed the results of the statistical chance one takes, going under the knife.

"The auto accident was a stinker from the start, but I never found enough conclusive evidence to go any further. Shoddy work on my part. I didn't dig deep enough to discover your long-standing relationship with your new wife. Certainly a common motive for murder...a beautiful, younger woman, and your wife's fortune."

Phil glared at the man. He wasn't going to let that bastard coerce him into saying something foolish. The policeman continued.

"I've conducted a more complete investigation of the so-called surgical accident. You failed to list on her admittance forms your wife's taking of barbiturates prior to the surgery. Handwriting analysis confirms it *was* you who completed those forms. Under the section requesting information about use of other drugs, you wrote 'N/A'."

"I forgot, that's all." Phil, chin lowered to his chest, avoided eye contact with the detective, who had raised a hand in the "stop" position.

"Mr. Maren, please don't respond until we've read you your rights." He flipped a page in his notebook.

"Now it seems highly unlikely you *could* have forgotten such a thing. Your maid, Miss Charlene Adams," he glanced at his notes, "will testify she clearly remembers you insisting your wife take two tranquilizers the morning of the surgery to 'calm her nerves'."

"So what's the charge? Filling out a form wrong?" Phil refused to return the man's stare. His ticking eyelid was doing the jitterbug.

"No sir. You're being charged with attempted murder."

"*What*! You're kidding!"

"We don't kid about murder. The D.A. is reviewing case law to see if, now that your first wife has died, we should upgrade the charge to Murder in the First Degree. That's a capital crime in this state.

"*Now*, I would like to advise you of your rights. You have the right to remain silent..."

Phil stood, frozen, his veins filled with liquid nitrogen. He couldn't move. He couldn't think. He couldn't breathe. Nothing worked. Then he began to shake, fired now by bitter flames of anger.

The blonde bitch was still trying to get him, even from her stinking grave. She hated him! It was really all *her* fault. She was always so prissy and sweet, and certainly no damned good in the sack. And *she* had the Goddammed money. *His* money! Any guy with balls would have killed her, even without someone like Rhonda waiting for him.

He'd show them. He'd get the best criminal attorney in the country. He could afford it himself, but the trusts would pay. That ought to really burn Osborn!

The detective finished reading from his card as Lieutenant O'Brien pulled Phil arms behind him and started to cuff him. Arthur Osborn stepped forward, looking every bit the Grim Reaper.

"All of your foreign accounts have been frozen. We have instituted actions to return those funds to the Webster trusts.

"Hey, you can't do that! It's my money. Those are private..."

"Oh, and where did it come from? Well over a million dollars? Certainly not from your salary."

"I... it... oh, forget it." Furious, his face red as a beet, Phil stammered to a stop. Stupid! He'd have to confess to stealing from the trusts to claim that money.

Stupid! Stupid! No way to do that without putting his feet in buckets of concrete and jumping off the bridge himself.

The two cops scribbled in their notebooks as Osborn, looking amused, continued.

"You apparently have few funds in your own name here. The court will appoint a Public Defender for you, if you wish."

"Bull shit! You're not going to make a patsy out of *me*, Osborn. I can still hire the best guy there is. The trusts will pay. How *that* for irony?"

"Apparently you don't understand those documents as well as you think. Two trusts are in your sons' names. The specific language, added by Mr. Webster before his death, requires them to be managed by the boys' *mother*, solely for their benefit. Certainly not to defend their father from charges of killing their biological mother."

"What? But you said..."

"That there have been no modifications since Mr. Webster's death? That's true. These changes were done before he died. I offered you an opportunity to examine them and you declined. I don't believe Chester Webster ever trusted you. I wonder why?" The attorney gave a mirthless chuckle.

"Mr. Webster also amended Jackee's trusts. In case of her death, her sons' new legal mother, whoever she may be, would inherit control. If there were no mother, than their legal guardian. But they *do* have a mother. Rhonda now controls *all* of the Webster estate, provided she follows the trusts' guidelines."

"Thank God." The first good news of the day.

"She'll pay for my defense."

"Don't be so sure. I've recently learned of your wife's background from Mr. Martin. She has managed, with considerable will and courage, to raise herself above her squalid upbringing. It might be expected she would seek a wealthy man to provide her all she longed for...someone exactly like you. A woman, coming from where she has will often make that commitment without love.

"Rhonda *does* seem like fine young lady, and you provided her the mythical brass ring. Now she owns it, all by herself. Maybe she does love you. Even so, when she hears everything, she may decide to distance herself. You've become superfluous to her needs."

How the Hell does the old bastard know all this shit?

His face beet-red, his twitching eye-lid doing sixty, Phil was about to explode. He wanted to slug the older man. Stuff his fist clear down his throat. Not possible, with his hands shackled behind his back. The lawyer bore on, taking obvious pleasure in the task.

"Frankly, I'll suggest she petition the court for an annulment of your marriage, due to your unsavory character and criminal activity. She will still be the boys' legal mother. If she still wishes to support you, I will contest any use of the trusts' money for your defense. I suspect she will seriously consider my advice."

"This is all Jackee's doing," he screamed. A throbbing vein on his forehead joined in tempo with the ticking eyelid.

"I don't know what you're talking about." A Cheshire-cat smile and steely-hard eyes regarded the younger man.

"How could that sweet, helpless woman have *caused* anything, although I am sure she would have some satisfaction with the results."

"You *bastard*! She did it, somehow. Screwed me and set the kids up with Rhonda. Maybe they planned it together. But I've got a monkey wrench to throw into their little machine."

"Oh?"

"Yeah. You'll have to find the kids *another* new mother."

"And why is that? Rhonda seems quite capable."

"Because if that bitch tries to dump me, she'll be in the same stew as me."

"If you're referring to some past conversation regarding a plot to kill your wife, we've already heard it from her. The police have discounted it as idle talk. There is no evidence Rhonda was in any way involved.

"No. Rhonda will not be charged. If necessary, she will be granted immunity to testify. She *will* be interested in knowing how steadfastly you stood in support of her innocence."

Phil sagged, knees buckling, his adrenaline rush spent, the last of his energy sluicing away. Head drooping, shoulders slumped, he was dragged stumbling toward a waiting police car.

His fairy-tale world has tumbled down around him, catching him in a sticky the web of his own design. Now it was Phil who was.....

Trapped!

CHAPTER NINETY

Rhonda Armstrong Maren met Arthur Osborn at the front door of her new home. He had called, briefly informing her of the charges against Phil, wanting to discuss the matter in person.

The conference with his newest, and definitely most beautiful client, lasted over an hour. She sat in pensive quiet for nearly a minute after he finished, before turning her gaze on him. He shivered imperceptibly with strange anticipation. Even an old fool was not impervious to her beauty.

"Frankly, Arthur," she said, "I was having second thoughts, even prior to the wedding. All his talk about somehow getting rid of Jackee? Jesus! I thought it was only that... *talk*. He actually tried to involve *me* with his plots? Unbelievable!" Coppery locks swirled with an imperious toss of her head.

"Boy, he had *me* fooled. Blinded by love, the same as poor Jackee before me. But it's over now. I don't want to have anything more to do with him. Love is too fragile to be treated so hatefully." She fidgeted for a moment, studying her hands. Looking up, her tawny eyes were filled with uncertainty.

"If I get an annulment, will that change the inheritance in any way? Tie up my sons' trusts? They're wonderful little boys. I've grown to love them very much."

"There's nothing to worry about. Divorce or an annulment won't affect their adoption and your subsequent control of the three trusts. I drew them myself, and the language is clear and unassailable. You *are* their mother, my dear, whether married to Phil or not. All the Webster trusts are in your hands now. Use them wisely."

"Oh, I will, Arthur. I will." She smiled.

So, the young woman from the Kentucky hills became caretaker and mother of two handsome little boys, and the sole mistress of a vast fortune.

Exactly as Jackee planned!

Rhonda lingered in the dimly lit den... Jackee's den...after the attorney departed, gazing at the frozen yard, lightly dusted with new snow. Osborn had confided to her that Kevin Martin gave him two envelopes as they left the courthouse on Christmas Eve. These contained messages from Jackee with the detailed information responsible for Phil's downfall. Arthur was impressed that, despite her incapacitates, Jackee still managed to bring justice to her cheating, murderous husband.

Rhonda smiled, stretching languorously. All of Phil's planning and intrigue had come to nothing. On the other hand, *she* had almost everything she had wished for.

Only a few things left to do...

CHAPTER NINETY-ONE

Kevin eased into the family room, finding Rhonda settled in an easy chair near the French doors, staring out at the snow-covered yard. She's demurely dressed in a beige pleated skirt and flowered sleeveless silk blouse

"Ya okay?" he asked.

"Yes, I guess. Just thinking about how things have shaken out. You know I've asked Mr. Osborn to file for an annulment of my marriage?"

He studied her, then nodded, plumbing those magnetic golden eyes.

Sighing, she shrugs, giving a small, dismissal shake of her head, causing a swirling russet cloud of hair.

"Phil's a liar, a cheat, and unbelievably, attempted murder... more than once! Rhonda Armstrong... Maren... whatever... can't love someone like that. That's over." She popped up, prowling around the room, arms clasped across her breasts.

"Got the boys to take care of. My sons! How beautiful. Don't know how to handle the name. They're Marens, after all, but I won't be one very long. Maybe hyphenated. 'Armstrong-Maren'? How does that sound?"

He rises, catching her by the elbows, stopping her restless meandering. They eyes lock, and his tongue sweeps across his upper lip.

"Whatever makes ya comfortable sounds right. Ya got the boys well-being to consider. I heard Osborn tell ya the annulment won't affect any of that."

"Yeah," she nods. "They'll still be my sons, thank God. And I've got all the trusts to use for their benefits. But what am I going to tell them about their father? I don't think there was any real bond there, but, my God, he tried to kill their mother. Can they ever accept that?"

"It ain't gonna be easy, but they're smart kids." He folds her gently into his arms, her head settling on his shoulder. "Ya'll figure a way to ease it in. I can see they trust ya."

"Yeah, Rhonda the interloper. I hope you're right.

"And then there's us...you and me," she says.

"Yeah. Us." His hands caress her back, savoring her touch and smell. "What about us? Ya know how I feel."

"Yes. And I think you know I feel the same." She kisses him lightly on the ear, then the cheek, as they separate. "But we've gotta take it slow for now. Mal and Bry have lost their mother, and now their father's going to prison. Us being together so soon might be a little too much."

"So this is it?" His voice a hoarse whisper. "The end?"

"Oh no, darling. No!" She takes his face in her hands, kissing him lightly on the mouth.

"This is only the *beginning*. I love you, Kevin. I told you that, even before...before..." She looked away for a moment, sighing, then straightened her spine, staring into his amber eyes.

"We're going to be together. Soon. Just not right now, not until I get the boys settled into this new life. In fact, I've got a wonderful surprise for you. Maybe a wedding gift, if you think we might..."

"Oh, yes. I've couldn't want anything more right now."

"Wonderful," she grinned. "Not exactly a romantic, on one knee proposal, but I love it just the same. It won't be long. I promise. I think I'll save the surprise until that day. It's something you always wanted."

"Gettin' Pappy off the farm in 'Bama?"

"You'll see. You're a good guesser, but you don't want to spoil it, do you?"

"Yer something else," he laughed. "So, now what?"

"So, now I have to work out how to tell the boys some part of the truth about their dad. I hope you'll stay on. You can move into Jackee's old room, but I think we have to cool it...you know, the physical stuff...for a while. I *do* think they'll be thrilled in having you for a step-dad, though. You showed them more love and affection than I think Phil ever did."

"Okay," he shrugged. "Yer the boss. I guess a little longer can't hurt. Anticipation'll make everything sweeter in the end. Gonna be kinda strange, sleeping in *her* bedroom, though."

He draws her into his arms, savoring the warmth and firmness of her against him, their lips meeting, a kiss more of tender love than raging passion. The fingers of one of her hands tangle in his curly, dark hair, the other caressing the back of his neck. He draws back slightly, his thumb stroking her cheek, their eyes linked. He sighs.

"Guess I'd better move my stuff down and get settled. Maybe help ya figure what to say to the boys."

She watches his depart, a small smile twitching at her lips.

CHAPTER NINETY-TWO

It is Saturday, with no school, when Malcolm and Bryan arrive in the family room, summoned by Rhonda. They settle on the hardwood floor, almost exactly where they sat when she first discussed their adoption, many months before. More carefully dressed nowadays, she's wearing a denim middy skirt and long-sleeve plaid flannel shirt, the tails knotted around her midriff. Mal and Rhonda sit cross-legged, facing each other, while Bryan lay on his side, head propped on one arm. Kevin is perched at the small desk by the window, supposedly working at his computer. He's really there for moral support, and to see how things go.

Rhonda's gaze sweeps from one to the other, her hands folded in her lap.

"It's time we have a talk, now that things are settled down some." Two blonde heads nod.

"We need to talk about your father. Explain what happened. Explain why he's not here anymore."

"He's never coming back, is he?" Malcolm asks.

"No, darling. He's never coming back. How do you guys feel about that?"

"He's... he's our daddy, but... but..." Bryan stumbles to a halt, looking at his big brother.

"Is it terrible that we don't really miss him?" Mal asks. "He's our dad, but he wasn't around much for a long time. Our friends' dads play ball with them, help with homework, read stories...or go fishing." The both glance at the big therapist, across the room. He smiles softly.

"Dad was always too busy. Kevin did more things with us than he ever did," Bry says.

"You're probably right." The redhead smiles, ruffling both blonde heads. "Kevin would make a pretty terrific dad, wouldn't he?" They're all looking at him now, watching him blush.

"Although your dad and I got married last year, in front of that nice judge, Mr. Osborn is asking that same judge to sort of cancel the marriage. It's call and annulment."

"Is it because daddy did a bad thing?"

"Yes, Bryan. A very bad thing."

"He tried to kill mommy, didn't he?" Malcolm's voice is choked, his eyes downcast.

"That's what the police say, honey. He'll have to go to court and have a trial. If a jury agrees with the police, which seem pretty likely, he'll go away for a very long time. Maybe forever. But I'm your mom now, and I promise to take very good care of you. And Kevin's going to stay and help."

"Are you and Kevin gonna get married?" Mal's eyes are wide. She burst out laughing, and Kevin can't contain a hearty chuckle.

"Why? D'ya thinks that's a good idea?" She wipes tears from her eyes.

"That'd be real cool. We'd all be a real family then. Right, Bry?"

"Yeah. Cool. I'd like Kevin for my dad."

"Well, we'll see about that. I gotta admit, Kevin's a pretty terrific guy."

His face now tomato red, Kevin lurches up, closing his laptop.

"I'd better find someplace else to work. This is getting kinda embarrassing. I'll be in my room if ya need me."

They watch him hurry off, then Rhonda turns back to her new sons. She winks.

"There something else we need to talk about, so you understand everything. Stuff we should have discussed earlier, but with so much going on, and this trouble with your dad, I was waiting for the right time. It's pretty complicated." The all settled back on the floor, giving her rapt attention.

"Here's the thing..."

The two boys sit, eyes wide, mouths open, as they listen to what Rhonda has to say.

CHAPTER NINETY-THREE

Spring arrived in a rush, with mostly mild sunny, and occasionally, rainy days. Malcolm and Bryan are busy with classes and the beginning of intermural baseball at Central School.

Kevin acquired two new therapy clients. Both are professional athletes, one a relief pitcher with the Cubs, and the other a wide receiver for the Bears. Still, he sets aside time to work with the two little boys on hitting and fielding. They're eager to try out for the school teams, so he's polishing their skills.

Rhonda's annulment was finalized in early March, and with nothing but time on her hands, she returned to teaching aerobics three days a week. Then she set out to take over Jackee's position as chairperson for the Northern Illinois United Way chapter. There was some doubt at first from local members, but she slipped into that role so naturally and effectively, that all doubts were quickly doused.

The redhead also helped Osborn with the mentoring of Miguel Gomez. Her own troubled childhood was all the impetus she needed to see this young man got every opportunity to raise above his dysfunctional surroundings.

Kevin... and Osborn... were pleasantly surprised at this young woman's maturation and restraint. Her control of the massive Webster wealth had not sent her on a wild spending spree.

Instead, as a wealthy heiress, she was becoming a responsible member of the community. And she set aside plenty of time with her new sons. She played games with them, helped with homework, went on week-end picnics, and attended school functions...all the things Jackee did before her.

"Looks like ya acclimated to this life, like a fish in water," Kevin said, one spring day. They just finished lunch and were nursing the last of their coffee.

"I guess. Lots of responsibility seems to come with so much wealth."

"Yeah, but the nice things is, ya've accepted it, rather than just trying' ta spend your way through it. I guess I shouldn't be surprised, but I'm betting' a lot of people are."

"Well, looking for the proverbial 'brass ring' doesn't automatically make you irresponsible. I'm enjoying doing good thing for people, and I'm really relishing being a family with the boys... and you."

"That's nice to hear." He rose, swiveling her chair to face him, fishing something from a pocket.

"So, maybe it's time for this, then." He takes her hand, dropping to one knee.

"The on-the-knee proposal, Kevin?" Her smile lit the room.

"Yep. Decided I gotta do it proper, and now seems a good time." A small grey felt-covered box appeared in his hand. He popped open the lid, displaying a simple emerald-cut diamond ring, probably less than a half-carat.

"This may not seem like much of a ring for a rich gal, but it was my ma's, and her ma's before that.

"Rhonda Armstrong-Maren, will ya do me the honor of adding Martin to that string of names?"

"No." She shook her head, those twenty-four carat eyes burrowing into his.

"No?" His lips draw into a disappointed frown.

"No," she repeated, grinning impishly.

"Not to a string of names. I'll be proud to be just 'Rhonda Martin.' Finally cut the ties to that messy past. Maybe Mr. Osborn can arrange for you to adopt the boys, and they can become Martins, too, if they wish. We'll leave that up to them, but I'm guessing they'll be thrilled to be your official sons. That may be doable, with Phil in prison"

"I love ya. More'n I ever thought possible." He slipped the ring on the third finger of her left hand and pulled her from the chair.

The kiss they share is so much more than passion.

"I feel the same. Never thought I could love anyone like this. I've got one thing to ask, though. I hope you'll understand." She caresses his cheek, setting him to trembling.

"Anything."

"We can be married in June, but I still want to keep it... restrained... til then."

"Restrained?"

"Yes. No sex. I know that may seem strange, with me having been Phil's mistress in this house. And maybe that's why. I don't want my sons...*our* sons..." she reaches up, kissing him tenderly on the lips, "...to go through that again. I know this is different, but it'll only be a few months. Can you do this?"

"Sure. Gonna be tough, but I've practiced a lot of abstinence most of my life, so I guess a couple more months won't be more than a little unbearable." He winked at her.

"It's going to be tougher on me. One thing Rhonda Armstrong never did was practice abstinence. But Rhonda Armstrong-Maren is a different person, and this will be best for everyone in the end."

"Okay. It's a deal."

"Good. Let's tell the boys this afternoon. I think they're going to be really excited. And now I've got a wedding to plan."

"Gonna need any help?"

"Nope. This is something I can do by myself. All you gotta do is show up. You'd better be there on time, buster." She pats him lightly on the butt.

"Count on it. Wouldn't miss it for anything. And as I remember, you promised me a surprise."

"I did, didn't I?"

"Pappy?" Kevin asked.

"You'll see. I think you'll be happy."

Grinning gleefully, she hurried from the room.

Kevin watched her whirlwind departure, his heart pummeling his breast. What a miracle the winds of Fate brought him to this totally unexpected point in his life.

And he's finally getting his father away from what amounts to indentured servitude from that worn out scrap of land in Alabama somebody calls a farm.

Life is, indeed, grand.

EPILOGUE

This early June Sunday dawns on a balmy breeze. The fickle Gods controlling the whimsical Chicagoland weather have provided a perfect day for a wedding.

Guests crowding into the stately old suburban church are a disparate lot. Sleek, young athletes mingle with medical professionals, ranging from hospital administrators to nurses and aides. Aerobic and physical fitness trainers commandeer the second row, while socialites from Chicago and the North Shore arrange their seating by some strange pecking order only they understand.

And there is the media, looking for new blood in the culminating murder trial of handsome ex-millionaire, Phil Maren. On Monday, the judge will give final instructions to the jury before they began deliberation. But this marriage is happening today, regardless of that verdict.

Music fills the sanctuary and the crowd hushes. A large, powerfully built man, handsomely dressed in a white tuxedo, enters from one side and stands by the alter, gazing down the aisle. His face, scarred and crooked-nosed, creases with a whimsical smile.

Intelligent dark eyes twinkle merrily under ridged, bushy eyebrows.

Kevin fidgets, awaiting the chords that will announce the procession, and the ultimate arrival of his new love. Gazing over the crowd, he reflects on the chain of events bringing him here this day... an unbelievable miracle, beyond his wildest dreams.

First Jackee, whom he'd inexplicably grown to love, despite never even hearing her voice...except maybe once at the end. She said she couldn't actually talk to him, but those words spiraling through his head had to be hers. Loving her was an impossible dream, except for the miracle that she, in turn, loved *him*! She told him so with fourteen blinks of her eyes, and at the very end, with her trust.

That this remarkable woman encouraged his growing affection toward his bride-to-be is just as unfathomable. How did the most gorgeous and exciting woman he had ever known come to love a big ox like himself?

Rhonda, of the burnished copper tresses and molten hazel eyes!

The second Mrs. Maren is about to become his wife. She entered his life as the interloper, mistress to the callous husband of the woman who had already enchanted him. Soon though, she seemed less a challenge to Jackee, and more a friend and kindred spirit to him.

Their relationship developed a warmth transcending friendship, each unable to stem a blooming but unspoken love. It just happened! There were those few erotic encounters...before, but they never again shared that ultimate intimacy after Phil imploded and their marriage dissolved.

In spite of Jackee's urgings, "U and R good," he'd never sustained a moment's hope of ever winning Rhonda. How could she turn away from all the money, and the commitments she'd made to the children?

But then Phil's deceitful house of cards collapsed, precipitated by two envelopes he handed to Arthur Osborn on the courthouse steps on Christmas Eve.

Kevin recalls, rather uneasily, the events of December 23, the day before they all gathered in the judge's chambers. Jackee asked him to write some messages to Osborn, but the thoughts were long and arduous for eye-blinking. Pausing for a moment, obviously exasperated, she studied him, a strange intensity in her eyes. Then she blinked a new message.

"L'st'n your mind. Write." It was a moment before he realized what she wanted. Then, frighteningly, words began rushing through his head, as if plugged in to someone else's brain. They came to him in his colloquial voice, but they certainly were *not* his thoughts.

Arthur Osborn must do an extensive audit of the trusts. Phil has been skimming money into a secret account in the Cayman Islands. Kevin blinked.

The Cayman Islands?

He should ask the police to reopen the investigation of Jackee's auto and surgical accidents. Phil planned it all, and by not telling the hospital about the sedatives he pushed on her, attempted to kill her. They should talk to Charlene about events the morning of the surgery.

He knew where all this was coming from, but still sat transfixed, mouth agape.

Investigate his past relationship with Rhonda Armstrong, who was an innocent pawn, as motives for murder. The Company might find interesting their several years affair while she was first Mr. Charles' and then Phil's secretary.

He sat there for a moment, mind totally blank, stunned by what had passed through his head. He looked at Jackee, eyebrows raised.

"Write," she blinked to him. She sent him these thought, as she had suggested was possible, just a few weeks before. But if she could do *this*, why rely on the difficult eye-code? She refused to discuss it with him.

He wrote down what could only be *her* words, sealing them in the two separate envelopes which he delivered the next day. That led to why he is standing here today.

Jackee's final signal to him before going to bed that Christmas Eve was, "I love U."

Fourteen treasured little opening and closing of her eyes. His own teared at the memory.

She was never strong enough to communicate again, after that night.

◆ ❖ ◆

Kevin stirs from his reverie by the beginning strains of *Here Comes the Bride*. His heart pounds, and he blushes with guilt. He has a fleeting vision of Jackee.

No, he *does* love Rhonda. Jackee was the first, but Rhonda and he are probably better suited, both coming from simple Southern beginnings.

The ushers, athletes he'd helped rehabilitate, and the bridesmaids, aerobics instructor friends of Rhonda, parade down the aisle. Seldom has any seen a more physically striking bridal party. They are followed by Kevin's father, 6'3" and at sixty-eight, still broad shouldered and straight backed, looking distinguished and proud as best man.

No one guesses he is still a poor Alabama sharecropper. Well, that change is surely Rhonda's surprise. On his arm is the Matron of Honor, Rhonda's widowed mother. Even at forty-nine, there's no doubt where the bride inherited her looks.

The two parents smile shyly at each other.

The music breaks into a drum roll, as Malcolm and Bryan appear, adorable in little white tuxedos, each carrying white satin pillows on which nestle the two gold bands destined to join this unlikely couple.

Finally, to the renewed strains of the traditional march, Rhonda materializes, luminous in gossamer white silk and lace. A murmur ripples through the crowd. Morning sunlight, streaming through a leaded glass window, bathes her in a radiant glow, shimmering like an angel.

She pauses, smiling brilliantly, and then, on the elegant arm of Arthur Osborn, proceeds slowly down the aisle to join Kevin in front of the alter. His heart swells so, he's afraid it will burst from his chest.

The ceremony is all a blur to the big man. He still can't grasp how his life has changed. His eyes feast on her. She grins, winking slyly. Finally, the minister completes the nuptials with the familiar phrase, "You may kiss the bride."

He sweeps his new wife into powerful arms, holding her close, relishing the promise of her lips, the heat of her body against him. Whistles and applause erupted from their friends. Separating slightly from the lingering kiss, he is swallowed by her hazel eyes. Her smile sends goose bumps racing up his back.

Then her eyelids began to flutter, and for a moment he fears she's about to faint. Her finger traces the line of his jaw, and sudden realization thunders over him, as her eyes blink again, fourteen irregular times.

Those magic words!

"I luv U."

Stunned, he stands frozen.

"Rhonda!" He sucks in a short, sharp breath.

"Yes, my love?"

Her mouth twitches into a whimsical smile. He searches her face, his bushy eyebrows arched.

"You never... how did... when did you... learn Jackee's code?"

"Twenty months ago," she whispers. Magnetic eyes of molten gold hold his.

"Twenty months? I didn't even know you then. I never... how...?"

"Yes! *You* taught me."

A chill races down his spine, his voice choked to a hoarse whisper.

"*Me!* No, I never... you weren't interested. I only taught... Wait! Are you telling me...?

She nods, her eyes devouring him. Kevin gulps, licking his lips before squeaking out a single word.

"Jackee!?"

She smiles seductively up at him.

Her eyes blink once.

"Surprise!"

The kiss is indescribable.

About The Author

George A Bernstein is the retired President of a Chicago company, now living in south Florida. "Trapped" is his first novel, and was TAG Publisher's contest winner, as "The Next Great American Novel." It has received high praise, gaining mostly 5-star reviews at Amazon & Goodreads, and is currently republished by GnD Publishing. His 2nd novel, "A 3rd Time to Die," recently published by GnD, is also gathering all 5 & 4-Star reviews, with high praise for the author's writing style and "voice."

George is now preparing for publication the first of his two Detective Al Warner (in the vein of Patterson's Alex Cross) suspense novels, that will debut in early 2014.

He's also a "World-class" fly-fisherman, having held a dozen IGFA World Records, and has published "Toothy Critters Love Flies" (www.pikeflyguy.com), the definitive book on fly-fishing for pike & musky.

Feel free to visit George at: http://www.suspenseguy.com.

If you enjoyed this book...

George A Bernstein's second novel, *A 3rd Time to Die*, is widely acclaimed, with loads of 5 & 4-Star reviews on Amazon. It's available at: http://www.amazon.com/dp/0989468100 in Paper Back & Kindle, and also at book stores.

Here is a brief excerpt:

~~*~~*~~*~~*~~*~~*~~*~~*~~

A 3RD TIME TO DIE

PROLOGUE

1695 AD

"Sound the assembly! The Sun's up, and time's awasting."

Charles Wallace stood in his stirrups, long, equestrian-hardened legs raising his tall frame high above the restless conglomeration of horses and riders, milling about the glade in front of the gray granite mansion-house.

The Earl of Devonshire's nostrils flared, savoring the pungent orders of trampled, dew-laden grass and fresh droppings. He tugged at the cuffs of his taupe doeskin riding gloves, massaging palms together, as a shiver tiptoed across his spine. Anticipation, not the chilled morn air, was its author.

'Tis a glorious day, full of promise! Puffs of cottony clouds spilled across a rich, aquamarine sky. Flexing broad shoulders, Wallace twisted in his saddle, scanning the melee.

What a bloody good turnout. Few local gentry dared miss the Earl's first spring foxhunt. Nobles and wealthy landowners converged from across southern England for this new, prestigious sporting event. Every guest room in his rambling country estate was filled, as were the stalls in his stables. Even George Villiers, the Duke of Buckingham, who recently popularized this sport, was hard pressed to compete.

Wallace's topaz eyes raked the crowd, all mounted and eager to be off. Sixty horse at least, edgily mincing and prancing in place, awaiting the blare of the hunting horn. Still, he scoured the sea of bobbing black and tan caps and flowered bonnets.

Ah! There—the copper-haired French seraph. He visualized her delectably curved long legs below full hips, cinched by a petite waist. Her heart-shaped face was illuminated by incandescent emerald eyes, hovering above a slender, tipped up nose. Arched cheeks bracketed Cupid's-bow-shaped lips. So deceptively feminine, slender and delicate she seemed upon her muscular white gelding.

Charles knew otherwise.

Victoria Chevalier was a passionate, willful maid, plainly disenchanted with her marriage to an effeminate dandy twenty years her senior.

When first he saw her, the young Countess du Beaujolais' sensuality swept over him, sucking away his breath and setting his heart thundering like the hooves of this very stallion he sat astride. Thick-limbed, masculine Clarice, his acidic, passionless wife, had never ignited lust in his heart... or his loins.

But this nymph, Victoria, was God-sent. During the week as his guest, they were drawn together, as bees seek succulent clover. Sharp-witted and charged with life, she was full of sport. Quick dexterity with a 16 gauge brought three flushed grouse to hand... just one less than he... while her effete spouse was knocked ass over heels by his 12 gauge gun. Clarice had stayed abed.

And Victoria must have otter in her blood, out swimming him, crossing the river in swim garb much too brief for local customs. Long arms and strong legs sliced the water with astonishing ease.

He felt stirring, despite his tight britches, at the memory of his arms around her, teaching her to cast a fly for trout. Her soft chuckle hinted at greater expertise with the long rod than she admitted. 'Twas sport neither of which their partners show interest.

Victoria Chevalier was truly akin in spirit, far different from either of their mates. This French beauty would be his that very day. His starving soul demanded it, boding a liaison far more intense than just a quick tumble in the grass.

How is it she was even wed to this foppish count? Arranged marriages! Bah! Neither Chevalier, nor the earl's icy wife will offer any real obstacle to their desires. Charles and Victoria had slyly courted for the entire week, and now was their chance to fulfill those promises silently made.

He smiled as she wound her horse through the mob. As she edged nearer, her devilish grin and sly wink snatched the breath from his lungs.

"We go," his strong tenor carrying to the page, standing atop a small stone wall. "Sound the horn, God blast it!"

The brass trumpet echoed three times over the glade, and then thrice again.

Shouting riders urged their steeds ahead, each vying for a place directly behind the Earl, a sea of horses, sleekly muscled hunters, surging into the lightly wooded countryside. The drum of hooves and the echo of lusty shouts echoed through the trees like rolling thunder.

Immediately, a stone wall bordering a creek loomed as the first challenges, and two riders were quickly down. The hounds had drawn far ahead, hurdling through the underbrush, noses skimming the ground, seeking fresh scent. It won't be long. The Earl had spied several fox in the area just last week.

A movement at his right drew his glance, as the copper-tressed angel closed to his side. A few light strokes from her crop urged her steed ahead. She grinned, a playful challenge in her eyes, tossing her head, loosening burnished bronze locks from beneath her flowered hat.

They were swiftly upon a huge downed oak, vaulted by both animals with little trouble. Just as they landed, a hound let forth a melodious wail, and charged off to the south, head high, the call ringing from his throat, joined in full harmony by his brethren. A familiar wave of goose bumps skipped down his spine.

"Tallyho! Tallyho!" Wallace yelled, as he urged his dappled mount hard after the quickly disappearing dogs.

"Tallyho!" the two-legged vixen riding beside him howled gleefully, putting her crop to her snow-white steed. The cry echoed behind him again and again, as the others, strung out over a thousand yards, strove to follow. None could match the abandon of their host and his reckless female companion as they surged even farther ahead.

Ten minutes of hard riding, spiced by arduous jumps, had brought them within a few hundred yards of the hounds, their calls saying the fox was not yet bayed. Much of the party had fallen prey to the many obstacles they had crossed in their pell-mell charge after the dogs.

The countess' fearless attack of the hunt had kept her slightly to the front. Charles happily hung back, watching her with an ever-escalating appreciation. She was magnificent! Never had he known such a wild and exciting creature, so fully invested in all he held dear. He could barely wait to gather her in his arms.

The hounds were clearly visible ahead, just beyond a low, stone wall. The riders vaulted it, almost as one, and as they landed on the far side, Victoria began slowing her mount, pulling off to the side.

"What's amiss," he asked, slewing to a stop beside her.

"Fa! This foolish beast has come up lame. I'm unable to continue."

"Damn the luck. We were hot on the little bastard's trail." Turning to Count Armand, surging to a skidding halt with several other riders, Charles pointed south.

"Her horse has gone lame. Finish the hunt without us. I'll see the Countess safely back to the manor house." The mud-spattered Frenchman nodded, tapping his cap with his crop, and charge off in pursuit of the fast disappearing dogs.

He may be an effete dandy, who can't shoot and doesn't fish, but the bugger can ride. Charles watched them vanish into the woods.

Dismounting, he took the lady's reins, starting back from whence they came. After a bit they found themselves in a shaded meadow, a small brook tumbling cheerfully along one side. Cottonwoods lined its banks, their flowers in full bloom, perfuming the air with a heady scent.

"Come, m'lady. We'll take our ease here for a time before we continue. 'Tis been a hot, thirsty chase."

"Ah, truly said, m'lord. Your every wish is my command."

His lust-filled eyes caressed her every curve, lingering over each erotic swell. He licked parched lips, smiling up at her.

"An interesting proposition. You'll accede to anything I ask of you?"

She gave a throaty laugh, as he plucked her from her sidesaddle mount... and into his arms. Once there, he had not the will to release her. The scent of lilies and musk sent him spinning.

She tilted her face, crimson lips slightly parted, eyes green pools of fire. The sweet smell of her hair laid waste to his senses.

His manhood, trapped in the confinement of skin-tight jodhpurs, struggled to attention.

"You are but to ask, m'lord," she whispered, panting softly. "I am willing--nay, eager--to heed your every desire."

He crushed her to him, hungry lips entangling, tongues darting vipers, his breath snatched away by the heat of her response. The fire of her kiss consumed him in delicious flames. They grappled with sweaty garments, and luckily, riding habit was infinitely less complicated than the normal fashions of court.

Welded as one, they slid down upon the soft grass, moist with dew. There was only sweetness in the salty taste of their skin. In a moment's time they were lost in wonder, soaring high above even Heaven's Gate.

For uncounted hours they bared their souls as well as their bodies to each other. Charles, reluctantly struggling with his unwilling libido, glanced at the sky.

"Come." His voice still husky with ardor, he snatched up their garments and pulled her to her feet. "We must be off before we are found out."

"Oui," she said, but her flaming body, clinging closely to his, disagreed, rekindling the blaze within him. She raised liquid eyes to his, honeyed lips parted, wetted by the tip of her tongue.

They were quickly lost in a heated embrace, slipping again to the lush green carpet. He worshipped her skin with tender kisses and wet caresses of his tongue before entering her, her long legs trapping him urgently against her.

Their hearing filled by the thunder of unquenched passion as they lay entwined, they never heard the heavy tread of quickly approaching footsteps.

A sudden vicious blow to the back of his head slammed Charles against her, showering her with blood and gore, pinning her down.

"No!" A fearsome beast hovered above her, swinging a weapon high above its beaked head.

"Mon Dieu! No! Please, don't hurt..." The thud of heavy blows, the crunching of bones and rending of flesh, continued unabated for many minutes in the otherwise silent glade.

It wasn't until four hours after the last of the hunt had ridden in, two foxes in hand, before it was admitted that something was amiss. A hastily organized search party gave up, finally, three hours into the night.

The entire village was out again at dawn, searching ahorse and afoot for the missing couple. Two hours after sun-up, a hunting horn was sounded from a thick forest glade. The dogs had found their master. Searchers gathered in silent wonder in the small meadow that, sixteen hours before had hosted an idyll of love and passion. The ground was torn, blood and bits of flesh splattered everywhere. Two broken bodies lay heaped together, limbs twisted askew, heads crushed, faces gone, barely recognizable as having once been human.

The huntsmen agreed it was the work of some great beast-- mayhaps an angry bear. Had an enraged sow destroyed them while protecting her cubs? Surely a plausible answer. They would hunt down and kill her, if they could.

So two lovers, newly discovered unto each other, died with love and life unfulfilled.

It was a passion that might have lasted an eternity, were it not cut short.

So brutally short.

◆ ❖ ◆

1850 AD

Morgana Quincy's hazel eyes, shaded by arched, inky eyebrows, squinted against the sun, watching the one-horse coach clatter around a corner before she started down the cobblestone path. Her white parasol, protection against the mid-day sun, draped casually over a slender shoulder. She shook her head, glistening onyx curls swirling and bobbing about her gentle, round-cheeked face. She needed time to clear her mind.

Her father, Jonathan Denton, had immigrated to the Americas only fifty years before, and had distinguished himself as a block- ade-runner in this new country's second war with England. Now, thirty years later, he owned a successful shipping business, with six sloops carrying goods to all the major cities of the World.

But a life that should be a cornucopia was not going well. She was a fortunate woman, raised in a warm and loving environment by her father, widowed now these past twelve years. She married eight years past to a handsome young pillar of Philadelphia society, something that should fill her life with joy. William came from one of the oldest families in the city.

At twenty-seven, the major thing missing from paradise was a child, but not for a lack of trying... at least during their first five years together. Sex with her husband... something she shamefully enjoyed... was far less frequent now.

Just last month she discovered the cause: his affair with a sultry, voluptuous singer from a "high class" saloon near the harbor.

How could that bastard do this to her? What to do now? Take revenge? Something not in her nature, but the lure was strong.

They could try to work things out, but did she even care to make the effort? For what? If he pledged penance, would she let him back into her bed? She imagined he would try. She'd begun to suspect William was more enamored with her father's fortune than her. And despite promises, would he really forsake that sensuous trollop? Nay, nothing good could come of this.

Now she was plagued by greater worries. Father, her stout oak providing shelter throughout her life, was ill. Seriously ill! Some foreign thing grew tenaciously in his chest, consuming him, sucking the meat off his bones, casting him into a mere shadow of himself. He'd become somnolent from heavy doses of morphine. She could only hold his hand, weeping incessantly during her daily afternoon visits. Conversation, while lucid, was brief and strained.

Head lowered, lost in thought, she was sent spinning upon colliding with someone on the walk. Strong hand caught her slender shoulders, steadying her until she regained her balance.

"Oh, I'm so sorry." She snatched a breath, her cheeks flushed, hazel eyes wide, as she glanced into a pair of fathomless, amber wide-set orbs. A long face, dominated by a strongly arched nose, smiled down at her. A mop of curly mahogany hair sprouted around the edges of his cap.

"'Tis I who owe an apology, Mrs. Quincy. I wasn't looking where I was about."

"Nor was I, sir. But how is it you know my name?" Her heart fluttered, her skin infused with a tingling heat. Who was this strangely exciting man? His was not a presence she would soon forget.

"I am your father's barrister. Robert Isaac, at your service."

"Oh, yes. Father mentioned you just today." Tears blossomed in the corners of her eyes. "T'was the most we have talked this whole week."

"'Tis a sad thing to see one so strong grow frail. It must be very hard on you." His long, smooth, tapered fingers magically encircled her hand, and honest compassion filled his eyes.

"Your father has been very kind to me. Few of this city's gentry show much interest in a Jewish lawyer."

"Father spoke of that as well, mocking their ignorance. You are the brightest of them all, he said... his gain and their loss. He also said you were the only compassionate barrister he'd ever met." *Can he hear the cacophony he has stirred in my breast?*

"He is too kind. Thousands of years of oppression have taught my people that virtue well. 'Tis a major tenant of our upbringing." Her hand still nestled in his, her knees trembled. A strange heat permeated her.

"He also instructed me to help you with any matter in which you might have need. He referred, rather obliquely, to something about your husband?"

"He knows, does he?" She sighed. "Well, I shouldn't be surprised. He always fathoms when something is amiss. I dare say, he's a lot less innocent than I."

"Is it something you wish to discuss, ma'am? I am available, and anything told me is strictly confidential. It won't be repeated, even to your father, if you wish."

She looked at her pale fingers, still ensconced safely in his tanned hand. She was flooded with the strange sensation she had known this man all her life. Her heart fluttered with the wings of a small frightened bird, but there was no fear in her. Finally, all that had been wrong would be set right.

She was awash with an inexorable sense Robert Isaac came from God to protect her, now that her father was unable. Her eyes turned to his. A delicate, bow-shaped mouth and aristocratic cheeks conspired to transform her smile... the first in many weeks... into a brilliant sunrise.

"I suppose I must confide in someone, although there's little enough to be done. Just talking to a person of trust would be a large load off my back. And I do sense you are someone to rely on, Mr. Isaac."

"There's a small cafe nearby," he said. "Quite secluded, and tables in the back allow for complete privacy. Shall we go there?"

◆ ❖ ◆

Settled beside a scared oak slab, perched on slick, dark leather benches in a dim corner of the sparsely occupied pub, she found herself pouring out her heart about things she had never before discussed with a single soul. His compassionate understanding of her grief over her father's illness and the illicit behavior of her husband were a strange catharsis. This was a connection she never felt with another person, especially a man.

Robert escorted her to her door, finally, as darkness began its approach, saying he had some ideas that might help in dealing with her husband, should things eventually come to an end in their marriage. She made an appointment to visit his offices the very next day.

◆ ❖ ◆

Almost a year to the day after she first met Robert Isaac, they rode his black lacquered surrey into the countryside for a picnic. Jonathan Denton had succumbed ten months past, leaving his fortune in trust to his only daughter.

William Quincy made many determined forays after a share of that wealth, but a phalanx of attorneys could not dent the ironclad instruments forged by Robert for his client. Denton had consigned Morgana's care and fate to the hands of this capable young man. It was a duty he would have taken seriously... even if he hadn't fallen hopelessly in love with her.

He had struggled to remain aloof and proper with his lovely client... until the beating. William, in a fit of rage, peaked by his family's failing finances and his inability to touch his wife's vast wealth, had taken a riding crop to her.

Robert summoned all his self-control to keep from thrashing the man. Instead, he charged Quincy with assault and battery, a rare challenge to a husband's right to strike his wife. Eventually, charges were dropped with the court ordering William to keep his hands to himself.

It was the impetus Morgana needed to begin pursuing a divorce.

"I've found love with another man," she had told Robert, a merry twinkle in her golden eyes.

"Who is the lucky fellow," his throat suddenly constricted, he could barely draw breath.

"Oh, he's a strong, handsome, gentle man of the utmost integrity. Completely unlike that lout I married."

"If you'll only give me his name," his eyes cast down to hide his despair, "I'll make inquiries to be sure he's as upright as you fancy him. 'Tis for your protection." He was resigned to step aside. Anything for the happiness of this angel he had grown to treasure so deeply.

"Oh, you ninny." She laughed, eyes alight, her face a picture permanently etched into the fabric of his brain.

"His name is Robert Isaac. 'Tis you I love, my sweet fool."

What? T'was he? How could this be? His wildest dreams fulfilled? Thunder hammered his breast as he took her hands, his eyebrow arched. Her smile dazzling his senses, she nodded, nestling in his arms, her face tilted, begging to be kissed.

They soon became lovers, enthralled by a familiarity and passion more profound than either ever expected. Now, months later, her divorce to Quincy soon to be finalized, they were about to celebrate. The picnic basket was filled with delicacies and two well-chilled bottles of wine... a fine meal, capped off with tender lovemaking under the shade of the great oaks that bordered this idyllic meadow.

They nestled, naked, upon a light blanket, spread over the dew-dampened meadow, shaded from the warm sun by mighty oaks, full with spring bloom. Robert rolled to his side, propping his head against a hand, gazing down at her, snuggled in the crook of his other arm. Her velvety fair skinned, slender body was still flushed and moist from their recent ardor.

"'Tis a miracle I still cannot fathom that I am here with you. That such an angel professes to love me as deeply as I love her."

"The miracle 'tis mine, my love." She stroked his face with elegant, crimson-nailed fingers, "that I could be shed of that cruel bastard, William, and find myself in the arms of one such as you. I adore you more than I can say. 'Tis as if I've loved you forever, in my dreams."

"Aye. So 'tis with me." He handed her one of their partly filled glasses of wine glasses.

"To our love, eternal. Nothing on earth will ever destroy it." They clinked their glasses together, sipping the warming brew.

"We are already one, Morgana. Marry me, to make it official."

Her smile stirred him almost beyond bearing.

"Yes, my darling. As quickly as I'm shed of William. Our child will need a proper name, and I love you beyond my ability to say."

"Our child? Are you...?"

"Yes! I missed my time, neigh three months past."

"But how? Eight years with William, and you never..."

"Aye, but apparently t'was his lacking, not mine." Her smile ignited him. Their hands, their mouths, wended on amorous explorations, and soon he was entering her.

Nearing a wondrous finale, the earth seemingly trembled at their exquisite ardor. Her ears twitched, and the flames of passion were suddenly chilled by an ominous sense of danger.

A vague image of a horned beast and blood-soaked beak bloomed in her head. Eyes flared wide, she struggled to glimpse the wood beyond her lover's shoulder.

"Morgana? What's amiss, my love?" He snatched a breath, struggling from the depths of ardor.

An approaching heavy tread was clearly audible, as the air humming with a strange whirring beat.

"Non! Mon Dieu, non!" *French?* Terrified, she wondered, *I don't speak French.*

Locked in the steel band of her panicked arms, Robert tried to turn but before he could move he was slammed against her, his full weight pinning her to the ground. Reeling from the impact, her face drenched by blood and splattered with small spongy gray particles, Morgana's eyes flew wide.

Paralyzed by terror and the weight of her lover, she cringed at large shadow above her, then the suddenly familiar fierce beaked head, the sun glinting off its silvery body, flailing the air with a spinning weapon.

"No, don't!" A terrifying flash of memory bloomed... a vision of being here before!

"Arret! Not again! Mon Dieu! Non! Non..."

The search party, led by Robert's brother, Aaron, found them the next afternoon. The small glade was a gruesome slaughterhouse... ochre stains and shredded bits of flesh scattered across the verdant lea. Two naked bodies, tangled together in a heap, were rent beyond recognition. Not a single man there held down his gorge.

It must be the work of some wild creature, probably a bear. Destruction of the two and the grounds around them were too vicious to be dealt by human hand.

Still, the Sheriff made a thorough investigation. William Quincy had been in his offices the entire day. No other possible perpetrator could be identified.

No, it had to be an animal. A hunt was organized to search for the beast, but none was ever found. It remained the mysterious end of a new and wonderful love, cut short.

So brutally short.

Chapter One

2013 AD

God, they're so beautiful!

Ashley Easton watched the big horses attack the course. Thoroughbreds, mostly. Few amateurs owned the more exotic breeds, like Warmbloods. Perched on the edge of cold metal bleachers overlooking the white-fenced jumping arena, gray eyes wistfully traced the action. She pressed forward, her knees squeezing imagined sweaty flanks as powerful brutes hurtled oxers and walls, and maneuvered through triple-bar in-and-outs.

She was breathless, filled with jealous nostalgia. So many years tip-toeing quietly by since she'd seen an Open Jumper class, much less ridden in one. Gently curled, shoulder-length locks swirled in a coppery cloud as she shook her head and sighed.

Training jumpers wasn't in the books while raising a family—and trying to make a life with a husband who seems more and more distant and self-involved. She leaned back, hugging herself. Things were different now. The kids were no longer babies.

How did we drift so far apart? We were so in love... so powerfully drawn to each other... despite all that went wrong. We don't even have anything to talk about anymore.

She stood, slender and casually elegant in tapered tan chinos and a flowered cotton blouse. Stretching her five-foot-eight inches frame, stiff from balancing on the hard metal seat, she ambled down from the bleachers, not really interested in the lower fence Novice Hunter class just beginning. She wandered aimlessly, musing, surprised to find herself at the entrance of the barn. A comfortable place, filled with happy vibes.

She turned, slouching against the railing, arms folded across a bosom surprisingly full for one so slim, idly watching a teenage girl work her bay mare over the low fences.

Moisture welled in her slate eyes at the memory of her parents cheering as she took Lady over the higher Open fences. Thirteen years had trundled by since she last showed a horse. Mama was always there and Papa usually came, despite his busy schedule at the mill. She missed them terribly.

But bad stuff happens. They were gone, wiped away in that one terrible instant. Now she and Keith seemed to have so little in common. Did they ever enjoy the same things... besides each other? She was into horses, and then home life, raising a family of happy children.

He was into... what? Keith, mostly. The world revolving around the Big Jock. He expected her to be the Moon, spinning around his planet. But his sphere of ego-centric gravity was repelling... not attracting... her.

Couples divorced for less, but Ashley was no quitter, eschewing the search for other solar systems. She'd keep her marriage together, if only for the children... make every effort... go more than half-way. The rest was up to Keith.

Of course, if he's rarely home, whatever she does makes little difference. She refused to give up her individuality, if it came to that. Pushing away from the railing, she shook herself like a dog out of a pond, casting off morose thoughts like droplets.

Ashley Easton functioned best happy rather than depressed. She glanced at the ring, the corner of her lips twitching up as an Appaloosa mare nimbly maneuvered through the Hunter course. How fulfilled and contented she was when riding and jumping.

Might as well visit the horses. Scratch a few ears. Enjoy the smells.

She entered the barn, kicking at straw strewn across the floor. Funny how the aroma of fresh hay and manure ignited a sense of happier times.

She strolled from stall to stall, stroking velvety muzzles and caressing behind ears. The animals rubbed her with their snouts and nibbled at her sleeve, recognizing her as a friend.

She paused at the stall where she'd boarded Lady as a teenager. A dappled gray leaned over the wood-rail gate, tossing its head, nickering. She sighed.

She came to Onwentsia Stables on a whim to watch the first Amateur Open Jumper competition of the Spring, and the banked embers of the old fire burned brightly in her again. Seeing those big muscular athletes bounding over rails and walls had her heart tumbling giddily.

Maybe it's time to get a horse... even start jumping again. Thirty-one's not too old, and it's such great therapy. One thing's for sure... a four-legged buddy will always be there for me.

Riding created a sense of peace and a bond with the animal that no one but an equestrian would understand. The pressures of rearing a family were minimal now, with Maria living in for the last year, there to care for the children if she were away.

Time to get out and do my own thing. It'll be daytimes, while Keith's at work, so it won't interfere with our being together. Besides, when was the last time he spent any real time with me, doing something fun? Something I love! She couldn't remember, but it'd been years.

Ashley ventured deeper into the gloomy barn, absorbing the ambiance.

I can even get back into show jumping, if I get a good horse. Wonder what was wrong with that huge chestnut? A redhead, just like me. He seemed so listless, even refusing fences. Hard to believe that big thoroughbred was unwilling to jump. You never know until you...

A horse squealing in apparent pain, somewhere deeper inside the barn, brought her to an abrupt stop. She spun around, looking for a groom, but all stable hands were near the show ring.

"Better take a look. May be an animal in trouble." She hurried back, checking stalls as she went.

There it was again. She circled into a wing for visiting horses, slowly approaching the end stall. Peering over the gate, she staggered back, a hand clasped over her mouth.

"OhmyGod." Her eyes flooded. "You poor baby. What's *happened* to you?" It looked like the big roan gelding that had jumped so poorly in the Open Class, its flanks lathered and striped with bloody furrows. The horse nickered softly, ears up, sensing compassion in her voice.

"Jesus! You've been beaten." Salty streams spilled down her cheeks, her heart pummeling her chest, a soft moan slipping between her lips. A horse should be your buddy and companion, not an outlet for anger and abuse. She held out her hand to him.

"Who *did* this to you?" The tall horse edged tentatively forward, ears flicking back and forth. She gently rubbed his satiny snout. He nuzzled her shoulder, nickering softly.

"Sweet boy." Her arms circled his neck and he brushed his face affectionately against her body. Why would anybody hurt such a lovely animal? Tears continued to gush, as she fished for a tissue to blow her nose and blot her eyes.

Damn, my mascara's running. I must look a mess.

"I'm gonna find some help, pretty boy. Somebody's gonna pay for this, I promise you." She hurried off. He neighed plaintively after her.

Ashley was turning into the main part of the stable when the horse trumpeted again. She skidded to a stop, searching again for help, but everybody was still out at the show ring. Another shrill whinny. Was some bastard beating that poor guy again?

"Looks like it's up to me." Gritting her teeth, Ashley hurried toward the stall, snatching up a nearby pitchfork. Who knew how crazy this guy might be?

She cautiously approached the stall on suddenly rubbery legs. The chestnut gelding was struggling to get away from a tall, lanky man in riding habit, brandishing a whip. A very *big* whip. He had looped a lead chain over the animal's snout for control.

"I got a real weapon now, you bastard! You'll never embarrass me like that again. I'll kill ya first." He hit the horse hard across the withers. The big gelding bucked and pawed, but without any real energy.

"Hey, quit that!" Her shout raspy, she banged the gate with the side of the pitchfork.

"Huh?"

"Stop beating that poor, defenseless animal!" Energized, adrenaline flowing at flood tide, she danced from foot to foot, a redheaded Valkyrie, brandishing her weapon over the gate, beating the air. Angry tears flowed unabated.

"Hey, put that thing down before your hurt somebody." Lowering his whip, he backed away in the face of this very agitated woman, her cheeks streaked with black mascara war paint.

"Then leave that horse alone, Godammit." She jabbed the pitchfork in his direction.

"What the Hell business is it of yours, lady?" His eyes never left the sharp metal tines.

"No animal deserves abuse like that. What's he done that was so terrible?" She sniffled, rubbing her nose with the back of her hand, tears drying up from flood mode.

"You see him jump today?"

"Yeah, so what." She caught her breath, lowering her weapon, having deflected him from his attack. "Any athlete can have an off day."

"Been more like an off year. Supposed to be a great jumper, but he's got no heart. I've had it." No longer threatened, the horse stood quietly, head hanging, breathing hard. Blood dripped in red rivulets off his flanks.

Maybe someone *did* sell this guy a clinker, as far as jumping went, but the animal didn't look at all well. So thin!

Shit! When I get back into jumping, I'll want a good Open horse. She almost smiled, despite her fury, realizing the decision had just been made. She studied the horse.

This poor guy may never qualify, but I can't leave him in the hands of this cretin. The reek of booze on him was overpowering. She skewered him with two gray lasers, burning out from below arched scarlet eyebrows.

"Well, you'd better leave him alone. You can get in trouble for this kind of abuse." Sighing softly, giving a small shake of her head, she leaned her weapon against the wall and entered the stall.

"What's his name?"

"Injun, but he sure ain't no warrior." He edged away, keeping a wary eye on this crazy woman.

She studied the big red horse, watching her with soft brown eyes. He nickered, and she could almost hear, *Please help me,* in the forlorn sound.

Oh, damn! Trapped. She glanced at the man, still holding his whip.

"Want to sell him?"

"Huh?"

"Do you want to sell him? You clearly don't like him. Beat him again, I'll report you."

"Yeah?" He studied her for a moment. "What'll you pay?"

"Look, I wanted an open jumper, and you said yourself he's not cutting it. I could probably low-ball you, as angry as you are, but I'll make you a fair offer. I'll pay you whatever you paid. Just show me the invoice. Deal?"

"You bet. I got it right here in my locker."

A half-hour later, check written, she called the vet most highly recommended by the stable's manager. Luckily, he was nearby and would be there in an hour or so.

Good. This poor baby needs his wounds cared for and a good general check-up.

Chapter Two

She was back in the bleachers, awaiting the vet and watching the Novice Open Jumper Class, struggling with growing apprehension.

How impulsive. Keith'll be furious. Have to deal with it. Couldn't let that guy maim that lovely animal. She sighed, giving a tiny shrug.

The Hell with him. At least the horse will give unquestioned love, which is more than I'm getting from my husband lately. She leaned back, arms akimbo, reflecting on the state of her marriage to Keith Easton. Her eyes pooled.

Where did our passion go? She blinked away moisture, thinking of their youth. Those were the times... sometimes exciting and sometimes painful.

Passion was the problem. She never imagined how, at the exhilarating age of seventeen, her life would change when they moved from Chicago to the suburban North Shore. A new house, new school, new friends... and the hopes of finally finding a boyfriend.

But things became unexpectedly complicated, especially after making the cheerleading squad. She smiled, remembering her new friend, Sue Malloy, talking her into to trying out...

"Cheerleading? Jeez, I don't think so," she'd responded to Sue's urging.

"Why not? You're a natural, with your, coppery-colored hair. And you're so tall. I wish I were tall."

"Oh, c'mon. You look great."

"Yeah, but my hair color's phony, and blue eyes are a dime a dozen. You got that hot-looking hair and those neat gray eyes, and you're really stacked. Who can compete with that?"

Ashley chuckled. Sue had made her sound like a movie star. But cheerleading was how she met Keith, as if Fate forced them together, and her usually blissful life suddenly became a lot more confused. Not so uncommon for teens, but even at its most tumultuous, she never expected this.

It was cheerleading, Keith, and of course, horses that filled her life. She had taken jumping and dressage instruction since she was a little girl.

"You're the most instinctive rider I've ever seen," her instructor had said. "As if you were born on a horse. For a usually reserved girl, you attack jumps with an almost wild delight."

Taking Lady over fences released a hidden recklessness in her then. She imagined being on a foxhunt, hurtling hedgerows and stone walls with startling ease. Somewhere in her head, a woman's voice (was it hers?) exalting in gleeful French. But she barely knew the language!

She blinked and sat up, casting away the web of memories, chuckling mirthlessly.

With a final wistful glance at the horses still performing, she strode toward the barn to check on Injun before heading home. Delaying a confrontation with Keith won't change anything. He was sure to go on a tirade over the horse.

Too bad. It's my money, and it's about time I do what I want for a change.

She thought of that fateful time in her youth. Cheerleading never proved a disappointment, but the complications stemming from it were unexpected. She had no inkling as an innocent, trusting girl, what joy... and misery... would follow.

No time to dwell on that now.

Made in the USA
San Bernardino, CA
19 May 2014